THE

WOMEN

OF THE

CASTLE

THE
WOMEN
OF THE
CASTLE

JESSICA SHATTUCK

ZAFFRE

First published in Great Britain in 2017 by

ZAFFRE PUBLISHING
80-81 Wimpole St, London WIG 9RE
www.zaffrebooks.co.uk

A CIP catalogue record for this book is
available from the British Library.

ISBN: 978-1-785-76269-7 (tpb)
ISBN: 978-1-785-76271-0 (hb)
ISBN: 978-1-785-76258-1 (tpb-B Format)

also available as an ebook

1 3 5 7 9 10 8 6 4 2

Printed and bound by Clays Ltd, St Ives Plc

Zaffre Publishing is an imprint of Bonnier Zaffre,
a Bonnier Publishing company
www.bonnierzaffre.co.uk
www.bonnierpublishing.co.uk

In memory of my mother, Petra Tölle Shattuck,
and my grandmother, Anneliese Tölle

THE

WOMEN

OF THE

CASTLE

BURG LINGENFELS, NOVEMBER 9, 1938

The day of the countess's famous harvest party began with a driving rain that hammered down on all the ancient von Lingenfels castle's sore spots – springing leaks, dampening floors, and turning its yellow façade a slick, beetle-like black. In the courtyard, the paper lanterns and carefully strung garlands of wheat drooped and collapsed.

Marianne von Lingenfels, niece-in-law of the countess, laboured joylessly to prepare for their guests. It was too late to call off the party. Now that the countess was wheelchair-bound, Marianne had become the de facto hostess; a hostess who should have listened to her husband and cancelled the party last week. In Paris, Ernst vom Rath lay in a hospital bed, the victim of an attempted assassination, and in Munich the Nazis were whipping the country into a frenzy for revenge. Never mind that prior to the event no one had even heard of vom Rath – an obscure, mid-level German diplomat – and that his assassin was a boy of seventeen, or that the shooting was itself an act of revenge: the assassin's family was among the thousands of Jews huddled at the Polish border, expelled from Germany, barred entry by Poland. The Nazis were not deterred by complex facts.

All the more cause to gather reasonable people here at the castle, away from the madness! Marianne had argued just yesterday. Today, in the rain, her argument seemed trite.

And now it was too late. So Marianne supervised the placement of candles, flowers, and table linens and managed the soggy uphill transport of champagne, ice and butter, potted fish and smoked meats, potable water and canisters of gas for the cookstove. Burg Lingenfels was uninhabited for most of the year, with no running water and a generator just strong enough to power the countess's Victrola and a few strings of expensive electric lights. Hosting the party was like setting up a civilisation on the moon. But this was part of what kept people coming back despite yearly disasters – minor fires and collapsed outhouses, fancy touring cars stuck in the mud, mice in the overnight guest beds. The party had become famous for its anarchic, un-German atmosphere. It was known as an outpost of liberal, bohemian culture in the heart of the proper aristocracy.

By mid-afternoon, to Marianne's relief, the wind began to blow, chasing away the day's gloom with gusts of clear and promising air. Even the stone walls and the moat's sinewy water looked fresh and clean scrubbed. The chrysanthemums in the courtyard glistened under racing patches of sun.

Marianne's spirits rose. In front of the bakehouse, an architect acquaintance of the countess's had transformed an old carriage horses' drinking trough into a fountain. The effect was at once magical and comic. The castle was an elephant dressed to look like a fairy.

'Albrecht,' Marianne called as she entered the long, low library, where her husband was seated at the imposing desk that had once been the count's. 'You must come and see – it's like a carnival!'

Albrecht looked up at her, still composing a sentence in his head. He was a tall, craggy-faced man with a high forehead and unruly eyebrows that often gave him the appearance of frowning when he was not.

'Only for a moment, before everyone gets here.' She held out her hand. 'Come. The fresh air will clear your head.'

'No, no, not yet,' he said, waving her off and returning his attention to the letter he was writing.

Oh, come on, Marianne would have normally chided, but tonight, on account of the party, she bit her tongue. Albrecht was a perfectionist and workaholic. She would never change this. He was drafting a letter to an old law school acquaintance in the British Foreign Office and had sought her opinion on alternate sentence constructions many times. *The annexation of the Sudetenland will only be the beginning. I urge you to beware of our leadership's aggression* versus *If we are not vigilant, our leader's aggressive intentions will only be the beginning* . . .

Both ways make your point was Marianne's response. *Just pick one.* But Albrecht was a deliberator. He did not even notice the irritation in her tone. His own emotions were never complicated or petty. He was the sort of man who contemplated grand abstractions like the Inalienable Rights of Man or the Problems of Democracy while shaving. It rendered him oblivious to everyday things.

Marianne restrained herself to a demonstrative sigh, turned, and left him to his work.

Back in the banquet hall, the countess scolded one of her young disciples from her wheelchair: 'Not Schumann,' she said, 'God forbid! We might as well play Wagner . . . no, something Italian. Something decadent enough to shock any Brownshirt idiot who comes tonight.'

Even in her old age, the countess was a rebel, followed at all turns by young artists and socialites. French by birth, German by marriage, she had always been a controversial figure. As a young woman, she had hosted evening salons famous for their impromptu dancing and intellectual arguments on risqué subjects like modern art and French philosophy. Why she had married the proper, fusty old count, a man twenty years her senior and famous for falling asleep at the dinner table, was the subject of much not-very-kind speculation.

For Marianne, who was the product of an oppressively proper Prussian upbringing, the countess had always been an object of admiration. The woman was unafraid to step beyond the role of mother and *Hausfrau* into the fray of male power and intellectual life. She spoke her own mind and did things her own way. Even from their first meeting years ago, when Marianne was a young university student courting her professor (Albrecht), she had wanted to become a woman like the countess.

'It looks wonderful out there,' Marianne said, gesturing towards the courtyard. 'Monsieur Pareille is a magician.'

'He is an artist, isn't he?' the countess proclaimed.

It was nearly six o'clock. Guests would begin arriving at any moment.

Marianne hurried upstairs to the chilly hall of bedrooms where her girls were holed up in an ancient curtained bed, a relic from the castle's feudal past. Her one-year-old son, Fritz, was at home in Weisslau with his nurse, thank God.

'Mama!' Elisabeth, age six, and Katarina, age four, shrieked with delight. Elfie, their sweet, mild-mannered au pair, glanced up at Marianne with a beleaguered expression.

'Isn't it true that Hitler is going to take back Poland next?' Elisabeth asked, bouncing on the mattress.

'Elisabeth!' Marianne exclaimed. 'Where did you get this idea?'

'I heard Herr Zeppel saying it to Papa,' she said, still bouncing.

'No,' Marianne said. 'And why would you think that was anything to be excited about? It would mean war!'

'But it's supposed to be ours.' Elisabeth pouted, stopping mid-bounce. 'And, anyway, Herr Zeppel said the Poles can't manage themselves.'

'What nonsense,' Marianne said, irritated that Albrecht had allowed the child to hear such talk. Zeppel was the overseer of their estate in Silesia and an ardent Nazi. Albrecht tolerated the man's nonsense because they had grown up together: Weisslau was a small town.

'But it *was* ours, wasn't it?' Elisabeth insisted. 'Before the war?'

'Elisabeth,' Marianne said, sighing, 'you concern yourself with what is *yours,* please – and that includes the book you are supposed to be reading with Elfie right now.'

The child exasperated Marianne with her endless obsession with possession. She seemed to have absorbed the national sense of aggrievement, as if she, personally, were the victim of some great unfairness. She had so many advantages but always wanted more – a newer dress, a prettier skirt. If she received a bunny, she wanted a dog. If allowed a bonbon, she wanted two. In her mind, the world seemed to lie entirely at her disposal. Marianne, whose upbringing had been characterised by firm parsimony and restraint, was constantly appalled by this demanding, presuming creature she had raised.

'Elfie –' She turned to the au pair. 'Will you see to it that the candles are out by eight? The girls may come down to the landing, but no farther.'

'But –' Elisabeth began, and Marianne shot her a look.

'Good night,' she said, giving an extra squeeze to sweet, quiet, dark-haired Katarina and kissing Elisabeth's maddening little brow.

On her way downstairs, Marianne paused on the landing to observe the hall below, its stone archways illuminated by candelabras. The flickering light lent the room an exciting, almost spooky glow. Early guests had begun to arrive: the men in waistcoats and tails, a few in uniforms with gaudy new Nazi insignias stitched on the lapels; the women in fine new dresses. Under Hitler, the economy was growing strong: people had money, once again, for silk and velvet and the new Parisian styles. From a throne-like seat in the middle of the hall, the countess greeted her guests, her wheelchair carefully hidden away for the evening. She was a mountain of blue and green silk, the likes of which no other German woman of

her age (or any other) would wear. Her laugh rang out strongly for
someone in poor health – had there ever been a woman who loved
a party more? And there, bowing before her, was the guest who
elicited this peal of laughter: Connie Fledermann. Marianne felt
a rush of excitement. Who else received such a welcome? Connie
was a great favourite of the countess's, a star in his own right, a
man whose boldness of character, wit, and intelligence rendered
him beloved by all – a charmer of ladies, a receiver of men's trust
and confidences. No one, from crazy Hermann Göring to somber
George Messersmith, was immune to Connie's charisma.

'Connie!' Marianne called as she approached.

He turned and a grin spread across his face.

'Aha! The woman I have been waiting for!' He lifted her hand
to his lips. 'You are looking lovely.' He cast his eyes up to the landing. 'Will I get to see my princesses or have you put them away?'

'Put away,' Marianne said with a laugh. 'I hope.'

'Alas.' He placed his hands over his heart and feigned collapse.
'Well, at least I get to consort with the queen mother. Come' – he
extended his arm – 'meet my Benita!'

Marianne's smile stiffened. In the drama of the past week, she
had forgotten. Martin Constantine Fledermann was to be married. It seemed impossible. Even with the date set (two weeks
from today!), it still had the ring of a lark gone too far.

But he was earnest, even nervous, as he took Marianne by the
elbow. 'You must befriend her,' he said. 'She knows no one. I told
her you would be her ally. And' – he turned to her – 'you know she
will need one here.'

'Why is that?' Marianne asked. 'You are among friends.'

'True,' Connie said. 'But she is not.'

Marianne frowned at his circular logic, but there was no time
to question it because suddenly there she was, Connie's Benita,
a strikingly pretty woman with the kind of flat, Nordic face that
emanated placidity. Her blonde hair was plaited and wrapped
around her head in the style so adored by the Nazis, a Wagnerian

Brunhilde in an honest-to-God dirndl dress. She stood between two young men who worked with Albrecht in the Foreign Office, both of whom looked delighted. Marianne felt an unusual pang of jealousy. It was not that she envied the younger woman's beauty or palpable air of sexuality (she herself had long ago carved out an alternate road to male regard), but at this moment, in the company of these three men – two silly, overeager boys and one dear friend, childhood sweetheart, luminary of the opposition – the other woman's beauty left her nowhere to go. At thirty-one, Marianne was an adult in a child's play, a schoolmarm among excitable students.

'Excuse me, boys,' Connie said, making a show of elbowing one of them aside, 'I need to reclaim her.' He put a hand on Benita's arm and pulled her towards Marianne. 'My love,' he addressed Benita (how odd it was to hear him say this), 'meet my – what shall I call you?' He turned to Marianne. 'My oldest friend, my sternest adviser, the person who keeps me most honest?'

'Oh pish, Connie,' Marianne said, trying to tamp down her irritation.

'Marianne,' she introduced herself, and extended a hand to the young woman, who, she judged, could not be much over twenty.

'Thank you,' the girl said, blinking like a startled deer. 'How nice to meet you.'

More guests arrived, and Marianne could feel them pressing towards her with hands to shake, welcomes to issue, politics to discuss. There was Greta von Viersdahl, already trying to catch her eye; since Hitler had invaded, Greta spoke of nothing but the winter clothes she was collecting for the Sudeten Germans, so recently 'returned to the fatherland,' so long 'oppressed by the Slavs' . . . Marianne wanted no part of Greta's politics. Impulsively, she took Benita's arm. 'Give us a chance to become friends,' she said over her shoulder to Connie, already leading Benita through the back door and into the lantern-bedecked courtyard.

'How beautiful!' Benita exclaimed.

'Isn't it?' Marianne said. 'Like a fairy tale. Countess von Lin-genfels has a talent for the amazing.'

Benita nodded, staring wide eyed.

'So tell me about yourself before we are swarmed with admir-ers,' Marianne said. 'Was your trip all right? Have you found your room?' She hurried through the necessary questions, half listen-ing to the girl's replies.

From all around, she could feel people's eyes. 'Remind me how you met Connie.' Marianne plucked two champagne flutes from a table and handed one to Benita, who accepted it without thanks.

'We just met in the town square, really,' the girl said. 'I was there with my troop – my BDM troop –'

'Good grief! The BDM? How old are you?' Marianne exclaimed.

'Oh no – not the one for little girls – for the older girls, Belief and Beauty. I'm nineteen.'

'Ah.' Marianne patted her arm. 'Positively ancient.'

The girl glanced at her.

'Aren't these lovely?' Marianne pointed at the white chrysan-themums and dark autumn anemones arranged in pots along the balustrade. High above, pale clouds scudded across the dark sky. And in the distance, the woods were inky in the twilight. 'So the town square . . .'

Benita sipped her champagne and coughed. 'It's not much of a story. We met and talked and then later we went out for dinner.'

Marianne rested her glass atop the courtyard wall. 'And now you are to be married.'

'When you say it like that' – Benita hesitated – 'it sounds odd.'

Marianne smiled and cocked her head to the side, knitting her brows. She had learned this scrutinising expression from the countess and found it proved helpful at drawing out confessions and explanations from children and family members, even grown men.

But it did not have the desired effect on the girl. Instead, she seemed to find her mettle, squaring her shoulders. 'There were a few things in between.'

'Of course,' Marianne said. Why had she taken this interrogative tack? The girl was to become Connie's wife. It would do Marianne no good to have started off this way. 'I'm sorry – I don't mean to pry.'

'Come.' She glanced around the rapidly filling courtyard for an opening and, with relief, spotted Herman Kempel, one of the rubes who had been so smitten with Benita earlier. 'Let's go and talk to your latest admirer.'

As the night wore on, a kind of giddy, reckless energy took over. A comical figure in lederhosen and knee socks played an accordion – was he someone the countess had hired or a local guest? – and people began folk dancing on the uneven cobblestones. Women even kicked off their shoes, despite the cold. And inside, the American jazz trio the countess had invited finally arrived. They played ragtime in the great hall while a number of the bolder, more cosmopolitan guests demonstrated dances with silly names like the Big Apple and the Lindy Hop. Somehow, despite the improvised stove and lack of running water, the chef presented a steady stream of delicacies: traditional pork meatballs with a delicate parsley sauce, plump white steamed dumplings, and silver-dollar sausage rounds. But also novelties – asparagus wrapped with paper-thin ham, jelly moulds, pineapple flambé, and caviar toast . . . like the music, the food spanned the gamut of German cultural life.

Marianne drifted in a haze, not of alcohol (the hostess never had more than one glass of punch – this too she had learned from the countess), but of relief. She had managed to continue the immodest tradition of the harvest party, even as the nation was swept up in this wave of rigid and peevish militancy. And she had managed to transcend her own upbringing (how mortified her father would be to see her throw a party featuring jazz dancing and champagne toasts) and provide these people with something lovely, liberating, and ethereal.

Buoyed along by this thought, she greeted guests, checked on the drinks behind the bar, the food on the buffet. 'The countess junior!' a jolly, quick-tongued cousin of Connie's cried, wrapping a thick arm around her shoulders. 'What a party! But where is your esteemed husband? And all his high-minded friends! I haven't seen a one of those trolls for the past hour! Are they holed up in some sort of elite gathering without their old chum Jochen?'

'No, no.' Marianne waved him off with a kiss on his cheek. But his question was a good one. Where *was* Albrecht? And for that matter Connie and Hans and Gerhardt Friedlander? She had not seen them for some time. Albrecht had probably pulled them into the library to review his letter. The thought irritated her. Albrecht's sobriety – his constant ability to focus on the world beyond what was directly beneath his nose – felt like a reproach. He was right, of course. Poor Ernst vom Rath lay in some hospital bed and thousands of Jews slept out in the cold borderland. Germany was being run by a loudmouthed rabble-rouser, bent on baiting other nations to war and making life miserable for countless innocent citizens. And here they were, drinking champagne and dancing to Scott Joplin.

In a state of defensive irritation she burst into Albrecht's study, where, yes, there they were – all her missing guests: Albrecht and Connie, Hans and Gerhardt, Torsten Frye and the American, Sam Beverwill, and a few others, many of whom, like Connie, worked as staff officers in the *Abwehr,* the military intelligence office.

'What's this?' she said, trying to make her voice light. 'A secret, serious party? The countess will not be pleased to know you're all skulking about in the study instead of dancing.'

'Marianne –' Albrecht said.

'Albrecht! Let your guests come out and enjoy the evening –'

As she spoke, she noticed a new person in their midst: a short, dark-haired man, balding, with a kind of intensity to his homely face. The energy in the room was odd; the men's faces remained grave and unchanged by her appearance.

'I'm sorry,' she said to the new man. 'I don't believe we've been introduced.'

'Pietre Grabarek.' He stepped forward and extended his hand. A Pole. Albrecht and Connie both had many contacts in the Polish National Party.

'Marianne von Lingenfels. The wife of your sober host here,' she said, gesturing towards Albrecht.

'Marianne –' Albrecht interjected again. 'Pietre has traveled from Munich with some alarming news. This evening –'

'Vom Rath is dead?' A chill swept over Marianne.

'Dead.' Albrecht nodded. 'But that is only part of it.'

Marianne felt uncomfortably at the centre of this small group now, all scrutinising her reaction. This was not a position she was used to: the ignorant one.

'It seems Goebbels has given orders for the SA to incite rioting, destruction of Jewish property. They're throwing stones through shop windows and looting, making a sport –'

'Not a sport – a battle! An organised attack!' the man interrupted.

'– of destroying people's lives.'

'How terrible!' Marianne said. 'Did Lutze condone this? What does it mean?' Lutze was the head of the police, the SA – an unpleasant man she had recently met and disliked.

'It seems so,' Albrecht answered.

There was a shifting of glances and bodies.

'It's descent into madness – Hitler is exactly the maniac we've suspected!' Hans exclaimed, but no one paid attention. He was a sweet, foolish boy. *There are thinkers and there are actors,* Connie had once said. *Hans is an actor.* Albrecht had balked at this dichotomy, though – so black-and-white, so reductive and unforgiving. Action should follow thought and thought should include careful deliberation. But this was not Connie's way. He was more of an actor himself, and his views, while informed and considered, were rarely mulled over and always absolute.

'It means shame for Germany in the eyes of the world,' Albrecht said.

There was a general swell of affirmation.

'And suffering,' Connie said. 'It means suffering for many, many people . . .'

Silence fell across the group as sounds of laughter and strains of the accordion filtered through the leaded windows.

'And it means reasonable citizens must take action,' Connie continued. 'We are not all thugs and villains. But we will become these, if we don't try to make change.'

It was a bold statement, a challenge almost, and Marianne watched it register on the men's faces with varying results. Hans nodded dramatically, captivated. Eberhardt von Strallen, clearly disapproving of such rash talk, flicked at the lint on his lapel. Albrecht frowned thoughtfully.

'It is our duty,' Connie said. 'If we don't work actively to defeat Hitler, it will only get worse. This man – this zealot who calls himself our leader – will ruin everything we have achieved as a united nation.' He continued, 'If we don't begin to mobilise like-minded people against him, if we don't begin to actively enlist our contacts abroad – the English, the Americans, the French – he will draw us into a war, and worse. If you listen to the things this man says – if you really listen, and read – it's all there in that hideous book of his, *Mein Kampf;* his "struggle" is to turn us all into animals! Read it, *really* read it, *know thine enemies* – his vision is medieval! Worse than medieval, anarchic! That life is nothing more than a fight for resources to be waged between the races – this "Master Race" he likes to speak of and the racial profiles he has devised – these are the tools he will use to divide us and conquer.'

Marianne had heard Connie's views before – how many times had they talked late into the night around the fire in Weisslau?

Hitler was a madman and a thug, they were all in agreement. Ever since the *Putsch* this had been clear. Connie, as well as Albrecht, had spent a good portion of the last years assisting the victims of the National Socialists – Jews who wanted to emigrate, imprisoned Communists, artists whose works were banned. *Without law,* Albrecht always said, *we are no better than the apes.* His work was as much to uphold and strengthen the law through practice as it was to win each individual battle.

But Connie had given up on the law, increasingly castrated as it was under the Nazis. He was a born dissenter and a believer in direct action. It was one of the things Marianne loved most about him – Connie, her childhood playmate, dearest friend, and the man she most admired, other than Albrecht, of course. He had always been an agitator, a passionate champion of what he felt was *right*. As children, he and Marianne had spent summers with their families at the Ostsee, and Connie had always led them on quests against injustice, plotting to reveal the hotel concierge's unkindness to dogs or some wrong-headed parental prejudice. And usually he prevailed, through sheer force of character or single-mindedness.

'. . . We *must* find ways to work against him,' Connie continued. 'Not only to bring the attention of the world to his ugly aspirations, but to take action ourselves. If we sit by and judge from behind the safety of our desks, we will have only ourselves to blame. So I suggest we commit to active resistance from this day forward. To trying to steer our country from Hitler's destructive path.'

Connie finished. Sweat had formed around his hairline and he was out of breath.

There were murmurs and nods among the men gathered.

'I agree with the principle.' Albrecht spoke slowly into the swell of support. 'But active collusion against our government – this government – is a dangerous thing. And we have wives and families to consider. I am not suggesting we should not, only that we think carefully –'

'Your wives and families will support you,' Marianne interrupted, surprising herself and the rest of the room. It came out
like a rebuke. Albrecht was always so measured, slow, and *thoughtful*. A plodding tortoise to Connie's leaping stag.

'All of them?' von Strallen asked wryly.

'All of them,' Marianne repeated. Von Strallen was a chauvin-
ist. He told his silly wife, Missy, nothing and took her nowhere.
Poor Missy, treated like a dumb fattened cow.

'And bear the risk?' Albrecht asked gently.

'And bear the risk,' Marianne repeated.

'All right,' Connie said, turning his intense gaze upon her.
'Then you will see to it that they are all right. You are appointed
the commander of wives and children.'

Marianne met his gaze. *The commander of wives and children.*
She knew he did not mean to belittle her, but it smarted like a slap.

The meeting – if that's what it was – broke up, and with a sense
of unreality, Marianne headed back to the party to resume her
hostess responsibilities. Conversations rose and fell, the jazz trio
played, and from the landing of the stairs someone recited Cicero
in Latin.

But outside, beyond the castle walls, terrible things were happening. Marianne could imagine Hitler's thuggish Brownshirts
swarming the streets, swaggering and shouting with their air of
unchecked violence. She had seen them marching in a parade
last summer in Munich. Two of the men had broken formation
and rushed towards her across the pavement. For a moment
she had stood frozen, afraid that she would be attacked: but for
what? Instead they knocked down the university student beside
her and kicked him as he curled into a ball, their shiny black
boots hammering at his back. It had happened so fast that she
simply stood. *Why? What did he do?* she asked a man standing
beside her when the SA were gone. *He did not lift his hand in a*

proper Heil, the man whispered as they bent to help the poor student to his feet.

For days afterward she saw those men's faces as they rushed at her: ordinary, middle-aged faces flattened and made stupid with violence.

'What is it? You look as if you've seen a ghost,' Mimi Armacher said, interrupting the memory. Mimi was a sweet woman, a distant cousin of Albrecht's whom Marianne had always liked.

'I've just heard –' Marianne faltered. What to call it? It was something from a less civilised time, and for which she had no vocabulary. 'We've received news from Munich that there is rioting – the SA – beating people, breaking down Jewish properties –'

'News?' Mimi repeated, as if this were the incomprehensible thing.

'From a friend of Connie's who's just arrived,' Marianne explained.

'Oh, how awful,' Mimi said, and her face fell. 'In all the cities?'

Others gathered around. Marianne was aware of Berna and Gottlieb Bruckner at the edge of the group, and Alfred Klausner: Jewish friends whose own positions here in Germany were increasingly difficult. Generations of assimilation no longer seemed to set them apart from the eastern immigrant Jews Hitler was obsessed with deporting. No one was safe.

Marianne felt exhausted suddenly. 'That's what I understood.'

'Destroying property?' someone asked. 'At random?'

'*Jewish* property,' Mimi asserted with chilling crispness. 'Only Jewish properties.' She turned to Marianne. 'Isn't that what you said?'

Marianne stared at her. 'I don't know.' She drew herself up. 'Does it matter? Our government is unleashing bands of thugs.'

'It is the beginning of the end,' the countess pronounced dramatically when she heard of the destruction that would later be referred to as *Kristallnacht.* 'That Austrian will ruin this country.'

With that, she went up to bed.

Marianne envied her freedom. She herself would have to shepherd this party to its bitter end.

As the news spread, guests with government roles or substantial properties in nearby cities took off down the hill, speeding drunkenly around curves, honking and flashing their headlights. They were followed, more soberly, by the few Jewish guests. A few voyeuristic idiots drove to the neighbouring town of Ehrenheim to see how far the rioting had spread.

By the champagne fountain, Gerhardt Friedlander argued with the Stollmeyers, a set of drunken, ruddy-faced twins who were devoted Nazis. The crowd cleared a nervous circle around them.

'The conspiracy of world Jewry will not stop at murdering vom Rath,' one of the Stollmeyers ranted. 'We must take action against them –'

'Don't be a fool,' Gerhardt spat. 'Vom Rath was killed by a deranged seventeen-year-old, not a conspiracy.'

'A deranged seventeen-year-old who was a Jew and a Bolshevik,' his opponent argued, 'who wanted to destroy the pride and unity of the German *Volk* . . .'

Marianne could not listen. This absurd Nazi blather was everywhere, ripe for adoption by the likes of the simple-minded Stollmeyers. How had those two ever made the guest list? Thank God Gerhardt was there to put them in their place.

In the great room, the jazz trio had disappeared (back to Berlin? Had they been paid?), and some dolt tried to play a Nazi marching record on the Victrola only to be pelted with a round of hot *Frikadellen* from the chef's latest offering. The gawkers who had driven to Ehrenheim returned and seemed almost disappointed to report that no, nothing was afoot. What did they expect? The town was thoroughly and pigheadedly Bavarian Catholic. It had no Jewish inhabitants or businesses.

Undaunted by the news or the departures, the cook continued to offer delicacies: a new round of pork roasts, apple tortes, a *Frankfurter Kranz*. And the bartender poured drinks.

Marianne wished the remaining guests would leave. They were all self-absorbed, and frivolous. But still the party limped along towards a slow death.

Around midnight, she allowed herself a moment of privacy in an empty trophy room decorated by some von Lingenfels hunter of yore. Its walls were bedecked with pale, delicate skulls of deer and mouldering taxidermies of boar, bears, even a wolf. A cruel room, but it would do. She would rest for five minutes. Any longer and she would never return. As she sat, the expression fell from her face and the slackness that replaced it made her feel old, a mother of small children in a suddenly savage land.

'Aha!' A voice came from behind, and two hands fell on her shoulders before she had the chance to turn: Connie. She had thought him long gone – either back to Berlin to repair the damage or off to bed with his fiancée, a changed man with a new set of habits. But here he was. His intransigence reassured her.

'Caught you,' he chided.

'Oh, Connie,' she said, turning. 'Should I tell them all to go home? It's so strange to have this party when beyond it, God knows –'

'Let them stay.' Connie sank into the chair opposite her own. 'They're too drunk to leave anyway.'

'I suppose.' Marianne sighed. 'What's happening out there?'

'Well,' Connie said, leaning back. 'Greta von Viersdahl is impersonating a goose on the dance floor, old Herr Frickle has found a new strumpet to sit on his lap, and someone I don't know is vomiting into the moat.'

'Oh dear.' Marianne smiled.

How many parties had they attended together? Too many to count since their days as children. And Connie was always an entertaining reporter – an interested observer of the human animal.

It was what had forged their friendship: the aptness of his perceptions, and her own appreciation for these as a person less gifted with insight.

'And Benita?' she could not resist asking. 'Is she sleeping?'

'She's a good girl,' Connie answered, stretching out his legs, the firelight creating comically long shadows of his shoes. His handsome face looked tired. There were circles beneath his eyes.

'Does that make it easier or harder for her to go to sleep?'

Connie shrugged. 'She was exhausted.'

Marianne pulled herself more upright in the chair and stared quizzically at her friend. 'What does she think? About this rioting and thuggery, about what's happening in the world?'

Connie rolled his head over the back of his chair to look up at her. Even exhausted, his face was strikingly handsome: the fine, clear features that had made him beautiful as a boy had never thickened or dulled. Instead they'd become sharper, and straighter – still capable of startling her with their symmetry.

'You don't approve of Benita,' he said. 'I knew you wouldn't.'

'That's not fair, Connie – why would you think –?'

'I know you,' he said.

'What – am I not an open-minded, accepting person who is happy to see her friend in love?'

Connie narrowed his eyes. 'Open-minded, yes. Accepting, no. You are exacting.'

Marianne frowned. 'Well, she *is* young.'

Connie laughed.

'Will she be a partner to you? In all you do?'

Connie sat up suddenly, and for a moment Marianne was afraid she had gone too far. But he did not storm off. He turned his chair to face her and leaned forward, propping his elbows on his knees. 'Not like you and Albrecht, no,' he said. 'But there are other kinds of unions. And I love her.'

She was surprised by the intensity of his declaration. Was there, in his assertion, an implicit criticism of her own marriage?

'You must promise me something,' Connie said.

'What is it?' Marianne frowned.

He reached forward to take her hand and a shock raced through Marianne at his touch.

'If things go wrong – and they may go wrong – you must help her. She is a simple girl and she won't deserve whatever mess I might drag her into.' An uncharacteristically diffident, almost boyish look passed over his face. 'And you must help her raise my child.'

'Your –?' Marianne began, astonished. 'She is –?'

Connie nodded. 'Will you promise me this?'

'Connie, of course I will, you know I will, but –'

'Is that your word?'

Marianne studied his face, as serious as she had ever seen it, and felt a chill of premonition.

'You have my word,' she said softly, and felt the full gravity of her promise well up around them.

And then, in a moment that Marianne would replay in her mind again and again, not just that night but over the years, long after Connie was dead, Albrecht was dead, Germany itself was dead, and half the people at the party were either killed, destroyed by shame, or somewhere between the two, he leaned forward and, with the same intensity he had used to extract her promise, kissed her. It was a kiss that dispensed with any trappings of romance or flirtation, that leapfrogged (and here was a question that would gnaw irritatingly, irrelevantly in her mind forever) maybe even over desire, straight into the sea of love and knowledge. Here were two people who understood each other. Here were two people aligned in something greater than themselves.

Who pulled away first? In all the replaying, this was never clear to Marianne. And had the moment lasted minutes? Seconds? It was both crystal clear and full of confusion. For days afterward she could feel the place where Connie's hand had brushed the hair from her cheek. It shivered in memory, hot and cold at once.

'Connie,' she said when they were once again apart. He leaned forward and brought her hand to his lips. But before she could think what to say, what to ask, he rose and was gone.

PART I

CHAPTER ONE

BURG LINGENFELS, JUNE 1945

The entire cart ride from the train station to Burg Lingenfels, Benita lay on the musty hay bales in a half stupor, no longer caring what she looked like: a slut or a vagabond reclining in the open air, making her way across the country with all the dignity of a sack of potatoes. She was sick. Her stomach churned, and the sockets of her eyes ached. Possibly it was from the sausage Marianne had brought – rich, flavourful meat, the likes of which had not passed through Benita's lips for years. She could not think of it now without retching.

The train trip from Berlin had taken them three days, including one night in a transit depot crowded with every wandering rape victim, bereft mother, and wounded soldier west of the Oder. Benita was sick to death of desperate people. Berlin was bad enough, with its carousing Russians and half-starved virgins hidden in cellars, its countless dead – some still buried in the mountains of rubble – and its stinking, overcrowded bomb-shelters-turned-refugee-camps. And the route west had been even worse, clogged with all manner of suffering and human detritus. It was as if the great continent of Europe had shrugged and sent everyone rolling. Benita had no illusions. She was an animal like the rest of them, no more concerned with their pain and suffering than they were with hers.

The cart bumped over the rutted hillside, and the clouds above bounced in time across the sky, round and friendly, as innocent as they had always been. They were the best thing she had seen in weeks. Her mind drifted in and out of exhausted slumber.

In Berlin, sleep had been rare. If it wasn't the Russian captain barging into what was left of Benita's bombed-out flat, it was some other bastard who didn't yet understand that she belonged to the captain. That was how it worked in the half structure once known as 27 Meerstein Strasse. And then in the mornings, the Russian soldiers played boisterous card games at the kitchen table, and Frau Schiller, frightened old bag that she was, banged pots and pans, cooking the illicit goods the soldiers gave her to prepare for them. Benita hadn't slept a full night since Berlin fell, which was a mercy, maybe. Because with sleep came dreams. And her dreams were a distillation of every horror from the past year.

When the cart stopped, Benita woke with a jolt. They had arrived at Burg Lingenfels. She scrambled to sit, and spots swam before her eyes. When they subsided, there it was: the castle, exactly the same and totally different from how she remembered it. Rough stones, deep-set leaded-glass windows, and giant, intimidating oak front door. The building itself was untouched – what was another war to this ancient fortress? But it possessed none of the grandness that had so overwhelmed her when she'd first seen it at the countess's party. All the candles and music and pretty dresses, the fancy cars parked helter-skelter along the hillside . . . it was hard to believe that was only seven years ago. It seemed to belong to another lifetime. Now the aristocrats and artists and intellectuals who had so intimidated her were dead, broken, or irrevocably guilty. And no better off than she.

'You remember it?' Marianne was saying, lifting Martin down from the wagon – sweet Martin, Benita's precious boy, love of her life, the child she had thought she would never see again.

She nodded and tried to climb out of the cart.

'Let me help,' Marianne said. 'You are exhausted.'

Benita willed herself to step over the side and drop to the ground. She would walk with her son. But Martin was already ahead of her, following Marianne's eight-year-old boy, Fritz.

'What a healthy child. That is a blessing,' Marianne said, taking Benita's elbow.

And despite the many years since Benita had seen her, despite the fact that she had never even known Marianne, really, that she had – if anything – been irritated by the older woman's assurance and quick tongue, she allowed herself to be guided.

When Benita woke the next morning, the sun was rising, pink behind the black outline of the chestnut tree, the stable, the crow perched on the roof. The scene reminded her of the silhouette cutouts she'd cherished as a girl: quaint two-dimensional forms of children frolicking, dirndl-clad maidens dancing, steepled churches rising over sleeping towns. She had always stopped before the artists' stall in the Saturday market and admired these black-and-white visions of an uncomplicated life.

She rolled over and surveyed her surroundings. The room had once been used as a pantry – the walls were lined with empty shelves and an ancient butter churn sat in the corner. It smelled of damp stone and, faintly, of pickling vinegar and Christmas spices. Old smells, baked into the walls.

Martin lay curled beside her on the thin mattress, his blond hair spread fanlike on the pillow, his sweet, perfectly formed features made fragile by sleep. He was such a handsome boy – beautiful, really. Even more so than Connie had been. And seeing him there, under the blanket (and to have not one but *two* blankets and *two* mattresses), Benita was seized with an urge to gather him up and press her face into the soft skin of his neck, to breathe in the smell of boy and youth and sleep. She wanted, almost, to consume him – this best, most perfect piece of herself. She wanted to *become* him and in so doing become herself again. Benita Gruber, town beauty, innocent nineteen-year-old, a girl out of a silhouette.

But she let him sleep. His breath stirred the fuzzy threads of the blanket. He shuddered as she watched. What haunted his dreams? The blare of bomb sirens and the screech of planes over Berlin? The dead bodies they had stepped over in the rubble? Or God knows what from the 'Children's Home' the Gestapo had sent him to after Benita was imprisoned. She had never seen it. It was Marianne who had – miraculously – found Martin when Benita had given him up for dead. *It was a typical Nazi establishment,* Marianne had said of the home, *lots of marching and no learning.* Being Marianne, she focused on the ideology and not the creature comforts of the place. Was there enough to eat? Were the caretakers kind? Had there been time to play? These questions remained unanswered. But Marianne had found Martin and returned him to Benita, and for that Benita owed her everything.

She must have drifted off again because when she next opened her eyes, the room was empty. Benita sat with a start. Where was Martin? The blood raced to her head and then away. Surely he was all right. The war was over. They were not in Berlin anymore, they were at Burg Lingenfels, in the American zone, and it was safe here. They were under Marianne's care.

But still, he had been taken from her once. She couldn't survive it again.

Benita pulled a skirt over her nightgown and raced down the dark stone hall. Breathlessly, she found her way to the kitchen. It was empty. No sign of Martin, or anyone. Then she spotted movement outside the window. Two little figures – Fritz, Marianne's boy, and Martin, crouched in the courtyard, poking sticks into a puddle. Relief flooded through her.

Thank you, thank you, dear God, for protecting my son . . . the prayer was involuntary, a nervous remnant of her Catholic upbringing. The religious pleas of her youth had returned to her in prison and served as an anchor in the endless sea of silence.

Without them, she was sure her mind would have drifted away. She did not believe in them, but still, they had saved her – not God, just the words.

She knew she was lucky to have been sent to prison and not a concentration camp after Connie was executed for his role in the assassination plot. Ultimately, this was how all her yearning for nobility and a good marriage had paid off: as the wife of a traitor with a noble Prussian bloodline, she had received solitary confinement rather than death. She could recognise, if not yet laugh at, the grim humour of this. But the blankness that had entered her during that time lingered. She had spent too many hours staring at the ceiling, the backs of her hands, the corner of her cell where the paint was chipped. It was only for Martin's sake that she now tried to overcome this.

As Benita stood watching the boys, Marianne banged into the kitchen, pulling a small cart of carrots and cabbages and even raspberries, which Benita had not seen in years. 'God bless Herr Kellerman for keeping up the garden,' Marianne exclaimed. 'There are not many men who were seeding potatoes and carrots last spring – and certainly not on someone else's property.' She was flushed, and her hair formed a frizzy halo around her head. 'Benita! How did you sleep, my poor dear? Have a bowl of porridge.' She gestured at a pot on the stove.

'Thank you,' Benita said.

Marianne was already removing a bowl from the cupboard – fine china, blue-and-white Meissen. 'I can't say it's tasty, but it's edible.' She plopped a helping into the bowl and set it on the table. 'Sit. You are meant to eat and rest.'

So Benita sat.

She watched Marianne empty the cart, a whirlwind of vigorous, chaotic activity. The war had not changed her as much as it had everyone else. She was still an enigma to Benita, a woman capable of tracking Martin to some obscure Nazi hideaway but incapable of managing her own hair. When Benita first married

Connie, she had marvelled at the woman's paradoxes. Marianne loved to entertain but cared nothing about food or fashion. She would slave away preparing the house for a fabulous party only to come down wearing last year's dowdy dress. She would invite the most distinguished members of the Foreign Office and intelligence corps to dinner and then serve her cook's homely *Sauerbraten* and *Wildschweingulasch*. She was an abstracted, disorganised mother to her children but an organised and efficient manager of adults.

She was not a beauty with her strong, almost mannish features and high cheekbones (a falcon face, Benita had once said to Connie and been thoroughly scolded). But she was compelling, and in moments, her face achieved a kind of graceful symmetry that was striking. It was a face you could not easily forget.

At the salons and weekend parties Marianne and Albrecht hosted in the beginning of the war, Benita had watched the handsome barons and counts and noble youths of Germany's most aristocratic families hang on Marianne's every word. They had jousted playfully in a style of speaking that made Benita feel stupid. Were they joking or serious? Teasing her or mocking one another? In the presence of Connie's fancy friends, Benita had found language an obstacle rather than a bridge to connection, but for Marianne it seemed a smooth and direct road that always rose to meet her feet.

'Why, you're still in your nightclothes!' Marianne exclaimed, glancing up from the vegetables she was unloading. 'Did you find the clothing I left in your room?'

Benita blushed. She had risen in such haste and completely forgotten to dress. 'I'm sorry – I was rushing.'

'Sorry! Pish. Nothing to be sorry for. It just doesn't seem like you. But then of course no one can be expected to be like themselves anymore, can they?' Marianne lifted the cart by its handles and pushed it back out of the kitchen door. 'As long as you have what you need.'

At that moment, Marianne's two daughters appeared in the doorway, carrying a bucket between them.

'Just in time,' Marianne cried. 'We have milk for you, Tante Benita!'

Benita was not sure which surprised her more – the presence of milk or the title *Tante*, 'aunt.' Somehow lowly Benita Gruber, last of a long line of toiling Westphalian peasants, had become *Tante* to the von Lingenfels girls.

'Say hello, girls, and introduce yourselves,' Marianne instructed.

The girls approached – dark haired and tall, maybe ten and twelve. Katarina and Elisabeth. And Benita remembered their two little heads peering down at the guests from the landing on the stairs at the countess's party. She had wished so fervently to have a daughter like them, a sweet girl to dress in dirndls and christen in delicate, frothy white. It seemed quaint now – an innocent dream. Who would want to introduce a girl to this world? Thank God Martin was a boy.

'Here,' said Katarina, the younger of the two, as she dipped a cup into the bucket and extended it to Benita. 'It's delicious.' She had a sweet, shy manner about her, with long, thick eyelashes and awkward coltish limbs.

'Where is Martin?' the older girl, Elisabeth, asked. She was the sharper of the two in both look and tone.

'Out in the courtyard – you didn't see him?' Benita sprang up to look. The puddle was now abandoned. 'He was with Fritz, playing –'

She started towards the door but was stopped by Marianne.

'Let him be,' Marianne commanded. 'It's good for a boy to be free.' Taking in Benita's face, she softened her voice. 'All is very safe here, Benita. Really.'

*   *   *

In her room, Benita pulled on the battered brassiere and the vest that she had washed and worn so many times its seams were nearly gone, the drops of blood across the belly now faded to innocent-looking brown splotches. She found a washbasin and a pitcher of water on an otherwise empty shelf. She splashed some on her face and pulled back her poor brittle hair, knotting it at the nape of her neck.

There was a loud rap on the door. 'I'm leaving shoes here for you,' Marianne's voice said. 'See if they fit.'

Benita's own were a badly worn pair of boots she had stolen from a bombed-out flat that she had joined the women of her building in combing through. No one asked what had become of its inhabitants – lying dead under the rubble of the bombing or safe in the countryside or killed in a concentration camp. The shoes had been cheap to begin with and were now nearly worn through.

Benita waited until Marianne's footsteps receded to retrieve the new boots. They were certainly the finest she had ever come into contact with: dark green, barely worn, with an elegant, distinguished heel. The leather was soft and smooth, and against it, her finger felt monstrously chapped. They were too fine for a woman with such hands, the kind of boots she had once dreamed of wearing. It seemed a cruel joke that this would be that day. *Be careful what you wish for,* they seemed to taunt. She could not put them on.

When she emerged, dressed, Martin sat at the kitchen table between Elisabeth and Katarina. His mouth was stained with raspberry juice, his eyes round at the sight of so much food.

'Ah, that's better!' Marianne said of the clean white shirt and wool skirt Benita now wore. 'The shoes didn't fit?'

'No,' Benita lied.

Suddenly there was a gurgling sound from Martin, and the little boy's face turned red.

On either side of him the girls blanched.

'Oh!' Benita exclaimed, feeling his shame as if it were her own. Of course his poor belly was not used to all this fruit. He had probably eaten God knows how many bowls of porridge, and now the berries, and whatever else. The stink was putrid – full of the bile of a dysfunctional gut.

'Poor boy,' Marianne said. 'We should not have fed you so much!' She held out a hand to him, taking charge in her usual calm, competent way. 'We will have to find you a new pair of pants.'

Slowly, humiliatingly, Martin rose, the back of his pants stained and the stench growing worse.

'Come.' Marianne nicked her head. 'I know just the thing.'

'Benita,' she added over her shoulder, 'would you give that pot a stir?'

Benita nodded and watched as Marianne disappeared with her son.

CHAPTER TWO

THURINGIA, LATE MAY 1945

In the Children's Home, Martin Constantine Fledermann was not Martin's name. He was Martin Schmidt, just as Berthold von Stauffenberg was Berthold Meister and Liesel Stravitsky was Liesel Falkman, and so on. All the children were given good, ordinary German names. And the shameful thing was that Martin had almost forgotten he was a Fledermann.

There were many things he had forgotten in the Children's Home. His father, for example: the shadowy figure Marianne later referred to as a hero and his mother never mentioned. And life before the war, before air-raid sirens and nights spent in the cellar, before the deafening roar of low-flying bomber planes.

But there were things he remembered in the home, too. How he'd arrived, for instance. A long train trip on a military transport, the pockmarked face of his SS chaperone, and the salty, tangy taste of dried meat on his tongue – it was the first time he had ever tasted such a thing, warm and a little gritty from its home in the SS man's pocket. He had thrown up afterwards, holding his head out of the window of the moving train so that the vomit spewed back in his face.

He also remembered the sunny flat in Berlin, air thick with dust motes, and the view over shady, elegant Meerstein Strasse, with its pale stucco buildings and café on the corner. And the warmth of his mother's body curled against his at night in bed. The cameo pendant that hung in the hollow of her throat. The words of the song she would sing to him – *Kommt ein Vogel geflogen, setzt sich nieder auf mein' Fuss, hat ein Zettel im Schnabel von der Mutter ein' Gruss.* 'A little bird comes flying, sits down on my foot, has a letter in its beak, from my mother a kiss.' But at the Children's Home there was no bird, no letter, and no kiss.

The home was not all bad, though. It was a cozy stucco house outside a village in the foothills of the mountains. It had a pleasant garden full of fruit trees and flowers, a broken fountain, and a high brick wall. The children were not allowed to leave.

Frau Vortmuller, the potato-faced grandmother in charge of the place, was not unkind. She was firm and orderly and saw to it that her charges were bathed and clothed and fed. Every night, she played the recorder for them: sorrowful folk ballads about poor millers' daughters and princes, witches and resourceful, neglected youngest sons. These were sweeter, softer melodies than the Nazi-endorsed songs the children learned from Herr Stulper, who supervised their reeducation. He taught them 'The Rotten Bones Are Trembling', 'The Horst Wessel Song', and 'Germany Awake', all full of verses about blood, slavery, and revenge; politics and war.

Every day, Frau Vortmuller wore the same tweed skirt and green jacket with a Nazi *Mutterkreuz,* which she had been awarded for bearing eight children, on the lapel. Four of these were dead: two killed in the war, one dead at birth, and another who had 'succumbed' in an institution for the 'feeble-minded.' Frau Vortmuller hung this one's picture in the pantry, where she could see his face every time she pulled out the ingredients for supper. Of those living, her sons had not yet returned from wherever they'd been fighting, and her daughters were married mothers themselves. Martin found the *Mutterkreuz* pin beautiful – with its gold points and shiny blue inset – and the pride with which she rubbed it clean and wrapped it in a handkerchief every evening lent it an almost holy significance.

In the weeks after the war ended, Frau Vortmuller, a religious woman, began to speak to the children about God. Once she was the only supervisor left at the Children's Home – Herr Stulper had taken off at the first sign of the Americans – who was there to reprimand her? The Americans, who held church every Sunday in their barracks and wore crosses underneath their uniforms? She included Bible readings and nightly prayers in the children's bedtime routine. Herr Stulper would have reported her. He had taught them about racial purity and German *Heimat* and the divine wisdom of their Führer and had no patience for what he called 'Christian superstitions'. Mostly the children hated him. Although he had led them on a few wonderful hikes in the mountains and let them listen to Nazi-endorsed radio programmes. Martin grew to love one song that was played often: 'Erika', which he understood to be a folksy ballad about a flower and a pair of childhood sweethearts. Until Liesel 'Falkman' whispered to him that singing along to it was as bad as spitting on his father's grave. Martin did not understand this. How could it be like spitting on his father's grave? The fathers and mothers of the children in the home had made 'mistakes', he understood. Now they were dead. And it was Frau Vortmuller and Herr Stulper's job to ready them for new families – rich, powerful Nazi families who would teach them to be good Germans.

Bullshit, Liesel said. *Our mothers aren't dead – they're in prisons or concentration camps.*

For what? Martin asked.

For plotting to kill Hitler, Dummkopf.

Martin was filled with shame. For plotting to kill the Führer, who Frau Vortmuller assured them in many ways was all-knowing, kind, and good? His own mother and father had done this?

At eleven, Liesel had a wider, darker sense of the world than Martin. When Frau Vortmuller extinguished the candles at night,

Liesel would climb into Martin's bed and whisper secrets. She was not supposed to be in the home with the others. Her parents were Communists, not aristocrats. Her bloodlines did not date back to Frederick the Great or Bismarck or anyone else of national significance. But somehow, when her parents were taken by the Gestapo, Liesel had been brought here. Maybe because she was pretty and blonde and blue eyed. This Martin understood. Liesel was the prettiest girl he knew. She would make a good child for an important Nazi family. Wasn't she happy then, that they had made this mistake? No, Liesel would scowl at him when he asked such questions. She didn't want to live with Nazi pigs.

Then, suddenly, it seemed Liesel was right. Their mothers *were* alive. The first to arrive was Adalbert 'Schmedding's' – a gaunt, hollow-cheeked woman with a dark-haired baby in her arms. She had cried and cried as she held her son, stuffing his face against her belly as if, rather than reuniting, they were saying goodbye. And then others came in batches: Claus and Gretel's glamorous aunt from England, who was taking them to their mother in Switzerland; the 'Beckers'' sweet, tired mother straight out of solitary confinement in Ravensbrück; the 'Hansers'' mother by way of a fancy American armed forces escort car. At first Martin's heart had leapt every time the gate bell chimed. His mother! He thought of her blonde head bent over the game of marbles they would play, her fine strands of hair catching the sun – and the tight grip of her hand as she walked beside him past the bombed fountain to the *Apotheke* or the market. He recalled how it felt to press his face against the stiffly washed fabric of her dress and, underneath it, the softness of her breast.

But Martin's mother did not come and neither did Liesel's.

My little sparrows, Frau Vortmuller called them, looking increasingly worried. It was the beginning of June. Her youngest daughter, Magda, had come to stay with them, along with her two mean little boys, who called them 'traitors' spawn'.

'Why don't you throw them out?' Martin overheard Magda ask

her mother one night. 'The war is over! Your responsibility here is finished!'

From then on, Martin was extra careful. He did not want to be thrown out. And he knew it was true: Frau Vortmuller did not have to stay with them anymore. There was no one commanding – or paying – her to do so. *She just wants the extra rations,* Liesel said. But he did not believe this. In her way, he thought, Frau Vortmuller loved them.

And then one day, a tall, stern-faced lady named Marianne von Lingenfels arrived. With her cape and high boots she reminded Martin of a toy soldier. *Is that your mother?* Liesel whispered, watching through the window with him as the woman strode up the path.

Then they heard her in the foyer. She had a loud, clear voice that carried up the tile stairway. She had come to claim Martin Fledermann (the sound of his name crackled inside like a spark along dormant wires: Martin Fledermann, of course that was his name). She was a friend of the family. She would take him to find his mother in Berlin.

Beside Martin, Liesel grew still. She would be alone if he left. Martin could see her thinking this, too.

The woman strode into the room, Frau Vortmuller scrambling behind her, wheezing up the stairs and looking alarmed.

'Martin Fledermann,' the woman announced, clapping her hands together. She had a long, intelligent face and startlingly bright brown eyes. Her hair was pulled back severely.

'Marianne von Lingenfels,' she said, bending to his level and extending her hand. 'You don't remember me. Your father was my dear friend.'

Martin stared back at her.

'And who is this?' The woman straightened, and her eyes moved to take in Liesel, whose pretty face grew petulant.

'Liesel . . .' Frau Vortmuller said, pausing, 'Stravitsky.' She cast a nervous look in the girl's direction. It was not a name Martin had heard before.

'Ah.' Frau von Lingenfels frowned. 'What was your father's name, child?'

'Bartosz,' Liesel mumbled, and then, seeming to consider something, she looked up. 'Do you know my mother? Johanna? Is she alive?'

Frau von Lingenfels looked uncertain. 'I don't know,' she said, finally. 'I didn't know her.' Martin had never heard these names. But he understood something he could not put into words and reached over to take hold of Liesel's hand.

'*Ach mein liebes Gott,*' Frau Vortmuller said, and crossed herself. Liesel snatched her hand away.

'Why don't you come with us?' the woman said. 'I will try to help you find your family.'

Liesel shook her head.

'*Nha!* Liesel!' Frau Vortmuller gasped at the rudeness, but the woman gestured away her protests.

'You can stay here with Frau Vortmuller, who obviously cannot do anything to help you find your mother, or come with me and I can promise nothing, but at least I will try.'

Liesel scowled, and then finally she nodded.

'It is settled then,' the woman said, clapping her hands to her sides. 'And' – she turned to Frau Vortmuller – 'you can do your explaining to the Americans.'

The journey from the Children's Home to Berlin was, for Martin, like a voyage to a foreign land. He had been nowhere and seen nothing in the year that he'd lived in the home. Herr Stulper's Sunday wanders were infrequent at best and always led the children *away* from civilisation, up into the hills. And like most of the children, Martin had arrived at night by car and never even seen the village.

So the morning they left with Marianne von Lingenfels, Martin and Liesel followed her with wide eyes. Bedraggled white sheets and handkerchiefs hung from windows of homes – left over from the capitulation, Marianne explained. *Have you not been to town since the Americans arrived?* Martin was suddenly embarrassed. How had they allowed themselves to be so thoroughly locked up?

Other than the sheets on the windows, the village seemed untouched by war. The half-timbered houses stood intact, geraniums growing from their window boxes. An old stone church stood in the small square and beside this a water pump fed into a stone trough. Two American soldiers sat in a jeep, handing out chewing gum. 'Would you like to ask for some?' Frau von Lingenfels asked. The idea of asking the soldiers for sweets struck Martin as preposterous. The dangers of America had been a great theme for Frau Vortmuller. In America, she warned the children, Germans had to wear swastikas on their lapels. Just like the Jews had to wear stars here. She did not have to elaborate. Obviously this was not a good thing.

The day was warm, and the satchel that held Martin's belongings (three shirts, an extra pair of trousers, a well-worn Loden jacket Frau Vortmuller had dug up from God knows where) bumped hotly against his back. It was beautiful out, though. Dandelions and morning glories blossomed along the roadside, and the flowering rapeseed fields were a sea of yellow. Frau von Lingenfels, or 'Tante Marianne', as she wished to be called, led the children in silence. Martin listened to the wind whistle in his ears and through the stands of trees between fields.

The next town along, which was bigger, had been bombed, and a church steeple jutted from a massive pile of rubble like a decapitated head. American soldiers and German women worked together scraping up the remains, pushing wheelbarrows, shoveling rocks onto an army transport truck.

When night fell, the moon was huge. Tante Marianne hired a farmer with an empty hay wagon to drive them to a town where she had heard there might still somehow be train service. And on the back of this bumping, clattering vehicle, Martin allowed himself, for the first time, to close his eyes and fall asleep.

When he opened them again, it was dark. People were everywhere, young and old, women and children, soldiers still in their Wehrmacht uniforms . . . all sitting on piles of belongings: suitcases and boxes and dirty sacks. He climbed off the wagon after Tante Marianne and Liesel, stepping around an old woman on a stool, cradling an intricately carved wooden clock.

But he and Tante Marianne and Liesel were not joining the masses on this side of the tracks. They crossed to the other side, in hopes of catching a train going east. The wrong way. Martin thought of Frau Vortmuller's warnings that the Russians were fierce, animal-like brutes who stuck German soldiers on bayonets and did unspeakable things to women (*What?* the children always asked, at which she would look aghast). They were going to find his mother. They were going to Berlin.

If his mother was alive, though, Martin wondered why she had not come for him. But he didn't ask.

'How were they killed?' Liesel asked Tante Marianne when they were seated on the platform, leaning against their bags. He knew who she meant: their fathers.

'That is no question for a child,' Tante Marianne said, her tone sharp.

'But I want to know,' Liesel insisted.

'Know that your father was a brave man. And that he did what he thought was right for his country.'

'Was he shot or hanged?' Liesel persisted in a hard and unfamiliar tone.

Tante Marianne sighed, a long, deep breath, almost worse than any answer. 'Hanged,' she said. 'They were almost all hanged.'

It was the first time Martin had heard it. He squeezed his eyes shut and pretended to have fallen back to sleep. His neck began to hurt, but he did not stir. It was essential to pretend.

When the train finally arrived, it was huge and violently loud, a freight train. Almost before its wheels ground to a halt, people hurled themselves at it, climbing hand over fist up the spindly ladders, scrabbling to the top of the open coal cars. There were only a few guards, all Americans, and they were busy unhooking the last car. One of them fired a few shots that whistled overhead: It was forbidden to climb aboard the freight trains, especially those hauling coal – it wasn't yet winter but the predictions were already dire. Coal would soon be as precious as gold.

'It's only the Americans,' Tante Marianne said. 'They don't mean to shoot anyone – if it were the British, we would have to watch our backs.'

Martin liked her optimism. When the train started, it blew her hair every which way. She looked younger and softer now. An old man passed her a flask, which she refused, but the generous spirit of his gesture was contagious. Another woman offered handfuls of raw oats. Marianne distributed a loaf of bread. The mood was jolly, even exuberant. Above them the stars were so bright and three-dimensional they seemed closer than the dark blots of towns and woods the train trundled past. Bombed church steeples, houses, and highways disappeared into an irrelevant jumble.

'Your father would have loved this,' Marianne said, startling Martin. 'He always was a troublemaker.'

Martin was confused. The image of his father was becoming more opaque rather than less.

'When he was a boy,' Marianne continued, 'he took up boxing to rebel against his father, who was very stern and very proper. A Fledermann boxing! It was shocking – it would be like' – she groped for an analogy – 'like you taking up tap dancing!'

Martin had never heard of tap dancing. It sounded frivolous. Like something a boy should stay away from. Boxing, on the other hand, was manly. He gave up trying to make sense. He could barely hear her voice over the wind. Beside him, Liesel had fallen asleep. He let Marianne's words wash over him. She had loved his father. This much he understood.

*   *   *

The train stopped at some point in the night. The tracks went no farther. The Berlin station had been bombed by the Allies and then flooded by the SS, who feared the Russians would use its vast tunnels to stage their invasion. Drowned bodies were supposedly still washing up onto the streets. They learned this from a grizzled old man who was eager to warn Marianne off. Liesel and Martin listened, half-asleep. *So we will walk*, Marianne responded, unfazed. Both children did not protest. Martin's wonder at being free had worn thin, though. His feet ached and the road was crammed with fellow refugees. In the grey light of dawn, the city's suburbs looked mean and haggard. Somewhere within all this crumbling brick, his mother waited. Martin tried to fill his mind with her but found he could barely conjure her face.

They walked all day through the suburbs and into the ruined city. They trudged down cavern-like streets piled high with debris. The fronts of buildings rose from the wreckage like jagged cut-outs. Had the buildings always been so fragile? Like sandcastles taken down by waves. At street level the remaining walls were covered with papers, scrawled names, and messages. Martin could see Liesel staring at them.

'Missing people,' she said in her defiant way. 'Probably dead.'

Makeshift chimneys rose from the rubble like waving arms.

For the final portion of the journey, Marianne flagged down a passing American army jeep. At first, the driver shook his head without even looking at them, but the soldier in the passenger seat jabbed him with his elbow. He slowed to a halt and extended his hand. Martin hesitated before accepting, but the sores on his feet and his general fatigue won over his doubts. Frau Vortmuller's warnings about the Americans already seemed like something from another life. Marianne sat with the soldiers in front and spoke English, while Liesel and Martin huddled in the back. To their amazement, the soldier who had waved them in turned around and handed them a chocolate bar. And after that, for some time all else fell away. There was only the unaccustomed sweetness of the chocolate, the slippery melting on the tongue. When was the last time Martin had tasted something so delicious?

When they arrived, Meerstein Strasse did not look like a street where anyone could live. No more tall, speckled plane trees lining the kerbs, no more lively café on the corner, no more gurgling fountain. But still, pockets of memory opened in Martin. The smell of damp stone, rot, and chemicals; the sight of people emerging from cellars covered in dust . . . the empty brass birdcage that hung in their shelter, the pee bucket in the corner. The horrible, glass-eyed elephant trunk masks.

Marianne climbed out of the jeep and thanked the Americans. Still sticky and slightly dazed from the chocolate, Martin and Liesel scrambled after her. She pulled a crumpled envelope from her jacket and regarded it for a moment before crossing the street to ask a group of women at a water pump for directions. The paper looked ancient and unpromising. But the script stirred something in Martin – it was familiar. His father's handwriting.

As Marianne spoke, one of the women tried to fill a woven basket. The water rushed out through its lattices, but she didn't seem to notice. On her hip, a baby stared at Martin.

'Over there,' another woman said, pointing to a building, if it could be called that.

Marianne looked back down at the letter as if hoping for some other indication, before she led Martin and Liesel towards the remnants of number 27.

'Building is full,' a Russian soldier barked as they approached. 'Move on.'

To Martin's surprise, Marianne answered in Russian. A wide smile spread across the soldier's face. '*Ty govorish' po-Russki?*' he asked.

More Russian issued from Marianne's lips and the soldier

bounced on his heels like a delighted child. 'Jiri,' he called, and soon they stood at the center of a small group of Russians, all grinning and slapping Marianne on the back.

Benita Fledermann – Martin distinguished his mother's name.

'Ah.' The man nodded, his face sobering. More Russian.

'This is where you lived?' Liesel whispered. She too seemed impressed with Marianne's Russian.

Martin shook his head. Where he lived was not like this.

The Russian gestured for them to follow.

What had once been a courtyard was now piled high with rubble and criss-crossed by narrow footpaths. 'Don't fall,' Marianne said as they walked. She was stern again; the freedom that had come over her on the train was gone.

They followed the man through a doorway, down a black hall, and up a staircase, climbing blindly. It smelled of mould and cabbage and human shit. Marianne's dry hand gripped Martin's hard enough to hurt. He was thankful for the pain; without it his body might disappear in the dark.

Then there was light. A man sat outside a closed door beside an electric lantern. He was terrifyingly ugly: swarthy and scarred and low-browed, wearing the uniform of a Red Army soldier. At their approach, he pulled a rifle across his lap. He and the man they followed exchanged words, and with a terse nod to Marianne, their escort departed.

The man outside the door was not moved by Marianne's Russian. He answered her in a short guttural grunt that did not sound like any language Martin had ever heard.

From behind him, a rich and salty smell of bacon wafted from the flat; also the sharp scent of alcohol.

The man rapped on the door, entered, closed it behind him, and then reemerged, opening the door for them. Inside, men clustered around a table, playing cards. Martin did not need to speak their language to understand that they were amused.

Was this where his mother lived? With all these men? Martin was confused. One wall was entirely gone, revealing the beams and brick and pipes, and old bits of newspaper insulation. Water dripped from a corner of the ceiling into a tub. But the smells – bacon, and onions, maybe even butter frying – were of delicacies he had not eaten in years. His mouth watered. Tins of beans and fruit lined the countertop.

But where was his mother in all this? A dreadful feeling grew inside him. *Smells of the devil,* Frau Vortmuller would have said. There was an old woman at the stove, and a girl with bright painted lips and cheeks stood beside her, wearing only a grubby silk robe that revealed her scrawny chest, the breastbones like a chicken's.

'Where is Frau Fledermann?' Marianne addressed the old woman, whose expression shifted from hostility to surprise.

'Dear God!' she exclaimed, looking at the children and crossing herself.

On the stove the potatoes began to smoke.

'I'll get her,' the woman in the robe said. She stabbed her cigarette out on a plate. As she passed, one of the Russians grabbed her wrist and said something that made her laugh.

Marianne was not amused. 'I will come, too,' she announced, shooing Martin and Liesel out into the hall.

Back in the darkness, beside the frightening man with the gun, even Liesel did not speak. The electric lamp cast long, spooky shadows.

Finally the door of the flat opened again. The woman who emerged after Marianne was almost unrecognisable to Martin: glassy eyed and thin and smelling strongly of perfume and sweat. She looked panicked and her hands – long, white, and trembling – reached for Martin, fluttering over his face and hair and shoulders, like a blind woman's.

'My boy! Oh, my boy!' she said, dropping to her knees. 'My sweet child!'

Martin wanted to speak – to reassure her, but he couldn't think how.

'Oh, my boy,' the woman, his mother, repeated, pulling him against her chest.

And Martin could only stand, stiff as a board, trying to keep them both upright.

CHAPTER THREE

FRÜHLINGHAUSEN, MARCH 12, 1938

The day Benita met Martin Constantine Fledermann was unusually warm for March. It was as though they were in Italy or Greece, she kept saying, hoping it made her sound worldly, like someone who had actually travelled to such places, experienced such heat, although of course everyone knew she hadn't, and they certainly hadn't been anywhere so exotic themselves, Frühlinghausen being what it was.

It was the day of the Anschluss. Five hundred kilometers south, Hitler had personally driven to his birthplace, the little border town of Braunau am Inn in Austria, to announce the country's 'return to the Reich'. The radio was filled with tales of cheering crowds, waving flags, and throwing flowers, of people dancing in the streets. Frühlinghausen officials, eager to capture a little gaiety for the town, organised an impromptu celebration – a rally to be led by their own mayor and a local band. Who wouldn't want to celebrate the union of two populations of German speakers? This was a great theme for Hitler, and therefore for Frühlinghausen, which was thoroughly in support of the man and his party: the quest to unify all ethnic Germans across the continent under one flag.

Benita Gruber was nineteen years old and dressed in her finest

Bund Deutscher Mädel uniform, a dark blue wool skirt and white blouse she'd saved her own money to buy – no longer the make-shift blue-and-white ensemble she'd worn for the first years of her membership, but the real thing, printed with the BDM mono-gram. She had braided her thick hair in two artful plaits and knew that she looked beautiful and healthy, the very picture of the cel-ebrated *Jungfrau,* or German maiden. It was young women like her who had inspired Hitler's vision of the master race. She was meant to become round with child, again and again, to populate the motherland with Aryan babies who would grow to be happy, healthy Germans, capable of hard work and loyal to their home-land. At least this was the idea propagated by Fräulein Brebel, the dour leader of Benita's BDM group, who had no children herself.

And so, after coffee, Benita arrived at the town square along with her troop of wide-eyed *Mädels.* The mayor of Frühlinghau-sen was a rising star in the local Nazi Party and was considered quite a catch. On that afternoon, at least among the girls of the BDM, there was a sense of Cinderella-at-the-ball anticipation as they took their places before the podium.

For all his promise, though, the mayor was neither handsome nor charismatic. His face was blubbery and wide, and as he spoke, rivulets of sweat dripped down his cheeks and hiccupped over his moles. But he was full of conviction.

'Today we usher in a new and important era . . .' He used an approximation of Hitler's own staccato, his words half lost in the wind, half swallowed by the stone walls of the seven-hundred-year-old church behind him. 'Today we embark on the road to a once again powerful and united Germandom . . .'

Benita was bored. She had no doubt she could attract this trundlehead's attention. But what was the point? The very idea of standing beside him, let alone kissing him, was unpleasant. She imagined he smelled like sweat and mildewed wool and, be-neath this, the pigsty. Like so many of the town's young men, he lived with his family on the farm they had operated with minimal success for the last however many hundreds of years. During the harvest season, he would be out in the fields alongside everyone else, pitching hay and sweating like a pig.

Benita backed away through the small crowd, careful not to draw Fräulein Brebel's attention. Once free, she ducked down the little pedestrian *allée* that led to the old millpond and Beiderman's Apotheke, where she could buy a bottle of the hand cream that promised to set her apart from all the other wash-powder-chapped girls of Frühlinghausen. For what? Who knew. For whom? Another good question. But the questions themselves excited Benita. She was destined for something better than Frühlinghausen.

Then suddenly, rounding the corner, Benita was confronted by the most handsome, most sophisticated man she had ever seen. He leaned against the wall of the millpond, lighting a cigarette and wearing a good suit. Benita recognised this immediately – it was made of some kind of English wool, and the shoes beneath it were of shiny oxblood leather. He was tall and slim and unmistakably aristocratic.

'Sorry,' he said, straightening and looking over his shoulder, as if to see whether he blocked her path. 'Am I—?'

Benita blushed. 'Oh no, I just wasn't expecting to see anyone.'

'Because they're all so engrossed in the mayor's brilliant oration?'

She laughed in surprise. His accent was refined, high German, and his sarcasm was as un-Frühlinghausen as his appearance.

'You were listening?'

The man shrugged and took a thoughtful drag of the cigarette he'd finally managed to light. 'I was present.'

They were both silent for a moment. Benita felt the urge to smooth her skirt, straighten the little neckerchief that had probably blown askew – but she stopped herself and stood still, staring back at him. 'It's boring,' she said, and her heartbeat quickened at her own recklessness.

The man smiled. 'The speech or the Anschluss?'

'Both.' Benita shrugged, feigning a sort of jaded sophistication. The man laughed. A jolt of fear snapped through her: Had she said something stupid?

'The Anschluss,' he said, pushing himself off the wall he leaned against, 'is not boring.'

He extended his hand. 'Connie Fledermann,' he said. 'May I buy you a coffee somewhere and we can debate this?'

The touch of his hand was warm and dry and sent splinters of excitement through Benita's veins. And his eyes were an almost eerie shade of blue – not pale like her own, but intense – the blue of the North Sea in the sun or of the tiny flowers that took over Frühlinghausen for a few magnificent days each spring.

But how could she say yes? She was bound by her own lack of imagination. Fräulein Brebel and the other girls would be looking for her. It was *Heimatabend,* and they were to go directly to Olga Meisner's parlour for a piano concert following the mayor's speech.

'I can't,' Benita said formally and with genuine sorrow, 'but thank you for the invitation.'

'Why not?' he pressed. 'You must get back to that bore?'

'No.' Benita blushed. 'To my group.'

'Your group – aha!' He narrowed his eyes and gave her an assessing look. 'Aren't you too old for Hitler Youth?'

'Oh, it isn't that – it's *Bund Deutscher Mädel,*' she said, surprised at his mistake.

The man shrugged. 'Any of these – *groups.*' He said the word with obvious disdain, and she blushed more deeply, feeling the full depth of the divide between them.

'Goodbye,' she managed.

'Wait – have I upset you?' he said. 'I meant no offence – it's just my own – well, never mind.' He bowed theatrically and doffed an imaginary hat. 'It was lovely to have met you, fair maiden.'

That night, Benita tossed and turned as she lay in the dingy bedroom she shared with her two brothers under the eaves of the mouldering thatched roof of Gruber cottage, replaying her missed opportunity and the tantalising possibility the man had presented. How had she let Fräulein Brebel's *Heimatabend* hold her back? This had been her moment, the chance fate had offered, and she had said no! In the face of this dreadful awareness, her family's cottage seemed particularly mouldy and damp, the blankets on the bed disgustingly pilly, and the snores of her brothers as low and dumb as the grunts of sleeping swine.

For the next few days Benita sulked, spending hours on the weedy patch of grass behind the cottage, staring at the sky instead of helping her mother with the wash she took in.

Even by Frühlinghausen standards the Grubers were poor. Benita's father, long dead, had been a mason like his father and his father before him, primarily employed by the town's mental hospital – a dank, rambling establishment housed in a building that had once been a monastery and was in constant need of restoration. Their home was one of seven that lined the north wall of its grounds like a row of grubby barnacles. On quiet summer nights the Grubers fell asleep to the moans and cries of the disturbed inmates.

Of the three children still at home, Benita was the only one not gainfully employed. Her two brothers had found work in road construction through Hitler's Four-Year Plan, and they were always quick to point out that Benita could find work through it as well. There *was* work for women. But Benita chose to assist her mother with the mending and washing instead. She did not want to commit to anything that might bind her to Frühlinghausen. Because for her real life, her real future, she would go to Berlin and find work as a typist or some such, she was sure of it, though she had never even handled a typewriter.

And Frau Gruber indulged Benita's dream, much to her other children's irritation. Benita was her mother's favourite – the fifth of six and the prettiest of the girls by far. Among her siblings she was famously incompetent and lazy. *Faulpelz* was what her oldest sister, Lotte, called her, meaning 'lazybones,' and it was not intended fondly.

The older children had each been sent to work at the age of fourteen and raised on spotty potatoes and dandelion-weed soup. Those were the desperate days, during and after the war. They begrudged Benita's privileged status as a member of Hitler's generation, a cohort filled with pride and idealism and, most of all, with excitement about the future.

Benita had little interest in politics, but she *had* absorbed the sense of possibility the new regime offered. And Frau Gruber, after so many years of hard and unemotive realism, seemed to have found in Benita's daydreams her own trampled capacity for yearning. She tolerated in her youngest daughter all the impractical nonsense she would have beaten out of her older children.

So it was fitting, in a sense, that Frau Gruber herself played a role in Benita's second encounter with Connie Fledermann. It was Saturday, market day, and Benita rose from bed with a grumbling commitment to help her mother buy and carry home their food for the week. Still in a sulk, she put on an old grey skirt and blouse and barely combed her hair. Who would she see, anyway? Ulrich Heschel? Mannfred Becker? In the wake of her meeting with Connie Fledermann, the voice in her head had taken on a sarcastic ring. She trudged along beside her mother, whose stoic German peasant silence seemed to Benita a hallmark of everything dull and cold and lacking in her life.

At the market, Benita dawdled, mooning over Frau Mullman's flowers and the artist's stall, until Frau Gruber returned, pulled at her sleeve, and reminded her that she was there to carry the wursts and flour and side of *Salzfleisch*.

So when, rounding the corner of the cheese maker's stall, Benita was suddenly confronted with the sight of Connie Fledermann, this time in full, handsome military garb, she was mortified rather than delighted. The horror of being seen so – in these awful clothes, carrying a bulging sack of smoked meats, and followed by her fruit-pinching, sniffing, hunchbacked mother!

He, however, broke into a wide smile. 'Fräulein of the Anschluss!' he said loudly, causing a few of the passersby to turn and stare. Benita's face went from cool and white to purple. 'I wondered if I would see you again.'

Then he turned with an air of great respect and formality to Frau Gruber. 'May I introduce myself? Staff Officer Martin Constantine Fledermann. I met your daughter here the other day and we discussed the recent event of the Anschluss.'

Frau Gruber bobbed her head repeatedly, like a deaf-mute.

Benita, still distracted by the bulging sack in her arms and the particularly ugly shape of her blouse, slowly registered the presence of two other men, both of whom appeared small and dull beside Staff Officer Martin Constantine Fledermann. In the focused light of his attention, all else seemed obscured in shadow. But she thought she caught them rolling their eyes.

'This evening perhaps? Can I take you to dinner?'

Benita stared.

'No?' His eyes twinkled.

'Yes,' Benita said.

'Yes?' he said, turning to Frau Gruber.

'Yah, sicher. Yes, of course,' Frau Gruber said when she finally found her tongue, and her response was so unquestioning – so utterly lacking in parental restraint – that something in Benita snapped to. From that moment on, a subtle but profound shift occurred in her relationship with this man who was to become her husband. In the face of her mother's mute, girlish awe, Benita realised she would have to act as her own parental figure – creating the barriers and slips that made the game of courtship alluring. It was something she had never even thought of with the various boys of Frühlinghausen who had made their interest known: there had been no game with them, no need for a game, she had taken none of them seriously, had no interest in more than the affirmation their interest provided.

'Then I will pick you up at half eight,' he said. 'At—?'

'Seven Krensig,' she said, cringing at the thought of him seeing the Gruber cottage. 'But eight o'clock would be better,' she added, beginning her new strategy as obstacle maker.

'Aha!' He looked satisfyingly surprised.

Benita stood a little straighter and held the bag with less of an apologetic tilt to her shoulders.

'Eight o'clock then,' he said with a bow.

That evening, in preparation for dinner, Benita luxuriated in a hot bath. The Grubers still relied on the old-fashioned assemblage of water heated on the stove and schlepped across the kitchen to a tub that sat behind a makeshift screen. Frau Gruber, as excited as Benita herself, had suggested the bath and put aside her own work to prepare it. Her mother was, in fact, gripped by such nervous energy that it calmed Benita.

She ran a comb through her hair and shook off Frau Gruber's offers to plait and wrap it around her head in her usual Sunday style and instead pinned it into a more modern, American fashion with three rolls at the base of her skull. Benita's younger brother made a racket knocking on the bedroom door and singing old love ballads in a falsetto.

When eight o'clock finally arrived, Benita wore her finest dress – a blue-and-red-flowered dirndl that had originally belonged to her sister – and her too-small Sunday shoes. She sat pretending to be engrossed in her needlepointing as her mother arranged a plate of cookies and uncorked the plum schnapps in an embarrassing display of ingratiation. By a quarter past the hour, when Staff Officer Martin Constantine Fledermann finally knocked, Benita had already experienced and overcome her nervousness, and she greeted him coolly.

'Staff Officer Fledermann,' she said, glancing at the clock. 'I wondered if you'd been caught by one of Herr Schulte's dogs.' Frau Gruber's mouth dropped open at her impertinence.

'They tried,' he replied with a smile, 'but I was too quick. Call me Connie, please.'

With no further back-and-forth, and certainly without partaking in pleasantries, cookies, or schnapps, Benita and Connie took their leave.

Outside the cottage the moon was bright and Connie's Horch sport car gleamed like an object from another world. She detected the strong smell of winter thaw – the hay that had covered the vegetable garden all season was thick with mildew and hoarfrost, a trace of dead animal. But over this the fresh, clean spring fragrance of the early blooming bloodroot and snow roses. And stepping through the door that Connie held open for her, Benita could barely believe her good fortune.

'To the Golden Onion?' he asked in a way that mocked the place and all its provincial pretensions even as he suggested it.

'Of course.' She smiled, in keeping with his tone, as if they were not two strangers pursuing some staid courtship ritual in a small town in an obscure corner of the Reich, but rather sophisticated, worldly lovers, known intimately to each other already and playing a game of pretend: Pretend we are two peasants in the backwaters of the empire, meeting for the first time. Pretend we know nothing of who we are or where we are headed. Pretend the conclusion of this chance encounter has not already been foretold.

Why had this faux familiarity been the starting point for them? It confused and flustered Benita, but at the same time seemed essential – vital to the excitement. She would wonder about it later, when the time to wonder about such things returned. By then Connie and old Frau Gruber were dead, and her brothers had been killed on the front. And there was no one left with any insight.

At the Golden Onion, Benita and Connie sat beside a pleasantly flickering fire, and Connie ordered them each a glass of the local cider and a schnitzel. It struck Benita as comical – a fancy staff officer from Berlin, ordering this. 'So tell me,' he asked when their cider was before them and the *Jägerschnitzel* steamed greasily on its plate. 'What do you really think of all this marching and saluting and repatriating the German peoples of Europe?'

Benita was shocked at his question – the implication and glib tone. It was, maybe, a trick, she thought. After all, had he not said he was here on some official business?

'I think it is a kindness by our Führer to bring them back into their motherland. And also the German people need more room and space,' she parroted Fräulein Brebel in a confused rush.

'Who told you that?' Connie asked, laughing.

'No one – it's what I think,' Benita said, drawing herself up straight.

'And what of all the opponents and Communists and Jews who've been arrested?'

Benita stared at him in disbelief. It was a traitorous line of questioning. And the basis for the question was fuzzy in her mind – certainly in Frühlinghausen no great number of people had been arrested. She stared down at her hands and could feel the blood racing to her cheeks.

'Oh no! I have upset you! My dear maiden,' Connie said, again using his cheerful playacting voice. 'Don't let my talk confuse you. Here – we will talk about Frühlinghausen's famous cider. Is it really as good as your arrogant distillers boast?' He took a swig and made a comically evaluative face. 'Do they put socks in every barrel?'

'Only in the barrels they save for visitors like you!' Benita recovered and was delighted to hear him laugh.

'Well, it's delicious,' he pronounced, setting his glass on the table. 'In Berlin we have only beer.' He made a face.

'And champagne,' she said. 'Isn't it so? There are bars in Berlin where they serve nothing but champagne?'

'Absolutely.' Connie leaned forward and took her hand. A thrill raced through her at the touch. 'Will you come to one with me, Mademoiselle Gruber?'

'You are an odd one!' Benita could not help exclaiming, and for a moment she worried that she had ruined their game. Connie threw back his head and laughed.

'I am sure you are right, fräulein. And you must promise to remind me of that whenever I am being a boor.'

The rest of the evening passed pleasantly. There was no further talk of politics, and Connie seemed truly interested in learning all about her. Benita had never been asked so many questions – about her family, her childhood, her town, and Fräulein Brebel's BDM group, about which Connie was remarkably curious. The cider made her feel free and light. And through Connie's eyes, she saw herself anew. Not only was she beautiful and young, a future bearer of bold and strong Aryan children, but she was also a woman who could tell funny stories. And her life – the boring, small-town monotony of Frühlinghausen – had become a subject worthy of this man's attention: the carnival at which she was crowned queen last year, the crabby town butcher who mixed up everyone's orders, the time Frau Meltzer's pigs escaped onto the mental hospital grounds. Connie had a seemingly bottomless appetite for her tales. And every time his knee grazed hers, she felt a jolt of electricity.

When they reached 7 Krensig, the windows were dark. Frau Gruber was not one to stay awake past ten, even on such an occasion. Connie ran around to Benita's side of the car and held her door as she climbed out. Then, as she stood there against the still-warm body of his car, he leaned down and kissed her – lightly and skillfully, one hand tilting her chin. It was entirely different from Herbert Schmidt's rough advances or Torsten Finkenberg's awkward kisses, and she felt her whole body thrill at the feel of his smooth-shaven chin and the height from which he approached. She leaned into the spicy clove scent of his aftershave and the pressed wool of his suit.

'Can I see you again?' he asked. 'I leave tomorrow, but if you say yes, I will come back in two weeks.'

'Yes,' she said, leaving aside strategy and coyness.

'Then it is decided,' he said, 'and I will wait until you are safely inside.'

With that, Benita made her way up the narrow path and into the ugly, comfortable squalor of her childhood home, forever changed. She was a maiden who had met her prince.

CHAPTER FOUR

BURG LINGENFELS, JUNE 1945

The little boy sitting on the counter in front of Marianne was a miniature version of his father. Same startling blue eyes, high cheekbones, and straight, elegant features. His demeanour was different, though, certainly from that of his father as a man, but also from what he had been like as a boy. *This* Martin was solemn, impassive, and self-controlled where *that* Martin had been exuberant, bright, and spontaneous. *This* Martin's face was a closed door. God knows it had good reason to be – Marianne would never forget her first sight of him, peering, wan faced, out of the window of that awful Nazi orphanage.

'Does this hurt?' Marianne asked as she straightened the battered leg they had come inside to repair.

No, he shook his head.

'Or this?'

He shook his head again. But this time he flinched.

'Well, then, we will wash and bandage it, and it will be good as new.'

Marianne dipped a rag into a bowl of water and then pressed it against the bloody gash. She could feel the grit in his broken flesh. But the boy did not cry.

It was a bad fall. He and Fritz had been playing some sort of game in the rafters of the old horse stable. Fritz's idea, of course. Her son could not stay out of trouble. It was as if all the hasty actions, wild ideas, and ill-considered nonsense he'd suppressed during their stressful journey west from Weisslau had returned to him doubled. Where had he come by his incautious streak? Neither she nor Albrecht had been impulsive or disorganised as a child. Even Elisabeth, for all her willfulness, was at least careful.

Luckily the floor of the stable was still the original packed earth. And Martin had landed like a cat. He seemed to have inherited the gift of luck from his father, who'd always had it in spades . . . until he didn't.

'You know not to play on those beams now,' Marianne said. 'I think we need not concern your mother with this so long as you promise to be more careful. And' – she raised her eyebrows – 'promise not to let Fritz get you into trouble – he can be a real gypsy.'

'I won't,' Martin said, his voice earnest and childlike. She forgot just how young he was sometimes. 'I promise.'

Martin was not easily brought to tears. She had seen this much when he said goodbye to the little girl from the Children's Home: Liesel Stravitsky. It was obvious he had loved her. But when they found her family, such as it was – a beleaguered aunt with three small children, her father dead, her mother last known to be in Auschwitz – Marianne's own eyes had not stayed dry. The poor girl had thrown her arms around Martin and bawled as if her little heart would break, but he had remained stoic.

Marianne tied the last strip of silk around the cut. 'Why don't you sit in the kitchen and help Elisabeth and Katarina shell the peas?'

Martin opened his mouth as if to speak.

'What is it?' she asked, placing a hand on his other, unhurt and chasteningly bony knee.

'When will I be able to see her?' he asked. 'My mother?'

'Soon,' Marianne said. 'I promise.'

Benita had fallen sick with diphtheria a week after arriving at Burg Lingenfels. They said this was what happened sometimes: as soon as one made it to safety, illness set in. Marianne and her children had been inoculated at the English hospital in Braunschweig. As the wife and children of Albrecht von Lingenfels, they were classified as *Opfer des Faschismus* – 'Victims of Fascism' – and treated well by the British authorities, who had waved their cart past the long line of fellow refugees queued at the border between zones. They were a wretched lot, mostly old people, women, and children fleeing from the east. It made Marianne feel guilty. What right to special treatment did she and her children have? They were lucky enough to have a wagon and a horse to pull it.

Benita, on the other hand, had received none of these advantages. She had not advocated for herself as the widow of Connie Fledermann, an active resister and a man executed by the Nazis. Though to be fair, it was different in Russian-occupied Berlin. A German was a German to most Russians. So she was simply a German widow, and a beautiful one at that, which had not worked to her benefit. Marianne would never forget the leering soldiers around the table in the flat on Meerstein Strasse or the horrible little bedroom with the closed windows and stink of sex. She had arrived too late. She had promised Connie that she would protect his wife and child, and she had failed.

Once Martin was safely settled in the kitchen, Marianne washed the bloodied rags that had once been Elisabeth's Communion dress. This had arrived last week in a giant sea trunk that was delivered, improbably, on the back of an American army mail truck. Her heart twisted when she saw the trunk. Albrecht had insisted, years ago, that they pack it up and send it to his cousins in Geneva for safekeeping – a gift from a foresighted dead man.

We live in the middle of nowhere, Albrecht! Marianne had complained when he suggested packing up their prized possessions. *It's not as if any army will bother with Weisslau.*

But Albrecht was right. The Russians had marched right through the town, determined to avenge their losses, taking everything from bicycles to grandfather clocks to Grossmutter von Lingenfels's maudlin needlepoints. Collateral for the toll the war had exacted – as if loot could bring back their dead.

You finally have your way with it all, Fräulein Communist, Marianne imagined Albrecht saying at the sight of the shredded Communion dress. It was their little joke. She had liked to proclaim fancy clothing and fine table settings bourgeois banalities – distractions from the real fineries of human life: music and poetry, theatre and art . . .

Which was itself a foolish, bourgeois statement. The war had made this clear. Music, poetry, and art were luxuries, too. *Everything* was a distraction from the basic struggle between life and death.

What Albrecht had not understood, though, when he packed their trunk, was that the culture that had given birth to these precious objects and endowed them with value would be so thoroughly self-immolated that its assignations were no longer valid. What was the point of a Chinese silk pinafore sewn by Weisslau's finest tailor when you didn't even have a pair of shoes? Or a Meissen china tea service, transported without so much as one chipped plate, when there was no tea, no bread, no table to eat at? He had anticipated disaster but not lived to see its depths.

'Mama!' The washroom door flew open and Katarina appeared. 'The American leader is here.'

'The American leader' was how the children referred to Lieutenant Peterman, the man in charge of rebuilding Ehrenheim and its surrounding area. He had been kind to the von Lingenfelses since their arrival, and he treated Marianne with a certain nervous respect based on his belief that she was descended from royalty (she was not) and that her husband had been a friend of the American general Patton (a vast exaggeration, as Albrecht had never even met the man). Marianne had not planted either of these ideas, but she didn't go out of her way to correct them. Peterman was a useful ally. She had enlisted his help in her search for fellow widows of resisters, the women and children she had sworn so passionately to protect at the countess's long-ago harvest party. *The commander of wives and children,* Connie had called her. The words had seemed demeaning to her at the time – an exclusion from the real business of conspiring, a reminder that she was, in the end, a woman, and therefore relegated to the work of picking up the pieces. But in the years since, she had come to understand his words differently: she was the last man standing, the decoy left holding the key.

Though what she was supposed to *do* with it remained opaque.

At the very least she could honour her promise and do her best to look out for the wives of the men present in the room that night.

'Frau von Lingenfels,' Peterman barked in his jocular way. On his lips *von Lingenfels* always sounded comical to her ears, the g hard and the syllables flat.

'Lieutenant,' Marianne replied.

Behind Peterman, she noticed another man – tall, thin, and wearing a ragged Wehrmacht uniform with the insignias removed. He stared down at his boots. A German prisoner of war. There were thousands of these in the British and American internment camps. 'Have you found one of my fraus?' Marianne asked Peterman lightly. It was the same joke he had made when she gave him her list of names. *So look for any of these names with Frau in front?* he'd asked.

'I'm afraid not,' Peterman said. A shadow swept over his face. Clearly he had not given the list a thought. 'But I've brought you someone to help out around the castle.'

Marianne looked from Peterman to the other man, who met her eyes for an instant. His own were a pale, almost transparent shade of blue, and he had a broad, unexpectedly handsome face.

'Herr Muller is one of the detainees from our camp. And I figure you could probably use an extra set of hands around here. Muller is handy. Worked on a farm before the war, right?' he asked, turning to the man. '*Bauernhof?*'

The man looked from Peterman to Marianne questioningly.

He was not a farmer, Marianne understood.

'That's all right.' She frowned. Marianne did not like the idea of relying on an ex-Nazi prisoner of the Americans for help. God knows what sort of person he was, what sort of soldier he had been. And on top of this, he was her countryman. 'We don't need any help.'

'I beg your pardon, Frau von Lingenfels, but—' Peterman stepped back and surveyed the castle edifice. 'You have broken windows up there and missing slates. And' – he looked at her – 'winter is coming. You'll need wood.'

Peterman turned to the man again and pantomimed an axe. 'You can chop wood – *Holz*. Right?'

The man nodded in assent.

'So?' Peterman asked, squinting at Marianne. 'Will that suit? I'd hate to have you freeze up here, especially with so many trees around.'

Marianne sighed. 'You make it hard to say no.'

'All right,' Peterman said. 'Next Thursday then. You have an axe?'

Dinner that night was their usual nearly unpalatable meal of soup. Marianne had never learned to cook. As a girl, she had been spoiled – the bright and favourite daughter of a wealthy widower who believed in women's education over domesticity. She had read Goethe and Schopenhauer and Schiller, rather than cookbooks.

'We are going to have a slave here? In our house? Once a week?' Elisabeth demanded.

'Oh, stop it. Certainly not a *slave*,' Marianne snapped. 'Why would you say such a thing?'

'Well, he *is*.' Elisabeth harrumphed. 'That's what prisoners of war are. I heard Herr Koffel say so. Slave labour. Against international regulations. How is that different from what we did when we were in charge?'

'"We"?' Marianne echoed, appalled. 'We were never Nazis. Don't forget that.'

Elisabeth shrugged. 'Still. He won't be getting paid for his work.'

'Right now, if you hadn't noticed,' Marianne said, '*no one* is getting paid for their work. And certainly coming here to cut down trees once a week will be a pleasant relief from the internment camp, which seems to be an impossible place.' There were rumours of men dying in such installations, barren fields with no shelter and no shade from the sun, of men sleeping in holes they dug out. Though Marianne did not trust most rumours the Ehrenheimers circulated.

She turned to her son. 'Fritz, sit like a man and stop fidgeting.'

'Did he kill many people in the war?' Katarina asked in a hushed voice. 'Is that why he is a prisoner?'

Marianne looked at this daughter: dark haired, plain faced, and thoughtful. Always slow and deliberate in her reactions. So much like Albrecht. 'I don't know, love.' She sighed. 'Lots of people are prisoners. Even boys your own age who don't know one end of a rifle from the other. I don't know what Herr Muller did.'

'Something bad anyway,' Elisabeth grumbled.

'Oh, Elisabeth, really,' Marianne snapped. 'I didn't *ask* for his help. But now we have it. He will cut wood to help us get through the winter, and for that you should be thankful.'

In the silence that followed, she mulled over her own words. *Is that how it works?* she could hear Albrecht asking. *Personal gain trumps moral decision?*

Yes. No. What was the difference between the man working here at the castle or for the Americans? Either way he was a prisoner. Connie would have supported her view, wouldn't he?

She doled out the last of the soup.

'Probably he had a Luger anyway,' Fritz offered. 'Do you think he still has it?'

'No,' Marianne said firmly. 'No Germans can carry arms. Now, could we sit and eat our supper in peace?' She turned to Martin, who had remained quiet through all of this. 'Wouldn't that be nice?'

After dinner, Marianne climbed the stairs to see Benita.

She had moved her to a cot in the warren of servants' rooms above the kitchen, where they all slept. These were the best rooms in the castle now. During the cold months, they would be warmed by the fire from the giant oven below. The formerly grand bedroom suites at the front of the castle were chilly and dim, littered with the hacked-up remains of ancient curtained beds. Marianne had been appalled to discover this when she arrived. Who would have chopped apart such antiques? In the great hall too the grand piano was mangled, its keyboard stripped of ivory, its wires splayed like a giant spider. Possibly the Nazis had done this; for a short time, before the end of the war, an SS unit had taken up residence in Burg Lingenfels. One corner of the courtyard was still stacked with their empty tins of meat and cherries and white asparagus. But it was also possible that the citizens of Ehrenheim were responsible for the destruction. In the last days of war, after the Nazis had left, many of the townspeople had holed up in the empty castle to hide from the approaching Americans, who they believed would rape and murder them. And Marianne would not put such destruction past the Ehrenheimers. They were an insular bunch, all married to one another's cousins and uncles and brothers, and locked into the mindset of medieval serfdom in which the castle folk were their oppressors. They had all been ardent Nazis, as far as she could tell. And to them, Marianne and her children were the family of a traitor, a man who had tried to kill their beloved Führer, in addition to being born von Lingenfels.

Marianne paused and reached into her pocket for the letter she was delivering. It felt cool and soft with wear and sent a rush of adrenalin through her. She rapped lightly on Benita's door.

Lying in the narrow army cot Marianne had arranged, Benita no longer appeared the rosy German peasant *Mädchen* she had once been. Marianne had chopped her blonde hair to help protect her from germs, and shorn like this Benita looked thin and world-weary – her full cheeks hollowed, the colour of paper, and her eyes huge and dark. She was still beautiful, but now in a painful, trampled way.

Marianne placed the tray of broth and water beside the bed, and Benita's eyes fluttered open.

'Is Martin all right?' she asked, and immediately began to cough.

'Shh.' Marianne raised a finger to her lips. 'He's fine. He and Fritz have been up to all sorts of healthy little-boy things.'

'He isn't,' Benita began but was again interrupted by her cough. 'He isn't sick?'

'Perfectly healthy,' Marianne said. She did not mention the fall.

Benita nodded, but her eyes remained anxious.

Before the war, Marianne had imagined that Benita would become mother to a horde of children, a robust and placid matriarch. Connie had always wanted a big family: five or six children at least, a different experience from his own as an only child. What had happened in the meantime? Miscarriages? Infertility? Connie had never confided in Marianne about his marriage, and she wasn't close enough to Benita for her to do so. How ironic that she, bony, flat-chested Marianne, would be the more fertile of the two women.

Marianne sat on the edge of the cot and lifted a spoonful of broth to Benita's lips, the last of the bouillon they had smuggled out of Weisslau.

Dutifully, Benita opened her mouth.

As Marianne leaned in to spoon the soup, the letter crinkled. It was time, certainly, to give it to her. But it was so difficult to part with! Connie had left it with her the last time she saw him: *To my wife, Benita Fledermann* was written on the envelope in his long thin script, surprisingly elegant for a man's. She was supposed to give it to Benita in the event of his death. And this time, when he'd enlisted her help, Marianne had not protested.

But when the plot failed and Connie died, Marianne found she could not deliver the letter. It was too dangerous with Albrecht in prison. Six months passed between the assassination attempt and Albrecht's trial and hanging. And Marianne had spent those months pleading for his release – visiting high-powered contacts, writing letters, and even, on three occasions, being interrogated by the Gestapo. Her possession of a letter from Connie Fledermann would not have helped matters. And then afterwards, when Albrecht was dead, it was impossible to gain access to Benita, who was sequestered in a Nazi prison. So she had held on to the letter the entire journey back from Berlin, waiting for the right moment, which never seemed to come.

'I have something for you,' she made herself say after Benita swallowed the last spoonful of broth.

Benita lifted her eyes.

Marianne pulled out the letter. It was dirty and crumpled. But it had survived – the Russians, the flight from Weisslau, the end of the war.

To her surprise, Benita did not startle at the sight of her husband's handwriting. She did not even move to take the letter from Marianne's hand.

'I've had this for too long,' Marianne began. 'I'm sorry – I didn't know how to get it to you, and when we were on our way from Berlin, it seemed so – it seemed that you should have a quiet place to read it.'

Still Benita said nothing. From outside, Marianne could hear the sound of the children playing.

'I didn't even know, you know,' Benita said finally, looking up.

'Know what?' Marianne asked.

'What they were planning.'

'They told almost no one.'

'But they told *you*.' Benita's tone was startlingly fierce.

Marianne searched the girl's pale face. It was both hard and hurt, tinged with petulance. For a moment, she felt the full weight of Connie's words to her that night after the party. *She is a simple girl and she won't deserve whatever mess I might drag her into.*

'It was different.' Marianne sighed. 'I was a part of their conversations. If I were a man . . . the Nazis would have hanged me, too.' She paused, considering. It was the first time she had spoken this aloud.

Benita looked away.

Between them the letter lay where Marianne had placed it. She felt its presence like a living thing. Like a child or an animal, waiting to be held.

'How did you—' Benita began, and then dissolved into a fit of coughing. 'How did you keep them from taking your children? And from sending you to prison?'

'I don't know,' Marianne said, though in truth she could guess. The Nazis had never liked Connie, whereas Albrecht had maintained the frustrated respect of a few among them until the very end – through his natural diplomacy, maybe. Or, more likely, on account of his deeper and more illustrious roots. Connie was from an old, once-rich Junker family, but Albrecht was a von Lingenfels, descended from a long line of revered German generals, a vital 'stem' of Hitler's beloved master race. 'We were lucky.'

'Ah,' Benita said, 'and we were not.' Finally she picked up the letter.

But the look in her eyes was neither sad nor loving. She regarded the envelope in her hands like an object from outer space.

'Here,' Marianne said, gathering the soup bowl and spoon. 'I will leave you to read in peace.'

Benita nodded.

But as Marianne closed the door, she saw Benita set the letter down unopened and lie back, flat as a corpse.

Marianne had spent a good amount of time considering Connie's marriage. After his wedding, she had seen him together with Benita from time to time – at the Bemelmans' Christmas party, at a few dinners she had hosted in Berlin, and once at a weekend gathering in Weisslau. It was a difficult match. The girl was quick to seem aggrieved (Connie had not fetched her from the station, or the baby was not sleeping, or no one had helped her with her suitcases on the train . . .) and Connie was oversolicitous. But even though he was attentive, he remained somehow apart from his wife, disconnected from her in a way that seemed to encourage her complaints. Marianne did not understand what had drawn him to Benita to begin with. She did not normally consider such matters, but this was not just any marriage. Benita was Connie Fledermann's wife. She was beautiful to be sure, but he had beautiful women all over Germany who fancied themselves in love with him. There was an innocence about her – an inherent lack of wit and sophistication that no amount of money or time in the city could transform, which was endearing in a certain way. But Marianne had never known Connie to be enthralled by this sort of simplicity. It was the Nazis who revered such quaint, unthinking *volkishness*, not forward-thinking men of the world like Connie. Yet Benita had captivated him.

Marianne had come across them once, alone on the terrace of a mansion in Dahlem, at a party thrown by one of Albrecht's colleagues. It was in the first years of the war, when there was still plenty of wine and gaiety to go around. She had hesitated in the doorway and something about their demeanour made her stop before calling out. Benita was smiling up at Connie coyly and was without little Martin, which was rare in those days. Connie's back was to Marianne. As she watched, Benita said something that made him laugh – a real head-thrown-back burst of astonishment, and then he caught her around the waist and pulled her towards him with an intensity that made Marianne catch her breath. It was forceful, even aggressive – a side of Connie she had never seen. Benita returned his laughter and allowed herself to be wholly enveloped in his embrace with a kind of softness and subservience that Marianne couldn't imagine emulating.

This was the closest she had come to understanding Connie's marriage: Benita made him a looser, more animal version of himself.

Marianne had felt a stab of sadness at the realisation and hastily retreated into the familiar comforts of the party, and the various like-minded people with whom she knew how to converse, but she was like a person masquerading at normality after receiving terrible news. And when Marianne found Albrecht, dear steady Albrecht with his soft eyes and stooped shoulders, his thoughtful, deliberate way of speaking, she felt lonely and irritated by the crumb caught on his cheek, the dandruff on his evening jacket. And the fact that he stepped back to make room for her rather than pulling her close.

CHAPTER FIVE

WEISSLAU, JULY 20, 1944

For Marianne the twentieth of July had unfolded slowly.

It was hot in Weisslau. The children mooned around in the late Grossmutter von Lingenfels's parlour, a cave of faded tapestries and heavily shaded lamps. They loved to lounge on the horsehair sofa in their light summer clothes, sucking penny candies and leafing idly through the collection of ancient illustrated books: Greek myths, Bible stories, German folktales, and obscure scientific tomes. And Fritz spent an unseemly amount of time examining prudish drawings of the human body in a great Victorian medical encyclopedia. Grossmutter would have been appalled. Their activities in the parlour always struck Marianne as slothful, and vaguely debauched.

On this day, the children were sorting a pile of scrap metal they had collected: valuables they planned to hand in to the local Nazi district head as their small contribution to the war effort. Marianne had no patience for such Nazi nonsense, especially when it involved turning her children into little warmongers. She had managed to keep them out of the youth groups despite Fritz's wheedling (he hated to be excluded from the local Hitlerjugend Sunday hikes and football matches), but even so they were caught up in the obsessions of their peers. Collecting scrap metal seemed particularly idiotic to Marianne. And it always led to squabbles – who had found what and how much they would get in exchange. As if any of them really needed pocket money. They were lucky out here in Weisslau – on the land, with their own source of food and no bombs to worry about. This was the fifth year of the war, and in the cities it was ugly now. There, children needed all sorts of things (safety, a roof over their heads, enough to eat, and coal to burn in their furnaces through the winter). It had been nearly a year since the bombing of Hamburg, yet the stories and images of the aftermath were still grim. The newspapers ran tales of or- phaned children living in the city's remains, surviving on rats and fetid water; of people who had boiled to death in the canals as they tried to escape the firestorm. It was difficult, of course, to discern truth from propaganda, and Marianne trusted nothing the Nazi press printed. But still, the photographs were shocking – the inner city transformed into a grey and cratered landscape like the surface of the moon. And she had seen firsthand the faces of those who had fled to find work and housing in the south: they were blank with shock.

On this particular afternoon, Marianne could not tolerate the children's bickering. All night, all week really, she was held in suspense. Any day now 'the plan' was to unfold. *Uncle Ulrich will join us next weekend,* Albrecht's latest telegram from Berlin had read. *Please prepare his favourite Semmelkuchen.* They had decided on the code words together. Since then sleep had been a delicate web she was too big and too clumsy to be caught in – she clutched at strands of it like a falling woman . . .

And despite the months and years of preparation, the argu- ments and discussions – *What justifies a murder? Can right be achieved through wrong?* – and despite the endless *how* and *when* and *where* and, most endlessly of all, *What comes next?* – it seemed incredible, impossible even, that their plot would unfold at last.

* * *

Albrecht had not approved at first. Assassination. Murder. It was not the culmination he wanted for the resistance movement. In his estimation, injustice could be fought only with justice – he was a lawyer to the core. Murder was evil. This was an absolute. *But if it would end the war and prevent the murder of thousands? Even millions?* They had debated this often, deep into the night with him probing his own convictions and Marianne playing devil's advocate. Although, in fact, she was *not* the devil's advocate. She believed Connie and von Stauffenberg and the others were right. Hitler must be killed.

For her, the case was sealed three years before, when Freddy Lederer returned from the east. He had stopped at Weisslau on his journey from the General Government zone of occupied Poland. And Freddy, an openhearted boy Marianne had known since childhood, always the first to jump off the dock at the lake and the last to come in for dinner at the Grand Hotel on the Ostsee, had been a gaunt shell of himself. He had recently returned from an intelligence trip for the *Abwehr,* and they had assigned him an SS escort, who had taken him to see an 'action' – a 'miracle of efficiency and dedication', as this SS man described it. The 'action' was being carried out by a unit of ordinary German reservists, older men for the most part, civilians with little or no training or military background. They had been instructed to 'cleanse' the area south of Lublin. *Lublin* – Freddy had shuddered pronouncing the name – *a kind of hell on earth.* They were rounding up Jewish women, children, and old men and marching them into the forest to be shot.

To be shot? Marianne repeated. *Are you certain?* She had heard rumours, of course, but had still believed (though not supported) the Nazis' Madagascar plan. All Polish Jews would be shipped to that island to form their own homeland. Other, darker stories trickled back from the front, but she had dismissed them as rumour or exaggeration. This was different, though. This was straight from the mouth of Freddy Lederer.

And he had seen it with his own eyes. German soldiers paired one-to-one: victims and their killers marched into the woods as partners. Children had been assigned their own executioners. He had watched one woman with three children – a little one, unable to walk yet, an older boy and a little girl, maybe seven or eight years old. The girl had refused to let go of her mother's hand, so she had been allowed to walk together with her and the baby, a tiny thing wrapped carefully in blankets, looking around with wide eyes.

'That one will make trouble,' Freddy's escort had said with indifference. 'Three shots for one soldier. It will slow the process down.'

When Freddy finished speaking, silence welled up around them in the comfortable library of Weisslau with its roaring fire and plush furniture, its dog snoring lazily on the hearth. Marianne sat frozen with a kind of stillness that aimed to stop time, to go back, to untell Freddy's story.

For a long time, Freddy said, *I could not grasp what I was looking at. I saw it, but I couldn't take it in. It was* – he groped for an analogy, his pale face haggard with the effort – *it was like one of those hidden pictures; you see a goblet not a face, a stairway not a flower, you can't see it even when it's right there in front of you. And then suddenly* – he raised his eyes and looked directly at Marianne – *you do.*

Marianne dreamed of them that night, the mothers and children walking into the woods. And the men, her own neighbours and peers, her fellow countrymen, marching them. This was what all Hitler's frightening rants amounted to: ordinary, middle-aged men marching mothers and children into forests to be killed.

For so long Marianne and Albrecht and many of their friends had known Hitler was a lunatic, a leader whose lowbrow appeal to people's most selfish, self-pitying emotions and ignorance was an embarrassment for their country. They had watched him make a masterwork of scapegoating Jews for Germany's fall from power and persuade his followers that enlightenment, humanity, and tolerance were weaknesses – 'Jewish' ideas that led to defeat. They had wrung their hands over his dangerous conflations, his fervour, and his lack of humanity. But Freddy Lederer's account was something new to Marianne. She lay in bed that night and knew Connie was right. Hitler must die.

For Albrecht, though, the answer still lay in the pursuit of justice. He too was deeply affected by Freddy's report. He redoubled his efforts to assist Jews in their attempts to escape, and to bring Nazi horrors like the one Freddy described to the attention of the British and the Americans, who he believed were the only hope for defeating Hitler. He was a religious person – much more so than Marianne – and he grappled with his faith. He lost sleep and barely ate. But he still believed the answer was to judge the man in the court of law. *Only when we prove that international law and the human rights of all mankind are greater than any villain can we vanquish evil.* He remained steadfast in this belief.

But this is impossible, Albrecht! Marianne argued. *How are you to bring Hitler to a court of law? All of Germany would have to rise up against him.*

With the support of the outside world, he would say. *And with time . . .*

He was a dreamer, though, Marianne felt. There was no time. And all of Germany would never rise up. They were too steeped in Hitler's rhetoric, too cowardly, too implicated in the horrors of his war to reject him.

Two weeks after his visit to Weisslau, Freddy hanged himself.

It was not until the news of the extermination camps reached Albrecht – not the rumours, but the undeniable firsthand accounts he had access to through his work in the *Abwehr* – that he agreed. Assassination was the only way.

Downstairs, Marianne sank into the cool leather of the chair at her husband's desk with the intention of going through their accounts. She had taken over the bookkeeping when Albrecht's work in government – and more important, in the resistance – became too demanding. Sitting here, at this great desk, where he had drawn up many plans and documents, Marianne was struck, as if for the first time, by the possibility that their plot might fail.

Outside the window, she caught a flash of black flapping across the lawn, followed by a brown-grey blur, which resolved itself into a cat chasing a crow. As she watched, the cat managed to bring one outstretched paw down on the bird's wing. The crow half flew, half jumped forward, wing crooked at an alarming angle, and the cat, satisfied with the damage, turned and streaked back into the bushes. The bird staggered and flapped. It began to utter a throaty, guttural sound. Three other crows flew down from the treetops and stood at a respectful distance, watching, heads cocked, as it hobbled before them with its terrible trailing wing spread out as evidence.

Then, as if they'd passed judgement and found their comrade beyond hope, they flew away.

The sight was at once horrifying and addictive; Marianne could not avert her eyes. It was just the two of them now, though the crow did not know she watched. She stood frozen at the window with a hard, knotted feeling in her chest. If the cat returned, she would open the window and shoo it away – or go outside and throw a rock. But it didn't. It was content to leave the bird to die.

Marianne was not a believer in signs and portents. These were the recourse of the powerless. But all the same, in that instant, she had the clearest sense the coup had failed. *In the end it will hang on chance*, Albrecht had said when she last saw him. She had nodded but had not understood it in her heart. She had never really allowed herself to consider the opposite of success. She had believed, almost superstitiously, that to admit doubt would invite failure, and to imagine success would bring it about. And her imagination was docile. It conjured what she told it to, no more, no less. She did not imagine crevasses and hidden boulders when the children skied; she did not picture an accident when Albrecht drove too fast. It was part of what made her confident rather than anxious. It was part of what made her an optimist.

She had pushed Albrecht to support the plan and championed taking action almost from the start. Inaction was impossible. Once you knew – *really knew* – of the women and children being shot in the woods, of the shower rooms constructed for the sole purpose of killing, how could you *not* act? But now, here was the obvious reason she had repressed: the cost. If the plan failed, all that she cherished would be lost.

Somehow Marianne managed to get through the afternoon, a blind woman fumbling her way down a familiar path. She filled out the ledger with the number of pigs born in the last month and the bushels of wheat harvested. She presided over tea. If the conspirators were intercepted, what would happen? Arrest? Imprisonment? Death? Albrecht's connection would surely be discovered. How could it not? He had hosted the plan's primary actors on many occasions and was a known critic of the Nazis. Of course, they had been careful – last month they had burned letters and buried notebooks and plans. Even the guestbook of Weisslau had been 'lost.' But there were countless threads to implicate him.

Meanwhile, outside, the crow staggered around in the dark margin of shadow between the woods and the lawn. Its wing dragged, its shiny eye blinked. She did not want the children to see it. *Don't look, don't look,* she told herself, but her eyes were helplessly drawn to where it hunched, damaged wing extended like a cape.

Before supper, Frau Gerstler, the cook, entered the study with a stricken look on her face: 'Our Führer has been injured! Our dear Führer! Assassins have made an attempt on his life, but praise God, he has only been hurt.'

Marianne clutched the arms of the chair to steady herself. It was less a shock than a confirmation.

'Our Führer, our Führer,' Frau Gerstler cried. 'Thank God he has survived!' Almost as if he were her own son or husband.

'What is it? What happened?' the children clamoured around her, drawn by instinct from wherever they had been playing.

'Frau Gerstler has heard rumours,' Marianne said, amazed she was able to speak.

'The Führer?' Fritz persisted. 'Did she say he was almost killed?'

'Don't eavesdrop on adult conversation,' Marianne snapped, drawing courage from the sound of her own voice.

'Frau Gerstler,' Marianne said when the children retreated in confusion, 'I would appreciate it if you kept such rumours out of our house.'

'But, madam,' Frau Gerstler said, 'it is on the radio.'

After that, there was no possible excuse for turning off the radio. Hitler himself was expected, at any moment, to give a speech.

The urgency forced Marianne to calm the storm inside her head. She had to be careful. From now on, every movement she made would be suspect. Frau Gerstler loved the family, but she did not love them *so* much that she wouldn't inform on them if the Gestapo asked.

So they listened to the broadcast as a group, Frau Gerstler at their centre, wringing her hands and shaking her head. Fritz too could barely contain himself, his eyes bright with anger and astonishment. But Marianne was too distracted to be rattled by her son's ignorance. The girls listened with less fervour. Elisabeth rolled her eyes at the hysterical tone of the announcer behind Frau Gerstler's back. Katarina sat quietly beside her mother, looking up from time to time with wide, perceptive eyes, trying to read her face.

When Hitler spoke, his voice was as absurd as always, but this time tinged with a special, bellicose fury:

The claim by these usurpers that I am no longer alive is at this very moment proven false, for here I am talking to you, my dear fellow countrymen. The circle which these usurpers represent is very small. It has nothing to do with the German armed forces, and above all nothing to do with the German army. It is a very small clique composed of criminal elements which will now be mercilessly exterminated . . .

The word *exterminated* repeated itself in Marianne's ears. There would be executions, certainly. Claus von Stauffenberg. Ludwig Beck. And Connie. Connie! There was no way he could escape. He was too central to the plot. She held her hands together in her lap so no one could see them shake.

But what of Albrecht? What of the children and Weisslau? What of herself? She had to remain calm and think straight. Albrecht had many powerful friends, even among Hitler's regime. It was possible this would help. And she had heard nothing from him yet. So she would need, first of all, to wait. They had discussed what she should do in the case of his arrest, but until she had confirmation, she must carry on as normal.

Somehow she managed to get the children to bed that night.

Then, unable to help herself, she looked out of the window for the crow in the semi-dark. The sun sank late this time of year; it was nearly ten and still the meadow glowed. The patch of woods beyond was enveloped in black. At the edge, a form distinguished itself. Still broken, still hobbling, no better, no worse.

Marianne pulled on her boots and jacket and quietly let herself out. There it was. As the door closed, the crow stopped. Her eyes adjusted to the dark. She approached quietly, and it remained still until she was a metre away. Then it swelled up, puffed its feathers, and seemed to sigh without lifting its head from its chest. It blinked, and its beak glinted faintly in the dark. The wing was beyond repair; a bit of bone protruded from the black feathers, which were stripped away by the cat's claws, revealing a patch of bluish, reptilian skin.

They stood for some time together. It observed her with wariness, even intelligence. Wind rustled the trees. Marianne hunched inside her jacket, chilly despite the night's warmth. The bird would die here alone in the darkness. Would it gradually starve? Or would the cat return to finish it off? Or some other night creature – a fox or weasel or barn owl?

She did not want to leave it.

You are not alone, she thought. *Don't be afraid. You are beloved.* And the words filled her mind, big enough to transcend and spread out into the night. Marianne was not a religious person, but she felt the presence of something divine. The bird was an angel. The bird was Albrecht.

No, she realised with star-bright clarity: it was Connie.

She spread her coat on the grass and lay down beside it, and at some point she drifted off to sleep. When she woke in the first grey light of dawn, the bird was gone and Connie was dead.

CHAPTER SIX

BURG LINGENFELS, JULY 1945

Lying in her cot at Burg Lingenfels, Benita did not open Connie's letter. Through her sickness, its presence on the bedside table exerted a ghoulish force. In her dreams, she would try to read it, but the words swam before her eyes, long and ponderous, so obscure as to be incomprehensible, or worse, dull. No sense would shake from its folds. And Connie himself hovered at the periphery of her sleep. She saw him across a crowded party or at the end of a hall, or even in the shadows here in her room, but it was impossible to connect. He would be engrossed in conversation with a colleague, or flirting with another woman, or simply slip out of her sight as she approached. When she woke, sweaty with fever, rattled by stress, she wanted nothing to do with his letter and blamed it for her nightmares. *I love you, I'm sorry* . . . It didn't matter what he said. Their marriage was what it was – and now it was over. Connie was dead.

'Can you put this away somewhere?' Benita asked Elisabeth one night when the girl came to deliver her evening soup in Marianne's place.

'Where?' Elisabeth asked. She was a stolid, literal girl and did not seem surprised.

Benita cast her eyes around the bare room. 'Anywhere that I don't have to see it,' she answered.

So Elisabeth stuck it in the chest of drawers that housed Benita's few possessions. And after that, Benita's sleep improved.

Benita had been sick for three weeks when she woke to find a strange man in her room. Her first thought was of what she must look like. The edges of her mouth were dry and cracked, and her nightgown sweat-stained. The sheets lay twisted at her feet. She scrambled to cover herself and became light-headed with the effort.

Marianne, who had come in with the stranger, was wrestling open the ancient window and made no move to assist her. 'This is Herr Muller,' she said, turning back to Benita, who remained huddled on the cot. 'He has come to help around the castle today, and I thought he could begin by taking you outside. The sun will do you good.'

Benita stared at Marianne. 'Could I—' She clutched the open neck of her nightgown. 'Could I have a minute first to dress?'

'Ah! Of course!' Marianne said. 'Herr Muller, would you give us a moment?'

It was so like Marianne to act first and then think. Even in the daze of sickness, Benita recognised this. Marianne had no patience for mundane concerns like appearance or propriety.

'Who is he?' Benita managed to ask as Marianne helped her tug a pair of trousers on under her nightdress.

'A prisoner,' Marianne said brusquely. 'Someone the Americans sent.' Her tone forbade more questions. A German. But Benita had already recognised this.

When he reentered the room, head slightly bowed and eyes averted, Benita felt a wave of shame. He was a good-looking man, too thin for his large frame, with a bold, strong-featured face and a square forehead. He seemed to understand her embarrassment. It confirmed that she was right to feel self-conscious. Sickness and the war had made her ugly and broken-down.

But when he lifted her – easily, as if she were an armload of feather ticking – she felt unaccustomedly feminine. The ginger-ness of his touch, the careful placement of his hand so that it would not brush against her breast, the heat of his forearm under her thighs brought something dormant in her to life. As her light, hot head bounced against his shoulder, she was filled with a sense of relief. His manner projected competence. In his arms she felt like a baby picked up and collected by its mother, purring with the pleasure of being held. To her embarrassment, her eyes filled with tears.

'Are you all right?' he asked as he navigated the curving stone stairs, and she nodded, unable to speak.

Outside, he laid her on a straw mattress underneath the chest-nut tree. The sun was beautiful and dappled, and the breeze brushed across her cheek like a breath, lifting her shorn hair from her scalp. She was not chilled and aching or struggling for breath, and she was filled with wonder at her own painlessness.

'Is this a good place?' the man asked, bringing her back to the moment.

'Thank you,' she managed to say, nodding.

His eyes glanced up at hers then – shockingly blue, like one of those eerie northern dogs, light rather than the deepwater blue of Connie's. And something like recognition, only sharper, passed between them.

Why are you here? she wanted to ask, but then Martin came running – her sweet, lovely boy, his cheeks pink from play, his forehead sweaty. He crouched before her and she lifted a hand to his face, the beautiful child she had lost and found. And she forgot all about the man who had just carried her down.

For the next few weeks, Herr Muller helped Benita downstairs every time he came to the castle – first carrying her and then, as her strength returned, supporting her as she walked. He was not a talker, but she questioned him anyway. He was from Braun-schweig, a city not far from where she had grown up, which perhaps explained his familiarity. Before the war he had been a carpenter. He had a daughter and a father still living in the home he had left.

And your wife? she asked, knowing she was being forward.

His wife was dead.

Mostly they proceeded in silence, which Benita did not feel pressured to fill. She found his quiet steadiness comforting. He reminded her of the men of Frühlinghausen, men who worked with their hands and ate dinner in silence. Men like her father, a quiet hulking presence in her childhood, falling asleep in his chair after dinner with his red hands splayed like slabs of meat on his knees. She had spent her girlhood scheming to escape such men, but now, in Herr Muller's presence, she found she missed the way they made her feel.

As she regained her strength, she began taking short trips around the castle, to the stables, the bakehouse, the kitchen garden. It had been so long since she'd been free to walk where she wanted. The openness of the countryside, the smell of summer grasses, the clouds of dust on the road were all suddenly beautiful to her. The war had quashed any romantic notions she once held of the city.

On one of these walks, she came across Herr Muller piling split wood under the eave of a dilapidated outbuilding that had once been the castle brewery.

'Frau Fledermann,' he said, straightening. 'Are you well enough to walk all this way? On your own?'

'Of course!' she said through her breathlessness. It had, in fact, been a little far.

'Ah.' Muller looked uncertain. He mopped the sweat off his brow. 'Here,' he said, levelling the stack of logs in the wheel-barrow and spreading his jacket over the top. 'Sit a minute and catch your breath.'

Light-headed, Benita complied. She could feel the sweat running under her arms and standing at the edge of her hairline. The barrow was in the shade of the building and beyond this, the sun was hot. Two huge dragonflies hung and swooped, attached head to tail, across this boundary of shadow and light.

Muller regarded Benita with concern. His pose struck her as clownish – this large man, peering at her so tentatively.

'I went to Carnival in Braunschweig once,' she offered impulsively. 'With my troop – my BDM cluster.' As she spoke, she remembered the parade – the colourful floats of costumed dancers and local school groups, business associations, and social clubs. There were giant papier-mâché caricatures of knights and princesses, tableaus of political figures and folktale characters. And everywhere the smells of beer, crisp potato pancakes, sausages, and sugary doughnuts. She had gone with a group of classmates and they had schemed to meet their future husbands. *Schoduvel,* they called Carnival in Braunschweig – 'Scare the Devil.' The city had seemed huge and magical and dangerous.

'Ah.' Muller smiled, and Benita felt him relax. He leaned back against the wood he had stacked.

'It was wonderful,' she said. 'Did you go every year?'

'When I was a boy.'

'And not after?'

'And sometimes after.' He smiled again, now looking sheepish.

'Of course!' she said. 'Why wouldn't you?! Did you ride the Ferris wheel?'

'Always.'

'It was amazing, wasn't it?' She remembered the rocking, and the exhilarating sense of danger that was not actually danger at all. 'I would have done it a million times if I could.'

'And then come down for a *Weissbier* and a plate of *Kartoffel-puffer.*'

'Exactly.' Benita smiled.

Companionable silence passed between them.

'I was the Carnival princess in Frühlinghausen once,' she said.

Muller raised his eyebrows and tipped an imaginary cap, bowing his head. 'Your Highness.'

'Did you have one in Braunschweig?'

'The mayor's wife.' He puffed out his cheeks. 'Too fat to ride in the parade carriage.'

Benita laughed. The dragonflies darted into the sun, frightened by the sound.

'It feels impossible now, doesn't it?' she said, and then wished she hadn't. The words invited melancholy. 'Never mind.' She shook her head. 'I should start back or Marianne will worry.' She extended her hand to Muller. 'Will you help me stand?'

He bowed slightly. '*Gnädige* princess.'

At dinner Benita found the courage to mention Herr Muller.

It was a change from their usual topic of conversation: whom Marianne had received a letter from, and where they were . . . She was engaged in a quest-like search for other widows like Benita – the lost wives and mothers and faithful secretaries (a category Benita found deeply suspicious) of Connie and Albrecht's fellow conspirators. Even now, with the country's infrastructure in shambles, Marianne managed to exchange letters and telegrams with friends and acquaintances from all over. Mostly these were women Benita didn't know or had felt snubbed by because she was so young, so uneducated, so unfitting a bride for Connie. But there were others still missing from Marianne's careful catalogue: the wives of men on the outskirts of the group, beyond Marianne's social circles.

'How long will the Americans keep their prisoners?' Benita managed to ask before Marianne could get started on the subject.

Marianne glanced up from serving the soup: a tasteless cabbage and carrot and potato that neither she nor Benita knew how to improve.

'I don't know,' Marianne said. 'I think they'll be sent to France for the rebuilding.'

'The terrible ones,' Elisabeth said.

'Really?' Fritz asked, wide eyed. The boy had a grim fascination with all the most horrible details emerging about the Nazis – psychopaths like Josef Kramer, the Beast of Belsen, as they now referred to him, a man who had personally gassed eighty Jews for his collection of skeletons.

'Elisabeth,' Marianne scolded, 'you have no idea who they send where. Don't give your brother wrong-headed facts.' She turned to Benita. 'Why do you ask?'

'I was just thinking of Herr Muller,' Benita ventured.

'Ah!' Marianne frowned. 'I haven't asked Peterman how long he'll be here – but we can get by without him, certainly.'

'Of course.' Benita nodded.

'They can't keep those prisoners forever,' Marianne continued. 'Too expensive. They'll need them to get back to work.'

'But I like Herr Muller,' Fritz said petulantly. 'I don't want him to be released.'

Elisabeth shot her brother a look. 'Do you hear what you're saying? You sound like Rapunzel's stepmother. If you like someone, you should want them to be free.'

The next week, a heatwave settled over Burg Lingenfels, a shaggy animal brushing against the hills, panting along the river, quieting the birds and making the castle sweat. The ditches were alive with milkweed, nettles, and creeping phlox. In the warmth, the forest looked soft and dense, a black lump against blue sky.

Benita decided she was well enough to walk down to the farm of Herr Kellerman, the castle caretaker, for the eggs he supplied. She had imagined going with Martin, walking down the hillside with her long-lost son, continuing their reacquaintance, which was still a work in progress. He was a different boy to the one the Nazis had taken from her – at six he seemed a young person rather than a child. But he had wanted to stay with Fritz. So Benita walked alone.

On her way, she noticed a figure below – Herr Kellerman, maybe. But the person was too tall to be Kellerman and walked without a limp. As she watched, the figure became clear: it was Herr Muller. She smiled and lifted her hand. He returned the greeting, though neither of them called out. She heard nothing but the sound of the warm wind in her ears. When he finally reached her, he stopped and removed his cap.

'Are you going to Burg Lingenfels?' she asked.

He nodded.

'But it isn't Thursday.' She lifted a hand to shield the sun from her eyes. She could smell the dust and sweat on his clothes.

'I came to give you something,' he said, reaching into his pockets. 'I made these for the boys.'

In his hand he held two wooden soldiers: intriguing, roughly carved figures, each around the size of a carrot.

'They're beautiful,' Benita said.

'Take them.' He held out his hand.

She hesitated. Marianne would not like her to accept a gift from him. She did not like Herr Muller. This much was obvious. 'I don't think—' she began. 'I don't think Frau von Lingenfels would like it.'

The smile on his face faded and he looked down the hill. Benita regretted her words. 'Never mind,' she said swiftly. 'She doesn't have to know.'

Muller regarded her. 'I don't want to make trouble.'

With growing conviction, Benita smiled. She slid the soldiers into her pockets, one on each side. 'They will make the boys happy.'

Herr Muller smiled back. And she felt her old self stir, the Benita who knew how to make a man smile.

CHAPTER SEVEN

BURG LINGENFELS, AUGUST 1945

Marianne did not discover the toy soldiers for some time, and then only because she was looking for the cat. The animal had appeared one day outside the kitchen door, an ugly thing, half its tail missing, unbeautifully brindled. Cats were rare these days – starved, or worse. Rumour had it that people in the bombed-out cities ate them. But this one was brave and proud and unafraid. The girls fed it scraps from a bowl they left beside the kitchen steps. So now the cat was probably better fed than most of Germany's children.

Then suddenly it stopped coming. The scraps lay in the bowl uneaten, picked over by the birds, which then twittered and shat all over the kitchen stoop. The girls were beside themselves. *Stop worrying about that creature,* Marianne chided them. *Don't create drama.* But secretly she worried, too. There was something cheering about the cat's pluckiness. Even Martin liked to play with it. It brought a certain lightness to their makeshift family – and its absence seemed unaccountable. It was far too pragmatic a creature to forsake such a good situation. So Marianne went looking. Perhaps it was trapped somewhere. God knows the old stables and barns were full of dangerous rotting floorboards and menacing holes.

This was what brought her to the stable.

When she entered, she was surprised to hear Fritz and Martin. Since Martin's accident they were forbidden to play here. She followed the sound to the back of the building and found them sprawled in a patch of sun. At her approach, they looked up guiltily, and Fritz tucked something behind his back.

'What are you doing here?' Marianne asked.

'Just playing,' Fritz said.

'With what?' She extended her hand. 'May I see?'

Fritz did not move.

'Here.' It was Martin who placed his carved soldier in her palm.

Marianne frowned. The little figure was beautiful – carved with rough tools but still quite detailed, a soldier crouching with a rifle. Reluctantly, Fritz handed her his as well: a soldier standing at attention, wearing a long coat.

'They're lovely,' she said, confused by the boys' diffidence. 'Where did you get them?'

Neither spoke.

'My mother,' Martin said finally.

'Why such long faces?' Marianne laughed. 'I thought you had something terrible. Did you think you weren't allowed to play?'

'*Tante* Benita said not to show you,' Fritz blurted. 'She said you wouldn't like it because Herr Muller made them.'

Marianne's face fell. 'Ah,' she said. 'I see.'

In her palm, the figures suddenly seemed heavy and sharp, their forms weirdly undefined.

'Well, you have them now. I won't take them away. But in the future—' She broke off. What did she want to say? *Don't listen to Benita? Don't take gifts from a Nazi? Don't hide things from me?*

'In the future, you are not to talk to Herr Muller,' she finished. 'Don't—' She raised a hand at the protest she knew Fritz was forming. 'I don't want to hear your complaints.'

Marianne brooded over this all afternoon. So Benita had cast her in the role of righteous humbug, and about something you couldn't expect two young boys to understand. And what was worse: Benita was right. Marianne *didn't* approve. And Marianne *didn't* want Herr Muller making things for the children. She didn't want him working his way into their family. Benita had *known* that and had given the toys to the boys anyway. It was bad enough that they hung around Muller as he worked. That they spent hours in the woods watching him split wood, talking about God knows what. The man was a prisoner of war, an ex-Nazi, and she knew nothing of his character. She did not want him playing a paternal role for these fatherless boys. She had been wrong to accept his help.

It wasn't until that evening that Marianne remembered the cat and went looking again. But like half the living creatures on the continent, it could not be found.

The following day, Marianne went to Lieutenant Peterman.

'I should have asked for Franz Muller's file before I accepted his help,' she said, standing before the man's cluttered desk.

Peterman looked amused.

'His file?' he said, leaning back in his chair. 'Do you think we're as organised as the Nazis?'

Marianne frowned. 'Well, presumably he has filled out a *Fragebogen*?'

Peterman sighed and turned to one of the overstuffed cabinets behind him. He opened a drawer and began rummaging.

The *Fragebogen* was a questionnaire the Allied occupiers used for denazification. It consisted of six pages of questions, ranging from height and weight to membership of the Nazi Party and whether the subject had ever been involved in the destruction of Jewish property. No one thought highly of it, including the Allies. What was to stop people from lying? But Marianne saw its value – weren't most Germans too literal and unimaginative to lie? And how else were the Allies supposed to begin sorting ordinary *Mit-*

läufer fellow travellers from true Nazi criminals? But apparently she was nearly alone in this sentiment. Even Peterman took a dim view of the forms, which were proving a great hassle for the Americans to process.

'Miraculous!' he announced, pulling a slim packet of stapled papers from the drawer. 'Here it is – his *Fragebogen*.' He extended it to her. 'For what it's worth. God knows what people make up on these things.'

Marianne scanned the pages. *Address, birthday, education* (he had finished school at fourteen), *party membership* (joined 1942). *Member of the Reserve.* And then there it was. On the third page. *Ordnungspolizei. District Kiel, District Mecklenburg, District Lublin.*

Her eyes stuck on the word *Lublin.* That was where Freddy Lederer had been.

'Not good?' Peterman asked, seeing her face. 'Let me see.' He took the papers from her hand and looked them over. 'Not even a member of the party until '42, probably because they made him when he was called up,' he said, flicking his finger against the page. 'A nobody. I wouldn't have sent you one of the real crazies.'

Marianne shook her head. In her mind's eye, she saw Freddy's face again – a sweet, unserious man, transformed by despair. The 'Jewish Action' he had witnessed was carried out by a unit of the *Ordnungspolizei. All those children marched into the woods holding their mothers' hands.*

Concern spread over Peterman's face as he watched her. 'Did he *do* something to you?'

'No.' Marianne looked at him. 'But they did terrible things in Lublin.'

'Ah.' Peterman looked confused. He stared at the paper, searching for information that would clarify her response. Finding nothing, he lifted his eyes to hers. 'So what do you want me to do?'

Marianne stared at him.

'Tell him to finish chopping whatever trees he has felled,' she said. 'And then not to come back.'

Peterman sighed. 'He's being transferred to a French camp at the end of the month, anyway.'

Marianne levelled her gaze. 'Tell him.'

Every day the American and British radio programmes broadcast new and grisly stories about the Nazis and the horrors of the camps they had liberated. But almost no one listened. The citizens of Ehrenheim made excuses: they had no radios, no money for newspapers; they were too busy clearing rubble, rustling up food, mourning their dead. Or they maintained that it was all Allied propaganda. *Look at how the Americans treated their German prisoners – locking them in open-air cages along the Rhine!* they argued. *What was the difference?* Marianne was enraged by their disinterest. Didn't they want to *know* what happened in the camps, especially if – as they all insisted – they didn't already? Anyway, the idea that they had been ignorant was hogwash. Wasn't that why the German troops had fought until the bitter end? And why the Ehrenheimers had holed up in the castle, terrified of the advancing Americans? They were afraid they would be punished for their country's sins. Goebbels and Himmler and Hitler himself had all but spelled it out in their absurd exhortations over the past year and a half: fight until the bitter end or pay the price. *For what we've done* was implicit. They had known but not *known*. That was closer to the truth. That was something Marianne understood.

In any case, she and her children listened to the radio. They needed to understand what their fathers had died fighting, especially Fritz, whose sense of right and wrong was fickle at best. They listened to reports of rotting piles of bodies, gas chambers, and sadistic guards. And of the arrests of high-ranking Nazis, like Ilse Koch, the wife of the commander of Buchenwald, rumoured to have turned the skin of executed Jewish prisoners into lampshades. In Lüneberg, Josef Kramer and forty-five other camp guards and workers were set to go on trial in September. Grisly pictures of camp victims ran in the papers, side by side with glamorous photos of Irma Grese, a sadistic concentration camp guard, rumoured to be Kramer's mistress.

Could you see a person's soul in their face? Marianne and Albrecht had often argued about this. *Yes,* she had insisted. *Didn't you know from the moment you saw Hitler's photograph that he was bad?* Albrecht wasn't sure. *If it was so obvious,* he pointed out, *how did he fool the rest of Germany?*

Some people are better than others at reading the signs, Marianne had said with a shrug. She was half joking, half serious. The conversation came back to her when she saw the photos of Irma Grese. The image on the paper's front page was of a woman who could have been a starlet, with her coy smile and stylish hairdo, while the mug shot inside revealed a repellant bully with a look of stupid hardness in her eyes – the same person, seen two ways. But even in the first one, if you looked closely, you could see the cruelty at the edge of her mouth, and the meanness in her gaze. And this was the version that sold papers.

In town, the Americans were showing a film: footage of the liberation of Buchenwald. Everyone was required to attend except for *Opfers.* Marianne went anyway. Wasn't it her – and every German's – responsibility? She made a demonstration out of her commitment, standing tall and solemn at the front of the line.

She already knew, of course. But it was one thing to *know* from documents and stories, horrifying in their own right, and another to *see.* When the movie began, Marianne had to dig her nails into her palms to keep from throwing up. Here on the screen were actual bodies, heaped like scraps of fabric. Here were fathers and mothers and children, starving and naked, lying in piles. Here were victims staring into the camera as individuals with all the sadness and despair of unique lives.

For all the horror of the official reports she and Albrecht had seen, with their language of 'extermination' and 'elimination,' they could not come close to conjuring this. How could they? There was no point of reference. Later, such footage would come to be so familiar it became unseen – a kind of placeholder for human evil. The first black-and-white glimpse of barbed wire, dirt, and nakedness cautioned viewers, *Look away*. But in this moment, in the first unveiling, it was like nothing she or anyone else had ever seen. And it was impossible to look away. She looked and trembled in her seat.

Exiting the theatre, two girls walked in front of Marianne. Young women, really, maybe sixteen and seventeen. As they jostled through the doors in the midst of the solemn crowd, Marianne overheard them talking about silk stockings – one of them had ruined her last pair. Now where would she ever get new ones? She pouted. 'Not from the Jews,' the other said, and they both giggled.

'For shame,' Marianne spat. 'Have you become such monsters that you can laugh at that?' The girls stared at her, not with shame or anger but with fear. And all around her Marianne felt the people draw close together, tightening their scarves and jackets, squaring their shoulders, fortifying themselves against her reproach.

A rumour had developed in Ehrenheim and elsewhere that the film was a piece of Allied propaganda and that the footage really showed German soldiers and collaborators killed and starved in Soviet gulags. In the last months of the war, the Americans had dropped leaflets with photos of concentration camp victims from planes and this was how Hitler had explained them. Being the sheep they were, the Ehrenheimers believed him. And they clung to this idea now – a thin protection between them and their own complicity.

It made Marianne livid with fury and shame.

*　　*　　*

Unlike Marianne, Benita did not go see the film. And she stopped listening to the news broadcasts with the von Lingenfelses.

'Ugh,' she said with a shudder on the third night when she joined them sitting around the radio. The subject was the liberation of Mauthausen, another concentration camp. 'Do you really think the children should hear this?' Benita asked.

Marianne turned and stared at her. 'Of course they should. They are Germans.'

The children fidgeted in their seats. Even Elisabeth knew better than to interject.

Cowed, Benita returned to her darning and listened to the rest of the broadcast in silence.

But the following night she begged off. She was too tired to listen and was going to bed. Marianne bit her tongue. Where was Benita's sense of moral responsibility? Where was her compassion? She seemed to have no feeling of commitment to – or belonging in – the wider world. She was as bad as the citizens of Ehrenheim. Marianne's anger rose as suddenly as a flock of startled birds. Connie had loved Benita, she reminded herself. She was the mother of Connie's son. This was what mattered.

But it was so difficult not to judge! Some deep seed in Marianne's being grew unstoppably towards fairness, pushing blindly through nuance and complication to extract a simple answer: wrong or right.

As a girl, roaming the Ostsee with Connie and Freddy and the other children of the Prussian aristocracy, she had been christened 'The Judge.' In the anarchic atmosphere of the summer holidays, the children had turned to Marianne to sort out their quarrels and issues of fairness. She had loved the role. It made her feel distinguished and powerful. And it was because of this privileged place she held that she and Connie grew close. He was a leader of the group too, an inventor of the best games and most exciting adventures, a charismatic Pied Piper to the children of the Grand Hotel. In the absence of nannies and governesses, who were instructed by their parent overlords to let children return to nature on these holidays, Connie and Marianne reigned together – king and queen of the wild things – Connie full of mischief, and Marianne (at fourteen) full of wisdom.

But then her role became a prison as the age of flirtation descended and Marianne found herself locked out of its frivolities. Her reputation made her self-conscious. How could The Judge bat her eyelashes and giggle? How could she feign the silliness necessary to play such games? She was not well suited to flirtation in a physical sense, either. She was tall and dark and awkwardly proportioned, with coltish long limbs, a flat chest, and a sombre face.

Even so, Marianne imagined that her connection to Connie was meant to transition into something more adult, more gendered. More romantic. What exactly that entailed, she did not consider, but she believed it was a given, as confusing as it was promising.

Then one night their little group went swimming in the moonlight. There was a ball at the hotel and all the adults were swept up in the excitement. It was a hot night and the ballroom was fetid with the stink of alcohol and perfume, waxy hothouse lilies and sweat. The children escaped to the beach, stripping their clothes as they went, giddy with the excitement of transgression. The sand was still warm from the sun, and the Baltic looked especially soft in the windless darkness, the waves barely lapping at their toes. One by one, they plunged into the water, laughing and calling out.

For most, the swim was quick. Despite the calm, they were frightened of the blackness, and they charged back up the dunes to pull on their dresses, shirts, and trousers, crouching and shrieking at the prospect of being seen naked. But Marianne and Connie remained. They swam as if it were a competition to see who would turn back first. When she finally stopped, her heart pounding, she became aware of her body, naked below the surface, suspended precariously over the depths. Connie noticed and turned and swam back to her, emerging nearby, shaking the water from his hair. Above them, stars twinkled through the haze, and in the distance, the hotel sparkled like a cruise ship. For a moment, Marianne was terrified. Of their distance from the shore and of the unknown deep, but also of Connie, her own nakedness, and her certainty that this was the moment that would change their relationship. Her whole body thrilled with anticipation.

But just as she began to swim in his direction, he dived under the water.

'I won,' he called when he surfaced, farther away. Then with confident, lazy strokes he started towards the shore.

One afternoon, Benita, Katarina, and Elisabeth returned from town, flush faced and laughing, their light moods discordant with Marianne's.

'You have a note, from Herr Peterman,' Elisabeth exclaimed. She held out a thin envelope. 'Maybe we're invited to one of their parties!' Elisabeth was preoccupied with the thought of attending an American army event and dancing with a soldier. Where did she get these ideas? Benita? The doltish Ehrenheim girls she had recently met? She was only thirteen.

Marianne took the envelope and tore it open.

It was not an invitation, but something of far more import.

We have identified the wife of the late Pietre Grabarek, whose name is on your list. Her name is Ania Grabarek and she is accompanied by two sons. She is currently at the Tollingen Displaced Persons Camp.

The news was exciting but also puzzling. Grabarek was a Polish name, and one Marianne did not immediately recognise. But apparently she had given it to Peterman. She had lifted the names directly from Albrecht's journal, and not all his associates and contacts were known to her. She felt a pang of disappointment that it was not someone she knew – Carlotta Biedermann, for example, whom she had always liked and had lost track of completely. But this was selfish. The list was not about providing her with friends. It was about finding the women she had sworn to help.

She read the note aloud.

'Oh.' Elisabeth harrumphed in disappointment. 'I thought it was an invitation.'

The children did not understand their mother's quest. They were, in fact, discomfited by it. Now that school had begun, such as it was, taught by the sorriest lot of old maids and barely literate numbskulls (all the old teachers had been defrocked as fervent Nazis, this being Ehrenheim), they were surrounded by people who mourned Hitler in secret and viewed Albrecht as a traitor. The children craved distance from their father's reputation.

'Who is Ania Grabarek?' Katarina asked politely.

'I don't know,' Marianne confessed. 'Do you remember him, Benita? Pietre Grabarek? '

Benita shook her head with disinterest. Of course Benita didn't remember. The girl had no interest in politics.

'The wife of Pietre Grabarek,' Marianne mused aloud.

Suddenly an image came to her: a short man, dark haired, bearing urgent news. He had brought word of *Kristallnacht* as it was unfolding across Germany. A Polish envoy, or some sort of diplomat. An associate of Connie's rather than Albrecht's.

'I think maybe I do remember,' Marianne said. 'He came late – straight from Munich.'

Benita shrugged and kept her eyes on the buttons she was counting. 'Could be.'

'He was a particular friend of Connie's,' Marianne persisted.

'That doesn't mean I would know him,' Benita said.

'No.' Marianne looked down. 'Well, we will find out who she is soon enough.'

CHAPTER EIGHT

BURG LINGENFELS, AUGUST 1945

To Ania Grabarek, it was clear that the woman leading them out of the Tollingen Displaced Persons Camp was accustomed to giving orders. She had a wide, confident stride and the sort of commanding tone Ania was not used to hearing from members of her own sex. Even her name conveyed forcefulness: Marianne Falkenberg von Lingenfels.

'Your father was a brave man,' the woman said over her shoulder to Ania's boys. 'It is my honour to host his family.'

Ania glanced at her sons with their pale, thin faces. They looked stricken. Fear and confusion had rendered them mute. Poor Anselm had barely spoken since Dresden, and Wolfgang – Wolfgang, her baby, her fierce one – had fallen into the sullen glower of a trapped animal.

Frau von Lingenfels moved on to the next subject. Then suddenly she stopped. 'What's this?' They were passing a low building from which people emerged like ghosts, covered in acrid-smelling grey chemical dust: the camp's delousing hall.

'Decontamination,' Ania answered.

'Horrible!' Frau von Lingenfels exclaimed. 'There must be a more humane way!' She was clearly a do-gooder, an advocate. It made Ania wary.

At the gate, a young man in a UNRRA badge waved them past. This was the agency in charge of Europe's DP camps – the United Nations Relief and Rehabilitation Administration: it seemed to Ania a miracle that such an agency could exist. The line of new entries waiting to be processed stretched down the road. Every day more people arrived from the east: ethnic Germans expelled from territories annexed by Russia and Poland, some who had settled there at Hitler's urging, some whose families had lived there for centuries; Russian Cossacks who had fought alongside the Nazis; Ukrainian nationalists who had fought against the Russians; and anyone else fearing Stalin's wrath. Last month the camp had run out of beds. Now, new arrivals waited to be assigned local 'hosts', who would provide them a place to sleep under their own roofs. Usually, these hosts were reluctant at best. But not Marianne von Lingenfels. She had volunteered to host the Grabareks. In fact, she had sought them out. They were meant to be grateful, Ania understood. But she wasn't. She preferred the anonymity of the camp.

'You speak without an accent,' Frau von Lingenfels said as they started in the opposite direction of the waiting people. 'Are you originally German?'

Ania nodded.

'Ahhh,' the woman said. 'But your husband was Polish?'

Ania nodded again.

'And you speak German, too?' Frau von Lingenfels continued, turning to the boys. 'What are your names?'

The boys remained silent. Anselm sent an anxious look in his mother's direction, Wolfgang glared at the ground.

'This is Anselm and this is Wolfgang,' Ania supplied.

The woman remained oblivious.

'Well, you will meet two other young men about your ages at our castle: my boy, Fritz, who is eight, and his friend Martin, who is six – another child of a resister. I am sure you will become great friends.

'Burg Lingenfels is not a castle as you might imagine,' she continued cheerfully. 'It's not *grand*. We live in the kitchen, really, because the rest of the place is empty and damp. And there's no more fine furniture – no one has lived in it for ages. But it has its advantages. A roof, for instance!' She laughed. 'And a great big oven we can light when it's cold. And there were once little princes and princesses living in it. Learning to joust and eating off golden plates and whatnot. Or anyway, my children like this idea . . .'

Ania let the woman's words roll over her. They were going to a castle, to live with a 'widow of the resistance,' as Marianne von Lingenfels referred to herself. Thrushes sang from the grass. Poppies bloomed in the field. There was no checkpoint, no scrape of strafers, no tromp of boots. This was the important thing.

'Before the war, the castle belonged to my husband's great-aunt,' Frau von Lingenfels continued. 'She didn't live in it, but she organised parties there, and picnics. She was something of an eccentric. Your father met her once – he was there for one of her parties.' She grew serious. 'That was the only time I met him. Did he tell you anything about it? Countess von Lingenfels? Albrecht, my husband? Or Connie Fledermann?'

'No.' Ania shook her head.

'Your husband was in the Polish Foreign Office before the war?'

'He was in the military.'

'Ahhh.' Frau von Lingenfels nodded. 'And then in the Home Army?'

Ania nodded.

'Was he arrested by the Nazis or killed in the fighting?'

'He was sent to a camp.'

A look of remorse, even pity, crossed the woman's face. 'I'm sorry,' she said. 'Albrecht always felt guilty that we were not able to do more to support the Home Army, that he was imprisoned before the uprising.'

Ania was silent. *No checkpoints, no strafers, no stomping boots,* she reminded herself.

*   *   *

Dinner consisted of potatoes, cabbage, and mushrooms the children had gathered in the forest, and, luxury of luxuries, three boiled eggs. At the camp, the Grabareks had eaten thin gruel and spinach soup every day. This was a more lavish meal than they had seen in half a year. The eggs, apparently, were a gift from the farmer at the base of the hill, a man named Herr Kellerman, whom Frau von Lingenfels referred to as 'our hero' with a glibness Ania understood was meant to be kind.

'But the eggs should be for you, not us,' Ania said stiffly, dredging up a trace of manners she had learned in another life. Anselm and Wolfgang looked alarmed.

'Nonsense,' Marianne said. 'You need them. We take turns.'

Besides Frau von Lingenfels, there were her two daughters – one dark and solemn, the other lighter haired, tall, and sceptical. And her son, a sturdy boy of about Wolfgang's age who would not sit still, and another woman and her son. The last two were confusing to her. Benita and Martin Fledermann. They too were refugees, Ania understood. Their husband and father had also been executed by Hitler for his role in the 20 July conspiracy. The rest of the connection was lost: Frau von Lingenfels had grown up with him, or her husband had grown up with Frau Fledermann, or someone had known someone as a child.

The von Lingenfels children spoke too fast. Frau von Lingenfels assumed too much. Their words raced over Ania like water from a hose. They too had come from the east, from Silesia. First, they had gone to Berlin. There had been an illness. There was a list of widows. Other wives of resisters. She, Ania Grabarek, was the second one they had found. The first was Frau Fledermann.

Anselm and Wolfgang kept their eyes down. Ania nodded and ate.

Frau Fledermann and her son were also silent. Both were pale and blond and beautiful – she in the fragile way of an injured bird, and he like a blinking, quietly startled fawn. They were not at ease here either. This made Ania like them.

When the von Lingenfelses were done telling, they began with the questions.

'Were you taken to a Children's Home, like Martin?' Fritz asked Anselm. 'Were you in a KZ?'

Anselm shook his head no.

'Were you in Warsaw when it was bombed? Was it worse than Berlin? Were the Russian soldiers as cruel as everyone says?'

Anselm and Wolfgang shook their heads, focused on their eggs. *No, no,* and a shrug.

They fielded the questions with one-word answers, shovelling food into their mouths. In the last months, they had become animals, used to sleeping in the open, foraging for sustenance, guarding against predators.

Ania felt exhaustion settle over her. If she closed her eyes for even a moment, she was certain she would fall asleep.

'Enough,' Frau von Lingenfels announced, pushing back her chair. 'We are overwhelming our guests. Elisabeth and Katarina, wash up. Fritz and Martin, bring in water. Grabareks, go to bed.'

With relief, Ania led her boys upstairs to the small room they had been assigned above the kitchen. In the middle, two mattresses were covered with sheets and two blankets each. When was the last time Ania and her boys had slept on sheets? The beauty of it, this simple sign of order and cleanliness, tightened her throat. She remembered learning to fold sheets as a girl, to wrap them around the mattress, pulling the corners just so – a realm of knowledge rendered meaningless over the previous months.

'Mama . . .' Anselm's voice floated out of the darkness. Disconnected from his body, which had grown tall and wiry, it sounded childish: a reminder that he was only nine. 'Are you going to tell them . . . ?'

Ania jolted awake.

'Tell them what?' Wolfgang demanded before she could speak.

'That you don't want to stay here? That you want to go back to the camp?' His voice was surprisingly harsh. Of the two, he was the leader despite the fact that he was younger.

'No,' Anselm said meekly. And then: 'Mama?'

Ania was silent. Through the dark she could feel both boys waiting for her to respond.

Outside, an owl hooted in the dark. 'Hush,' she said finally. 'Time to sleep.'

CHAPTER NINE

THE WARTHEGAU, JANUARY 1945

In sleep, Ania returns to the march. Not so much in her dreams as in her memory. It waits there for her to relive – a weird middle point, the journey from one life to another, her personal metamorphosis.

The road to Breslau teems with refugees. Mothers, children, old people, sisters . . . all flee before the advancing Red Army. Some are from as far away as the Black Sea and have been on the road for months. There are few men among them – only the crippled, sick, and elderly. The war is not over yet and the rest of the men are fighting – for the Germans, the Russians, the local partisans, or whoever is the most expedient to fight for. Even more of them are dead.

Occasionally, Ania and her sons pass groups of boys around their age, unaccompanied by any family. They are from the *Jugend* camps and lagers, the various *Kinderlandverschickung* (children-to-the-land) programmes set up across the conquered east to remove children from the embattled cities. They are sullen creatures who have been without their mothers for too long, now half-moulded into Hitler's fantasy. The German youth should be *as swift as a greyhound, as tough as leather, and as hard as Krupp's steel.* Ania knows Hitler's rhetoric. *I want a brutal, domineering, fearless, and cruel youth. . . . The free, magnificent beast of prey must again flash from their eyes.* These boys make her nervous. When she sees them, she takes pains to melt away.

Ania and her children have only the clothes they wear, the coats on their backs, and a few extras: a good pot, a tin cup to share, a paring knife. She also has a small book of photographs and a sack of pilfered food: a blood sausage, a scrap of butter, one dry loaf of bread, a precious jar of last summer's plums. Anselm has his favourite book, Wolfgang his precious pocketknife. Unfortunately, they have no papers. This is a problem. All along the road SS men are stamping, sorting, and turning people back. It is not only the sad-sack German soldiers at the front who are supposed to hold their ground against the enemy. The German civilians are supposed to stay too – a kind of human obstacle to the Russian advance. And so the SS devote their efforts to preventing flight. What cowards these supposed *über*-Nazis are, avoiding the front and hiding behind bureaucratic responsibilities! As if placing all these poor, terrified souls in the path of the Russians will change anything. The war is already lost in everything but name. At the front, only the last members of the Home Guard remain.

Whenever they hear word of a checkpoint, Ania and her boys are forced to tromp into the forest with every other paperless refugee. Their progress is painfully slow. They are not the only ones frustrated by this. The woods are full of anger and panic. Everyone talks about the Russians: they will eat German children, rape German women, burn German houses to the ground. At least these fantasies distract them from the cold. What is frostbite when compared to the threat of being eaten by a hungry Russian? They are suggestible masses, used to basing their beliefs and actions on ideology rather than experience.

As it is, the cold causes enough trouble: chilblains and frostbite, sores on the fingers and lips and eyelids that won't heal. People strip clothing from the corpses of less fortunate refugees and huddle together in woodsheds and haylofts, pressing their bodies

against those of strangers to survive. In the north, where the refugees are forced to cross the frozen Haff, there are rumours of
horses stuck in the ice, and whole wagons of families who have
disappeared into the freezing lagoon.

Ania is less afraid of the cold or the Russians than she is of
being sent back. The Russians are not individuals but an army.
And in her experience, armies are less interested in individuals than the individuals think they are. The stream of refugees
is like blood from a severed arm – a troubling side effect, not a
root cause. The Russian army is after the German army, not this
human by-product of their fighting.

She and her boys move south as well as west, and the front
grows closer. At night, they can hear the shelling and drumroll
of the big guns. The more frightened travellers scramble to their
feet at one, two, three in the morning and resume their march in
the dark, clutching their sacks, pushing their handcarts. No one
has wagons here. The horses are all gone. If the Nazis didn't whisk
them off to the front, the Russians have stolen them.

For a few weeks, Ania has noticed a sympathetic-looking
woman among the crowd of fellow travellers. She is of average
size with light brown hair that she keeps tucked under a grubby
scarf. Her face is kind – not old, but timeworn – and intelligent.
She has a son, a boy of about Wolfgang's age, but smaller, and
sickly. Ania has seen them several times sleeping in the abandoned barns and train stations in which they take refuge along
the way. She finds solace in the woman's presence: a reasonable-
looking person, someone with whom she might have, in another
lifetime, become friends.

Ania does not have warm feelings for the other familiar faces.
The Polish grandmother in jarringly shiny men's riding boots,
the Ukrainian mother accompanied by six children and a dim-
witted young man she smacks on the head and gives only the
smallest portions of food, the bone-thin young woman with the
lifeless baby wrapped against her chest, the old man pulling his

listless, swollen-legged wife on a wheelbarrow. *Her legs look like they're going to explode,* Wolfgang remarked when they first saw her. Ania can barely look at any of them. Instead, she concerns herself entirely with her boys: whether they need to stop, whether they are sick. For two weeks, Anselm suffered from terrible diarrhoea and they had to camp in place. She is responsible. It was her choice to flee.

For the most part, people on this journey do not share. They do not establish camaraderie in their misery – their supplies are too meager, the mood too grim. They are fleeing *from,* not *to,* and the uncertainty of their destination renders them mute.

Then one night, the eastern front falls and the Russians overtake the village in which Ania and the others are hiding. The ground reverberates with the weight of human footsteps – an entire battalion approaches, accompanied by the rumble of tanks. Panic runs through the crowd sleeping in the nooks and crannies of the village. For the first time Ania can recall, people begin to run, even stampede. Shots are fired. And the road, narrow here in the village between the ancient barns and stables, becomes clogged with human beings.

Ania and her boys remain hidden in the hayloft where they have taken shelter. They are nearly the only ones left. 'Shouldn't we leave, too?' Anselm asks. He looks at her, eyes wide – he is anxious by nature and has developed a tremor on the march.

From the street below they hear screams. 'Better to stay,' Ania says with confidence she doesn't feel. But at least here they will be safe from the human avalanche.

When the Russians finally enter the village, the beams and girders of the barn shake. Several heavy artillery vehicles precede the soldiers and can barely fit down the narrow street. Without speaking, Ania and her boys creep towards the shuttered hay chute to watch. Only then does she realise they are not alone. The woman she's noticed these last few weeks and her son are at the opening, already peering out. Without speaking, the woman shifts to make space for them, patting the floor beside her as if they are old friends.

Outside, the scene is one of absurd chaos. After the vehicles, the Russians press down the street on foot. They are in high spirits, shouting back and forth in their rough language, singing, and passing flasks. Scattered through the stream of soldiers are the last of the fleeing civilians, small and grey and terrified, clutching their bundles, pressing back against doorways, crouching, even covering their heads. But the Russians barely see them, and it strikes Ania as perversely funny – here are the troops that sent these masses scurrying ahead for weeks and now they simply march past. After all the panic, their disregard is almost insulting.

'They can't be bothered,' the other woman says, as if she has read Ania's thoughts.

'Look at that one.' Wolfgang points to a stocky, bearded soldier, singing, dancing a Russian jig.

'Like a trained bear.' The woman laughs.

The situation is weirdly cosy, with all of them clustered around the window, and they remain for hours, until the last of the Russians have passed. From time to time a soldier or two bangs into the barn below in search of livestock, knocking open the empty stall doors, firing unnecessary shots. In the loft, they hold their breaths. One particularly persistent man starts up the ladder, then is shouted down by someone outside. In the hayloft, relief makes them giddy.

Ania is the other woman's name too, although she has always been called by her middle name, Gerda. 'I knew there was a reason I liked you,' Ania says when she learns this. It is the first time she has made anything resembling a joke in God knows how long. The boy's name is Olgar. He is sweet with bright eyes and a mischievous sense of humour. His cough is alarming. It sounds like a scraping Tomahawk plane. He doesn't complain, though, and carries a pack of cards in his breast pocket. He teaches Anselm and Wolfgang to play poker while they wait.

When the last of the battalion finally marches past, Ania, her boys, and their new friends climb down the ladder.

In their wake, the Russians have left massive confusion. A farmer who guarded his pigs with a rifle has been shot; his pigs have been taken and his wife is wailing in the street. Another woman claims she has been beaten, and her two daughters raped. Several people have been trampled in the chaos. And they find three Ukrainians in German uniforms slumped at the bottom of a brick wall – apparent victims of an impromptu firing squad. The Russians show no pity, even for their own soldiers who have been captured and conscripted to fight for the Germans.

On the bright side, they have not bayoneted women through their private parts or cannibalised Germans or hatcheted the children and cooked them on spits as Goebbels forecast. Ania hopes they at least bayoneted a few SS men at the checkpoints. She leaves her boys with her new friend and helps pull the Ukrainians' bodies off the street. They will be buried in the local graveyard unless someone comes looking for them. Which seems unlikely at best.

When evening falls, Ania and Gerda and their boys retreat to the hayloft. Gerda shares a heel of black bread and Ania cuts into the blood sausage she's been saving. Outside, a layer of frost covers the village rooftops and they glitter in the moonlight. Smoke from a burning house billows towards the sky, and the boys take turns naming the shapes it makes. *A mermaid, a leaping deer, a dog's head.* It feels like a celebration – of what, they're not sure. Certainly nothing is over, and they have a long way to go. A celebration of camaraderie, then. It has been years since Ania felt such a thing.

A family of refugees from distant Galicia lights a fire in the woodstove downstairs with straw and foraged wood. The boys, basking in the rising warmth, fall asleep and the women talk. Mostly they speak of their journey west, sharing only the banalities: the nasty, apple-faced woman who screamed at passers-by on the bridge, the family with scarlet fever, the way people flocked to a barrel of rotten chestnuts on the roadside like a swarm of flies. 'No, like SS men to a checkpoint,' Ania corrects, and they both laugh. When was the last time she laughed? Anselm startles awake, unfamiliar with the sound.

In the morning, they set out together. When they reach Breslau, they don't even bother with the train. They have heard that Karl Hanke, the gauleiter of Lower Silesia, has ordered the city evacuated so they can transform it into a military 'fortress.' The crowd of people waiting at the station spills so far beyond the platform they can't even see the tracks.

As they walk in the other direction, a train rumbles into the station: a line of open goods wagons filled with what appears, at first, to be sacks of food.

'Mary, mother of God,' Gerda says, looking back. 'Those are prisoners.' The sacks of food are human beings in striped uniforms, half covered with snow.

But Ania does not look back.

'Which would you rather: sit in an armchair and sew or kneel in a sunny garden and pull carrots?' Ania's new friend introduces this game and they play often. 'Which would you rather: eat *Sauerbraten* or fresh cream?'

It distracts them from their bleeding feet and grumbling stomachs.

Over the next weeks, they fall into a rhythm. Wake, share what little they have to eat, and play a game like this to still their minds. In the afternoon they submit to the bare necessity of walking, continuing towards the next piece of bread or mouldy potato Anselm and Wolfgang manage to dig up, left over from last year's harvest. Occasionally they come across stations set up by the National Socialist People's Welfare, where boisterous volunteers hand out soup and propaganda: the Germans are merely waiting for the newest installment of weapons before they turn back the tide; the

Russians are so desperate they are conscripting women; the supposedly kindly American troops advancing in the west are only
the frontrunners – they are followed by Jewish *Einsatzgruppen*
eager for revenge. That is why it is imperative to continue the
fight. The Germans must triumph or be killed. No one believes it.
The Germans are losing. This is clear from the flood of humans
marching west.

In bits, the women learn more intimate details about each
other. Gerda is an ethnic German, born outside Warsaw to parents who were both chemists. She studied music at university,
where she met her husband, a gifted trumpet player. He is now
dead. Killed by the Nazis.

She shares funny, romantic stories about her husband – the
time he serenaded her from outside her dormitory window at midnight and woke the matron, who ran outside brandishing a stick.
How they honeymooned aboard a barge on the Danube. About
the kitten he gave her when they first met. And while the children
sleep, the women exchange darker, more painful stories about the
families and homes they have lost. This way they fall asleep.

Gerda is heading to Dresden with her son, where she hopes to
stay with her cousins. 'Come with us,' she urges Ania. 'I'm sure
they will put you up, too.' It seems a promising destination. *Flor-
ence on the Elbe,* as it is known, a beautiful city still largely intact.
Everyone says it is safe from Allied bombing on account of its
lack of heavy industry, the International Red Cross station, and its
cultural significance. There are also rumours that Winston Chur-
chill has a favourite aunt who lives there, and that the Allies are
preserving it so it might become the capital when the war is over.
Ania is happy to go along.

It is January 1945.

Their journey to Dresden takes three weeks. They are not
happy weeks: misery is the prevailing sentiment. But somehow,
in Ania's mind, they are lighter than the rest of the time around
them – the years before and those that follow. They are like the

last odd burst of energy from a dying man. The weather becomes kinder – it is cold but suddenly sunny. They are hungry, but they have their combined food and the little fat left on their bones – and they have their precious boys, while so many other women do not.

Every night, they fall asleep curled together – an economical row of bodies: Ania on one end, her friend on the other, and the boys in between. Sometimes Ania falls asleep midsentence. Somehow she is capable of this. She doesn't battle the usual *what ifs* and *hows* and *what thens* that tend to dominate her thoughts at night.

And so despite everything that follows, this is the improbable oasis Ania returns to in her dreams.

CHAPTER TEN

BURG LINGENFELS, AUGUST 1945

A week after the Grabareks came to Burg Lingenfels, the Russians arrived.

Their approach was eerily silent, a collection of dark figures climbing the hillside. Three of them fanned out like scouts in front of a platoon – but they were not a platoon. Though maybe they once had been. Now they were a kind of human wreckage: gaunt, tattered, hungry eyed.

For weeks in Ehrenheim, there had been talk of roving bands of ex-prisoners, released from one of the Nazi stalags. Nearly seventy thousand prisoners of war had been held by the Nazis in the camp at Moosburg alone: some French, some British, Dutch, and even American, but most were from the Red Army. Not only Russians, also Ukrainians, Estonians, Latvians, and other Baltic peoples, first conscripted by the Russians, then captured by the Germans. Many of these men were afraid to return home to lands now subsumed by Stalin's Soviet Union. The *Hausfraus* of Ehrenheim were convinced they were all rapists, murderers, and degenerates – and that they were after revenge. No one talked about why.

Total hogwash, they're men like any others, just hungry and mistreated, Marianne had said when her daughters returned from town with their heads full of such talk. *The people of Ehrenheim know nothing about Russians.*

The Russians had arrived in Weisslau in January and made themselves at home. Unlike many of her neighbours, Marianne had not fled. It would take more than a few drunken soldiers to make her leave the home she had been so happy in, the land that connected her to Albrecht. For the most part, the rumours of the horrors the Russians would inflict proved false. Yes, they came banging on doors at night, looking for schnapps and women, but Marianne found them easy enough to dissuade. You had to push back. Show them you were not afraid. Once she had come to the door in her bathrobe brandishing a frying pan, and how the Russians had laughed. But they had not barged past. They were thieves, of course, but who could blame them? The Germans had killed twenty million of their countrymen. So they took everything from bicycles to kitchen kettles to feather pillows, and, most prized of all, any kind of radio. But they were not monsters. Marianne had not fled until it became clear that they would also take her estate.

But now, watching these men climb the hill to the castle, she felt a prickle of fear. They did not look like the Russian soldiers she remembered from Weisslau.

'Will they kill us?!' Elisabeth asked. 'There are so many of them.'

Next to her, Katarina began to cry.

'Don't be ridiculous,' Marianne snapped. 'They're just hungry.'

Behind the girls, Benita had gone pale. Marianne thought of the apartment in Berlin where she had found her: the hideous man with the Kalashnikov guarding the door. The poor girl had her own experience of Russians. Marianne felt a pang of guilt. Benita was right to be petrified.

'You go down to the cellar,' Marianne said to her daughters. 'I will greet them when they arrive.

'Go on,' she added, more kindly, to Benita. 'You take care of the children.'

Wordlessly, Benita followed the girls.

'We will stay,' Frau Grabarek said. Marianne had almost forgotten she was there. In the week since she had arrived, she and her boys had barely spoken. Who knew what traumas they had endured? For the most part, Marianne just let them be.

'That's all right—' Marianne began to protest, but stopped. It might be useful to have the boys here. And Frau Grabarek herself had a quiet, determined strength to be reckoned with.

'Thank you,' Marianne said, surprised at her own relief.

And so they waited. It was a curiously intimate thing. They did not speak, but there was solidarity in their silence. Until this moment, Marianne had felt only a sense of unease about the Grabarek boys. Their reticence made them seem shifty. They were so unlike the boys she was familiar with – the bright, boisterous children of the German aristocracy. Despite Fritz's best efforts, Anselm and Wolfgang did not play. Instead, they followed their mother like silent, restive Dobermans.

The knock, when it came, was firm but not belligerent. They were only men, only *Russians,* Marianne reminded herself, as she had reminded her girls. Human beings, wronged by the same regime that murdered Albrecht and Connie.

She wrestled the heavy front door open, and two men stood before her. One was tall with skin stretched over his cheekbones like the thin layer of fat on the surface of boiled milk, the other short and healthier, with a beard and bright uneasy eyes. The tall one had a blanket over his shoulders, despite the warmth of the day.

'We need food,' he said, in a rough approximation of German, his voice much lower than seemed possible from a man so thin. His pants were too short, and beneath them his bare feet were caked with dirt. 'And water,' he added. Behind him, the rest of the men assembled at the mouth of the bridge over the moat. At the front of the line were the more robust-looking prisoners, and behind, still arriving, a collection of sorrier souls, emaciated and close shorn, with wide, haunted eyes. A mix of newer arrivals and those who had been held in the stalag by the Nazis for God knows how long. There were maybe fifty in total, all silent, and all staring at her.

'I speak Russian,' Marianne said in Russian. 'You are Russians, no?'

The tall man looked at her without blinking. Neither he nor his partner evidenced the surprise or enthusiasm that usually greeted this announcement. 'Most of us,' the man said, speaking Russian now. 'We need food and water and a place to rest.'

'I will bring it to you,' she said. 'And there is space and straw in the stable for you to rest.'

The shorter man nicked his head towards the castle and spoke in a low, guttural dialect. The tall man translated. 'How many people live here?'

'The beds are full,' she said, squaring her shoulders. 'But the stable has room. We will bring you food.'

'And water,' the tall man said.

'And water,' Marianne repeated.

Only after she shut the door did she realise her hands were trembling.

In the kitchen, Ania and her boys had already begun paring potatoes. 'We can cook these together with the barley and carrots,' Ania said. 'It will thicken with a handful of bread.'

Marianne nodded, grateful for the woman's calm. And the fact that she actually knew how to cook. In the week since she had come, the castle had already benefited from her competence. She knew how to grind spoonfuls of rapeseed into oil, darn stockings, pickle the vegetables to last through winter, and preserve fruit.

And she had taken over meal preparation, to Marianne's relief. It had been so long since she had shared responsibility. Benita had been sick and had never seemed a real grown-up anyway. And it had been ages – a lifetime – since Marianne shared a household with Frau Gerstler in Weisslau.

While Frau Grabarek – Ania, as Marianne had begun to think of her – chopped and cooked, Marianne filled buckets and pots with water from the cistern, which was troublingly low. Once a week, Herr Kellerman filled his 'water wagon' and hitched it to his poor long-suffering horse, Gilda, so they could have water at the castle, which was without a well. It had been five days since their last delivery.

'Carry the water,' Ania ordered her boys after Marianne filled the first pails.

'I'll take one,' Marianne began.

'It's better if you wait,' Ania said with an authority Marianne had not heard before. 'Let them see you have help.'

Marianne stopped short. She was not accustomed to being told what to do, but the woman was right.

So the boys made their way to the stable, shouldering the heavy buckets, stepping carefully along the uneven ground. As they neared, the Russians started forward, but the tall man held up his hand, gave an order, and they fell into a neat, practised line.

Through the window, Marianne and Ania watched.

Some of the men wore the striped garb of KZ prisoners. So they were not all prisoners of war, but also prisoners from concentration camps who had been driven to the local stalags as the Russians advanced. Marianne had seen these wretched marchers on her own journey west: ghost-like lines of people stumbling through the fields, driven by black-clad SS guards, kept apart from the other refugees. *Untermenschen,* an SS man at one of the checkpoints had snarled when she had asked who they were, why they did not march with everyone else.

'God help us,' she murmured.

Beside her, Ania remained silent.

And in front of the stable, the Grabarek boys stood back.

When the potato-and-barley gruel was ready, Marianne carried down one pot herself, with the boys following her.

As she approached, the men rose from where they had been sitting and lying, their hunger rising off them like a smell, and the smell itself was pungent: one of unwashed bodies, sickness, and human waste.

'Put the food down here,' the tall man instructed, and behind him the men began to fall into line. Marianne and the boys did as he said and stood back.

The tall man gave a signal, and the first in line stepped forward and dipped the ladle.

'My husband was murdered by the Nazis,' Marianne said in Russian. It was what she had planned: it was important to draw connection between them, to make the men understand she was on their side. To her surprise, her voice shook. And the words felt strange and shocking on her tongue.

'He wanted to stop the war' – she paused, steeling herself – 'to stop the camps, and the killing, and the madness.'

Her voice rang in her ears. The next in line took the ladle and drank hungrily, the soup catching in his beard. The tall man remained silent.

'They hanged him,' she continued. 'They hanged him and all his fellow resisters. From meat hooks.' She had never said this out loud before. Instead she had closed her mind around it, divorced it from its physical reality. Suddenly, saying it here rendered it vivid: Albrecht, her tall, dignified husband, swinging, his legs kicking, the worn shoes and black socks he always wore – the line of white skin between his socks and trouser cuffs. She had never allowed herself to imagine this.

A few of the men darted glances at Marianne. There was the sound of bodies shuffling forward, soup being slurped, and her own breathing, loud in her ears. She waited for some recognition of her own suffering.

Finally the tall man spoke. He said: 'The soup will not be enough.'

Marianne blinked and stared. Maybe he had not understood her Russian. An odd shame washed over her. It was as if she had stripped down and proffered herself, naked, before him – dry skin, stretch marks, raw elbows and all, in the bright sun – and he had merely looked away.

She drew herself up and swallowed. 'It's all we have.'

The man looked at her. 'There is a horse.'

For a moment she did not understand.

'Where is it?' he asked. 'It was here recently. Its shit stinks.'

She stared at him. He was talking about Gilda, Herr Keller-man's horse.

This was what her soul-baring had led them to: he was suggesting they eat Gilda.

Her shame congealed into stunned, irrational fury. She had shared something sacred and essential, and this was his response.

'The horse is old,' she said, as calmly as possible. 'The farmer needs her.'

The man levelled his gaze. 'So do my men.'

More of them stared at her now. They were not really men, she felt with a burst of anger, but animals. They had been boiled down and stripped of anything that made them human.

'There are rations for liberated prisoners at the DP camp in Tollingen,' she said coldly.

The man said nothing for a moment. 'We have had enough of camps.'

The shorter, burlier man who had first come to the door stepped forward. In an abstract way, it occurred to Marianne that he might harm her. To him, she was no better or worse than any other German. They were victims and she the agent.

But the blood beating in her head made her fierce.

'I can offer you shelter and all the food we have,' she said, crossing her arms recklessly. 'But I cannot offer you the horse.' She steeled herself.

But then their focus shifted. It became clear they were not looking at her, but beyond her, towards the castle. Turning, Marianne saw Ania hurrying down the hillside with a stern, concerned expression on her face.

'Can I help with something, Frau von Lingenfels?' she called when she was close enough.

'We are hungry,' the tall man answered before Marianne could open her mouth. 'We would like the horse.'

Ania slowed to a halt. 'The horse?'

'Herr Kellerman's,' Marianne said, folding her arms. 'It's not possible.'

Ania looked from Marianne to the men and back. Then she spoke slowly and reasonably. 'The men are starving. There is no more soup.'

Frau Grabarek went with the group's leader to Herr Kellerman's to make the request herself. Kellerman did not put up a fight. He was too old and pragmatic to engage in futile argument. Gilda was decrepit and expensive to feed. He had a younger gelding he used for the harvest.

So Kellerman led the old horse up the hill, and when he reached the castle, he simply ducked his head and handed the reins to Marianne. He was not a sentimental man. He had lost the movement of his right arm in the last war, and his wife to childbirth, and his only child to scarlet fever. He offered no parting words to his horse.

Marianne had pulled herself together while she waited. The men were starving, the horse was not hers to spare. Her own strange effort to connect her suffering to theirs had been foolish. These men had no room for the suffering of others. And why should they? They had seen God knows what in recent years. They were far from home. And many had no home to return to: their villages had been destroyed, their families killed, their countries swallowed whole by the Soviets.

Herr Kellerman handed her Gilda's reins and she accepted.

But the horse sensed menace in the great pyre the men had built before the stable and resisted for possibly the first time in her life. She pulled backwards and stamped her feet.

'It's all right,' Marianne said, although obviously it was not. She tugged at the reins and Gilda stepped forward cautiously, then stopped and strained her neck to look back at Herr Kellerman, who had owned her for some twenty years. This was how she was to be repaid for her unquestioning service.

What sort of benediction could Marianne offer? Herr Kellerman was right to turn and leave. There was nothing to say. Gilda looked wild and stupid with fear now, reduced to her most animal self. They were all in the time of animals: the men, her own frightened children hiding in the cellar, Herr Kellerman's horse. Marianne handed the burly man the reins.

'Don't make her wait,' she said in Russian, thankful not to have to say it in her own language.

All night the fire crackled and spat. Sparks sprayed towards the sky. As the moon rose, the men began to sing – a rollicking, boisterous song with an unfamiliar rhythm and tone that drowned out the echo of the horse's weird, horrible screams.

In the corner of the kitchen, Katarina and Elisabeth sat clutching each other, crying. Benita was a bundle of exposed nerves, sewing a hem into an old pair of Fritz's pants so they might fit Martin, stitching, restitching, and then ripping the stitches out. Fritz stood at the window, watching, spellbound and horrified. Somehow Martin slept.

'The men will soon come looking for schnapps,' Ania said. She and Marianne exchanged a glance.

'Why don't you sleep in the cellar tonight,' Marianne suggested to Benita and the girls. 'We can bring down the pallets.'

And so it was decided – everyone would go down except for Marianne and the Grabareks, who would keep watch upstairs. Only Fritz protested, half-heartedly. Marianne could see that he was fighting back tears. For the first time in ages, she wanted to hug him to her and kiss his head – her little boy, Albrecht's son – he was only eight years old. Instead she said, as gently as possible, 'Go on with them, Fritz, there's no point in staying up.'

And when all were settled in the fruit cellar, which had a door that could be locked, she and Ania sat in the darkened kitchen and waited, listening to the singing and the fire and the occasional shouts.

When the men came to the door, as predicted, the women answered it together and handed over the last of the Weisslau plum schnapps. Already men were passed out on the cobbles and retching in the corners on all fours. Gilda's body looked obscene, legs tied to the spit, head hanging unnaturally, abdomen blackened and hacked.

Schnapps in hand, the men retreated, and the women once again sat in the dark. Despite everything – the horse, the men, the raw exposure of her own emotions – a weird peace descended on Marianne. In this mysterious, pragmatic woman beside her, she had found a partner. And for the moment, this was enough.

When she finally slept, Marianne dreamed of the Polish labourers. All day they had stirred in the crevices of her mind, rattling tinnily in the corners where she had buried them. Now they marched forward like a ghostly jury in her sleep.

There had been maybe twenty of them, assigned to live on the estate in Weisslau when all the local boys and men who usually worked the fields had been sent to the front. They were from far-ther east, a part of Poland that had become the General Govern-ment, Polish citizens deemed unfit for Germanisation. So in the parlance of the Nazis, they were to provide labour to the master race. A lot of Nazi garbage. But the von Lingenfelses had not re-fused their services. How else was the farm to be worked? And to refuse would have thrown suspicion onto Albrecht's activities.

Provisional quarters were erected in the old pigsty. Marianne recalled a delivery of cots, some tables requisitioned from the old servants' kitchen and the appearance of barbed wire across the windows.

The labourers wore *P* for *Polen,* or 'Polish worker', stitched onto their ragged uniforms. They reported to Roland Zeppel, the farm overseer. *Untermenschen,* he called them. 'Underpeople' – the Nazi term for non-Aryans – the Gypsies, Slavs, and Jews at the bottom of the lot. *They are people, too,* Marianne had said when she heard him use the word. *You must treat them with dignity.* Roland Zeppel whipped out a Nazi pamphlet about managing foreign la-bourers. *'Do not confuse Polish workers with Germans. They are not allowed at the table. Fraternising is punishable by law.'*

Marianne glared at him.

She had never liked the man. He had been a member of the party from the beginning, and even before that, he was not well liked. He had no skills or talents or education to distinguish him, which made him just the sort to be taken with the notion that he belonged to a master race. But despite Marianne's objections, Albrecht did not fire him. He had known Roland since childhood; they had gone to the same elementary school in Weisslau, played in the same football matches, danced at the same town dances. For Albrecht, this connection was larger than the man's politics. He was loyal to Herr Zeppel, and Herr Zeppel was loyal to him.

And so, with this man at the helm, their beloved estate became part of a system that had introduced slaves overnight. Suddenly Roland Zeppel carried a pistol and commanded twenty men from a different part of the continent. Marianne saw it as another piece of Nazi ugliness. Yet in her own day-to-day existence she had accepted it. She sent extra blankets when the weather grew cold and ensured the men had enough soup and potatoes, but still, she benefited from their work.

And now, lying in her cot at Burg Lingenfels with the Russians gathered outside, Marianne realised that she could not remember the faces or names of any of those Polish labourers. Unlike the local boys and men who had toiled in the fields before the war, she knew nothing about where those men had come from. Chelmno camp, yes. But who they were beyond this, whether they had families, what sort of lives they had left behind, she had never bothered to ask.

When the Red Army arrived in Weisslau, she had liberated the labourers. She had given each bread and potatoes and a small handout of what reichsmarks she had left, but she did not find out where they would go after this.

On neighbouring estates, there were labourers who killed their landowners and overseers after the Russians arrived. Revenge was their first action upon being freed, and the Russians didn't care. They had their own agenda of revenge. The Weisslau workers did not come for Marianne. But Roland Zeppel hid in his sister's attic for days.

Remembering this made Marianne sit bolt upright in her cot. Zeppel had held the pistol, but it was her farm that both he and the labourers worked.

Outside the castle, the Russians began to sing again. This time it was a strange, unearthly song full of heartache and low, atonal notes. Something about the Volga River, the tapestry of time and the bright thread of suffering that ran through it. It was a kind of collective keening – a primal, soldiering sorrow rising from their souls.

Marianne lay on her narrow cot and listened in the dark.

CHAPTER ELEVEN

BURG LINGENFELS, AUGUST 1945

When Benita awoke, she confused the cellar walls with her prison cell. How had she ended up back here? Horror flashed to the roots of her hair, the ends of her toes. To be back in prison meant she had lost Martin.

But no, here he was, his warm body curled beside hers.

She reoriented herself: she was in the west, the countryside, with Marianne, at Burg Lingenfels.

Yesterday a gang of Russian prisoners had descended on them. They were not as terrifying as the dream. She wrapped her arms around her sleeping boy and said a silent, involuntary prayer of thanks for his young life.

Benita had been pregnant with another child when she was sent to prison, although she hadn't known it at the time. But when she found out, the life growing inside her had been a source of comfort: Connie was dead, and Martin had been taken, but she was not alone. She had passed her days whispering prayers and rosaries and lullabies to the baby: a little sister for Martin. She felt certain it was a girl.

And then the baby died. Lifeless, its small body huddled stubbornly inside her like a stone. She knew it was dead long before her body expelled it. The delivery was horrific. Her womb became infected, and she remained in the prison hospital until the Russian soldiers arrived.

And while she lay there swimming in and out of fever, she had immersed herself in a strong, oddly sustaining fury at Connie. It was his fault that she was there. His fault that Martin had been taken. His fault that the baby had died. If she had not been in prison, surely the baby would still be alive. He had abandoned her for his lofty ideals and secret conspiracy – and his affairs with other women. Gigi Flagstaff, that brassy American, who had the gall to court Benita's friendship; Margarete Vederlander, the notorious Berlin glamour girl . . . and who knew how many others? And meanwhile, Benita had miscarried one baby after another.

She and Martin had spent countless long nights alone in their hot, unlavish flat (so different from the one she had imagined when she married), staring out at the empty city streets. Connie hadn't sent them to the country, like the other aristocrats' wives and children. His widowed mother did not invite them to stay with her in the drafty old Fledermann estate, and Benita was too proud to ask. Anyway, it was a horrible, formal place that would ultimately be destroyed by the Russians, his mother shot along with what staff remained. But in Berlin, Connie was always busy, always travelling. So Benita and Martin were abandoned to the roar of bombers, the endless trips to the bomb cellar, and the increasingly stark governance of the city.

All this she resented while she lay mourning the baby in her hospital bed. And beneath this, she was angry at her own ignorance. Why had Connie left her in the dark about his work when so many other widows had known so much? Did he think she was too stupid to understand? It was the final proof of their estrangement. She had listened to the radio report on 20 July, 1944 with only the faintest inkling of unease.

Later still, Benita would be ashamed of her own oblivion. And of the rage and self-pity she had wrapped around herself during those feverish months. But at the time, it had kept her alive.

*   *   *

From her pallet in the fruit cellar of Burg Lingenfels, Benita began to hear a dull thunk, repeated rhythmically. It was faint but distinct. Grey light glowed through the casement windows. It was a new day. Thursday, to be exact.

Thursday! She realised with a start that the sound was Herr Muller's axe. It was his last day in these woods. Next week he would be transferred to a camp in the French occupation zone. And anyway, Marianne did not want his help. This morning, he would have approached the castle from the back side of the mountain, through the woods, and not seen the prisoners. If he *had* seen them he would have turned around. Or if they had seen *him, they* would have turned *him* around. Or worse. They would not take kindly to the sudden appearance of an ex-German soldier, an ex-*Nazi*. Benita did not need rumours to tell her this.

Gingerly, she rose to her feet. It was important she not wake Martin or the von Lingenfels girls, asleep on the pallet they had dragged downstairs. They would only get in her way. With rare clarity, Benita knew exactly what she must do: warn Herr Muller before the prisoners discovered him. She took her shoes and the paring knife she always carried and tiptoed out of the door.

Upstairs, the kitchen was empty. Marianne and Frau Grabarek had apparently gone up to their rooms. Outside the window, in the grey light, Benita could see the smouldering bonfire and the blackened carcass above it, an obscene thing. Around it the men slept, splayed out like corpses on a battlefield.

Herr Muller's axe was louder once she was above ground. Pulling her cardigan close, she hurried out of the kitchen door to the courtyard. On the other side was an old bakehouse with an opening for shovelling waste into the moat. She had often seen Fritz and Martin climb through it and down to the murky bottom. From there they splashed along to a ladder of footholds carved into the moat wall, then up to the meadow between the castle and the woods.

Moving too swiftly to allow time to reconsider, Benita jogged to-wards it. The morning was fresh and cool, and the wild morning glories climbing along the wall were still closed. From the roof over-hang, swallows began to stir, darting out in missile-like feints and swoops. They reminded her of something from her childhood – the swallows in the eaves of the asylum outbuildings; the baby birds that would fall out of their nests to the ground. One year she had tried to care for them, feeding them milk from a medicine dropper, offering them the worms she had dug. They had been so soft and fluffy and pitiful – their tiny bright eyes blinking up from her palm. It had never worked, though. One by one they died.

Inside the bakehouse, all was dim and rotten. It had not been used in years. The opening was not difficult to find; it was not even covered. Benita dropped to her hands and knees and low-ered herself through. The drop was farther than she trusted, but she closed her eyes and let go. She staggered upon impact but remained on her feet. From here it was easy to make her way through the muck to the footholds in the wall. In a moment, she had scrambled up and out. Then she was free of the castle with only a short stretch of field between her and the woods.

Again, Benita heard the thunk of the axe.

She did not stop to look beyond the castle to what was visible of the stable, the fire, the sleeping Russians. Instead, she ran across the shaggy grass until she reached the safety of the woods. A scramble of weeds and low brush edged the forest, prickly and sharp, but she barely noticed. She was going to save Herr Muller. It was in her power to do this. The knowledge made her palms sweat and her heart race – but also filled her with a potent deter-mination. She had been saved so many times – by Marianne, by her neighbour Frau Kessler in Berlin, by the prison warden who kept her in the hospital instead of a concentration camp . . . even, at one time, by Connie, her knight in shining armour, who had saved her from her life. But who had she ever saved? No one. Not even her own son.

It took a moment for her eyes to adjust to the dim light of the wood. She knew the clearing where Herr Muller worked and wound her way there at a half run, barely registering the brambles scraping her legs, tearing at her skirt.

Not until she was almost to the clearing did Benita realise the sound of the axe had stopped. She could hear voices. She paused and strained to listen over her own ragged breath. It was Herr Muller and another man. A Russian. And the exchange did not sound friendly.

She was too late! The thought struck her physically. It was impossible. She could not be. She would not allow it. She ploughed forward into the clearing. At the centre stood two men: Herr Muller and a Russian soldier with blunt, stubby features, wearing a bedraggled Red Army uniform. He spoke in a harsh, guttural voice.

'Herr Muller!' Benita called, and both men whirled to look at her.

'I came to tell you' – she panted – 'to go back.'

Confusion spread over Herr Muller's face.

The Russian grinned. '*Shlyukha,*' he swore. *Whore.*

This word Benita knew.

More Russian followed – words she did not understand, but she grasped their meaning from his leer. For a moment, the Russian seemed to forget about his fight with Herr Muller and moved towards her.

Staring at his ugly, smirking face, the acne pits half covered by a growth of stringy beard, Benita felt something inside her explode and this man, advancing on her now, became not just the prisoner who had reached Herr Muller before she could, but every other man who had ever called her a whore. Every man who had ever pummelled and beaten and clawed his way into her with stinking breath and rancid sweat and rage about things for which her body had no responsibility. Of course he had reached Herr Muller first! How could she have imagined herself powerful enough to intervene? She was nothing but a lump of flesh to be tossed between fighting dogs. She was half-dead already, torn up, chewed on, spat out. This was how he saw her. She could see it in his eyes.

But it was not true! She was a mother with a son, a woman who had escaped once already. She was the wife of a resister, a friend of Marianne von Lingenfels. She was no longer little Benita Gruber – a pretty, expendable peasant girl with no money, no father, and no power. She drew herself up and spat as hard as she could at the man's feet.

The look on his face turned from amusement to irritation. He did not understand. He saw only her old self. With a torrent of fury sweeping through her veins, she reached into her pocket for the knife.

CHAPTER TWELVE

BERLIN, LATE APRIL 1945

Benita's first time was not the worst. The soldier had been clean, relatively speaking, and had given her food – a roll, with jam even – and beer. He had taken the satchel of belongings she carried and steered her into the courtyard of a bombed-out building in Neukölln. She had not even made it home from the prison hospital. He chuckled and grinned and rubbed her feet like a devoted husband. Never mind that the outcome of his advance was fixed. It didn't matter if she acquiesced. He *tried* to win her over anyway, which, under the circumstances, seemed tantamount to romance. When he finally pressed her against the courtyard wall, he was disgusting but not cruel, only avid and self-absorbed.

During the second, third, and fourth times Benita came to really know revulsion. And pain – such bloody, cramping, screaming pain as she had not imagined possible outside childbirth.

This was still the beginning of The End, when there was fighting in the streets – blasts of machine-gun fire, skirmishes between the last terrified Wehrmacht holdouts and the Allies who had them surrounded. They fought for control of the city, block by block. But the Russians on Meerstein Strasse knew they had won. They tramped up and down the building's staircase bedecked with stolen watches, drinking looted whisky, searching for girls.

The grandmothers on the sixth and third floors of her building hid their granddaughters in the bomb cellar and treated Benita and the other women who went outside during daylight as lepers. But Benita couldn't remain in hiding. How would she find Martin if she was hiding in the cellar? And she didn't have a mother or grandmother to slip her drinks of water and scraps of bread. Frau Gruber, bless her poor, stolid heart, had been dead for five years.

You too? Four times? Six times? The Mongolians are the worst. No, the Cossacks. They broke her leg. She cannot pee. She lost her mind. Everyone talked of it. Talk, talk, talk . . . and the questions. Not from the victims, but from the old women and the men. The men, the few who remained, were the worst. They feigned sympathy and anger but really only wanted to listen, to *imagine*. It made her sick.

And still there was no Martin, and no one to ask for help. Every passing day Benita felt her will to live fading. The Nazis who had taken her son had now vanished into the night. The Russians knew nothing of the stolen children and had no interest. What was another lost child in this war that had already killed so many?

There was a soldier who 'loved' Benita: a tall, skinny boy from Georgia with a wide grin. He brought her chocolate and sardines and canned peaches – delicacies his unit had raided from some local Nazi lair. He wanted her to be his wife. This she deduced from his mix of broken German and pantomime. He was a naive boy when it came to anything but killing people. He had grown up with nine siblings in an apple orchard.

It was with his help that Benita gained access to the 'captain' of the district, the only man who seemed to have any contact with the world beyond this measly corner of Berlin.

The captain was a large, stern man from St Petersburg – a real Red Army official, not a ragtag conscript from some country that had become a province of the Soviet Union. As a teenager, he had taken part in the October Revolution. His men were awed by this fact. He was a real Bolshevik. And the Bolsheviks, Benita understood, wanted to annihilate the Germans.

The captain had set up shop in what had once been Mulman's Bakery, on the ground floor of an intact building around the corner from 27 Meerstein Strasse. When Benita was presented, he rose from behind the flour-clouded counter like a general rising from behind a great desk. He had a shrewd, intelligent face. Standing before him, she felt naked and unnerved.

Ah, he said, bowing his head when she finished explaining her search for Martin. *I will make inquiries.* Then he looked at Benita and her Georgian escort. It was clear that he was not a man who did favours for nothing. So this was how she became 'his,' which was, in its way, a mercy.

He was a hard man, but not a cruel one. And his affection, if it could be called that, protected Benita from the others. The Georgian was forced to retreat, tail between his legs, back to his dreams of the apple orchard.

But it didn't matter. Nothing mattered after the news. Martin was dead. This was what the captain told her. He was among a number of 'orphans' from a Nazi Children's Home sent on the last train to Buchenwald. The captain delivered the news matter-of-factly. He was not a man to mince words, and even if he had wanted to, he did not speak enough German.

Benita stared at him and felt the world darken around the edges. Everything she knew seemed to fall away until she was left perched on some last, invisible outcropping of solid land in a great and empty universe.

After that, when the captain came to her, she left her body – the body that no longer meant a thing to her, that would soon turn to rot. Instead, she went to her boy, to her little Martin, and curled around his sleeping form, stroked his fine blond hair, and kissed the crown of his sweet head. She hummed the lullabies she used to sing at night when he was frightened and crawled into her bed. And she filled him with all the love he would ever need in his next life.

That was the end of Benita Gruber, the girl who grew up at 7 Krensig and dreamed of marrying a rich man. That was the end of Benita Fledermann, Connie's wronged wife, silly little chicken locked up in her flat, feasting on her own disappointment. The grim details of Connie's execution, the time in prison, the miscarriage of her daughter – these were nothing compared to the loss of her son. For Benita, 'The End' that Germans spoke of in the years to come boiled down to this.

CHAPTER THIRTEEN

BURG LINGENFELS, DECEMBER 1945

Martin was too young to remember Christmas before the war. The stories Elisabeth and Katarina told sounded as improbable as fairy tales to him. Roasted goose for dinner, *Glühwein,* and baked *Zimtsterne,* oranges pierced with cloves. Packages filled with new socks, hair ribbons, chocolates, and books. Once, Elisabeth told him, her father gave her a real white rabbit in a painted cage.

Martin was especially interested in the parties – so many people coming together in celebration, rather than fear. The only large gatherings he could remember took place in bomb cellars or rallies or on crowded, terror-filled streets.

'We will make a fine Christmas this year,' Marianne announced on the first day of December. Never mind that it was freezing and that food, even here at the castle, was in short supply. This was her plan. On the first Sunday of Advent she was determined to bake a *Stollen.* Everyone was sceptical, not only on account of the rationing, but on account of never having seen Marianne bake. But she insisted. She had been setting aside flour and sugar for this purpose since September.

So the children decorated the kitchen. The girls crafted delicate stars out of straw and bits of yarn from an unravelled sweater and hung them on freshly cut evergreen boughs.

'Dear Lord, we thank you for all that we have when so many people have nothing. We have each other, we have food, we have our health and a roof over our heads,' Marianne had begun saying before dinner each night. This was new. Before – meaning before The End, not before the war, but certainly before she came to the castle – Marianne had not been a religious woman. Elisabeth and Katarina did not like this new piety. But Martin enjoyed the sound of Marianne's voice listing the things they had to be thankful for, talking about the misery of others. It was always good to know there were people more miserable than you.

'Do you believe in God?' he asked his mother one night as they fell asleep in their little room above the kitchen, his breath puffing out in white clouds.

'I don't know,' she said, and even in the dark he could sense that his question had brought tears to her eyes.

It made him angry – her readiness to cry. She was always on the verge of tears, trembly, red eyed, and uncertain. It had been worse in the days after the Russians came, but even now it took almost nothing to set her off. Including, apparently, the mention of God.

Martin believed in God, though. How could he not? It was unbearable to imagine there wasn't something better out there, a divine balm for all the havoc he had seen here on earth. He believed in God not as an explanation, but as a salve – a wise, stern figure on a throne in the clouds, watching out for those below. *Nice job he did for the last seven years*, Elisabeth said when he admitted his belief. But it wasn't God who caused the war and all the horror. It was people, he thought. He knew better than to argue with Elisabeth, though. God ruled only in heaven, he would have said. But apparently Elisabeth expected to see more of his hand on earth.

Outside the temperatures reached record lows. Snot and breath and tears froze as soon as you stepped outside. All over Germany people were starving. *A taste of their own medicine*, the British radio declared. *During the war we starved so Germans could eat – let them reap what they sowed.* It was the first time Martin thought of enemy children – not just soldiers but boys and girls.

Fair enough, Marianne said, though you could see uncertainty in her eyes. *Bastards,* Fritz swore, and was sent to his room. In Berlin, people chopped down what was left of the bombed-out Tiergarten for firewood. And in cities all over the country, people were rumoured to be eating slugs and rats and other small animals. Every weekend townspeople from Tollingen and Momsen flocked to the land to beg for scraps of food.

Here in the castle, though, they were warm and relatively well fed. They didn't venture far from the kitchen and their small rooms above it. There was frost on the damp north wall of the great hall and ice at the bottom of the moat, but their lamps burned bright and the giant oven blazed with Herr Muller's firewood. They took turns sitting against it, warming their backs. And everyone wore clothes on top of clothes.

In the months since the Grabareks had arrived, life at the castle had become more comfortable and orderly. Frau Grabarek was a good cook. She knew how to turn coarse meal into palatable porridge, how to boil syrup from sugar beets, how to bargain shrewdly on the black market. She would return home from town with real wheat flour for baking, sugar, and even black tea. She was also more practical than Martin's mother or Marianne: She made the boys chew spruce bark to ward off germs and mended the holes in Martin's pockets and undershirts that no one else noticed. She thought to rub lanolin on Martin's chapped cheeks, and when he developed a nagging cough, she made a poultice for his chest. She was a caretaker of regular, bodily needs. In this way, she reminded him of Frau Vortmuller from the Children's Home, who sometimes he secretly missed.

The Grabarek boys, Anselm and Wolfgang, were even more silent than their mother, which was fine with Martin, who grew tired of Fritz's endless chatter. And they knew real survival skills:

how to find potatoes missed in the harvest, how to trap rabbits, how to lie.

And they knew how to split wood, which was important now that Herr Muller was gone.

Something bad had happened the night the Russians killed Herr Kellerman's horse. Something so terrible no one even asked what it was. In the early morning, Herr Muller had appeared at the kitchen door carrying Martin's mother. She was like a baby in his arms, with her own wrapped around his neck and her face buried in his chest. And she was covered in blood. It was everywhere – on her hair, blouse, even her face. Martin had never seen so much blood.

For a moment they had all stood and stared – the sight was too much to absorb – and then Marianne began to ask questions: *What is this? Where have you been? Are you all right? Oh my Lord, good Lord, Mary, mother of God . . .* And the girls began screaming and everything was chaos until Frau Grabarek sent the children back down to the cellar.

When she called them upstairs, Martin's mother had been quarantined in her room, Herr Muller was gone, and there was no sign of the bloody clothes.

We must never speak of this, Marianne had said that night, and they were all too frightened to ask: *About what?* Even Elisabeth.

The next day the Russians left. One of them had disappeared. The leader came to the castle door to ask if they had seen him, and standing in the shadows, Martin heard Frau Grabarek say, *Yes, actually; I couldn't sleep and was looking out of the window at midnight; I saw a man walk down the hill.* Martin was the only one to overhear the exchange.

For the next few weeks the von Lingenfels children whispered about what had happened, but they fell silent in front of Martin, whom they seemed to regard with renewed pity. It was a pitiable thing, apparently, to be Benita's son. Was the blood hers? And why had she been outside and not in the cellar? How had Herr Muller found her? These questions gnawed at Martin, but he did not ask them. The answers did not matter. Herr Muller had saved her. Martin was certain of this. So why had Marianne told him not to return?

Afterward, Benita had remained upstairs for two weeks. When she came back down, she was as jumpy and tentative as she had been when they first found her in Berlin. *My sweet boy, my dear boy,* she would say over and over, reaching for Martin.

On the day before Christmas, Marianne presented the children with packages sent by American Quakers. They were full of fabulous items: oranges, toothbrushes, candy bars, a tin of something called Kraft cheese, and chewing gum. These were accompanied by handwritten cards from American children – pictures drawn in bright wax crayons. Martin's card had a drawing of a fat brown-and-white cat with a red-and-white-striped bow. It read *As a token of our country's goodwill* and was signed by Amy (age eight) and Roger (age six). Martin tried to imagine Amy and Roger and the box of colours they had used to create this card. He pictured them wearing crisp store-bought clothing and new shoes with thick soles and no worn-out places. He was sure they each owned their own bicycle and left food uneaten on their plates. Martin pictured this not so much with envy as with wonder – what an amazing thing to be an American!

'Enjoy half of what is in the package, and then find someone to share the other half with,' Marianne instructed. They had received these gifts only because they were *Opfers*. There were not enough for all the children of Ehrenheim. And despite Marianne's disdain for the townspeople, she did not like the inequity.

Only Elisabeth had the courage – or the foolishness – to protest.

'For that, you just lost half your portion,' Marianne announced. 'You already have it better than most of Germany's children.' From then on, no one complained.

So that afternoon, while Marianne visited the DP camp and Ania prepared the Christmas stew and Benita rested, the children, minus Fritz, who was in bed with a fever, bundled into even more layers and walked to Ehrenheim, bearing their half candy bars and chewing gum sticks like the gifts of the three kings.

'I'm going to eat mine myself,' Elisabeth announced.

But Katarina looked so shocked that Elisabeth was forced to take this back. She was thirteen now. If it weren't for the war, she said, if it weren't for everything, she would be learning to play piano and reading interesting books and going to dancing school. Instead she had only the Bible and two volumes of Goethe, which she had read a million times. And she had only her 'numbskull brother' to dance with. Her rant semi-politely excluded Martin and the Grabarek boys.

Katarina and Elisabeth decided to head to the children's centre at the DP camp to share their gifts. They had visited often enough with their mother, who had begun to volunteer there, and knew some of the children. The decision was certain to please Marianne.

'Martin, do you want to come with us?' Katarina asked.

Martin declined. He would join Anselm and Wolfgang. He had spent enough time with the girls, who were always chattering and worrying and bickering with each other. The Grabareks, on the other hand, were silent and knowing. They shared a language of glances and nods, by which they communicated. They could walk across the fields kicking a stone back and forth, making a game of it without ever stating the rules. Martin admired their self-containment. *Cut from a different cloth,* Frau Vortmuller would have said. Not as a judgement, but as an observation. Martin had earned their trust through his own silence and ability to assimilate. And so they told him things about their journey west – about finding their way around the SS checkpoints and sleeping in cold Polish forests. About escaping from an overheating bomb cellar in Dresden the night of the famous bombing – the fire in the streets and the trees lit up like dancing torches, the pools of pavement melting in the heat. *What was it like before, where you lived in the east?* he asked them once, but they grew silent. He did not ask again.

On this Christmas Eve, the town was quiet. Usually there were crews of locals digging and raking and clearing the remains of the porcelain factory, which the RAF had mistaken for an armaments plant, but the Americans had given everyone the day off. In the absence of the clatter and bang of reconstruction, Martin could hear new, more ordinary sounds: a baby crying, a door opening and shutting, a gutter rattling in the wind, and a whole host of some hearty, fearless species of bird chattering wildly from the branches of a bare tree.

Martin followed the Grabareks without asking where they were headed. He would do whatever they did – it was an unspoken understanding between them. Wolfgang was the leader. He was younger than Anselm, but stronger and bolder. And they accepted Martin only because he didn't try to manage their activities or corral them into games the way Fritz did. When they were all together, Martin was the bridge.

They made their way past the church, the frozen millpond, and the bombed factory, through the town square with its billboards plastered with American posters. THESE SHAMEFUL ACTS: YOUR GUILT was emblazoned over photographs of dead bodies, naked, and emaciated, piled like sticks. In one, a boy stared at the camera, squatting behind a barbed-wire fence, his skeleton visible through his skin.

The boys passed these without looking. They had already seen them. When they were first posted, Marianne had marched them all down from the castle to look. 'This is what Hitler and his people did,' she said. 'Don't let anyone tell you his death was a tragedy.' Katarina had begun to cry, and the people walking through the square had glared in their direction. You were not supposed to stop and stare, Martin understood. To stop and stare was to admit guilt: YOUR GUILT, the sign read. You were only 'You' if you were the one reading.

But Martin wanted to look at the horrific pictures. *Propaganda,* the people of Ehrenheim said, but Martin believed Marianne. And in the images he saw the hugeness and menace of the world beyond what he knew – a threat and horror even larger than any he had experienced. The boy in the photograph stared at him like a face glimpsed through a sheet of pond ice. It was as if he lay beneath Martin's own feet.

Today he kept the brisk pace of Anselm and Wolfgang, though. They continued to the far side of town, down the narrow pedestrian passageways, past the row of fine villas once owned by Ehrenheim's most prominent Nazis, now appropriated to house DPs. And finally back out in the countryside. The sky stretched above them, as cold and grey as the underbelly of a dead fish. They followed the road through the frozen meadows in the shadows of craggy, snow-covered mountain peaks. They were heading west towards the French zone. The border was not far. And finally Martin understood: they were going to the French camp for German prisoners of war.

'Qu'est-ce que vous voulez?' a French guard asked when they arrived at the gate. The camp was housed in some sort of military barracks – a collection of low buildings surrounded by a chain-link fence. Wolfgang answered in German – 'We are here to see our father.' Martin looked over at him, confused. NO VISITORS EXCEPT FAMILY MEMBERS, the sign read.

'The greeting area is over there.' The guard waved them through and pointed towards a stretch of fence to the right. A number of people, mostly women and children, waited there with gifts – cigarettes, potatoes, lard, and slices of salt pork, wrapped in bundles small enough to press between the links.

Prisoners were lined up on the other side of the fence.

'Who are you looking for?' asked a thin, long-necked prisoner in a tattered Gestapo uniform with all the insignias cut off.

'Franz Muller,' Wolfgang answered with a glance at Anselm. Martin was filled with a combination of nerves and embarrassment. They had not seen Herr Muller since the Russian incident.

The long-necked man called the name over his shoulder, where it was picked up by another and another until it disappeared into the barracks. Then they waited, claiming a small section of fence for themselves. On the other side, small groups of prisoners walked past with their hands buried deep in their pockets, their breath escaping in clouds. Others leaned against the building despite the cold, caps pulled low over their eyes. And then, almost miraculously, Franz Muller appeared and walked towards them, his broad, impassive face transformed by surprise. It was awkward to see him here, among this sorry lot. Behind the barbed wire, he was more intimidating now than he had been while chopping trees in their woods. Martin glanced over at Anselm and Wolfgang. But to his surprise, their eyes had already moved on, as if they were looking for someone else.

'Here!' Martin was the first to speak. 'We brought this for you.' With frozen fingers he pushed his half candy bar and tin of cheese through the fence.

'For me?' Herr Muller asked, studying their faces.

Martin nodded.

'Do your mothers know you came here?'

Martin shook his head.

'Ah.' Muller seemed to consider this. 'It was kind of you.'

The boys stamped their feet against the cold.

'Have you met anyone named Brandt?' Wolfgang asked, and his words were slightly breathless, as if he had pushed them out.

Muller frowned. 'I don't think so. From where?'

The Grabareks exchanged another glance. 'The Warthegau.' Anselm answered this time.

Muller shook his head.

'Your father?' Martin asked, unable to stop himself.

'No,' Wolfgang said, his tone harsh. 'Our father is dead.'

Who, then? Martin wanted to ask, but didn't.

Muller regarded them in silence. 'Well, thank you,' he said finally. 'Take care of yourselves. And your mothers. And don't come back here.'

On Christmas Day, the Catholic Church of Ehrenheim offered an open mass, and all the inhabitants of Burg Lingenfels traipsed down the hill through the cold. Never mind that aside from Martin's mother, they were all Protestant.

'Catholic, Protestant, Jewish – such nonsense,' Marianne responded when Elisabeth pointed this out. 'These divisions have never caused anything but grief.' Apparently her own new-found religion existed outside these lines.

Tonight was different, though. The vespers service was open to all and would feature the Ehrenheim orchestra, performing together for the first time in years. 'They are quite good,' Marianne conceded. 'The conductor studied in Berlin as a young man. No one thought he would come back.'

Even Martin's mother, who never left the castle in the cold, bundled herself into an old fur coat of Marianne's and walked down the moonlit hill with the rest of them. They made their way through the streets towards the church's famous crooked steeple – a tall shingled spire built hundreds of years ago to point straight to the heavens but that, through some fault in its construction, instead curved slightly south. *Like the German soul,* Marianne joked. *Aiming for heaven but stooped towards hell.*

The whole town seemed to have turned out for the gathering, shuffling up the steps of the unheated church in their warmest coats and blankets, nodding greetings. Mostly women and children and the elderly, but some men now too, as Germany's soldiers gradually came limping home from hospitals, enemy combatant camps, and wherever else.

Inside, the air was solemn but festive. People carried lanterns and tallow candles – a precious commodity these days – and the shadows of their flames leapt and danced across the rafters. They reminded Martin of an illustration from Frau Vortmuller's Bible – the spirits of the damned burning in hell. Beneath the shadows, the faded frescoes on the walls were illuminated in bursts: the trailing robe of St Paul; Jesus's bare and bloodied legs; the stern, pinched face of an angel that Martin would have been terrified to encounter. There was a jagged hole in place of the rose window – shattered in the bombing – and outside the sky was dark and dotted with clear winter stars.

Then the service began – a wholly foreign experience for Martin, who had attended church only a few times in his life, and never a Catholic mass. It was full of chanting in Latin, the smell of incense, and unintelligible prayers. The stone floor and walls magnified the cold, and Martin's breath froze as soon as he opened his mouth. Slowly, the priest climbed to his pulpit and spoke. He was old and his voice echoed confusingly. 'For our celebration of the Feast of Christ the King. That it would be a time of reflection on our crucified Lord, and an opportunity for us to imitate his attitude of humility . . .'

People coughed and shifted in their seats. Martin glanced at his own family, if they could be called that. Marianne sat stick straight, brow furrowed, closely attending to each word. Beside her, Elisabeth cast her gaze around the congregation, taking stock of who was present. Katarina leaned against her sister for warmth. And Fritz, bending his head in apparent concentration, scratched a design into the rough fabric of his pants. The Grabarek boys, shoulder to shoulder, dark heads nearly identical, were an island unto themselves, passing something between them – a note? A pebble? It was impossible to tell. And Ania was as unreadable as always, her eyes on the minister but seeing something else inside her own head. Martin's mother sat on his other side. Of them all, she seemed the most absorbed, gazing up into the bit of sky framed by the broken window, lips parted, eyes soft, like a woman coming face-to-face with a benevolent God. Martin reached over and took her hand. She startled, as if seeing him for the first time. But the smile that followed was like a flash of sun across a darkened field. And for once Martin felt sustained rather than terrified by his own capacity to bring her joy.

When the priest finished, a palpable sense of relief swept through the crowd. His words had brought no one peace – *penance, forgiveness, justice, sin* – these were still papery abstractions that could not begin to address the everyday realities of their lives.

Then the orchestra musicians took their places on chairs brought from their own homes and began tuning their instruments. Where had they managed to hide these over the past years? It seemed a miracle that the war would have spared anything so delicate as a harp or violin. When all were ready, the church fell silent. The bundled forms onstage sat poised with bows raised, breaths held. And the conductor, a small man wearing a battered felt hat, raised his baton. The stillness intensified, and the silence had a particular starving quality. This was why the people were here. To hear music. It had been so long.

At once, the conductor jerked his baton upwards and the orchestra gathered itself and dived in. The music, Beethoven's Ninth, opened with a blast: violins, trumpet, an explosion loud enough to knock thought and worry from the mind. It was reminiscent of war – thundering footsteps, the rumble of tanks, the screech and crack of planes overhead, an exploding bomb. The audience sat at attention, gripping their seats. Something small and gentle might have lost them. Something tender and they might have begun to cry and never stopped. They were there, but they were not strong. They would do anything to protect themselves from sadness.

Martin was swept up in the sound – no longer blood and bone, frozen feet and hungry belly, but an empty vessel filling with notes, carried by something older and bigger and more permanent than himself. This music had been played and heard before and would be again, not only here in this church, but in places all over the world, by people living in different circumstances and different times. These musicians and this audience were allowed, for a fleeting instant, to climb on its back.

When it was over, no one spoke. The clapping faded, and the church was once again jammed with clumsy shuffling and cold. Frozen fingered, one of the violinists dropped his bow. An icicle of snot hung from the conductor's nose.

But leaving the church, they found the night was blacker, the stars brighter, the outline of fence, roof, and road clearer and more beautiful – and the people's faces looked oddly exposed.

In the future, Martin will recall this night as the first time – and one of the only times – he ever saw Germans crying in public, not at the news of a dead loved one or at the sight of their bombed home, and not in physical pain, but from spontaneous emotion. For this brief time, they were not hiding from one another, wearing their masks of cold and practical detachment. The music stirred the hardened sediment of their memory, chafed against layers of horror and shame, and offered a rare solace in their shared anger, grief, and guilt.

Years later, as a professor, Martin would try to find the words to articulate the power of togetherness in a world where togetherness had been corrupted – and to explore the effect of the music, the surprising lengths the people had gone to to hear it and to play it, as evidence that music, and art in general, are basic requirements of the human soul. Not a luxury but a compulsion. He will think of it every time he goes to a museum or a concert or a play with a long queue of people waiting to get inside.

In the moment, though, he was simply buoyed along.

The walk home was magical. No one was glum. For this Christmas night they were lifted from the damning particularities of their own lives and invited to be a small piece of eternity.

PART II

CHAPTER FOURTEEN

TOLLINGEN, MAY 1950

Benita loved the flat she and Marianne had moved to in Tollingen, which was practically a city compared to Ehrenheim. It was on the town square, in a gracious turn-of-the-century building some-how left intact by the war. Now, a Danish businessman owned it, and he had polished the honey-coloured floors to a sleek, post-war shine, plastered over shell wounds in the façade, and rented the apartments to the town's most established citizens. Their flat was full of light and space and the air of aristocratic elegance that Benita had once imagined for herself.

Tollingen had come back to life since the war. After years of hunger and shortages, the storefronts once again advertised sewing needles, matches, oranges, and stylish shoes. The bakery windows displayed fresh loaves of bread. The pharmacy shelves were stocked with creams and medicines.

'Oh, but we Germans can work, can't we?' Marianne liked to say as she observed the new plenty. 'Give us a task and we'll complete it – and waste no time looking back.' She said it with a sort of Marianne dryness, as if it were actually a fault, and one for which she condemned her countrymen. Benita did not understand this. So the Germans were hard workers! So they did not look back! Given the circumstances, why would they? And anyway, wasn't Marianne one of them?

But, deep down, there was a part of her that appreciated Marianne's scorn for German industry. Benita's own dreamy laziness had always been held over her head as a moral failing, and here was Marianne, a hard worker and moral example in all ways, turning the table, imbuing her sloth and imagination with a kind of virtue.

On this particular morning, Benita, Marianne, and the children – Elisabeth, now eighteen; Katarina, sixteen; Fritz, thirteen; and Martin, who, at eleven, was still her baby – were all headed to Ania's wedding. Ania was to marry Carsten Kellerman, a match that pleased Marianne and depressed Benita. For the rest of her life, poor Ania, thirty years Kellerman's junior, would have to lie beside his club foot, breathing in his stench of cabbage and tooth rot. *Is it what you want?* she had asked Ania when she first heard the news. *Of course,* Ania answered. *Carsten is a good man, and my boys can help with the farm.* 'Can help with' Benita understood to be a euphemism for 'inherit'. Herr Kellerman had no children, and Ania Grabarek was a pragmatic woman. She was marrying to create a decent future for her sons.

Marianne, on the other hand, delighted in the match. Herr Kellerman had been a loyal neighbour and the caretaker of Burg Lingenfels ever since she had first arrived. And, furthermore, he had never been a Nazi, which, in Marianne's opinion, automatically made him good. The fact that he was old and taciturn and unattractive was of no consequence to her when compared to his loyalty and sound politics.

In Marianne's enthusiasm, Benita detected a double standard. Marianne was a born matchmaker, especially for those she had taken under her wing, which applied to both women. But she had much higher expectations when it came to a second marriage for Benita, whom she steered towards members of her own circle – distinguished survivors of the resistance, for example, vetted already by their politics and social standing. So why was she content for Ania to marry an elderly peasant? Ania's husband had been a resister, too. Was it because he had been Polish? Or was it something about Ania herself? After all, Benita was no less a peasant than Ania, as Marianne had made clear when they'd first met. Whatever the root of her bias, Benita knew Marianne would be ashamed to acknowledge it.

At times, Benita still found it comical that she and Marianne were flatmates. How impossible this would have seemed to her that long-ago night at the countess's party. The von Lingenfels and the peasant, the odd couple of the castle. It would have made her laugh.

No one lived in Burg Lingenfels anymore – it was too cold, too big, and too remote. And it was still without running water or electricity. Marianne had always hated Ehrenheim; she liked their new home as much as Benita did. It was closer to the DP camp where she spent so many hours, near the train station, and an easy trip to Munich. Their new *Bürgermeister* was an old friend of Albrecht's. And there was plenty of space in the flat. *What is the point of two widows raising their children alone?* Marianne had asked when she first proposed the idea. *The children are like siblings now, why tear them apart?* Left unspoken was the fact that despite the restitution – finally – of Connie's pension, Benita and Martin depended on Marianne's largesse. Left to their own means, they would be living in some colourless and cramped new apartment block on the outskirts of town.

'Benita,' Marianne called, tap-tapping down the long hall of their flat with her particular, Marianne-ish determination. 'Benita!'

'Coming!' she called.

Benita folded the letter she was rereading and pushed it hastily into a small wooden chest. *What is that?* Marianne had asked when she first caught sight of the chest, as if it were one of the mangy feathers or dead butterflies the children used to collect at the castle. *Something I picked up at the Christmas market,* Benita lied. Marianne had tilted her head to the side in a show of critical bewilderment – it was an odd little thing, carved of rough wood and unpainted – but she had accepted the explanation. Marianne did not expect sound judgement from Benita anyway. And for Benita, the chest had one simple purpose: it locked. She turned the key and slipped it behind the mirror on her dresser.

When she opened the door, Marianne was wearing something Benita had never seen before: a dress with ribbons at the cuffs and throat. It was pretty, but too frivolous for Marianne. Another item resurrected from Albrecht's sea chest. Marianne was diligent about reusing all her old things. The woman had no vanity or fashion sense.

'Ready?' Marianne asked. 'The children are waiting in the foyer.'

'Ready,' Benita repeated. 'What a pretty necklace!' she added, noticing for the first time.

'This?' Marianne glanced down. 'Here—' She lifted it over her head, a silver fleur-de-lis with a tiny amethyst inset. 'You wear it. It will suit you better than me. And' – she turned back almost slyly – 'Helmut Kressing and his sister will be there. He always asks after you.'

'Oh no—' Benita began, but Marianne shushed her protests. Dutifully, Benita put on the pendant. She did not attempt to explain that Helmut Kressing would never be more than an acquaintance. Or that the necklace did not match her dress. When it came to defying Marianne's wishes, it was better to keep a low profile.

For the trip to Herr Kellerman's farm, Marianne splurged and hired a car and driver. The bus to Ehrenheim was slow and unreliable – another strike against the town – and it was a long walk from the bus stop to the farm for women wearing their Sunday shoes. Besides, it was not every day they went to a wedding! At the smallest extravagance, Marianne put herself through these rounds of justification. It was admirable, but tiresome. If

Benita had Marianne's resources, she would enjoy them without such hand-wringing. And a car would be her first purchase. There was a new Volkswagen dealership on the edge of town with a park full of beautiful, rounded 'bugs', as they were called – row after row, gleaming in the sun, pleasing in their sameness. These were the cars Hitler had once promised everyone. Benita felt a personal spite towards the man. He had duped them all with his promises of cars and jobs and self-respect. Connie had been right to hate him from the start.

Connie had become confusing in her mind. She was not angry anymore. She was embarrassed, actually, by how angry she had been. He had been unfaithful, this was true, but she had been a difficult wife. The last time she had seen him, she had not even looked up. He had come to say goodbye, she now understood. It was the night before the assassination attempt. And she had been sitting at the window of their flat with Martin asleep behind her in the bed. Connie knelt and tried to take her hand. *I'm sorry,* he said. *I'm sorry I have left you alone so much.* But she had pulled her hand away. *I love you,* Connie said. And she had never even turned to look at him.

In the hired car, Elisabeth, now in her last year of school, argued with her mother about politics. Adenauer, their new chancellor, was right to end denazification, Elisabeth insisted; the denazification process was merely turning Germans back into angry nationalists. No, he was wrong, Marianne maintained: expedience could not take precedence over the pursuit of justice.

Benita did not participate. Neither did she play the guessing game with Martin and Katarina and Fritz. She stared out of the window at the green fields, the cows, the red-roofed villages, and the jagged mountains rising behind this like a row of teeth.

When they arrived at the Kellermans', there were no outward signs of festivity. But in recent years, the farm had undergone its own sort of metamorphosis. There was a pungent stench from the new pigsty Kellerman had built, and a red tractor gleamed from the stables where Gilda used to live. Under Ania's care, the gardens were full of more than mere essentials like potatoes, cabbages, and carrots. There were peas, parsley, and leeks, even a small gooseberry bush. Along the fence, a line of sunflowers bobbed their clumsy heads. When Ania and her boys had first moved to the farm as tenants, she had taken over the gardening in lieu of rent. *Well, that living arrangement worked out well for Herr Kellerman,* Elisabeth joked.

Benita, Marianne, and the children climbed out of the car and carefully removed the serving dishes Marianne had brought: a white soup tureen with lion heads, three platters inlaid with pink roses, and an elegant, gold-rimmed glass punch bowl that had belonged to Albrecht's grandmother.

'They don't need any of this,' Elisabeth grumbled, unloading it. 'Frau Grabarek is only being polite saying yes.'

'Don't begrudge,' Marianne scolded, with a cutting look that reduced Elisabeth's point to one of mere selfishness. Which was not fair. Benita understood what the girl meant: Ania would be embarrassed by her connection to Marianne's fine things. She would not want to stand out from her guests. Ania did not like to set herself apart. Marianne could not grasp this.

'*Guten Tag, guten Tag,*' Ania greeted them nervously.

Benita kissed her on both cheeks in the manner of Connie's high-society friends, which made Ania blush. And, for a moment, her face was transformed into something shy and girlish. Benita squeezed her hand.

'Congratulations!' Marianne said, beaming and hoisting the punch bowl aloft. 'Herr and Frau Kellerman!' They were already husband and wife, wed in the town hall that morning. The party was simply a celebration. 'Put us to work,' Marianne directed, depositing the bowl on the kitchen table, where it looked completely out of place.

'But you're wearing such fine clothes.'

'Don't be silly. What do you think, we can't roll up our sleeves and work?'

*   *   *

The wedding guests began to arrive around four o'clock: somberly clad farmers and townspeople, like pigeons in their grey and brown suits. They brought strawberry jam and beeswax candles, meat loaves, sides of ham, and fine tortes. Benita knew these people. If she were dropped back into Frühlinghausen right now – God forbid – it would be just like this.

They clustered around the parlour table, drinking beer and local wine and Herr Kellerman's homemade plum schnapps. Their faces began to come alive beneath their impassive masks. The men loosened their new polyester ties, removed their jackets, and lit cigarettes. It was still remarkable to see so many men gathered in one place. Even the longest absent had returned from their various prisoner-of-war camps – thinner, balder, absent eyed, and closed faced. Benita wound her way through the crowded rooms, nodding and murmuring hellos but mostly keeping to herself.

In the dining room, Herr Fetzer, the local butcher, pulled out his fiddle, and festive music filled the space. Even drunk, the young men hung together in uneasy clumps. Wives and sisters and mothers chattered while keeping nervous watch. There was a sense of latent menace. Who might come undone? Who might turn belligerent?

Marianne sat in the corner with Helmut Kressing, her latest matchmaking case. He was a widowed friend of Albrecht's who had spent the last year of the war in Buchenwald for his role in the resistance. Poor man. He deserved better than to be dragged into this awkwardness. Benita would never marry him, but she could go and sit beside him.

As Benita made her way across the room, a young man with a wild look in his eye pulled her into an aggressive dance. Johannes Kraisler, one of the bad ones. Benita had heard of him: a boy who'd always had one screw loose. He had joined the SA while still in school and had recently returned from a Siberian POW camp.

Thank God Martin had been born when he was! He was scarred, yes, but not corrupted by the war. He had never even marched with the Hitler Youth. *Why did Hitler want to make war?* he had asked her recently with an earnest, quizzical face.

The vigorous whirling of Johannes's dance made her sick. 'Please excuse me,' she said, but he only tightened his grip.

'Really,' she said, and he grinned, swinging her towards the corner with a hostile yank that made her flinch.

'I know who you are,' he hissed into her ear. 'The traitor's wife.' She could feel his penis hard against her leg through his pants. 'I know your secret.'

Startled, she looked up into his face.

'Aha! You see, I am not as stupid as you think!'

'I have no secrets,' she said, but her heart gave an anxious lurch.

'You *ladies* of the castle think you're better than everyone else,' he said with a dry laugh. 'But I can smell a cunt lover a mile off.'

'Ah.' Benita relaxed. 'You'd like to imagine that.'

With a quick stab of her elbow to his ribs she managed to loosen his grip. But she could not continue over to Marianne and Herr Kressing now. She needed to compose herself.

Benita wound through the dancers and stepped out into the courtyard behind the house. It was so ugly. The peace and plenty of this time were like a thin quilt spread over a pile of shit. No one was innocent. The Russian prisoner in the woods flashed in her mind: the inhuman sound he had made when she struck him, the squeak of air into his cut throat. Her own personal pile of shit.

She straightened and pushed the hair off her face. Above her, the moon was high and round, laying a coat of silver over the young wheat. And the air was cool, thick with the smell of roses and pigs, slightly damp.

Movement caught her eye – a figure in the entrance to the barn. No, it was two figures, leaning together, hands entwined, white against the darkness, lovers seeking a quiet spot. How amazing that this could still exist. It made her think of her own love. And of the letter she had stowed away in the little wooden chest.

Without it, she would be lost.

CHAPTER FIFTEEN

EHRENHEIM, MAY 1950

Ania surveyed the party from her seat at the head of the long table, which Wolfgang had assembled using planks from the old hayloft. There were so many cousins, neighbours, and old friends of Carsten's in line to shake her hand and offer congratulations in their formal small-town manner. Beyond Marianne, Benita, and the children, there was no one here from Ania's own life. *Is there really no family?* Carsten had pressed. *No aunts and uncles? No friends from childhood?* Ania stood firm. *Family dead. Friends lost. It's only a party,* she had reassured him. *I have my boys.* This last part she meant. It was the most important thing, the thing from which all others stemmed. This marriage was for them, although she had not seen either of her boys since the party began. Wolfgang was probably outside somewhere, his stiff new shoes cast aside, playing soccer with his school friends. And Anselm – shy Anselm – was probably holed up in his room studying. Wolfgang would take over the farm someday. By the old German laws, it should have been Anselm as the oldest son, but Anselm wanted to attend university and become a scientist.

'*Herr und Frau Kellerman.*' An old man doffed his cap and beamed – the ageing father of the town dressmaker, and a known pervert. 'To be married is to be closer to heaven,' he said, a strand of spittle gleaming from one corner of his mouth.

This was rich, coming from Herr Betz. The town was full of pretence. No one here demanded truth. Which was fine by Ania. To them, she was simply a DP from the east, one of those desperate people they had been forced to make room for in their homes and invite into their children's schools, and support with their hard-earned deutsche marks. And now she was Carsten Kellerman's wife. They did not want to plumb the depths.

God bless you, may God keep you . . . The guests approached with their pieties and gifts. Now that Hitler was gone, they had all returned to being devout Catholics. But who was Ania to judge? Ania clasped their hands and ducked her head and gave thanks.

'What a lovely party,' Marianne said, suddenly standing beside her.

Ania smiled, happy to see her friend. Marianne was much taller and bonier than the Ehrenheim *Hausfraus* and looked out of place in her fine dress. Out of her element too, as a guest. The woman was most at ease when she was in charge – striding around the DP camp with donated blankets, conducting interviews, or dictating letters for Ania to type.

'Don't get up,' Marianne said. 'You are the king and queen of this celebration. You must stay on your thrones. Herr Kellerman' – she turned to Carsten – 'you have outdone yourself.'

This was not Carsten's kind of talk.

'*Gnädige Frau*,' he stammered. 'We are honoured to have you here.'

'And we are honoured to be here,' Marianne said, slipping into her more formal, talking-across-barriers voice.

'Will you bring some of the food home, Marianne?' Ania began, and then stopped as she saw a short, round-faced man approaching with his camera: Herr Bremer. At this point in the evening, she had thought she was safe.

'Frau Grabarek!' Herr Bremer called, and then stopped. 'No – Frau and Herr *Kellerman*.' He swept his cap off his head and folded himself into a theatrical bow. 'My apologies for being late. But there is an excuse—' He reached behind his back. 'My new flash! In the paper you will look beautiful and bright as day even in the middle of the night.'

Ania blanched. It had been Carsten's idea to have their photo accompany the wedding announcement. Ania had protested. But the decision was made. In his desire for their marriage to be recorded, she had stumbled on some hidden strand of vanity in him, a wish to show the world his new life.

'This will be a fine place for our work,' Herr Bremer said, his eyes twinkling as he set the camera down and attached the flash. He was an insidious little man, the former photo editor of the local Nazi paper, famous for his extensive catalogue of 'racial portraits,' though of course no one talked about this. Ania shifted uncomfortably in her seat.

'A few casual pictures first,' Herr Bremer said, lifting the black box to his eye. Ania blinked and the camera flashed. Beside her, she felt Carsten draw back. The guests began to gather around, and the fiddle player stopped.

The camera flashed again, and Ania gripped the edges of her chair as if she might fall off.

'Now, one standing – over here,' Herr Bremer directed, pointing the camera into the circle of guests and taking a few candid shots. Several of the men drew back.

'Like an interrogation,' someone grumbled.

Ania tried to smile.

'Ready?' Bremer said.

'*Jawohl,*' Carsten answered with surprising strength.

Then they stood together, side by side against the wall like victims of an execution, pinned by the flash.

CHAPTER SIXTEEN

TOLLINGEN, MAY 1950

So there were to be new chapters. This was the happy feeling that filled Marianne after Ania's wedding. To see her friend married to a good man, a good *German* man (almost an extinct species!), this was a hopeful thing. Her dear Ania – stalwart companion, comforting presence, perpetual enigma – was to begin a new life.

But if she was honest with herself, Marianne also felt a twinge of grief. It was the end of their partnership. In the past years, she and Ania had volunteered together at the local displaced persons camp. Even now, two hundred thousand refugees remained in German camps. But Carsten would need Ania on the farm. It was half the reason he had married her, anyone could see that. He was ageing, and Ania was strong. She would have to work like a horse. And she would have no more time for Marianne's schemes and projects and lists. Marianne would have no one to bounce her ideas off, to type up her letters, to help her sort boxes of library books.

Today, Marianne was hosting a send-off party for the last DPs at the camp, a group of Estonian Jews. This was the camp Ania had first landed in, recreated in the last years as a camp for Jewish survivors. In the beginning everyone had been mixed up: Nazi collaborators thrown into the same dormitories as Polish nationalists, Gypsies, and Jews. Concentration camp guards with former inmates. Thank God they had changed that.

Over the past year, Marianne had completed enough paperwork on the Estonians' behalf to sink a ship. And her efforts had finally paid off. They were granted entry to the United States.

Signor Carfolo, the International Refugee Organization official responsible for the camp, had been sceptical about the celebration – *For such an emotional thing, the last refugees, the final survivors of their small community . . . a party?* The man was not very Italian. But Marianne knew that if she planned it, he would enjoy himself.

It was the Tuesday after Ania's wedding: blustery and cool. Marianne waited at the camp's front gate for Ania and also for Benita, who had reluctantly agreed to help them set up. The area looked desolate now – the barracks empty except for the building where the Estonians lived, the delousing station long since shuttered and the cook fires replaced by kitchenettes. Good riddance. But today, as Marianne stood in the silence, she missed the old bustle and restless energy. It had served as a physical manifestation of the war, evidence. And now it too would be erased. With the departure of these last refugees, the camp would be demolished and rebuilt as modern apartment-style housing.

What would you think of all this? she asked Albrecht. And Connie. Connie would have been especially disgusted by the town's proposals. After all, before the DPs, the site had been a Wehrmacht barracks and training camp. *Burn the place down, erect a terrible monument,* he would have declared. He had never been a pragmatist.

You're not a real German, Marianne had so often teased him on account of this. He was a romantic and an idealist.

Just as her thoughts turned glum, Marianne saw Ania arrive, driven by Herr Kellerman. Two fine new horses pulled his wagon, but the wagon itself was the same one he had first met Marianne and her children with so many years ago.

'Won't you join us for the celebration?' Marianne asked as he helped unload the food.

'*Nha.*' Kellerman shook his head with a sheepish smile and offered no excuse.

'What a feast you have prepared!' Marianne exclaimed, seeing the two cakes her friend had baked. There was a whole pot of sausages, and bread and cheese as well. Ania always knew how to feed a large group. *Where did you learn to cook in such quantities?* Marianne had once asked. *Just instinct,* Ania demurred.

'Let's set up in the library,' Marianne said. 'The dining hall is too gloomy for a party. Never mind what Signor Carfolo says. After all' – she turned to Ania slyly – 'it's our library, isn't it?'

The library was nothing fancy, a large room with bookshelves and a comfortable table and chairs. But it had been Marianne's idea, and she had been right – it was a great success. The DPs had relished access to books. And Marianne had collected and organised them herself.

As Marianne and Ania approached, a few children ran towards them – Aarne Alver, Lev Pulvel, Janna and Eha Masing. These last two were sweet, rosy-cheeked twins born right here in the camp, members of a surprising peacetime baby boom.

'Have you brought things for the party?' Lev asked in his near-perfect English.

'*Kuchen?*' Eha asked, bouncing with excitement. This was a German word all the children had learned, whether or not their parents approved.

'Cake, yes,' Marianne corrected, in deference to their mother, Jutta, who stood in the doorway of their apartment. 'And lots of spinach soup.' The children squealed and shrieked in mock horror. Spinach soup was what they had eaten for breakfast, lunch, and dinner during the early days of the camp.

'*Süssigkeiten?*' Janna tugged Ania's skirt. *Sweets?* The children loved Ania, who spoke little English, and no Estonian, but somehow seemed, always, to grasp what they wanted. In the presence of these children, Marianne saw her smile far more than she ever did with her own sons.

Ania had cared for some of the children since they were new-borns. When the camp administration had placed an ad in town for local women to serve as nannies for babies whose mothers were too sick after the war, or too traumatised, Marianne had pressed Ania to apply. And Ania had proved a deft and patient nanny, swaddling the babies in old army blankets, coaxing them to swallow their sugared vitamin water from medicine droppers. Her silence put the families at ease. *You're so good at this!* Marianne had once remarked, and was startled to see tears spring to her friend's eyes.

'Let us arrange the party and we'll call you in,' Marianne said to the children. She nodded her head towards the residence where she could see Jutta waving. How tall and strong the woman looked – so different from the diminished figure she had once been. Marianne waved back, surprised to find tears pressing at her own eyes. All the men in Jutta's family were dead: executed by one of Hitler's *Einsatzgruppen*.

'Now,' she announced, once they had entered the library, 'we must make a beautiful end.'

The party was set to begin when Benita burst through the door. 'There you are!' she exclaimed, her cheeks flushed. 'I can never find my way in this place!'

She looked particularly lovely this morning – and the waft of high spirits she brought with her was contagious.

'Ania,' Benita said, beaming. 'How *is* this new married life?'

'Not so different than before.' Ania shrugged.

'Oh *really*,' Benita said with a twinkle in her eye. To Marianne's surprise the other woman did not blush.

'A man wants what he wants,' Ania said demurely, and they both laughed.

Marianne busied herself with the tablecloth.

'Marianne, you're shocked,' Benita said, some combination of her light mood and Ania's presence making her brash.

'Me?' Marianne asked, although it was true. She had never shared this sort of banter with Ania – or Benita, for that matter.

'Of course!' Benita smirked. 'Ania can't very well shock herself.'

'Don't be so sure,' Ania said, surprising Marianne into laughter that chased away the echo of her old schoolmarmishness.

'*That* I'd like to see,' Benita said. '*Frau Kellerman* shocking herself.'

Their laughter subsided into comfortable silence. From outside they could hear the children playing. And with the tablecloths and food unpacked, the library took on a festive look.

'I almost forgot!' Benita said. 'I brought us *Eiswein!*' She reached into her bag and held a bottle aloft. 'Herr Reiner said it was the best.'

Benita opened the bottle and poured them each a glass. 'To you two,' she said. 'And all the hard work you have put into this place.'

'Pish. We can't drink to ourselves. To the travellers—' Marianne began.

Benita cut her off. 'Then to marriage. To *love*. And to whoever is next.' With a coy smile, she brought her glass to her lips.

Marianne regarded her, suddenly curious. 'Why – is there someone—?'

Benita shrugged mischievously. 'Who knows? Where Ania goes, we may follow.'

'You don't mean Helmut.' Marianne frowned, perplexed. The wine had gone straight to her head.

'How do you know I mean me and not you?'

'Benita!' Marianne exclaimed. 'What on earth can you be talking about?'

Benita sashayed over to the window and rested her forehead against the glass. For a moment, Marianne was reminded of the girl she had first met. Then Benita straightened, cocked her head, and smiled. 'Nonsense,' she said. 'And daydreams. Don't you ever have those?'

'Oh, Benita.' Marianne shook her head. She stabbed a knife into the cake on the table and began slicing. 'Isn't it time for the party to begin?'

'You should.' Benita smiled, ignoring the question. 'A few daydreams would do you good.'

CHAPTER SEVENTEEN

MOMSEN, JUNE 1950

As far as Marianne knew, Benita was going to visit her sister.

'Bring her this,' Marianne had said that morning, thrusting a bag of expensive oranges into her hands.

It gave Benita a twinge of guilt. Marianne was a good woman. She knew Benita's sister Lotte had four children and worked long hours in a canning factory. She did not know that Lotte was an ignorant, hard-hearted bitch and her husband was not dead, but locked in some Siberian camp for ex-SS.

Or that Benita was not actually going to see Lotte.

In Momsen, Benita stood for a moment on the makeshift train platform, blinking in the spring sunlight. Then she spotted him: Franz Muller, always taller and broader in person than he was in her mind. It was as if he belonged to another species – all parts of him well proportioned, but larger. A superhuman. She loved this.

When he saw her, a shy smile spread across his face.

'Franz!' she called, and ran towards him.

Circumspect as always, he extended his hand.

'Oh, stop,' Benita said, wrapping her arm around his waist. She turned her face up to his. 'You can at least give me a kiss!'

He obliged with a furtive peck on her lips.

'You would think *I'd* be the one who didn't want to be seen!' She laughed.

'Come.' He swung her bag over his shoulder, where it perched ridiculously.

Benita thrust her hand into his. Wrapped in the warmth of his calloused palm, her own felt like some small, vulnerable mollusc. She trailed a step behind, enjoying the feel of following, of being led by someone so much bigger and stronger than herself. And of knowing it was an illusion. When they were together, she was the one in charge.

When Franz had been released from the internment camp, he was a thin, hollow-eyed man with an apologetic stoop. He had hitched a ride to Braunschweig – first with a transport of American soldiers, who called him 'old man' and offered him a candy bar that later had him retching in a ditch, and then with a friendly Tommy driving a jeep. This was the freezing winter of 1946. Benita knew all this from the letters he had written to her soon after his release. Such sweet, simple letters, asking how she was, what Martin was doing, whether the castle was warm enough . . .

At first she had been self-conscious about writing back. She had never been good with words or spelling in school. But then it had seemed cruel not to answer. And she liked Franz Muller. She missed his strong, quiet presence in the woods. So she had made herself respond.

And what fun this turned out to be! It made her notice more, think more, and find the humour and interest in little things. The chickens Marianne was raising proved endlessly entertaining – it was a miracle that they survived under her care! And Fritz and Martin's mischief became less galling when she wrote about it. Life was so much brighter and more vivid once she had a reason to observe it closely.

Everything was fodder for her letters. Except for the Russian.

But of course he hung between them, their personal ghost. A

man she had killed and Franz had buried. To everyone else he didn't exist. He had simply vanished from the face of the earth. On that day in the woods, Franz had seen Benita's most hideous self, and still he did not hate her. Somehow it saved her from hating herself.

Through their letters, they learned more about each other. Franz was the oldest son of a carpenter, who made fine cabinets and furniture. At nineteen, he had married the daughter of his father's partner in order to consolidate the business. She was a sickly girl, five years older than he was. They had one daughter, Clotilde, and his wife died two years later. So Franz and his father had raised the girl, who was now eleven, the same age as Martin. He was not conscripted until 1942; he was older, for one thing, already thirty-five when the war began, and the sole proprietor of a business. But finally he had been sent east as part of a local group of reservists. What it was like there, where he had been . . . he did not write about this. Anyway, she knew where he had ended up: Burg Lingenfels, cutting down trees.

After he was released from the internment camp, he had gathered up his small family. Their flat had been bombed, his business destroyed, and he found Clotilde and old Herr Muller living in a dank, overcrowded apartment with neighbours. So he had packed their things and moved south to the American sector, where there were more opportunities. And there was Benita.

In the city of Momsen, he could find work as a carpenter. *Why not Tollingen?* Benita wrote. *Come back as a free man!* But Franz had a cousin who had a friend who owned a coffin-making business in Momsen, and Franz was assured of work there. Demand for coffins was steady, he joked. And it was not far from Tollingen.

So their letters had continued. But now there were also visits.

Over the last two years, Benita had been to Franz's flat above the coffin business several times. She had met old Herr Muller, who was bitter and unpleasant and spoke to his son as if he were still twelve years old – how did Franz stand it? – and little Clotilde, who was a sweet thing, all skin and bones and large, soulful dark eyes. She clearly needed a mother – someone to teach her how to put her hair back in something other than a plain braid, how to look people in the eye, how to keep the house. They had sat on the makeshift furniture Franz crafted from coffin scraps and eaten Clotilde's homemade, nearly inedible, cookies. And Benita had daydreamed of all the ways she could improve on this.

Today, Benita and Franz were alone. Clotilde and her grandfather had taken the train north to visit Franz's ailing sister.

As soon as they entered the flat, Benita turned and hooked her hands into his waistband.

Franz took her fingers in his and brought them to his lips. Still holding them, he walked her backwards to the brand-new sofa – yellow with stiff cushions – under the open window.

'What are you doing?' Benita laughed, pulling away her hands.

'Bringing you to the sofa,' Franz said. 'Making you sit. Getting you a cup of tea.'

'But I don't want tea!' she protested, catching his hand as she sat back, with a poof, on the cushion.

'I insist,' he said, pulling away. 'A lady deserves tea after a long journey.'

'Oh, *a lady*!' she said. 'How fine. And how has the gentleman been?'

'Lonely,' Franz said, lighting the gas under the kettle. 'Waiting for your visit.'

'But now he wants to wait even longer?' Benita teased, batting her lashes and watching him blush. A widower, a soldier, a man nearing forty-six, and still such an innocent! With him, she adopted the old role of flirt and temptress that had once been her signature. She slipped off her shoes and tucked her feet underneath her on the sofa.

'How was the wedding?' he asked, measuring tea into the

strainer. He was so careful and considerate – traits she would have hated in her young life, but that now endeared him to her. His carefulness made her feel safe.

'Wonderful,' Benita said. 'The bride wore a grey suit and the groom his best lederhosen.' She laughed aloud at the image of Herr Kellerman in a pair of short pants. 'No, but really it was nice. Ania looked happy – at least secretly.'

Franz handed Benita a steaming cup – thick white china, the kind one could buy at any market now, so different from Marianne's fine Meissen. Benita would miss those when she became Frau Muller – their refinement and air of bygone elegance. But she held no more illusions; she could eat off fine china, but she would never be an aristocrat.

'Franz,' she said, hooking her foot around his leg as he started back for his own cup. 'Franzl.' She loved calling him that – it was such a boy's name, so inappropriate for the man before her. 'When will you make me a good woman? Have you been looking at flats?'

His face slackened, and immediately Benita wished she had not teased. Franz would find one when there was enough money – she had no doubt. And then they would be married. It was only a question of time.

'Not yet,' he said as if breaking terrible news. 'I'm sorry – I think it will be another month.'

'Hush – never mind. I'm only teasing.' She ran her stockinged foot farther up his leg. 'But now you must stop teasing me.'

Slowly, Franz leaned down and took the cup of tea from her hand, placing it on the side table. Then he pulled her to her feet. She pressed her breasts against his chest, delighted by their regained roundness in her new brassiere – a white lace shelf that created real décolletage. It was the first piece of lingerie she had owned since before the war. In it she felt young again and excited by her own beauty.

'That's better,' she murmured against his lips and unbuttoned her dress.

*   *   *

They made love four more times during the twenty-four-hour visit. It was never enough.

Benita had always cultivated her seduction skills – Connie was not her first – and her husband had benefited from her experience. There was Heinrich Kohl and Karl Josef before him, handsome, fresh-faced village boys with whom she had practised, with the explicit intention of gaining expertise. She was a dreamer, but she was not naive. She had always known that it was not her brains that would get her out of Frühlinghausen. And so she had learned how to slip her tongue into the rim of a man's ear just so, how to graze her nipples against his chest, a titillating reminder of their presence as she slid one hand down over his belly to the ridge of his hip.

With Connie, all this had come together in an impressive bit of theatre that he had loved. For a man of experience – which Connie Fledermann certainly was – he had been oddly enthralled by her simple games. And she had used that to every advantage. But for her, the benefit was only his addled affection, never any pleasure of her own.

With Franz it was different. There was no pretending. After Berlin, sex was something she had never thought she would want again. Yet somehow she did. She wanted him. And around him, she had no shame.

'Franz,' she said, rising on her elbow sometime before dinner on the second day. Her stomach rumbled. They had eaten nothing except Marianne's oranges and chocolate, and the sugar made her light-headed. 'Let's go to Lufner's. I could eat five schnitzels.'

Franz rolled onto his back. They were pressed against each other and lying on his cot – a rudimentary thing that he didn't entirely fit into even on his own. He slept on this, his father on the couch, and Clotilde in the bedroom. The flat Benita envisioned for the future Frau Muller was to be much bigger, with a room for each and a proper wardrobe for Clotilde. She had spent hours daydreaming of this.

'*Jawohl,*' Franz said, swinging his giant legs off the bed. 'Whatever Frau Fledermann wishes.'

While Franz was in the washroom, Benita scribbled a note to tuck into his underwear drawer. It was a silly little thing on a scrap of package paper – *I love you* and a picture of a goat with hearts for eyes. She did not mean to snoop. But suddenly, when she pulled out the drawer, here were his most intimate things – not only underwear, but a framed photograph of a woman who must have been his mother (square jawed and regal faced, with Franz's high forehead), another of Clotilde as a baby, and a box full of letters Benita had sent to him. Beneath these, she noticed the corner of another letter, something official and typewritten. Almost without thinking, she pulled it out. It was a directive from the *Spruchkammer,* the local denazification council, dated *August 1946. We have found Franz Muller to belong to Group III, Lesser Offenders, subject to sanctions accordingly.*

Group III was an unlucky designation, a step beyond *Mitläufer,* or 'fellow traveller,' which was the title every German liked to think he deserved. It was not as bad as *Belastete,* or 'loaded,' meaning guilty (a strange term in itself). But it signified guilt nonetheless. A Group III designation entailed restrictions; you could not, for instance, teach or play a role in politics. Why had Franz kept the letter? In the last year, under Adenauer, such designations had become nearly irrelevant. Germany was in the Cold War now. The Soviets were their enemy once again, not the Nazis.

'I'm sorry,' Franz said, his voice startling her.

'For what?' Benita asked, colouring. The letter was still clutched in her hand.

'I should have told you.'

'Told me what? That everyone is guilty?' Franz did not seem

angry, to her relief. 'Don't you think the Americans have made that clear?'

Franz remained solemn. 'You've never asked me about the war.'

'Why should I?' She approached him. 'You were in the reserve – you went to the east. You fought the Russians. I don't need to know any more.'

Franz was silent.

'What? I don't!' Somewhere inside a small pod of fear split open, sending doubt rattling. 'Do I?'

'I don't know, Benita.' Franz sighed. 'I can't tell you what you need to know.'

Benita stopped a metre away and felt the distance between them open like a vice. It filled her with panic. She could not lose him. She could not survive this.

'I know *you*,' she said, flinging her arms around him. 'That's all I need.'

Franz stiffened and averted his face.

'Franzl,' she pleaded. 'We are new people now. This is our second life.'

For a terrifying moment he did not move. Then slowly, as if navigating some viscous substance, he lifted his arms and wrapped them around her and touched his lips to the crown of her head. Thank God! But as she held him tight, she could feel the presence of the past – a great unknowable continent of experience pushing up between them, full of treacherous mountains and dry valleys. She did not want to explore it.

When they returned to the flat from Lufner's Biergarten, the door opened from within.

'Papa!' Clotilde cried. Her eyes lit up and then widened as she noticed her father was not alone in the hall.

'What happened?' Franz stuttered. 'You came home early – is everything all right?'

'Barbel was sick – not terribly sick, just not well, and so we took the earlier train to allow her peace and quiet.' She continued to stare at Benita.

'You remember Frau Fledermann,' Franz said, collecting himself.

'Frau Fledermann,' Clotilde said, politely ducking her head, then raising it to peer curiously back and forth between Benita and her father.

'Don't let the draught in,' old Herr Muller called from within.

'Have you bought the meat for supper yet?' he asked as they entered. He was reclined on the yellow sofa, facing away from the door.

'Father—' Franz said, and, turning slightly, Herr Muller caught sight of Benita. His eyes widened and his mouth fell open.

'You remember Frau Fledermann?' Franz said, placing a hand at her elbow.

Herr Muller nodded but remained speechless.

'Don't get up,' Benita said, crossing the floor with her hand extended. The old man stared at her. He was tall, even now, and his face was much like Franz's, although not as handsome or as kind. A series of emotions – confusion, anger, and suspicion – passed across it. And Benita remembered her valise, lying open on Franz's cot. Had Herr Muller seen it?

'Have you had a comfortable trip?' she asked hastily. For a moment both Clotilde and the old man stared.

'Frau Fledermann is on her way to the train herself,' Franz interrupted. His own face had turned a florid red. 'I will take her to the station and pick up the meat on my return.'

Herr Muller gave a peremptory nod. In his manner, and in Franz's sudden uncertainty, Benita saw their history. Here was the domineering father for whom Franz had married a sickly woman and become a carpenter.

'May I come, too?' Clotilde asked, breaking her silence. 'Please?'

'I don't think—' Franz began.

'Oh, why not?' Benita said warmly. 'We can hear all about your trip.'

'Please,' Clotilde pleaded.

'All right.' Franz ducked his head.

'Is that your valise?' Clotilde asked guilelessly, pointing to the cot.

'Thank you!' Benita answered smoothly. 'We stowed it there for the day so we could walk in the park. Franz?' She turned to her lover, who had suddenly become an overgrown boy in his awkwardness. 'Can you get it for me?'

'Ah, of course.' He crossed the room in three great strides.

Benita smiled brightly at Clotilde.

Franz rejoined Benita at the door with the valise. 'Frau Fledermann and I are betrothed,' he announced, almost fiercely, taking her arm. And for a moment, they – Benita, Herr Muller, and Clotilde – all stared at him gape-mouthed.

Clotilde was the first to speak. 'Congratulations!' she said shyly.

'Thank you,' Benita said, smiling broadly at Franz, surprised at the enormity of her own happiness.

CHAPTER EIGHTEEN

EHRENHEIM, JUNE 1950

The photograph in the newspaper made Ania look frightened, and Carsten proud and foolish.

'You were right,' he announced bitterly. 'It would have been better not to invite that photographer.'

'No, no,' Ania lied. 'No one looks at those pictures anyway.'

A month had passed and, so far, this seemed to be true.

But each night she had terrible dreams. In these, she was no longer on the march. She was a girl, in her father's house. *Ania, Herr Doktor Fortzmann would say in his stern, sonorous voice, it is vanity to think you can change fate.* She would wake in a sweat, her feather bed soaked. And when she saw her own dim reflection in the mirror, she mistook it for a ghost.

Married life was not very different from her life as a tenant. As a paying boarder on Carsten's farm, Ania had grasped his intentions early. He was certainly not flirtatious – God forbid! Even the idea was alarming – but he was solicitous. And her responsibilities were already those of a wife: cooking, cleaning, ironing his shirts . . . So Carsten's unadorned offer of matrimony had not come as a surprise. And once she agreed, there was no sense in abiding by old-fashioned traditions of propriety. Neither of them was religious. Neither was a virgin. And for both, their union was a utilitarian arrangement. Carsten favoured swift, silent encounters with no pretence of romance. They slept in separate bedrooms, but from the first day of their engagement, he had maintained a regular schedule of visits: Tuesdays and Fridays. He had not deviated from it once.

Which explained why, at the start of her marriage, she found herself undeniably pregnant. Five months along, the village doctor confirmed with unsubtle amusement. *Herr Kellerman will certainly be pleased*. He grinned.

But Ania was not amused. Denial had shielded her from the fact for as long as possible – her cycles had been irregular since the war and she had convinced herself she was too old to have children. Meanwhile, her belly grew round and she was hungry all the time. There was a flush of fat on her cheeks. Her pregnancy was too far along to escape.

Even so, she tried. She rode the wagon over rutted fields, scrambled up ladders and jumped down from the odd places the hens laid eggs, initiated a rigid programme of bitter teas and scalding baths. She did not tell Carsten the news. But the baby was stubborn. It clung to her like a barnacle; she imagined its tiny fists grasping the soft tissue of her womb. It was determined to survive.

When she finally told Carsten, he was both delighted and embarrassed. He never spoke of the pregnancy by name and made no changes to their daily life – except for the conjugal visits, which immediately ceased. Ania did not tell anyone else. Let Carsten and Doktor Schrenke, the old gossip, spread the word.

In the evenings, Carsten liked to sit with her in the parlour – an uncomfortable, dark room with nothing but the fire in the brazier to recommend it. They listened to the news on the radio and he forced himself to read the Bible, self-imposed penance for a man who never went to church. As he read, his lips shaped the words. Ania sat beside him in the reclining armchair he had given her as a wedding present, darning socks and half hearing the news.

Sometimes Wolfgang ventured into their little cocoon with a question about schoolwork. Unlike his brother, he was a terrible student. He hunched over his books like a man flinching from a blow. The softer subjects were of particular difficulty – the vague but cautionary parables of history, the dense imaginative formulations of literature. He could not wait to work full-time on the farm and genuinely enjoyed making the rounds with his stepfather, learning how to stack the baled hay, when to hose down the pigs, where to reinforce a fence. He didn't even mind Carsten's finicky and exacting commands. Next autumn his official apprenticeship was set to begin. Yet Ania always felt a twinge of sorrow at the sight of his dark head bowed over his schoolwork.

He was her mistake, poor child, born at a time when only wickedness was being ushered into the world. He was the product of her hungry, ration-fed womb and thin, insufficient breast milk. As a young mother, she had not had time to care for him. When he was sick with scarlet fever as a toddler, she had tied him to the bedpost on a leash to quarantine him. Carsten's farm was her way of making amends.

'Here is something for you,' Carsten said from his armchair one evening, extending an envelope with *Frau Ania Kellerman* written across the front. The baby hiccupped in her belly.

'Thank you,' Ania said, her heart suddenly pounding. She did not recognise the address – a street in Momsen. But the name – *R. Brandt* – took her breath away.

She sat rigidly still, terrified that Carsten would ask her about its sender. The torrent of chemicals in her womb made the hiccupping stop.

Thankfully, Carsten was engrossed in a seed catalogue.

Ania resumed her mending. The minutes sagged. The pages of

Carsten's magazine rustled. It was weaning season, and outside the mother cows bellowed for their calves. Across the pasture, in the barn, the calves cried back.

When enough time had finally elapsed, Ania excused herself.

Behind the closed door of her room, she tore open the envelope.

Inside was a thin sheet of airmail paper, the script written in a shaky but familiar hand.

Ania? it read. *Do I recognise you?*

Yours, as always,

Rainer

The words swam before her eyes. She tried to focus on the uneven ink, the fussy elegance of the *A* and the *D* – a kind of pidgin Old German script he had taught himself. After everything, apparently, this pretence remained.

From where had he emerged? *Missing, presumed dead.* This was what she had found at the Red Cross office. *Dead,* she had thought. After all, she knew the Warthegau. And she knew Rainer, or at least she once had.

But here he was, on this scrap of paper, slipping into her life.

The truth will out, her father had always said. Though, so far, in Ania's experience, this was not quite right. The truth was in God's hands. Or the devil's, more likely. The very word *truth* seemed quaint. Where had it been hiding during the reign of *obedience, pride, and duty?*

Ania lay on her bed and counted the rows of tiny flowers on the curtains to still the chaos in her head. But it seeped through. In her mind, doors banged open and shut. The stench of mud defrosting in the spring, the long blank horizon of the east. The cruelty of boys playing games in the cold. A baby's hand absently pulling at her ear. Beneath this were other, softer pieces. Rainer, not as the man she had last seen, but as a boy, sitting on the horsehair sofa in her father's waiting room, waiting for his own prematurely aged father to emerge with a new round of pills. Already he had been the man of the house. Dark haired and dark eyed, his feet barely reaching the floor, still he was in charge.

She rose abruptly and went to the desk. She had to write back. If there was one thing she had learned, it was that you had to *act*. To rise up and meet obstacles thrown in your path. To sit and wait was death.

She pulled a sheet of airmail paper from her desk.

I'm afraid you are mistaken, she wrote. *I know no one by the names of Ania or Rainer Brandt. Best of luck.*

For a long moment she sat, staring at the words and at the once intimate name, *Brandt*. Then she sealed the envelope and tiptoed down the hall to the room her boys shared. She stood before their door and listened. She could hear their voices within – Anselm's low murmur, Wolfgang's faster, more heated tone. What would they make of the news? Her boys, for whom she had done too little and from whom she had asked so much – total faith, total amnesia, total forgiveness.

Something made her hesitate. As she stood in the darkness, a new intention formed. She would shoulder this new uncertainty alone. It was hers, after all. So she listened a moment more, allowing her courage to be bolstered by the trappings of this ordinary life she had arranged: homework, supper, chores, bed.

Then, moving swiftly and quietly, she turned and went back down the hall.

CHAPTER NINETEEN

TOLLINGEN, JUNE 1950

Marianne was in the middle of a dream when the doorbell rang. A sweet, long-ago dream from her last life, of sitting in the garden at Weisslau, a picnic under the chestnut tree with her children, the dogs, and Albrecht. And then all the gaiety disappeared. She was not in Weisslau but in her flat in Tollingen. The plot had failed. Weisslau was lost. Albrecht was dead.

Marianne sat up. Late-afternoon sunlight streamed through the windows, illuminating dust motes and uneven layers of floor wax. It was still day. Without her work at the camp, she found herself napping at odd times and reading deep into the night. It was embarrassing. She swung her legs off the sofa. It was likely Benita, having forgotten her key, of course.

'Welcome home!' she said, opening the door, hoping there were no telltale wrinkles from the pillow on her face. 'Where are your keys?'

'I'm sorry.' Benita blushed. 'I must have left them on the table – or when I was—'

'Come in, come in,' Marianne commanded. 'It's too cold in the hall. How is your sister?'

'My sister.' Benita looked surprised. 'Oh, yes – she's well. Thank you.'

'She's well?' Marianne asked. 'I thought she was ill again.'

'As well as possible.'

Marianne studied Benita. She was, as usual these days, in a state of heightened spirits. She seemed *overexcited,* in fact. Something had happened. She could not step over a dead cat on the pavement without it appearing hours later on her face.

'Here, you must be tired from the trip. Come and have some coffee and raisin cake,' Marianne said, starting towards the kitchen. 'The children ate almost all of it, but I asked them to save some for you.'

Benita followed her.

'Have a wash and I'll make the coffee,' Marianne said, as if Benita were a child. And like an obedient daughter, Benita did as told.

'I've been thinking,' Marianne began as soon as she returned, 'that we should take a trip together with the children, show them something of Germany. We could go to Berlin first and visit Georg Bucher – did Connie ever introduce you to him? They were always such dear friends . . . or maybe into Munich to see Marienplatz and the Asamkirche? The boys are getting so old and what do they know of their country? Nothing but all the bad things.'

'All right.' Benita nodded, poking at her slice of cake.

'Or,' Marianne ventured, 'we could visit Helmut Kressing – What is it?' She broke off at the sight of Benita's face. 'Do you really dislike him so much?'

'No! No, no,' Benita said, shifting in her seat. 'I just – there is something I need to tell you.'

'Of course,' Marianne said, sitting back. 'You look so serious.' She laughed. 'Is it a matter of life and death?'

To her surprise, Benita did not smile.

Marianne could not sleep that night. She tried to believe it was the nap. But of course it was not. Benita's news was like a mouse crawling around in her head, nibbling on the wiring, pissing and shitting on her memories, creating electrical storms. Benita Fledermann, wife of Martin Constantine Fledermann, was to marry an ex-Nazi, an ordinary carpenter turned member of the *Orpo*, a man with God knows how much blood on his hands.

In Marianne's mind, he appeared as he had the morning he carried Benita back from the woods: a giant man cradling a girl in his arms, covered in blood. Like some monster from a legend. What had happened that morning was something she had never understood. Benita had ventured out to warn Herr Muller of the Russians camped in front of the stable and had been attacked. She had stabbed her attacker. And the man had run off. Herr Muller had found her and carried her back. This was the garbled story that Benita recited. But Marianne never believed it. The next day, the Russians had come looking – one of them was missing. Marianne had said nothing, but of course she wondered. She could not imagine birdbrained, fragile Benita stabbing anyone. No, Marianne felt certain it was Herr Muller who killed him. Possibly in defence of Benita, possibly not. What was one more murder to a man who had served in Lublin? She had been right to tell Peterman to reassign him. Only she had been too late.

But now suddenly he was back. This time, even closer, popping up beside the little skiff of a family she was steering. All these years, he had been swimming alongside, beneath the surface. It was a shock and a betrayal.

I have failed you, Connie, Marianne thought. It sounded melodramatic. But it was true. *Take care of my wife,* Connie had instructed her. *Look out for my son.* Don't let her marry a Nazi pig, don't let a murderer take my place. That was implicit.

Marianne swung her legs out of bed, pulled on her dressing gown, and went to the kitchen. To her surprise, light streamed from under the door – the faintly greenish glow of the fluorescent coil on the ceiling. She hesitated for a moment – what if Benita was there? The idea that this would keep her from her own kitchen gave her a righteous surge of adrenalin.

She swung through the door, grim faced and prepared for battle, but was met with the sight of Martin sitting at the table, reading.

'Tante Marianne!' he said, his expression guilty. His face shifted as he took in her countenance. Dear Martin, poor Martin, sweet boy – Marianne tried to smile and amend whatever anger he had seen.

'What are you doing up at this hour?' she asked. 'You have school tomorrow!'

'I couldn't sleep,' he said simply, and it occurred to her that for him this was not an unusual occurrence.

'Have you had milk? Warm milk?' She padded over to the small icebox and removed the bottle. 'That always helps.'

He shook his head.

Marianne poured enough for them both and set the saucepan on the stove. 'What are you reading?'

'Karl May.' Martin held up the book; it was Marianne's own ancient copy of *Winnetou*, its cracked leather binding and faded gold embossing as familiar to her as an old friend. 'I borrowed it from Fritz.'

'Do you like it?' Marianne asked.

'I love it.'

Marianne felt a swell of love for him. He was more like her than her own son, who had pronounced the book unrealistic and dull.

'It was my favourite,' she said.

They were silent. The milk simmered on the stove, and the light ticked overhead.

'You're happy here, aren't you, Martin?' Marianne asked. 'I mean living with us – all together, you and your mother and my family?'

'Of course!' The boy looked surprised.

'You don't wish' – she turned off the milk, placed two cups and saucers on the counter – 'that your mother were remarried, that you lived somewhere else with a stepfather?'

Confusion crowded across his young face. For a moment, Marianne regretted the question.

'No,' he said. 'Why – do you think my mother and I should be on our own?'

'Oh, no! No, no,' Marianne exclaimed, nearly scalding herself. 'Certainly not. I just wondered how you felt about it.'

She studied his already shockingly handsome face. He looked away from the intensity of her gaze.

'Martin,' she said seriously, 'you know your father would have wanted it this way.'

When Marianne awoke some hours later, she was hungry and filled with a sense of resolve. It was nearly eight o'clock. Fritz and Martin had already left for school. Benita was sitting stiffly at the parlour table, making one of those hideous stuffed dolls that had become her hobby of late. When Marianne entered, she looked up and her face was pale, her eyes swollen from crying.

'Marianne—' she began. 'I'm sorry I never told you before – I couldn't sleep. I—'

'Never mind.' Marianne cut her off. 'I cannot give you my blessing to marry Herr Muller,' she continued. 'I have thought about it and it is not right.'

Benita regarded her with a plaintive face. 'Why? Because he was a Nazi? But everyone was a Nazi. He is a good man—'

'Because it isn't right that you should marry someone who worked for everything your husband died fighting against!' Marianne could hear her own shrillness.

Benita began to cry. She looked childish and delicate in her distress. It made Marianne feel old. Here she was, cast again as the stable, unemotional foil to Benita's damsel in distress.

'Do you even know what he did in the war?' Marianne asked. 'Do you talk about it?'

Benita wiped her eyes. 'I don't know and I don't care.'

'He was in the *Orpo*. You know that much, don't you?' she demanded. 'But do you know what they did there, in the east?'

Hastily, Benita rose and moved to the window. When she turned again, her face was illuminated by a new desperation. 'Don't you ever want to put it away, Marianne? To be done with it? I don't *want* to know what they did. I don't *want* to look over my shoulder forever. It was a horrible time. And now it is past!'

Marianne stared at her. It was so selfish and cowardly! It made her blood boil. Benita was always looking out for her own interest, her own *comfort*. 'You think the past is like one of your dolls? That you can just – tear it up and begin over again? Like that! And you are the wife of a hero! A man who died to make the past a little less horrible than it is. Don't you think you owe him at least a little respect?'

Now Benita began to cry in earnest. Her shoulders shook, and ugly, sputtering sobs escaped from her throat.

'Do what you want.' Marianne sighed. 'But I won't let you draw Martin into this.'

At this, Benita looked up. She reached into her pocket for a handkerchief and blew her nose.

'Think it through,' Marianne said, softening slightly. 'It is easy to mistake—'

Benita interrupted. 'You are cruel, Marianne. Connie always said so, but I never saw it.' She looked directly at her. 'But now I can see it.'

All day, Marianne felt the words like an ache. When would Connie have said this? It was a betrayal. *Tough*, she could imagine him saying. *Discerning*. Even *hard*. But not *cruel*. It was an arrow to her heart.

'Katarina,' she asked when the girl came to say goodnight, 'do you think of me as cruel?'

Katarina's dark eyes blinked in surprise. It was not like her mother to ask such a thing. 'Cruel?' she repeated. The word shocked her: she was a true von Lingenfels. 'Of course not! Why do you ask?'

Marianne sighed. 'Maybe we are all cruel sometimes without intending to be.'

'Not you,' Katarina said, with such earnestness it made Marianne smile.

'Even me.' Marianne put an arm around her daughter and rested her cheek against the girl's side. Despite everything, she was still only a child.

Marianne longed for the reassuring voice of an adult. She would ask Ania when she saw her next.

CHAPTER TWENTY

EHRENHEIM, JUNE 1950

Ania received another letter the following Saturday. This time it was not delivered by the mailman but by Frau Metzger, the woman who brought their cheese.

'From a *man*,' Frau Metzger said with a coquettish smile, pulling the crinkly envelope from her bag. 'He came to the market last week.'

Ania stared.

'Well?' Frau Metzger grinned. 'Aren't you going to open it? . . . Or maybe you already know who it was.' The woman winked.

'Of course not,' Ania said.

'Ah.' Frau Metzger sighed, obviously disappointed. 'He did not look well. Recently back from the east.'

'Hmm.' Ania frowned in an approximation of confusion. 'Thank you very much.'

This time there was no return address.

I forgive you. You did what you felt was best. But you are not finished with me yet.

The letter, if it could be called that, was wrapped around a photograph. A young man and woman wearing formal clothing, standing side by side at the bottom of an imposing set of steps. Wind blew at their hair and lifted the woman's skirt. The man gazed off to the side as the woman smiled bravely in a manner that was as openly uncertain as it was direct.

And Ania was there, with the wind blowing in her ears and her best shoes pinching her toes and a sense of great import leading her, irrationally, towards giddiness. She was like a person jumping from an aeroplane, experiencing the lightness of commitment to an unchangeable path. It was like remembering a character from one of the novels she had read in her youth.

Ania set down the photograph. Outside, the afternoon sun yellowed, and bits of dried linden blew in the wind. It was time to prepare Carsten's coffee and send Wolfgang out to the field with it. In the pasture, the bereaved mother cows bellowed for their babies still. They were not finished mourning yet.

The next day, Ania visited the return address from the first letter. The trip required a bus, a train, and a long walk. Ania left Inge, the house apprentice, in charge of supper, afternoon coffee, the wash, the cucumber pickling, and tending the garden – and set off.

It was an uncomfortable journey for a woman six months pregnant. On account of the heat, her swollen feet, and the sharp pain that shot up her spine, Ania had little time to think en route. So when she arrived in front of 19 Mauer Strasse, she was filled with a sense of shock. It was a real place, with real windows, and a real door. There was a front bell and a list of names beside it: a rooming house. The neighbourhood was shabby; it stank of urine and cabbage soup.

An older man emerged from the door of the building as she stood there. Not Rainer, but certainly someone who had fallen on hard times. He scowled at her with blind resentment.

'Nha?' he said rudely. 'Does it look good enough for you?' It took her a second to realise that he mistook her for someone looking for a place to stay.

Ania squared her shoulders and mounted the steps.

A hard-looking old woman came to the door. 'No children allowed here,' she said, looking pointedly at Ania's belly.

'No, no – I'm not looking to stay,' Ania said. 'I'm looking for someone—'

The woman's frown deepened. She had small, scrutinising eyes. 'I'm not an information service,' she snapped.

'I'm looking for a man—' Ania withdrew the envelope with the return address and showed it to her.

'This is a personal matter?' the woman said.

Ania coloured. 'It's not—' she began and broke off. What did it matter? 'Personal, yes,' Ania said. 'Rainer Brandt.'

The woman's eyes glanced briefly at the name without recognition. Rainer had always been the sort to slide by unnoticed, a man with an unremarkable manner and face. The woman shrugged. 'There is no one by that name here anymore.'

'Did he leave a forwarding address?' Ania asked.

The woman cocked her head to the side. 'What would I do with that?' she asked. 'Go on.' She shook her head and her voice softened slightly. 'Finding him won't be worth much.'

So Ania was forced to wait for Rainer to show himself. She went about her daily life half-present, botching her usual tasks. She cut herself pitting cherries, burned the potatoes she was boiling, left a pail of milk to sour in the barn.

'Are you all right?' Inge asked.

'Just wait until you are this pregnant,' Ania replied, more harshly than she intended. It was a convenient excuse. The weeks passed, and with each one she grew more irritable. Daily, she was tempted to confide in Anselm and Wolfgang, and then stopped herself. Anselm was locked in his studies, and Wolfgang spent his days with Carsten, preparing for the harvest, feeding the livestock.

Carsten himself noticed nothing. He treated her with embarrassed caution, darting glances rather than direct looks her way. During their half hour after supper he made a great show of turning on the radio for her, helping her to her chair. It would have driven her crazy if she weren't so distracted. As it was, she barely registered his ministrations.

And she saw Rainer everywhere: outside the bakery, driving Herr Darmler's gleaming new combine harvester, walking up the road from town. Every time the dog barked, Ania was certain it was at him. What would she do and say when he arrived? She had a million thoughts and none. She could see his hard, slight body, and the jerky way he looked over his shoulder, the firm set of his mouth when he embarked on unpleasant tasks. He was a body washed up in her mind, dragging the tangle of her own bad choices like so much kelp.

One day, Marianne came to visit with a basket of fine rolls from Bemmelman's. It was still strange to receive her as *Frau Kellerman*, farm mistress rather than tenant. Ania was embarrassed at the disorder of the kitchen and her own rumpled dress. As she looked at her familiar friend's face, she was oppressed by her own secrets. Dear, difficult Marianne, who had been so generous and optimistic from the start. She had taken in Ania and her boys without hesitation, without question, and never looked back. This blessing had turned into a burden. At any moment, it would blow up in Ania's face.

Awkwardness made Ania formal. She pulled out Carsten's precious supply of tinned cookies and arranged them prettily on a plate.

'Don't make me feel a visitor,' Marianne said, waving them away. She seemed distracted herself. 'I have to ask you something,' she blurted, and Ania's heart raced.

'Have you ever known me to be cruel?'

Ania almost laughed. 'Never.'

Marianne sighed.

'Why do you ask?'

Marianne turned from the window she had been staring out of. 'Did you know Benita stayed in touch with Herr Muller? The prisoner? Do you remember him?'

Herr Muller. In Ania's mind, an image presented itself. A tall man, square jawed, pale eyed. She saw him as he had been the morning of the Russians, carrying Benita: a man with a guarded, uncertain face. A fellow keeper of secrets.

Marianne waited.

'I remember him. Why?' she asked, glancing out of the window. The barnyard was empty. Her constant checking had become a nervous tic.

'Apparently she has been seeing him. All this time – writing letters and visiting – he lives nearby – in Momsen! And she imagines she loves him!' Marianne stopped. 'I never even heard a word about it. All this time.'

Ania poured a cup of coffee and set it before Marianne. She was surprised but not shocked. She had wondered whether there was something between them at the time. But she had not imagined that their affair would have continued from that life into this. Benita, unlike the prisoner, was no keeper of secrets.

'When did she tell you this?' she asked.

'Just this week. As if I would be happy!' Marianne stared down into her coffee and then up at Ania. 'She never told you either?'

Ania shook her head.

'All this time she was lying!'

Ania hesitated. 'She didn't *lie*,' she said. 'She just didn't share the truth with us.'

Marianne frowned. 'She *concealed* what she was doing. What's the difference?'

Ania busied herself with drying dishes, feigning nonchalance. 'It could be like a photograph with the faces blacked out. What you see is true; it's just incomplete.'

'But who are people without their faces?' Marianne was impatient. 'How could you know a man if you can't see his face?'

When Rainer finally came, it was mid-July, and the weather was hot. Ania sat in the shade under the chestnut tree shelling peas. Sweat dripped down her sides and made her thighs sticky. Heat rose from the limestone of the barnyard in slippery, distorting waves.

He was halfway across before Ania saw him. She had imagined this moment so many times that the reality was strangely flat. A single burst of adrenalin shot through her, followed by something like relief.

It was clear that he was unwell. He was thinner than ever and walked with a limp. His face was waxy, and there were dark hollows beneath his eyes. His breathing was laboured.

At about four metres away, he stopped.

Staring at him, Ania saw a stranger. Not someone she loved, not someone she hated. Just someone she no longer knew. It was frightening but uncomplicated.

For a long time neither of them spoke. There was the sound of his breathing, the buzz of bees in the branches, and the mild rustle of leaves.

Rainer stared at her round belly. She placed a hand over it.

'What do you want?' she asked.

Removing a dirty cloth from the pocket of his even dirtier jacket – much too hot for this weather – Rainer wiped his forehead and squeezed his eyes shut. He looked like a man who needed to lie down. He looked like a man who was dying.

And suddenly, after all the time she had spent dreading this moment, Ania knew what to do.

He opened his eyes again and regarded her. 'Am I speaking to Ania Kellerman or Ania Brandt?'

CHAPTER TWENTY-ONE

MOMSEN, JULY 1950

Before Benita awoke, Marianne rose and took the train to Momsen to see Franz Muller.

No matter how many times she made this trip, the landscape remained foreign. The craggy mountains and flat green valleys dotted with cows, the patches of woods and hay huts were like something out of a fairy tale – complex, shadowy, and intricate. So unlike the wide open farmland of Weisslau. How she still missed it. Nothing could hide on the flat plain of northern Silesia – armies, visitors, weather, all were apparent from kilometres away. And Marianne felt at home with this transparence.

For a brief stretch, the Isar River ran alongside the tracks. It came down from the high mountains, fast and pale, full of some mineral that turned it a livid, almost unnatural whitish green. To Marianne, it reeked of menace. The ashes of Ribbentrop, Keitel, and Frick – those architects of Nazi horror – had been scattered along its banks. By whose decision? The random assignment of some government automaton? Or by their own wishes? Was there some symbiotic energy these men had felt? On the far side rose the jagged mountain peaks.

When Marianne had first arrived in this area at the end of the war, a freshly mounded pile of earth ran alongside this river. As she rode into Momsen with Carsten Kellerman for the first time, she saw men and women scrabbling around on its banks, digging.

What are they doing? she had asked.

Looking for their people, he had answered, his eyes inscrutable.

This was the grave of hundreds of marchers, he explained, the end point for those wretched collections of prisoners driven west from concentration camps. Why? For what reasons were they marched? At that point, the war was as good as over. Everyone knew. But still the SS had marched those prisoners until they dropped from exhaustion and then shot them when they fell. So the dead had lain here until the townspeople buried them, under this pile of earth. And after capitulation, some small number of brothers and fathers and friends and cousins returned to look for their loved ones. Marianne would never forget that.

But the townspeople went about their business as if it had never happened. They fished and washed in the river and walked alongside it in the evenings. No one spoke of the prisoners they had watched stumble and die along its banks. No one erected a marker over their bones.

At Momsen station, Marianne got off. She had steeled herself for the encounter, but now that she was actually here, her hands were cold and clammy and her face felt hot. Better to be quick and done with it. The children would wonder where she was and, left to their own devices, they would certainly forget their studies. Fritz would get into trouble . . . Benita was as good as another child when it came to discipline.

Marianne had intended to confide her plan to Ania, but something had stopped her. Ania had seemed surprised to learn of Benita's affair, but not shocked. It was clear she did not share Marianne's moral outrage – and why should she? She had never known Connie. And from what Marianne could discern, her own husband's life as a resister remained opaque. Ania was deeply silent on the subject. Marianne suspected marital tragedies that went beyond the man's death. And it was her philosophy not to disturb them – what good was opening a wound that had sealed itself shut? So she let it be, though deep down, she was disappointed by Ania's indifference. Marriage to Kellerman had put distance between them. But, unlike Franz Muller, Carsten Kellerman was a good man, at least.

In the month since Benita had announced her engagement, a stilted, awkward air had settled over their flat. Marianne and Benita skirted each other and exchanged cool, polite conversation only when necessary. Fortunately, the children were too absorbed in their own activities to notice the chill. Martin and Fritz would soon depart for the boarding school Katarina and Elisabeth attended, and they were busy roaming the hills and fields around Tollingen, enjoying their summer holiday.

But this silence in their flat could not go on forever. Even in her anger, Marianne loved her friend. Benita needed protection. She was easy prey – so fragile and romantic and readily swayed. For all Marianne knew, Muller might harbour a false sense of her fortune and believe her to be rich. After all, when he'd met her, she'd lived in a castle. And who knew what his debts were, or his prospects?

It was easy to find the shop where Herr Muller worked. There was only one coffin maker in Momsen. It sat on the first floor of a hulking, coal-smoke-stained building, still pocked with bullet holes. In the final days of the war, the local Hitler Youth and Home Guard had put up a fierce, irrational fight, losing countless lives, destroying buildings and bridges. And the mad captain in charge of this motley group was now a town councillor. Momsen was as bad as Ehrenheim, in Marianne's view.

To the left of the shop, Marianne found a doorway with a list of names. MULLER, one read. So he lived here, too. Marianne could not imagine Benita calling this home. She was a woman who lived for creature comforts and pretty dresses. It bolstered Marianne's sense of rightness to think that she was sparing her friend from such a fate.

A little girl opened the door when Marianne knocked: pale, dark haired, and unusually slim with wide, wary eyes.

'Can I help you?' the girl asked.

'Is this the shop of Franz Muller?' Marianne asked.

The girl nodded. She looked about Martin's age. 'Would you like to come in?' she asked. 'Papa!' she called into the shop.

Marianne was taken aback. So the man had a daughter. It rendered him less monstrous.

The door opened into a gloomy alcove and from somewhere inside, she heard the grating of a saw, which at this moment knocked off. 'Clotilde?' came a man's voice, and heavy footfalls across the floor.

And then Franz Muller stood at the entrance. In the flesh, his face looked dismayingly ordinary, free of the darkness Marianne had attached to it in her mind's eye.

'You can invite our visitor in –' he began, and then broke off, recognising Marianne.

'Frau von Lingenfels,' he said in surprise. 'Come in.' He held open the door. 'Can I offer you something – we don't have much here – but a cup of tea? Some biscuits?'

'That's all right,' Marianne said. 'Just a moment of your time.'

'Ah.' He nodded. 'Clotilde, will you leave us? You can go upstairs and see if Grosspapa needs help.'

The girl's dark eyes passed from her father to Marianne with curiosity. Then she grabbed her coat off a hook. 'When shall I come back?'

'I will come get you,' Franz said. 'Go on – but say goodbye to Frau von Lingenfels first.'

'Goodbye,' the girl said. 'Please come again.'

It seemed such a curious thing to say – come again to a coffin shop? Did they have many repeat visitors? Or had she mistaken Marianne for a friend? The girl's innocence was disarming. Marianne watched as her narrow back disappeared.

Marianne followed Herr Muller into the shop. It was a long,

narrow place, with coffins lining one wall, and the planks and boards they were made of stacked high on the other – so much wood and so many supplies for preserving the dead. It was an ugly business. In the corner was a modest table and four chairs. Perhaps this was where Herr Muller sat to sell his wares to vulnerable, grief-stricken clients. This too shored up her resolve.

He pulled a chair out for her and sat down.

'Herr Muller,' Marianne began. 'I won't waste your time – you are a busy man, I can see. I wanted, however, to tell you that Benita has informed me of your plans.' She made an effort not to look away. In all the hopeless meetings with Nazi officials that she had conducted when Albrecht was in prison, she had learned how to return a gaze.

'Our plan . . . ?' he asked.

'Your plan to *marry*.' She let the word sit between them. 'And I would like you to know that I am against it.'

'Ah.' The man looked stricken.

'Benita's first husband was my good friend,' she continued. 'A very dear friend, and a man of great character. He gave his life fighting against Hitler and the Nazis, and I don't believe it is right that his widow, and more importantly, his son, be joined' – she hesitated, gathering courage – 'to a man with your past.'

Outside, a wagon clattered down the street. But in the room full of coffins, Herr Muller mounted no defence. He had shockingly blue eyes. Marianne had forgotten this.

'Does Benita know you're here?' he asked finally.

'No.' Marianne swallowed.

'Ah.' He nodded.

Marianne waited for an outburst of indignation. She had prepared for this. But still he said nothing.

'I hope to keep this conversation between us,' she said into the silence. 'I promised her husband before he died that I would look out for her. And that I would look out for his son.'

'I understand.' Herr Muller nodded.

'You understand?' Marianne repeated.

The man lifted his eyes.

'I love Benita,' he said. 'She is a good woman and she deserves a good life. And I . . .' He paused. 'I wish it were different. I wish my life had not been as it was.' His blue eyes flashed at hers. 'And I am deeply sorry for the loss of your husband and hers. They were brave men.'

Marianne stared at him. To her horror, she felt that she was going to cry. Or worse – that she was about to snort and sob and explode with all the ungraceful, unholy sadness that she had locked up inside her. And once she started she would never stop.

She could not let this happen. So she sat straight as an arrow and focused on the coffins – the dark knots of pine and the stippling of oak, the gleam of the hinges. Silence welled around them, this time not awkward but necessary, like a cocoon. From upstairs came the sounds of footsteps, muffled voices – the sweet chirp of the girl and the lower, grumpier tone of the grandfather, whoever he was. Marianne held on to these like a lifeline, trying to make out the words of their conversation. The effort calmed her. The hard knot in her throat dissipated.

With as much dignity as possible, she rose.

Herr Muller followed, jumping to pull back her chair. When they arrived at the threshold, he bowed. 'I will consider your words,' he said.

'Thank you,' Marianne managed, bowing her head.

When she was around the corner she stopped, her chest heaving. She had intended to mention the Russian, Muller's time in the east, and the fact of Benita's innocence, her trust, her naïveté. What had happened? Somehow Muller's lack of argument had rendered her preparations irrelevant. She had got what she wanted.

Albrecht, she called out in her mind, *I did what was right, didn't I?* But it was almost as if she were talking to herself.

CHAPTER TWENTY-TWO

TOLLINGEN, JULY 1950

Benita was meeting Franz to talk about the future. She had not seen him since their engagement – first Clotilde had been sick, then his father, and then work had been too busy (too many dead people, Benita joked in a moment of lightness). But she had finally managed to corral him. Their marriage plans would need to be accelerated. Marianne's response to their news was even worse than Benita had imagined, and she hated living with her in this new, uncomfortable silence. Every day was like a punishment – and for what? Loving a man Marianne did not approve of? It was insulting, and worse, condescending. As if she had no right to her own future. Benita owed Marianne gratitude for finding Martin when she had given him up for dead, and for that she would be forever grateful. But she did not owe Marianne the rest of her life. She waited for Franz at Bemmelman's Café in a state of agitation, clinking the spoon in her cup of coffee.

Usually Bemmelman's made Benita happy. It was new, for one thing, and she liked new. She liked the high, gleaming windows and chic metal tabletops. She liked the sweetened cream and the selection of modern tortes with their bright out-of-season fruits and glossy layers of gelatin.

Benita held no reverence for anything old or historic. History was horrible, a long, sloppy tail of grief. It swished destructively behind the present, toppling everyone's own personal understanding of the past. It was, in part, why she felt such an urgent need to remarry. For Marianne, history came above all else; for Benita, it was death.

From the moment Franz walked in, though, Benita knew something was not right. His usually calm, placid face was edged with worry. And he looked as though he had not slept in weeks.

'Franzl,' she said, wrinkling her brow. 'What is it? You look like a man who has swallowed a monster.'

He shook his head and sat across from her. 'It isn't right' were the first words from his mouth. Not *Hello* or *How are you* or *You look beautiful*. The rudeness was utterly unlike him.

'*What* isn't?' she asked.

Franz looked out the window at the drizzle. 'I can't marry you, Benita.'

Benita pretended that she had not heard him.

'You can't what?' she asked.

On the street, a group of jabbering teenage girls scuttled past.

'I can't marry you, Benita. It wouldn't be right.'

For Benita, the whole world lurched.

'*Right?*' she managed to ask. 'For who?'

'For you.' Franz sighed. 'For Martin. You deserve better.'

'Better than what? Is this about the flat?' The thought flooded her with relief, and she grasped it like a life raft. 'I don't care about the flat – we will move someday, and in the meantime, we can find a place for your father – a room in the house on the corner, maybe, or—'

'I don't mean that,' Franz interjected, his voice harsh.

Benita sat back.

'You are the wife of a resister. You deserve a man who has done better with his life.'

Benita stiffened. This was not a term Benita had ever used: *resister,* referring to Connie and Albrecht and the others. It was Marianne's word. 'Why do you say this?' she asked, reaching across the table for his hand. 'Did Marianne say something to you? Did she come here—'

Franz looked away, and his voice was tired. 'It's the truth.'

'According to who?' Benita demanded. 'According to Marianne? She came here, didn't she? She talked to you! Look me in the eye and tell me she didn't!'

'This is not about Marianne,' Franz said. 'It doesn't matter what she did.'

'How dare she! She came here and talked to you behind my back! As if I were a child – smaller than a child, a toy – something to move around as she likes! She *never* liked you.' She lowered her voice to something like a hiss. 'She blames you for that dead Russian in the woods, and you know what? I would kill him again if I had to! Just to show her it was me who did it—'

'Benita—'

'It's true, Franz. You *know* that. She doesn't understand – she sees everything through her principles and ideas. And it doesn't matter! It doesn't matter what she thinks! What about *you*? Aren't you happy when we are together? Don't I make you happy?' She paused. 'Connie is *dead*!' It came out harshly, catching in her throat. She was aware that her voice had risen but didn't care. Let all the sheep-like patrons of Bemmelman's be shocked. Let them whisper and avert their eyes. 'But we are alive! And we have suffered, too! Don't we deserve this happiness?'

'Deserve?' Franz asked quietly, his eyes remote. 'I don't deserve anything, Benita.'

'You had to leave your family! You had to march into the east and nearly starve and freeze, and God knows what else – and now it's over! The war is over! And finally we can begin something new!'

'Stop!' Franz commanded. 'You can't say this! Your husband, Marianne's husband, they died for something they knew was right – and the rest of us followed along, did as we were told, and looked away. I can't *erase* that – I can't just begin again—'

'Why not? Is there any other choice?'

Dishes clinked and voices murmured around them. The cash register chimed. Someone laughed.

'There are always choices.' Franz looked at her. 'I can choose to let you go. *You* can begin a new life.'

'But I don't want to begin a new life.' Benita was crying now. 'Not without you. I don't care what you did! It doesn't matter! I would love you if you were Hitler himself!'

Franz stared at her and his face was a stranger's.

'You have no shame, Benita,' he said finally. 'And for me, shame is the only right way to live.'

Benita sat back.

This was the end. Her own stupid words repeated in her head. In the silence, Benita could see the future: no pleasant homely flat with flowers in the window and a place for Clotilde and Martin to study; no wide, soft bed to sleep in; no lovemaking; no new, ordinary, from-scratch life, full of simple things like cooking and marketing and Sunday walks along the river. No mornings of sunshine and coffee and growing old together.

For Franz there was only the motion of these things. His soul was already in hell. It was not Marianne who had come between them, but the past.

CHAPTER TWENTY-THREE

MOMSEN, AUGUST 1950

When Ania's waters broke, the convent hospital in Ehrenheim was still under construction. So Carsten drove her to the American military hospital outside Momsen. It was nearly empty. And as soon as he handed her off to the nurses, he turned around and drove home.

Then Ania could moan and clutch her belly and stop gritting her teeth. The nurses were kind, albeit alarmed. They were young American girls trained to bind wounds and dress amputations, not deliver babies. The doctor arrived and proclaimed it too late to induce the 'twilight sleep', and the nurses squeezed her hands and smoothed her forehead in terrified support. But Ania was not concerned. She had already delivered two babies without such interventions – she knew only that she wanted to return home as quickly as possible. She had secrets to keep.

Improbably, she had managed to keep Rainer hidden. Like some awful Rapunzel, he was locked in the castle, only he was free to come and go as he pleased. From the moment Ania saw him, she had understood what he wanted. It was not exposure or revenge. For all his anger and despair, he did not wish to destroy the life she had created for their sons. He wanted to see his boys. He was deathly ill and, like a shamed and beaten animal, he was looking for a safe place to die.

Burg Lingenfels was closed down. Last autumn, Carsten had boarded the windows as she and Marianne had covered what little furniture remained. They had planned to reopen it this summer, but then had not. Marianne was busy with her new project – sorting Albrecht's papers – and travelling a great deal. And last year, the local teenagers had used the empty castle to get into trouble. It was better to keep it shut up. There were only mice and swallows nesting in the stone walls, water rats and frogs burrowing into the chinks of the moat. No one went there except for Wolfgang, whom Carsten had tasked with checking on it from time to time.

Ania had been forced to involve her boys in their father's return. Ever dutiful, but simmering with resentment, they had half walked, half carried Rainer up the hill from the Kellerman farm. Wolfgang had arranged a straw pallet in the castle's kitchen, along with a supply of water to drink. Anselm brought him a plate of food every night – he barely ate. Presumably, while she lay here giving birth to this new baby, her boys tended to their father – locked in some weird reversal with the man who had never cared for them.

Ania's contractions sped forward until the pain was as constant as her heartbeat – rhythmic and all consuming, it obliterated worry. She was almost grateful. Rainer would be discovered or not. Her boys would tend to him or leave him for the ravens. Their life would explode or continue on the trajectory she had wrestled it onto. There was nothing she could do.

The baby came fast. In thirty violent minutes Ania pushed her out. Even four weeks early, she was as plump and smooth faced as an Eskimo. With her round dark eyes, she regarded the world impassively and then fell asleep. This was, apparently, what a child of Carsten's was like. Or maybe this was simply a baby of peace-time: satisfied, round cheeked, and enigmatic. Swaddled in US Army-issue blankets, she seemed to belong to some promising international future rather than a defeated Germany.

Ania handed her to the nurse and attempted to rise to her feet.

'No, no,' the nurse protested in alarm. 'Rest now, because you'll need your strength when you go home.' What did she know?

The nurses plied her with glasses of lukewarm water and sleep-ing pills. Carsten would not return for her until morning anyway.

Ania did not want to see the baby. So she took the pills they offered and drifted in and out of a thick, dreamless sleep, waking now and then to stare through the window at the courtyard, the bleached white paths across the grass like a criss-cross of bones.

The next morning, she woke to find Benita sitting at the foot of her bed.

It took Ania a moment to remember where she was.

'Benita,' she managed to say. 'Did you come to see me?' The idea seemed incredible. She had not seen Benita for so long – possibly not since the wedding.

'Why else? I went to the farm yesterday and heard the news.'

Benita did not look well. Ania could see this. She did not have her usual rosy cheeks and neatly arranged hair. She was wearing a shabby brown cardigan. And there were dark circles under her eyes.

'Is everything all right?' Ania began, but a nurse appeared, holding the baby. Her baby. The idea was still unaccustomed. Ania regarded the swaddled creature and felt nothing.

'*There* she is!' Benita exclaimed. For a moment, enthusiasm restored her beauty. She was the sort of woman who lit up in the presence of an infant. Her love of Martin had always made Ania feel sorry for her own sons, both loved so much less lavishly.

'Can I hold her? Please?' Benita asked.

Ania nodded.

The nurse laid the baby in Benita's arms.

'You're so lucky,' she said, her eyes filling. 'She's beautiful! And you can enjoy her. No wars and bombs to protect her from, and all this . . .' She hesitated, then landed on the word: 'Safety. Do you know, when Martin was a baby I was so worried he would be crushed in a bombing that I turned our icebox into a crib. I thought it would save him if the ceiling caved in – as if an icebox would have protected him!' She shifted the baby, who made a faint purring sound. 'I was such a child.'

'We were all children.' Ania sighed.

'I didn't intend to disrespect Connie, you know,' Benita announced with sudden ferocity. 'If I *had* married Herr Muller, it would not have harmed Connie's memory.'

'If you had—?' Ania repeated.

'We were engaged.' Benita sat back. 'I thought Marianne told you.' She looked at the ceiling, and tears slid down her cheeks. How seamlessly she cried, as if she went through life filled to the brim.

Ania shook her head.

'Marianne didn't approve.'

It required no more explanation. Benita's will had never been a match for Marianne's.

'So you have decided not to . . . ?' Ania ventured.

'Decided!' Benita snapped and stood up, still holding the baby. She went to the window and then turned back. '*I* decided nothing. But Marianne told Franz she was against it and he – it doesn't matter. I was stupid to imagine I could be happy again.'

'It's not why I came anyway.' She adjusted the baby and wiped her tears with the back of her hand. 'I came to say goodbye. After we take the boys to Salem, I am going home to Frühlinghausen.'

'To Frühlinghausen?' Ania repeated. This surprised her as much as anything else Benita had said. 'To take care of your sister?'

Benita tried to smile at the baby in her arms. 'It's where I belong.'

Ania stared. Benita had always hated the town where she was born. 'What does Marianne say about this?'

'She doesn't know.'

Ania regarded this woman she knew so well and yet not at all. Their lives had become entwined during such a strange time – without context, severed from the past, before the future. A time dictated by basic needs. What did they really know of each other?

'Are you sure?' she asked, the words sounding obtuse even to her own ears.

The baby's little hand clasped and unclasped against Benita's neck.

'Nothing is sure, is it?' Benita said, almost dreamily. 'That's what Marianne doesn't understand.'

The baby began to cry.

'Here.' Benita bent and placed her in Ania's arms.

The nurse appeared in the doorway. 'Do you want to feed her, Frau Kellerman? Or should I give her the bottle?'

'Feed her,' Benita said to Ania with sudden surprising authority. 'Take care of her. That is the most important thing.'

'*Auf Wiedersehen*.' She leaned down to kiss Ania's cheek.

'*Mach's gut*,' Ania said, and caught her hand. *Make it good* – an old expression her own mother had used.

'You too.' Benita squeezed her fingers and brought them to her lips. And then she was gone.

'Does the baby have a name yet?' the young nurse asked after Benita left.

Ania began to shake her head no. Then a name occurred to her, first as a joke – almost a joke, and then real – a name like a talisman, the name of the strongest, stubbornest, most difficult, and wisest woman she knew.

'Marianne,' she said. 'Her name is Marianne.'

The nurse smiled. 'Marianne,' she repeated in her American accent. 'Pretty!' She looked down at the baby, who had latched onto Ania's breast hungrily. 'Be a good girl, little Marianne.'

CHAPTER TWENTY-FOUR

SALEM CASTLE, SEPTEMBER 1950

The day the boys were scheduled to start Salem Castle Boarding School was clear and crisp and sharp edged in a way that was unusual for the region, which was known for its soft, moist air and bouts of low pressure blamed for headaches and illnesses and despair. A brisk autumn wind blew off the Alps, scattering sunlight across Lake Constance so it looked like an audience of people clapping hands.

Marianne had hired a driver for the trip. She sat in the front, straight backed, long necked, craning around every so often to remind the children of a piece of history or point out a landmark. And sitting in the back, sandwiched between Martin and the door, Benita hated her.

You think you know so much! she wanted to say. *But you know nothing! You have never even been in love!* It was something Benita understood after all these years of living together: Marianne, who had once seemed so intimidatingly wise, was in fact ignorant. She was her own kind of dreamer, a blind mathematician skating along the thin surface of life, believing in the saving power of logic, reason, and information, overlooking the whole murky expanse of feeling and animal instinct that was the real driver of human behaviour, the real author of history.

Since that awful day when Benita returned to their flat from Bemmelman's, Marianne had, several times, attempted something like an apology. *You know, if you would like, I could go back to Herr Muller and tell him I had no right to speak as I did,* Marianne had said one evening when Benita staggered blearily out of her room at suppertime, emerging for the first time that day. Benita only stared. Did the woman really believe it was so simple? That a few well-chosen words could make everything right? Or was this simply her shrewd play for forgiveness – a way to exonerate herself without ceding the territory she had won?

No, Benita had replied. Unlike Marianne, she understood that what had happened was not caused, but exposed, by the other woman's interference. There was a tight black cave where Franz Muller's heart, or something more than his heart – his *personhood* – should be. He had lost it in the war, and there was no getting it back. There was only a careful sidestep around the place it had once lived – a dance of ignorance that she had mastered without even knowing it. And there was no going back now.

Marianne was elated by the fact that finally all their children, Martin included, would be settled at the fine German boarding school that Albrecht and Connie and their fathers before them had attended. Salem was a school remarkably untarnished by affiliation with the Nazis – attended by the aristocracy, founded by a Jew. Marianne believed anything could be solved by a good education. *Look at the vast ignorance of the Nazis!* she liked to exclaim. If only they had understood music and art, if they had read Kant and Goethe and listened to Mozart instead of burning books, the world might have been spared. Benita understood but did not agree. Look at that hate-mongering Goebbels – he was a doctor of philosophy!

In the back of the car, Fritz and Katarina argued fiercely. Elisabeth rested her head against the window and feigned an air of has-

sled sophistication. Martin, absorbing his mother's despair, was
silent. For his sake, Benita tried to rouse herself. 'Do you suppose
they'll give you a hot supper tonight?'

'It's never a hot supper on the first night,' Elisabeth informed
them, rousing herself enough to answer. 'Dried fish, smoked
ham, brown bread.' She wrinkled her nose. 'I hope you aren't too
hungry.'

As they rounded the final bend in the road, Salem Castle
sprang into view, its angular red roofs and white walls rising from
the fields like an elegant mini-city.

Fritz let out a whoop and Elisabeth a theatrical sigh of relief.

'Aha.' Marianne turned around and beamed. 'You see, Martin?
Isn't it beautiful?'

Martin nodded, but his face remained sombre.

'Welcome,' Marianne said grandly, turning to face forward
again, 'to your new home.'

Benita placed her hand on her son's leg and squeezed, but
being a young man now, he moved it away.

At the castle entrance, there was a throng of students, attendants,
prefects, and other foreboding-looking officials giving orders.
Fine pieces of luggage, instrument cases, and steamer trunks
were piled in small mountains. The von Lingenfelses were immediately absorbed into the scene – Elisabeth and Katarina calling
out to friends, Marianne greeting teachers; even Fritz appeared
at home, scrambling towards some coveted position in the crush.

Martin and Benita alone stood beside the car.

'Come along, come along.' Marianne strode over, seeing their
inaction. 'The bellboys will unload.' Benita and Martin followed
her through the sea of bright young people, a whole eager generation of Germans. They would be spared their parents' sins, as Adenauer promised. No one even spoke of the war, the concentration
camps, the millions of murders. The parents themselves looked

relieved, if sceptical. They were signing their young over to an institution – one that was venerable, sanctified, and thoroughly vetted, but they understood the perils of indoctrination. Even Marianne, for all her bluster, was not immune to doubt. Benita detected strain beneath her show of cheer. All three of her children would now be out of the house. Any mother would feel the smart.

Benita, on the other hand, felt oddly empty and cried out. She had resigned herself ages ago to this peculiar aristocratic fate: Her boy – her baby – would be swallowed whole by this austere castle, occupied for centuries by the class of people her own humble peasant family had toiled to serve. He was to be admitted, completely, into their ranks. This was progress, wasn't it? Even if it created distance between them.

'Here he is,' Marianne called out to an officious young prefect, pointing at Martin. 'Martin Constantine Fledermann.' The full name was jarring – Benita never used it. 'Ah.' The prefect introduced himself in the clipped manner of an ex-Hitler Youth. 'Follow me to your quarters,' he instructed. And for a moment it seemed this would be their goodbye.

But then Martin turned and embraced his mother with all the fierceness of a younger child. 'Goodbye, Mama,' he said as Benita held him. And the word filled her with happiness. *Mama.* If nothing else, she had given birth to him.

Benita and Marianne were silent on the drive to the inn. Marianne knitted, her needles tapping. She had learned this skill in the last few years from Ania and approached it as if it were a quaint, mildly entertaining art form rather than a tiresome matter of necessity, which it had always been in the Gruber household.

The inn was shabby – an ugly, half-timbered house with a crooked roof and narrow yellow-glass windows on the ground floor. 'I'll have dinner sent up,' Marianne announced. 'You can join me if you wish.'

Benita demurred. She was happy to be left alone. And anyway, she was not hungry.

They parted at the bottom of the stairs.

But once Benita closed the little slanted door to her room under the eaves and saw the plain wooden cross mounted on the wall, the brown shaded lamp and worn coverlet, she knew she would die if she sat down.

So instead, she descended the stairs and walked through the dingy foyer and out onto the street. The inn was located on a narrow pedestrian throughway, and people walked past, shuttling children home to supper, carrying shopping bags. Benita felt raw and exposed. She was stripped of the love she had wrapped around her like a protective cloak. No more Franz. No more Martin. Suddenly, she saw everything in its harsh, naked state. She felt the pulse of the lives lived inside the mean little houses she passed: selfish or generous, kind or unkind, ugly or tolerable, almost all of them sad. And she saw the histories of the people passing by like x-rays stamped on their faces – ugly, mutinous tracings of dark and light: a woman who had informed on a neighbour, a man who had shot children, a soldier who had held his dying friend in his arms. Yet here they were, carrying groceries, holding children's hands, turning their collars up against the wind. As if their moments of truth – the decisions by which they would be judged and would judge themselves – hadn't already come and passed. What a sham this new German present was! An irrelevant time – a mad scramble to cast votes after the verdict had already been reached.

From behind the inn's gate, there was the dull thud of a beer stein knocking against another, a clatter and an outburst of scolding. Benita turned her feet towards the noise and discovered a meager *Biergarten* behind a stone wall, long roughly hewn tables arranged over gravel. It was nearly empty: a group of older men sat in the corner, another group stood at the bar. The heavy smell of stale cigarette smoke hung in the air. Benita sat at the end of an empty table and ordered a schnapps.

She thought of her mother, poor hardworking Ilse Gruber – how she had loved her glass of schnapps before bed. And now she was dead. Benita had never even said goodbye. *To you, Mama!* she thought as she swallowed the rough, tangy liquid, flinching at the burn. She felt a rush of sadness for her own loss, and for the decidedly unsparkling life of her mother, a woman who had existed entirely outside the reaches of love. And now she, Benita Gruber, would become just like her. She would return to Frühlinghausen in shame and be consumed by her own roots.

Benita finished her first schnapps and ordered another. The world grew less bleak. She caught the bartender eyeing her curiously: a middle-aged woman in a proper dress, drinking alone. Did he see some trace of the girl she had once been? The Benita who Connie had boasted could turn even a blind man's head? A woman whose smile made Franz Muller blush? Her knees began to feel watery. And the harsh tragedy of the world was enveloped in a soft, forgiving haze. The beer garden was filling up. A small group of teenagers sat at the end of her table. They were boisterous girls and boys, poor kids, workers' children, the girls in their new American-style full skirts, but their hair still worn in plain farm-girl cuts.

A man sat down beside Benita. He was young, a boy really, and handsome with a particular blooming sort of handsomeness that would not last, was even now beginning to thicken and dissolve. 'Another schnapps for the lady,' he called, 'and a beer for me.' He had the air of a posturing teenager. How amazing that such an impulse could still exist! That a young man could still care enough to pretend to be something he wasn't. And the girls, too – she saw it suddenly, these young women, self-consciously sipping their beer-and-lemonades, affecting worldliness. It was at once horrible and marvellous. It made her feel a thousand years old.

'What is a beautiful woman like you doing drinking by herself?' the boy asked. His curls poked out from underneath his cap, small and sweaty and distinct. Under the table, Benita felt the warmth of his leg against hers.

'What is a young man like you doing with a beautiful woman drinking by herself?' she found herself asking, her old sharp-tongued self returning.

In a moment, two other boys joined them – straight from work at a building site, plaster dust on their jackets and under their fingernails. And all of a sudden it was a party! More schnapps and beer and wursts with curry ketchup and crusty *Brötchen*. When was the last time food had tasted so good?

The night grew cool and when Benita shivered, the boy – the man, now that she was playing along – gave her his jacket. It was warm and smelled of paint and sawdust and, beneath this, of him. It had been so long since she had been drunk. Franz had never drunk more than one, maybe two beers, which was like a thimbleful of water for an ox, and it had never occurred to her to outdrink him. Before that, during the war, with the Russians and their stench of vodka, she had never wanted to touch the stuff. Now she was reminded of those early, heady days of her romance with Connie, when he had filled her with champagne and berries, *Sekt* and peach juice, and Brandy Alexanders, delicious, exotic drinks. She had the same lovely clumsy feeling, a sort of numbness in her face and jerkiness to her vision. Dear Connie. She felt a swell of warmth for him – he had shown her a good time in the beginning. Once, he had presented her with a fox stole that wrapped around her shoulders with a glimmering, silky softness that made her feel like a film star. A woman everyone envied. And Connie, confident, sleepy eyed, with one arm draped around her, had enjoyed the attention as much as she did.

In the middle of this reverie, Marianne appeared.

She stood in the doorway of the grubby *Biergarten*, a homely shawl clutched around her shoulders, her eyes searching the crowd. For an instant, her eyes met Benita's and a look of surprise, even shock, registered so transparently in them that Benita felt a corresponding jolt. There was no joining these two worlds – Marianne's ordered existence on one side, and these boys, this place, this buoyant, drunken feeling of irresponsibility on the other. And so Benita looked away. It was not so much a decision as an instinct. She threw her head back and extended her neck in a way she knew was loose and inviting. She laughed an indiscreet laugh. Out of the corner of her eye, she saw Marianne hesitate as if considering whether to barge in.

But she didn't. And a moment later she was gone.

Benita was disappointed and relieved at once.

The boy placed his hand on her knee, rubbing the fabric of her dress against her thigh in a way that made her skin feel rough. What did it matter? Benita rested her head against his shoulder – she was the slut and idiot Marianne had always thought she was. She was nothing but a stupid girl. The empty doorway where Marianne, her friend, her flatmate, her coparent, really, had stood, was like a black hole.

Upstairs, in her room under the eaves, what happened was quick and unclear. Benita floated through it as if from above: the sweaty hands on her breasts and the boy's wurst breath, the hot, surprising baby smoothness of his belly, the hard strength of his thighs. He was no expert. And more surprising, he had a false leg below his right knee, a hard stalk of wood that pressed against her shin through the pants he kept up around his knees. Did she imagine it? She reached down, but he pushed away her hand. And so she let him finish without knowing for sure.

Only after he was asleep, with one arm thrown gratefully across her breasts, snoring slightly, did she verify. Gently pushing up the leg of his pants, she felt the smooth wooden shape of the false limb and ran her hand to the end where it attached to his leg with primitive leather straps. A delicate nub of scar tissue covered the bone, dimpled and uneven, yet still smooth – as delicate as the head of a penis. She winced and the boy stirred in his sleep. Benita sat beside him for a while, in the lamplight that shone through the window, beside his clumsy, damaged body. A war injury, probably, despite his youth. Maybe he had been one of those hapless boys ordered to the front when no one else was left, shot on the spot if they so much as looked the wrong way. Or maybe he had been a cruel child soldier and performed some God-awful task.

As quietly as she could, she gathered her things, the small bag she had packed, the shoes she had kicked off, the skirt she had dropped to the floor. Stepping carefully, she slipped into the hall and down the stairs, this time without question as to where she was going, and with the cold, relieving calm of purpose; and when she shut the door of the inn, there was a satisfying finality to the click, severing her ties to this strange in-between life.

CHAPTER TWENTY-FIVE

BURG LINGENFELS, OCTOBER 1950

Without Benita and the children, the flat in Tollingen was too quiet. No more Fritz scuffing the skirting boards in the hallway, no more piles of shoes by the door, no more Martin lying on the sunlit parquet with his books. And no more scent of Benita's coffee in the morning or *eau de gardenia* perfume wafting from her bedroom at night. No more strains of sentimental music drifting down the hall from her precious Victrola, though the player was still there. Theoretically, Marianne could have listened to a record. She herself had given the Victrola to Benita, but it wasn't in Marianne's nature to select an album, place it on the turntable, and play. Some innate self-consciousness, or even an inexplicable anxiety, held her back. One evening, she went to the shelf and hesitantly flipped through the collection of records – almost all were unfamiliar names and faces – until she landed on Benny Goodman. She knew who he was. But when the needle touched the record, the notes that blared forth were startlingly loud and by the time she had managed to adjust the volume, she was too jarred, too *caught*, really – a person mucking about in someone else's business – to want to hear more.

Now there was only the light tap of her own house shoes as she walked through the flat. For dinner she ate a roll spread with jam or butter and a thin slice of ham. Instead of using the wide kitchen table, she ate at her desk – a grand, polished Biedermeier she had inherited from one of the von Lingenfels cousins. She had moved it into the middle of the parlour, where she could look out of the bay windows to the town square below and write letters to the children – one each night.

The desk was her new home. And from behind it she threw herself into a fresh project: documenting a history of the German Resistance. Every day she drafted plans, wrote lists, and took notes. She wrote to old friends and acquaintances, asking for journals and photographs, copies of their letters. She organised Albrecht's papers but was too restless, too unsettled, to actually read them.

Benita had returned to the town where she was born, where Connie had 'discovered' her. Beyond this, Marianne knew nothing about the place. She had written to Benita asking how she was and when she would be back, but received no response. Marianne's last image of the girl, sitting on the lap of some loutish *Biergarten* youth, was a horrible one.

Alone in the flat with no one to distract her, Marianne was left to deliberate over Benita's departure. She had overstepped. She should not have gone to see Franz Muller. She had allowed her own sense of betrayal to influence her actions. And when she had tried to apologise, something in her apology fell short.

In their letters from school, the children asked why Benita had moved. Only Martin was silent on the subject. So far, he had written two dutiful little letters detailing his life: early-morning chapel and cold showers and endless maths. Obviously, he wrote to his mother, too. What did she tell him of her decision to return to Frühlinghausen, a place she had only ever spoken of with scorn? Marianne was afraid to ask.

She began to compose another letter to Benita, one that sought to offer a more complete apology. But where to begin? *Our flat feels* empty without you. *The flowers on the balcony have shrivelled without your care and when I noticed, I soused them and now they look both shrivelled and waterlogged, if that is possible. Herr Dressler asks after you every day when I walk past his flat.*

I owe you an apology, she wrote, and crossed it out.

I was wrong to intervene in your plans to marry and I am sorry, she wrote instead. *If you would like, I will return to Herr Muller and apologise myself. I did what I thought was right, at the expense of your happiness. I see now that it was not my place.* This did not sound right either. Too implicitly scolding. Too righteous.

The truth was that Marianne had misunderstood their relationship. She had imagined Benita's affair with Franz to be a mere diversion, a flight of fancy. She had not grasped how fundamental it was to Benita's happiness. If she had *known* . . . then what? Should she have applauded the choice? An ex-Nazi for a resister's wife? She could never celebrate this. But she had been wrong to interfere. This was what she needed to convey.

But it was so hard to say both what was true and also what was required! At her desk in the lonely parlour, a thick, doldrumy feeling threatened to descend on Marianne. Through her friendship with Benita, she found herself dragged into the quagmire of complexity. *Don't overcomplicate,* she had always advised Albrecht. *There is a right and a wrong in every situation, and it is our job to extract it.*

She stood abruptly and shook her head, capped the pen and folded the letter. She would finish it later.

A warm breeze blew through the open window. It was an unseasonably warm autumn day. The kind of day in which late field poppies bloomed and bees worked frantically to finish their work for the season. Years ago, she would have been preparing for the countess's party – ordering wine and champagne, cakes and cuts of meat. The thought made her want to climb the hill to Burg Lingenfels. She had not visited the castle in ages, not since they had boarded it up.

*   *   *

It was strange to climb the hill alone, no children running alongside her gathering flowers, throwing stalks of wheat, no Benita
trailing behind, stopping every so often to rest. But the sunshine
and Herr Kellerman's new herd of cows grazing on the hill went
a long way towards dispelling Marianne's loneliness. *What shall
we do with the castle?* she asked Albrecht as she walked. *Give it
to the state,* she imagined him saying, his voice unusually clear
in her head. His answer was easy to guess: he was too much the
aristocrat to suggest selling it. The very thought made her laugh.
Albrecht von Lingenfels, intellectual, revolutionary, hero, yes . . .
but a terrible businessman.

And then there it was – squat, yellow, and impervious. On this
day, Marianne felt only pleasure at the castle's intransigence. It
was like a steady friend. She quickened her pace. Here was the
old linden. Here was her favourite patch of stone wall. Here was
the footbridge, and the grand opening, like a wide dark mouth.
She tracked around the side to the smaller bridge that led to the
kitchen and stopped short.

There were voices coming from within. Marianne could not
make them out clearly, but one belonged to a woman. Arguing.
She froze and listened. It was Ania.

Marianne's heart gave a contradictory flutter – relief that it was
her friend and not some intruder and dismay at the awkwardness
of having arrived in the middle of a dispute. Who was Ania arguing with? She had never heard the woman so much as raise
her voice. Her tone was tense. Possibly she had come to check on
the castle and been accosted by some dangerous vagrant holed up
within its walls. They should have locked it up more thoroughly!

Marianne stooped to grab a large stone and tried the door
handle. It was unlocked. She threw it open, her heart racing.

But the scene in front of her did not appear violent.

At the table, a man sat before a bowl of soup. He was gaunt

and hollow eyed and obviously sick. Ania stood across the room, leaning against the old dry sink. A series of emotions crossed her friend's face. Shock, dismay, and then something like resignation.

Marianne stood, still holding the stone, and gaped.

'I'm sorry—' she began. 'I didn't know—'

The man looked from her to Ania and back again. With a frail hand, he pushed away the soup. 'This is your castle,' he said to Marianne.

The words sounded strange. Burg Lingenfels was not really *hers*.

He was a land surveyor, maybe, a tax auditor, a salesman of some sort? Her mind leapt towards possible explanations.

Still Ania did not speak.

'And Ania has not told you about me,' he said, dashing the possibilities.

Marianne looked at her friend, whose face was now turned to the floor. Milk spread in two dark stains from her breasts.

Marianne felt an overwhelming need to sit. From outside she could hear the swallows. Inside, the room was dark and close as a crypt.

'I was going to,' Ania said, finally lifting her eyes. 'You must believe this.'

Marianne stared at her.

The face that stared back was unfamiliar – sagging with despair and a chilling sense of calm.

'This is my husband,' Ania said.

When Marianne left the castle, the day outside was shockingly unchanged. The afternoon sun lay thick across the stubbled fields, the poppies bloomed . . . But she didn't see this. Her mind circled and darted like a bird whose nest has been destroyed.

Her own actions in the castle were a jumble in her mind.

He can't stay here, Marianne had said, coldly regarding the man Ania had just referred to as her husband. Ania had bowed her head.

Even in his sickly state, the man emanated cruelty. He narrowed his eyes and shrugged. *Where would you have her take me? To her new husband's home? To some American hospital?* They were more like threats than questions.

But maybe this was what Ania deserved? She had lied to Marianne, to Carsten, to everyone in her life. She had thrived under their misconceptions, abused Marianne's generosity, and taken advantage of her desire to help. She had married a man under false pretenses. And now she had brought this stranger to die at Burg Lingenfels. For this, she should be exposed.

But there was Carsten to consider. Surely the knowledge of his wife's deception would kill him. And he deserved better, even if she did not. He deserved to end his life in the upstanding and peaceful way in which he had lived it. And those poor boys, Anselm and Wolfgang, whom Marianne had never liked – suddenly she felt compassion for them. They were harnessed to their mother's lies.

So Marianne summoned her largest self and walked away. She left the man, this Rainer Brandt, whoever he was, to die in Burg Lingenfels. And she left Ania, who was not really Ania, who was in fact a liar and a false friend – a woman who had pretended to be something she wasn't – shackled to his death. Whoever Ania really *was*, Marianne did not care to know. Let her rot with that man in the castle.

The only thing Marianne could do was turn her back on them.

PART III

CHAPTER TWENTY-SIX

DORTMUND, JANUARY 11, 1923

One of Ania's earliest memories is of the day the French soldiers arrived in Dortmund.

She is twelve years old and her father has forbidden her to leave her room.

But from outside, she can hear the rumble of the troops. First the tanks, then the horses, then the African soldiers the French have brought from the colonies to help with the occupation. Frau Richter, the Fortzmanns' cook and housekeeper, says they are blood-thirsty men, ready to spear and eat German children at a signal from their French overseers. She says the shortest of them is nine feet tall, that they can breathe fire and throw flames, and will march half-naked across the continent, their heads bald as bladder balls. In comparison, the French soldiers will look like milkweeds – seedy, slender little men with devious faces, here to make off with the first valiant sputters of output from post-war German industry.

Ania is old enough to understand that Frau Richter is an ir-rational, superstitious woman with no education. But also that her husband and son died in the war, which they will all come to think of as the First War, but for now is still simply (optimistically, really) defined by a finite *the*. This loss grants Frau Richter a cer-tain authority about all things military.

The French are here to commandeer the coal factories that employ much of the city. It is the finest industry in all of Germany. *Reparation* is the bad word on every German's tongue. *Just like in the schoolyard,* Frau Richter says, rolling her eyes. *We took their lunch money, now they must take ours.* Last month, eight men were arrested – fancy men in top hats and tails, the owners of several local factories. *For shame,* Frau Richter said, looking at their picture in the paper. *Is it not enough to take away their businesses? Do they also have to take their dignity?*

Most of what Ania understands about politics comes from Frau Richter. Ania's father, Herr Doktor Fortzmann, is a man of the old kind and believes children should be silent before their superiors. He is against politics in general and longs for the restitution of the monarchy. They have seen nothing but rioting and inflation in the five years since Wilhelm II abdicated. And Ania knows not to mention the Communists. Her father has not recovered from the shock of their brief takeover of Bavaria, which, for a few weeks in 1919, became the Bavarian Soviet Republic. If he begins on the subject, no one will hear of anything else for days. For Doktor Fortzmann all was better under the kaiser. And he is the kaiser of his own home.

Because her father is a doctor, Ania's small family is able to live relatively well on a currency of traded goods – eggs and potatoes in exchange for stitches, help stacking wood or cleaning gutters for treating a sick child. And there are always sick children because the local coal factory workers live in such poor conditions. Unlike the many locals relying on cash wages in a period of food shortages and inflation, the Fortzmanns are at least warm and well fed.

Frau Fortzmann has not left her bedroom since Ania's younger brother died. Back pain. Chest pain. Her delicate constitution. She does not venture beyond the confines of her sitting room. *My sweet Ania,* she says when Ania brings the breakfast tray Frau Richter prepares each morning. She runs her hand through

Ania's hair and her eyes fill with tears. Ania can barely stand to look at her. Her breath smells of the chamomile tea she drinks, and underneath of something sour – the essence of inaction. *Tell me what is happening,* she asks. And Ania is nothing if not dutiful: *Frau Richter has a new cosy for the kettle, knitted by her sister. Father read from Corinthians last night. In school we studied fractions. Some men in Munich tried to kill the president.* All news is equal. She has no idea what to tell her mother, no idea what she might be most interested to hear. Frau Fortzmann listens without really listening. She pats Ania's hand if she stands nearby, or smoothes the soft skin with her thumb. For Ania, the act of recounting feels like vomiting. When she finishes, she immediately flees to the relative warmth of the kitchen and to more of Frau Richter's salacious talk of politics.

On this day, when the French troops roll in to occupy the Ruhr, Ania has already visited her mother and completed her daily quota of embroidery. Frau Richter has gone out on 'errands' and can certainly be found among the crowds gathered to watch the advancing troops. Herr Doktor Fortzmann is reading in his office, frowning over the latest news of German indignities. Only Ania is at a loose end, trapped in her room with the oppressively dark armoire, the stark painting of her paternal grandmother, and the tightly made bed she is not supposed to sit on. Out there in the world, not two blocks away, a conquering army is taking over her city, and here she is, locked in a chamber of relics.

Standing at the window and picking at the pills on her stockings, she has an idea. The most radically transgressive idea she has ever had in her life. She will climb out of the window, across the roof of the kitchen, down the mirabelle tree, and into the garden. If someone catches her, she will certainly receive the beating that lurks behind all her father's commands, implicit in the switch that peeks out from behind his umbrella stand and his perpetual air of restrained violence. She would rather die than catch this beating. So she will make sure she is not caught.

Ania crab-crawls along the window ledge to the flat roof, a move so nimble she is surprised at her own ability. At the edge, she shimmies down the rough tree trunk and drops to the ground. From there, she dashes along the bushes at the far side of the garden and into the alley. And with a heaving chest, she looks around. She has done it. She has escaped. It is the first time she has ever disobeyed her father; the feeling is thrilling and sickening.

Ania draws closer to Uhland Strasse and hears the booming rumble of tanks receding – she has missed it! – and the hard clip-clop of horses' hooves. But rounding the corner, she comes upon everyone: here are the citizens of Dortmund, lined up on both sides of the street, watching restively.

The French ride through the middle of the street on proud, high-stepping horses, bayonets poised on their shoulders like oversize needles. Underneath their helmets, though, they are disappointingly ordinary looking. There are no nine-foot Africans. No fire breathers or weasel-faced French overlords. But the soldiers' disregard for the crowd is an open insult. The air is thick with anger and hostility.

Ania edges her way forwards. She reaches the front line in time to witness a humiliating spectacle. One of the foot soldiers marching at the front of the battalion breaks formation to lunge towards a man in the crowd who has forgotten to remove his hat. The soldier knocks it to the ground.

The man, who is young, stocky, and strong looking – the kind of boy Frau Richter would call *ein richtige deutsche Bursche*, a real German lad – attempts to fight back, striking at the soldier, but the people around him grab his arms. It sends a stir through the crowd, a collective intake of breath. Once the soldier has moved on, the people release the young man's arms, and Ania watches him scurry forward to retrieve his hat, now rolling dangerously close to a set of stamping hooves. As he darts before the great beast, he nods at the mounted soldier – a small, demeaning act of self-preservation.

It is nothing in the grand scheme of things (they have just been through a war, after all), but at the time, Ania is shocked. The rough way the soldier swatted the hat from the man's head – it was as if he were an unruly child, or worse, an animal. It alters her understanding of what it means to be a German. This is a personal manifestation of defeat. This is what it means to be a member of a defeated nation.

Ania's next transgression is more complicated.

The chancellor of Germany has encouraged citizens in the Ruhr to engage in acts of passive resistance against the occupiers. The girls' troops at the Munich Gymnastics Installation carry signs proclaiming WE DON'T WANT TO BE YOUR SERFS. Workers at the steel and iron plants are on strike. In the south, there are violent clashes between Communists and right-wing *Freikorps* militias. Maybe Ania is influenced by all this protest. Or maybe she has simply reached the age of rebellion.

On the first Sunday of Lent, Ania is supposed to accompany her father to visit her grandmother and aunt. It is a tradition, like most in the Fortzmann household, that Ania hates. Aunt Gudrun believes it is her singular responsibility to mould Ania into a proper young woman. Since her mother has decided to become a useless invalid, Gudrun teaches Ania to wash and scrub and 'learn household responsibilities' and to sit absolutely straight and silent while the adults eat. So Ania is forced to perch on her aunt's horsehair sofa and nibble digestive biscuits while the adults eat slices of cream-topped gooseberry tart. The oppressive tick-tock of the clock, the sour air of the room, and the dry, shaggy bits of skin that hang from Grossmutter's face all make Ania think, in an oppressive, suffocating way, of death.

So, on this particular afternoon, when the time comes to leave for Gudrun's, she hides beneath the weeping willow in the back of the Fortzmanns' garden. Its branches hang to the ground and provide a thick, leafy cover.

The smooth patch of earth here is one of Ania's favourite places. She loves the smell of the garden wall's decaying stucco, the damp ground, her own warm hands after playing with the twigs and leaves and worms. She hides things under the willow's branches. For instance, the cheap novel she found on a park bench that she knows her father would disapprove of – too modern, too sensational. He believes in reading only the Bible and Schiller. Even Goethe is too liberal for him. Ania has also hidden the candy she pilfered from her class graduation party, a snake skeleton, and a colourful mosaic brooch she stole from her mother's dresser three months ago.

Why is this willow here in the Fortzmanns' orderly suburban garden? There is no pond, no stream, no river to quench its thirst. The tree is a leftover, someone told her once – maybe Frau Richter, who is, at heart, a romantic, or her uncle Dierck, who is young and bad and recently ran off to find work on a ship. The tree is left over from a time when the whole neighbourhood was marshland, dotted with ponds and sloughs and great waterbirds. Its bent, grief-stricken shape is a product of its longing. While Ania lies under its grand draping branches she feels that same longing – her own cells thirst for the disappeared body of water, her ears fill with the ghostly burble of an extinct stream.

On this particular Sunday, Ania does not go into hiding alone. She is accompanied by her best friend and neighbour, Otto Smeltz. When she hears Frau Richter calling, she grabs his hand and squeezes it.

Shhhhh, she whispers fiercely, and Otto's eyes widen in surprise.

He is a little nymph-like boy: thin and pale and dark haired, and he and Ania often play for hours under the willow, making hospitals for sick animals. Sometimes Otto pretends to be a girl and lets Ania braid his shaggy hair. They carve games in the cool, smooth ground, using pebbles as pieces.

No one else on Langebein Strasse plays with Otto Smeltz. For one thing, his father is not a doctor or a lawyer like the other men on the street. He is a shopkeeper who runs a small speciality goods shop in the city centre. For another thing, the family is bohemian, at least compared to everyone else. And also they are Jewish, immigrants from Poland.

Sometimes, when the weather is nice, his family plays music in the garden. Herr Smeltz has a fiddle and his wife a mouth harp. Their daughter, Susi, a wild girl with messy hair and an insolent expression, plays her accordion. It is considered unseemly – *like a carnival,* according to Frau Richter, who would have a heart attack if she knew how much time Ania spent with little Otto. On warm summer evenings, Ania opens her bedroom window and listens as she lies alone in bed.

This afternoon, Ania's rebellion makes Otto nervous. *When will you come out?* he whispers. *What if they don't leave without you? What will your father do when he finds you?* His questions nip at her high spirits. *Shut up,* she hisses, suddenly aware of her own power in their friendship. She is a year older and taller and also in possession of a more intangible authority. *Be still.*

Ania – Otto tugs at her sleeve and she shakes him off. *Shut up* – Ania clamps a hand over his mouth and watches an instinctive, animal-like fear jump in his eyes. Reluctantly, he stays with her and does not call out.

Later, when she is finally discovered by the policeman neighbour Frau Richter enlists to help with the search, Ania is both terrified and jubilant. *Why did you do this?* Doktor Fortzmann asks gravely, sitting in the big leather chair in his study. *You should know better.* He uses his deepest, most moral voice. The switch is propped against his chair.

He made me, she says, squirming and looking down at the carpet.

The Smeltz boy?

The policeman found Otto, too. But, unlike Ania, he was dragged by the ear to the police station.

She nods her head, thinking of the officer's expression. *It was his idea,* she says, and her heart races. *He wouldn't let me come out.*

Something changes in Doktor Fortzmann's bearing – his hands spread over his knees and tighten slightly.

What do you mean by this?

Ania's story gathers steam. *He held on to me. He put a hand over my mouth when I wanted to call out.*

Herr Fortzmann's brows lower. *You are not to play with him again. Do you understand?*

Yes. She nods. *I understand.*

To Ania's surprise, the switch remains untouched. She is sent to her room without supper, and later that night Frau Richter slips her a bowl of pea soup with a slice of ham. *Poor child,* the woman says, shaking her head, clucking her tongue against her teeth. *We should have guarded you against that boy.* It leaves Ania with a peculiar feeling, as if the lie is a physical object stuck in her gut. And though she is hungry she can't eat. The night is beautiful, but there is no laughter or music from the Smeltz house.

Afterwards, people throw stones through the Smeltz family's windows. Someone paints a slash across their door. Word has got out. Otto does not return to school.

In fact, Ania sees him again only once. He is walking across the park, his shoulders hunched against the cold, and she is surprised at how small he looks. It gives her a funny feeling – the way his dark hair flies up like feathers in the wind, and the thinness of his legs in short pants, like delicate twigs. So Ania tells herself the story she has concocted: he is a manipulative child who forced her to disobey her father and clamped his sweaty, dirty hand over her mouth. She imagines it so carefully that it feels real.

Then one morning the Smeltz family disappears. In the middle of the night, they load up their wagon from Herr Smeltz's shop and leave their home for the Jewish neighbourhood.

On the long, boring afternoons at 34 Langebein Strasse in the days and years to follow, Ania misses her friend. And at night, she lies in her silent bedroom and attempts to recall the music his family used to play. It makes her heart ache. She knows it is her own fault the music has disappeared.

CHAPTER TWENTY-SEVEN

DORTMUND, 1934

By the next time Ania runs away, Otto Smeltz has faded to no more than a whisper in her childhood memories. This time she decides to leave home for a convent, the Sisters of the Holy Sacrament. She is now twenty-three, a young woman, but under her father's roof she is still a girl. She has finished high school with high marks and honours but is not bound for university. Herr Doktor Fortzmann does not believe in higher education for girls. He believes it is Ania's duty to keep house for him now that her mother has died. One day she will marry and have babies, so what is the point of a higher degree?

Ania, on the other hand, is not interested in housekeeping or marriage or, for that matter, babies. She is an athletic girl with a quick, literal mind, accustomed to spending most of her time alone. In a crowd of girls, nothing about her stands out. She is of average height, has average blondish hair, and ordinary features. Her eyes are maybe a little wide set, her lips a little thin, her legs gangly. She doesn't care. Her body is strong and healthy and in her gymnastics troop she runs faster and hurls herself higher than any of the other girls. Her steadiness of character and good citizenship make her well liked. She is always invited to the young people's dances at the Guild Hall. But she accepts the invitations only to be polite. What is the point of romance? It seems like a distraction from the important things in life.

Which are, in order: the wider world (not Germany, but the whole planet, full of all the odd varieties of human life – she has devoured every book in Herr Doktor Fortzmann's collection on foreign civilisations and anthropological research), science, and physical fitness (or her membership in the local Girls' Sport Training Group, to be exact).

So Ania leaves home for the convent not because she wants to be a nun, but because she wants to go to Africa. The convent has a mission there, in the former Hapsburg colony of Namibia. She imagines herself teaching chubby native children how to read and boil their vegetables, and falling asleep under mosquito netting listening to monkeys' cries. She hungers for an opportunity to see the wider world. And also to get out of Dortmund.

Ania does not ask her father what he thinks of her idea. She knows what his answer will be. For all his criticism of the current state of government, the Nazis and the Communists alike, Herr Doktor Fortzmann has never set foot outside Germany. It is his home, his *Heimat,* and, in his opinion, the only truly civilised nation on earth.

Since his wife's death her father has become even more remote. At dinner they eat in silence, listening to the clink of their own cutlery. It makes her miss the days when he lectured her about the sins of the Communists, the glories of the kaiser, and his favourite German heroes – Hermann, Karl der Grosse, and General Bismarck. Even his patients are deserting him. The Nazis have opened a new hospital on the other side of town that provides free care for the factory's workers. Herr Doktor Fortzmann locks himself in his study for whole afternoons, reading and scowling over the newspapers.

Meanwhile, the world beyond Ania's stifled childhood home is blossoming. There is excitement in the air; it is a new day for Germany. The young Hitler – so handsome, so vibrant, and so unlike the tired old intellectuals who, for the past fifteen years, have muddled the nation through riots, unemployment, and political strife – has been named chancellor. The papers are full of his bold plans and ideas. He has the vision and energy to make Germany great. He has rounded up the Communists who burned down the Reichstag and averted the revolution so many Germans have feared for years. Even Herr Doktor Fortzmann gives him credit for this. And Frau Richter is an ardent supporter. *Thank God for Herr Hitler,* she says. *He will save us from the Bolsheviks.*

Under him, Germany is to be one nation rather than a collection of rivalrous factions sniping at one another in the face of defeat. Together, they will create the finest, strongest, and greatest civilisation on earth! And Hitler says it is the young people who will accomplish this.

It would be death to stay locked up in the Fortzmann house.

On the day Ania leaves, Rainer Brandt waits for her on the corner. He is, what? Her friend? Her beau? Her unlikely confidant? There is no label that quite covers their relationship. She has known him since they were children. They have attended the same school and church. They have waited in the same lines for bread and gone to the same funerals and played at the same carnival games. His father, a bricklayer at the hospital, is a patient of Doktor Fortzmann's. As children she and Rainer played backgammon in her father's waiting room during old Herr Brandt's weekly appointments.

'Last chance,' Rainer says, pulling himself off the low wall he has been sitting on. 'Instead of joining those religious zealots, you can run away with me.'

'And go where?' Ania asks, trying to keep her voice light, though actually she feels as though she might collapse. She has said goodbye to no one – not her father, who would forbid her from leaving, or Frau Richter, who would cry and wring her hands. She is no longer a child, but she is still, effectively, running away.

Rainer takes her suitcase from her hands. 'Why go to Africa when there are so many Germans who need your help? Seriously.'

They have debated this often. Rainer is a recent convert to the Nazi Party. He plans to be on the front lines of Hitler's wonderful new empire. He has already signed up to become a leader of a *Landjahr Lager,* or camp – part of a national service programme in which young people spend a year on the land, developing the necessary skills they will need if Germany is to return, under Hitler, to a great agrarian society. Soon it will be compulsory for all the country's youths. Rainer will be poised to rise in the programme's ranks.

Ania sees the beauty in his dream, but all the same, she would like to go abroad. She would like to travel farther than the German countryside. Africa beckons with its promise of lush jungles and primitive tribes.

'Just think of what you will miss here,' Rainer continues. 'The beginning of a whole new Germany!'

'Oh, Rainer.' Ania sighs, unable to think of anything but her father sleeping like an old man on his narrow bed. She peeked in through his door on her way out and was surprised by how rumpled he looked, mouth open, snoring – his shirt loosened at the collar, his stockinged feet on the bedspread. 'I've already chosen my path.'

Rainer lifts his eyebrows. He has always been a quiet boy, cowed by his family's poverty, his father's poor health, and his mother's rough Swabian German. But now that he is a Nazi, he glows with an appealing, new-found confidence. Girls have begun to take note. He is not handsome – his face is too angular and long, and there is something truculent about his chin – but he is compellingly intense. And he has eyes for no one but Ania, his childhood friend.

'I give you three weeks in the convent,' he says, kicking a stone down the street. 'You'll come around.'

*   *   *

As it turns out, Ania lasts only two. The nuns in the cloister are realists. 'You will be sick most of the time,' Sister Catherine tells her. 'The people don't speak German, so you must learn French. There are no potatoes. Everyone will want to touch your hair.'

Ania could not care less. She is familiar with discomfort and sickness. She is genuinely curious about the natives. The problem for her is God. 'You must keep him close to your heart always,' says Sister Anne Marie. 'If you don't, he will forsake you.'

But when Ania tries to keep God close to her heart, she is filled not with warmth and reassurance, but with emptiness. Every night she says her prayers, and each morning she goes to chapel. She feels her habit rough against her elbows, the risers cold and hard against her knees, but she does not feel God. In his place she feels dread and fear of death. And this worries her. She is an earnest girl. She takes the nuns' admonitions seriously. She is Herr Doktor Fortzmann's daughter, after all.

On her second Saturday in the convent, Rainer invites her to come and see a presentation of a local *Landjahr* lager. The day is bright and lovely, and the air outside the convent walls seems to crackle with energy. A great many people have assembled outside the city hall, and, unlike the cranky, embattled crowds she remembers from her youth, they are not here to fight or protest. They are here to celebrate. They want to capture a little corner of this new spirit of possibility and togetherness for themselves.

And the presentation is marvellous! The fourteen- and fifteen-year-olds on the improvised stage look happy, healthy, and innocent in their matching short pants and thin dark neckties, their hair cut with a floppy fringe in front. They march in remarkable unison and sing spirited songs and traditional ballads, paeans to the beauty of nature and the joys of wandering. They enact a skit they have written themselves about the great German hero Hermann overthrowing the Romans. The costumes are basic, the lines are not particularly poetic, but the acting is committed and they have even worked in a few good jokes. When it is over, the actors stand straight and tall beside their leader, a handsome young man who can't be much older than Rainer, as he speaks about pride and self-control and discipline, and, most of all, togetherness – sons of steelworkers and department store owners, fishermen and nobles, all brought together through a year spent living on the land. Behind him, five boys wave Hitler Youth flags with their single, elegant lightning streak. It is, possibly, the most beautiful thing Ania has ever seen.

They close with a devotional song to mother Germany.

We are all connected, under our flag of solidarity
Since we found ourselves as one people
No one is alone anymore, we are all obliged,
God, our Leader, our blood.
Raised in our faith, happy in our work that everyone does
We all want to be as one
Germany, we are brightly standing by your side
We want this high alliance seen in all our glory!

Ania is surprised to find tears filling her eyes. She has not realised, until this moment, how isolated she has been. She has been alone every moment of her life. She goes to sleep alone and wakes alone – she has no siblings since her brother died and no experience of a mother's touch, nothing more than Frau Richter *tsk-tsk*ing about whether she has swallowed her spoonful of cod liver oil. And she imagined herself content in this solitude!

Before today, she has always understood togetherness as factional: the rioting groups of her post-war youth, drawn together only because of whatever they were against. But she is against nothing. And neither are these young people onstage, who seem so sincerely lifted by one another's company. They are *for* something – for solidarity and Germany.

This must be what Hitler means when he says *Kraft durch Freude*: 'strength through joy.' Strength through community and song and happiness. It is the opposite of everything Ania was raised to believe. The feeling she experiences at this realisation can only be described as religious.

So? Rainer says, after the youth march offstage. She feels a thousand kilometres from the nuns, the musty, damp-smelling cloister, the whole creaky missionary enterprise.

Yes, Ania says, breathless. *You're right.*

And so it is not as a conformist but as a rebel that Ania Fortzmann joins the Nazi Party.

CHAPTER TWENTY-EIGHT

DORTMUND, 1935

Ania and Rainer are married at city hall. She wears a sensible blue suit and he his best *Landjahr* leader uniform.

The solemnity of the occasion strikes Ania as funny. She feels like a child playing at being a grown-up. But Rainer is serious as death. He remains two steps ahead of her as they climb the building's steps. Even when she hurries, he won't quite allow her to catch up.

Following this new, stiff, and humourless Rainer, Ania feels the chill of doubt. *Do you love him?* her friend and gymnastics partner Ulrike asked her when Ania told her they were engaged. The question took Ania by surprise. She and Rainer have known each other since they were children. They share a passion for the work and for improving Germany's future. And Rainer says he has always known he would marry her. His certainty is compelling. Ania is used to following the lead of opinionated men. But is she 'in love'? She is not even sure what this means exactly. In novels, love seems to be a stormy and irrational thing, full of chaos and bodily urges. Ania has never experienced this. And it is not something she wants. What she wants is a partner.

She is marrying Rainer because as husband and wife, they can lead a lager together. They will be assigned their own troop of boys from all over the country. They will teach them how to till the land and grow vegetables and be proud, unpretentious, able-bodied citizens of the Reich. Never mind that neither she nor Rainer knows much of anything about farming. They have acquired some simple skills in their training and will work alongside local farmers. They will bring their passion for the movement and its ideals of togetherness, class equality, and national pride.

When Rainer reaches the top step, he turns and offers Ania his hand. 'My almost husband,' she says, smiling and panting slightly. He steps back and gestures for her to precede him. Together, they make their way down to the musty basement and the town clerk who handles such matters.

Their first two lagers are idyllic, really. They are the best years of Ania's life. She knows this is true, even much later when it is shameful to admit. Of course, in time, she will never say the best years of her life were spent running a Nazi youth programme. Her sons would never forgive her; her daughter would die of shame. But truly, her memories of those first years are fairly benign: full of the clean, satisfying feeling of physical labour, the joy of song and dance, and the camaraderie of teamwork . . . When they are not busy with farm chores they engage in vigorous exercise. In accordance with Nazi philosophy, Ania and Rainer believe in the civilising power of sports. What better way for young people to learn persistence, group allegiance, and self-sacrifice?

The first lager is in the south, outside Saarbrücken, in a beautiful country estate abandoned by its original owners. *Abandoned*, Ania will later realise, does not mean anything as lackadaisical as she imagined then. *Vacated under duress* is probably more accurate: the former owners were Jewish, and the Nuremberg laws now in place. But at the time, she grasps only that the owner was an imprudent debtor who has emigrated to America. Why would she look a gift horse in the mouth? The land around the estate belongs to a handful of prosperous local farmers, descendants of the serfs who originally tilled these same fields. How far Germany has come since those days! Rainer and the boys set off each morning to assist at one farm or another. There is much to do in the late summer and autumn, and relatively little in the winter.

At night, like the dwarves in the famous fairy tale, they return to the lager, where Ania, their Snow White, has made a wholesome dinner and a pudding for dessert. They eat together at one long table, do their chores, and then assemble for songs, stories, and games.

The manor house is beyond beautiful with its grand high-ceilinged rooms, gilt mouldings, and painted frescoes of Greek gods and solemn-faced cherubs. When Ania wakes each morning, she can step onto the private balcony off her bedroom and look out over the grounds: the charming overgrown lawn, the orchard with its pretty, blossoming trees, the tennis court (imagine!), and the impressive vegetable garden she has planted. It is hard work, certainly, but satisfying. She discovers she has a knack for coaxing strawberries from the cold earth and growing lush, deep green and red fronds of rhubarb, bumper crops of green beans and peas. In the Fortzmann house she never had a garden – there was only a scrubby plot of potatoes and gooseberries that fell under Frau Richter's charge. The science of growing appeals to Ania, as does the physical labour. Rainer allows her to plan the boys' fitness regimen. She challenges them to compete in hurdle jumping, sprints, even obstacle courses, which she bases on her favourite gymnastics troop exercises.

And the boys are sweet and fresh faced, younger than Ania imagined, only twelve and thirteen, on the cusp of their teen years. They are dear creatures, excited to be sprung from their homes in cities and from the boring, traditional subjects of Latin, arithmetic, literature, and geography.

In the evenings, when it's hot, she and Rainer take the boys on the hay wagon to a nearby lake with cold black water that reflects the hillside and the sky. The boys make a game of swimming to a float and throwing one another off. The biggest, strongest boys are always 'King.' Ania lies on her blanket on the grassy bank and watches their horseplay. Sometimes Rainer swims out and joins their wrestling, his pale, wiry body so different from theirs – more mature and also sharper somehow, harder and more determined, frizzled with fine black hairs.

She does not enjoy the physical element of their marriage, but she tolerates it. And Rainer himself is not an avid lover: He turns to her only sometimes, in the darkness, quickly and without preamble. Their lovemaking is over in a moment, and neither of them speak of it.

On Saturday nights, Rainer builds a wonderful bonfire and the boys sing and have contests – who can spring the fastest, jump the farthest, balance the longest on a fallen tree limb. Rainer is in his element here with so many adoring young people looking to him for guidance.

In the future, Ania's daughter will send her son to an American summer camp. *It's all about archery and soccer and fishing and camping, how to be a good citizen and good friend, how to be a confident young man,* she will tell Ania. She will say it in a wry tone that suggests she sees something amusing about this. *But that's beautiful,* Ania will say. *It's like what we did in our lager.*

Except they don't teach them to kill Jews at Camp Wykona! her daughter will exclaim. *My God, Mother! You can't seriously compare a New England summer camp to a Nazi youth lager!*

But we didn't teach them to kill Jews, Ania will protest mildly. *We didn't even* talk *about Jews.*

Her daughter will stare at her as if she is insane.

But Hitler did, she will say, as if speaking to a child. *Didn't you hear what he was saying?*

No, Ania will say, shaking her head. *I was too busy. Or too stupid.*

But this is not exactly true. She was busy, but she was not stupid. And she *did* listen to Hitler, though she does not recall what she actually *heard*. She remembers gathering around the radio in the elegant dining room with murals of pastoral farm scenes painted on the walls. She remembers the boys in their pyjamas, exhausted from a day of physical exertion, sprawled across the wood floors, smelling of fresh hay and dust and clean sweat. There was great excitement about listening to the Führer. She remembers his exhortations and energy, his talk of building and unifying the Reich, the unique and wonderful qualities of the German *Volk*. But she does not remember the ugly quotes her daughter confronts her with.

Maybe because at the time what she heard did not seem radical.

Listening to the radio at that first lager in 1936, Ania believes Hitler's assertion that Jews are rich businessmen who have profited from Germany's troubles and taken the best jobs in Germany. And that those who are not rich, which is to say mostly the eastern Jews who have immigrated here from Poland, Romania, and the Baltic, are freeloaders and Bolsheviks. They are Trotsky followers, the same people who set the Reichstag on fire and created the 'Bavarian Soviet Republic.' Her grasp of the details is vague, but she understands this last group of agitators is dangerous. She accepts this in the abstract, of course. The actual Jews she knows are different. Herr Goldblum, the grocer, or the Cornbluth girls from her grammar school, for example, are neither rich nor Bolshevik. They are kind, ordinary people who happen to belong to a bad group. But how can Hitler know who is a 'good Jew' and who isn't? Easier to evict them all and prevent infiltration. Where they will go – back to Poland, Romania, wherever they came from? America? Israel? Madagascar? – is not Ania's concern.

In the countryside around the lager, there aren't any Jews. There is only the ghost of Otto Smeltz. In Ania's mind, the boy has fused with the story she told. He has become an uncomfortable hybrid that she would rather not think about.

Ania also accepts Hitler's statement that Poles and Slavs and easterners belong to a lower race, disproportionately represented

in civilisation's criminal elements. In her training as a youth
leader she learned the science of this: genetics and brain size
and forehead measurements, statistics of their incarceration for
stealing and rape and murder. The *Völkischer Beobachter* runs
disturbing stories about their poor hygiene and laziness. They
breed like rabbits and live on the best, most arable plots of land,
much of which, until the last war, belonged to Germany. They
need German order, modernity, and management. And Hitler is
just the man to bring this to them – look at what wonders he has
done for Germany's crime rate! It is not just unemployment he
has fixed; under his leadership the country has become a much
safer, more peaceful, and more orderly place.

*Weren't you alarmed by all the racist talk? Hitler's rants about the
'Jewish virus' and 'the noble German' . . . You can't read more than
four sentences by the man without knowing he was a racist fanatic,*
Ania's daughter will press.

I didn't notice is all Ania can say. And it is true, as outlandish
as it sounds. She has never been taught that drawing distinctions
between races is dangerous. In Germany, there is no great history of equal rights. For thousands of years, the population was
divided into an impoverished and disenfranchised peasant class
and wealthy, ruling aristocrats. The only teaching that gives her
pause is the Christian precept of kindness and tolerance. But the
churches themselves are not making much fuss about Hitler's
harsh rhetoric. Christianity is superstition, Hitler says – a pallia-
tive against life's brutal realities.

This is before the war. Before the Jewish star badges, before the
roundups and mass deportations and extermination camps.

And, really, Ania is busy with her own life.

This lager is where Ania has her babies: first in 1936, sweet
Anselm, an easy infant, content to lie in his cradle while she
washes and cleans and cooks. Ania has no mother around to

teach her how to swaddle and burp him, how to apply salve to his chapped skin to keep it from splitting, how to add pea soup to his bottles to keep him full. So she has to learn these things herself. But she manages. And she takes pride in this.

In 1937, Ania gives birth to Wolfgang, who is more difficult. In her heart, she blames him for the downgrade in their quality of life. He is jaundiced at birth, and often sick. His stools are thin and endless – she has enough laundry to do without an extra ten napkin cloths a day. And she has Anselm, who is a toddler now, to run after – and all the other boys in the lager. Often she has to let Wolfgang cry himself to sleep.

When the boys are two and three, Germany invades Poland. No one wants war – it has been only twenty-one years since their last one! – but Ania believes the stories she reads in the German papers, which call it a war of self-defence. According to the papers, the Poles have made a number of incursions onto German soil, murdering innocent citizens and taking over their radio station in Gleiwitz. She is an intelligent woman, but she is not a sceptic. It must be true if the paper reports it.

Their next lager is also fine. It is 1940. Germany is at war. Most German papers still call it a war of self-defence. As allies of Poland, France and the United Kingdom have declared war on Germany. No one wanted it to come to this. But so far, for the Germans, it has gone swimmingly. This lager is in Luxembourg, which is now a conquered country, rolled over in the rapid and remarkably successful German invasion of France. But *conquered* is not how she and Rainer and the rest of the Germans they know think of it. Luxembourg has become 'Luxemburg' and been welcomed into the Reich. Its people have little to complain about. Their casualties amounted to all of seventy-five when the German army invaded. And now they have the opportunities afforded to citizens of the Reich, including participation in these lagers. As long as they don't speak French.

This time, the lager is housed in a modest barracks-like building. It is not as splendid as the one outside Saarbrücken, but it is comfortable. The work is good, life is wholesome, and the war still distant. Suddenly, from Paris, there is an influx of fine things: At Christmas, Rainer gives Ania silk stockings (where is she supposed to wear these?), and also a beautiful, sturdy watch. There is goose liver pâté for the boys to taste, and champagne for the adults. Everyday food is now rationed more strictly – eggs and pork and milk are set aside exclusively for the troops. But the lager receives a portion of the food they help produce – flour, potatoes, barley, fresh fruit in the summer, carrots, and beets. It is a shame to be at war, of course, but Ania relishes the order and fullness of her life.

They are still in this lager when Germany declares war on Russia in 1941. This is an unsettling turn of events. Ania is not the only one to feel the first real grains of doubt. *A preventive war,* the Nazis call it. *Better to attack than be attacked.* But the German army is worn out. Anyone can see that it is dangerous for a country to wage war on two fronts. And the Allies have begun bombing in earnest – air raids are the new measure of urban life.

Ania knows Rainer will be called to the front, but even so, the order comes as a shock. She and her boys are to return home. But where is home? Herr Doktor Fortzmann is dead. Old Herr Brandt is dead. Rainer's mother is an invalid. And their lager is to be shut.

The following week, Rainer must escort the lager's boys to the train station, and from there he is to report for duty. On the morning he is scheduled to depart, he rolls over and climbs out of bed without even pausing to look at her. He has never exhibited affection for his wife and young sons in front of his charges, and he doesn't change this. 'Take care of yourself,' he says, nodding. So Ania is left to pack their belongings and find them a new home. Soon, she and the boys are on a train heading towards Dortmund, where her aunt Gudrun has agreed to take them in.

The trip is long. The RAF has bombed the tracks, and they sit in the September heat for hours awaiting repairs. Four-year-old

Wolfgang is sick with scarlet fever. His body is as hot as a fireplace brick.

'The boy should drink much water,' an older man says kindly as he passes them on the platform in Frankfurt. He is followed by his wife, who wears a heavy winter coat and clutches a number of suitcases. They are Jews, Ania realises when she sees their gold stars. The stars are a new requirement, and it is the first time she has seen one. For that matter, it is the first time she has seen a Jew in a long time. She is taken aback by the man's kindness. In the absence of contact, her idea of Jews has unified with the images on the Nazi posters: beak nosed and nefarious. But this man and his wife look ordinary and sad. She thanks him and thinks suddenly of Otto Smeltz, her one-time friend and partner. Where has he ended up?

In Dortmund, life is not as easy as it was on the land. Aunt Gudrun sets her jaw when Wolfgang cries and beats Anselm's knuckles with a ruler when he scuffs his feet, or forgets to say thank you, or accidentally breaks a dish. The bombings come in spates, sometimes every night for a week, then nothing for a month. They become accustomed to the routine of tramping up and down the cellar stairs half-asleep.

Anselm starts school and Ania and Wolfgang remain at home with Aunt Gudrun's sharp tongue and demonstrative, beleaguered sighs. They eat boiled cabbage and potatoes and sleep under the thin blankets they brought with them from the lager, huddling together for warmth. On Gudrun's crummy People's Radio, Goebbels and Hitler proclaim their successes on the Russian front, but on the streets, other stories circulate. The German army is freezing and the battles are bloody. For every Russian they kill, two more spring up in his place. And there are even darker rumours: in the ghettos where the Polish Jews have been sent, people are dying of disease and hunger; the SS and local Poles are killing whole villages of Jews; and the Wehrmacht is shooting Russian prisoners of war, or worse, locking them up in starvation camps. Ania would like to tune in to foreign broadcasts, but she has no radio of her own, and anyway, if she tried, Gudrun would report her. Rainer sends back short, opaque letters: his boots are worn out, they are stuck in some small Russian town or another awaiting orders, a man in his unit comes from nearby Aplerbeck. What he is *doing,* how he *feels* – she can only guess.

One day, after nearly a year in Dortmund, Ania passes the local *Winterhilfswerk* – Winter Help – headquarters and notices a sign for blankets, coats, warm clothing, and other necessities. She hesitates – she and her boys are no charity case, after all – until several well-dressed women precede her. Inside, the canteen has been remade into a shop with piles of goods arranged for perusal, carefully sorted by size and type: warm wool coats and sweaters, feather beds, pillows and leather boots. Volunteers distribute tickets to those waiting: two coats per family, two pieces of bedding, shoes for everyone. What a windfall! Thank goodness she has arrived early enough for the best picks. She selects a lovely camel-coloured wool coat with silver buttons for Anselm (much finer than any he has ever owned), a thick green wool cape for Gudrun, two feather beds, and a practical pair of shoes for each. The question of where all this has come from does not even occur to her until she checks out. *Redistributed,* the volunteer stamps on a paper listing the items Ania has selected.

'Redistributed from where?' Ania asks.

'From deportees,' the volunteer says curtly.

So these are belongings Jews sent east have left behind. The thought is dismaying. Some little boy had to leave this handsome coat. But then it confirms what the Führer has been saying – the Jews of Germany have made themselves unreasonably rich. Who would leave behind such a coat unless they owned an even better one they could bring along?

Bring *where* is an increasingly uncomfortable concept, though it is still outside the realm of Ania's immediate concern.

In the beginning of the war, Ania imagined the resettlement

camps to be humble, organised places like her lager, focused on
reeducation and run with German efficiency. Early in her *Landjahr* training, she received a glowing booklet about a camp for Jews
in Poland, a clean, orderly place, with a hospital and vocational
training programmes. The word *resettlement* conjured an image
of a village emptied of its inhabitants, who had been resettled to
another village, emptied of *its* inhabitants, who had also been resettled, and so on – with each population pushing farther into
the wide and roomy east. A continent of people shifting to make
Lebensraum, living space, for their bursting population. There is
an easy logic to it. After all, there are *eighty million people living
on five hundred thousand square kilometres in Germany;* Ania has
memorised Hitler's facts. They need more space, more resources.

But now, everyone knows the 'settlements' are really just
camps, and the camps are no better than the squalid 'Jew houses'
where the few remaining Jews in German cities have been con-
fined. Last month when they 'cleaned up' Dortmund, the citizens
were told to cover their mouths with cloth or stay indoors while
the soldiers marched the last Jews to the trains.

Many years later, in another lifetime, Ania will enter an American second-hand store with her daughter and be overcome with
instinctive horror. *Do you know where all these clothes come from?*
she will ask.

People who don't need them anymore, her daughter will say with
a shrug. *Why do you ask?*

When Rainer returns home on leave, he is distant, harder, and
more aloof. This is to be expected, of course. How can you fight
a war and come back cheerful? Ania knows this. But still, she
misses his old jokes, even the ones at which she used to roll her
eyes. And she wishes he would offer some affection to his sons. He
addresses them with curt formality, sometimes even disdain. One
day, when Anselm comes home from school in tears because an

older boy has stolen his new pencil, Rainer boxes his ears. 'Don't let yourself be beaten again, you understand?' he says roughly. 'The future is not for boys who don't know how to fight.' Ania tries not to mourn the old Rainer, the one who knew how to inspire and instruct with humour, and to bring out the best in young men.

They make love, if it can be called that, only a few times. Rainer is rougher and less cautious physically. More than once, Ania bleeds afterwards. But this too is to be expected, isn't it, from a soldier on leave? She stifles her revulsion. It will only make her pity herself.

In the spring of 1943, Rainer is discharged from service. He has been wounded, and after three months in a Danish military hospital, shrapnel is still embedded in his knee. He cannot return to combat duty. So he is given a new assignment: to lead a lager in the Warthegau, a German district of conquered Poland. The boys will be older this time – ages thirteen to seventeen. And the lager will be part of the *Wehrbauer* 'soldier farmer' movement used to hold the eastern territories. They are meant to bring modern farming practices to the backward Polish countryside and pro-duce much-needed grain to feed the Reich. They will be at the forefront of Hitler's *Blut und Boden* plan – members of a superior race united with superior soil (rich, black stuff that slides between your fingers like silk) and ready to defend it if attacked.

The assignment has a frightening, warlike ring to it, but then again so does living in Dortmund. The Ruhr is under constant siege now, and British and American bombs wreak havoc every night. Those people remaining in the city have become mean and desperate: they report one another to the Gestapo for not offering the proper *Heil Hitler,* or listening to foreign broadcasts, or for 'de-featist' talk. 'Our poor soldiers,' Ania says while reading the news-paper one night, and Gudrun gives her a harsh look. 'Our *brave* soldiers,' Gudrun corrects. 'You could go to prison for such talk.'

The presence of slave labourers has become ubiquitous – mostly Russian POWs working in the city's coal and munitions plants. Tramping through the streets, they look thin and haunted – a hungry, miserable lot. But in Russia, German POWs receive the same treatment or worse, according to Rainer, Hitler, Goebbels, and every Nazi *Kreisleiter*. Ania is growing sick of men and their talk, though. In the last year, she has seen groups of female prisoners, too. Pretty and young Polish and Ukrainian girls are hawked at the train station for use as nannies and household help. And a group of malnourished-looking women in striped uniforms walk through the city to the munitions plant each morning. Jews from a temporary labour camp. Their presence has no German analogue in Russia.

Rainer evidences no joy at the prospect of leading another lager. He wakes screaming almost every night. When the doctor prescribes pills to help him sleep, he takes them right after supper and falls immediately into a sluggish, absent state.

So again it falls to Ania to pack up their small family. They are allowed one bag each, just like the Jews. This gives her pause.

In the last year, Ania has heard new horror stories: of KZ inmates worked so hard they drop dead, of women and children shot to death in the woods, of giant ovens where Jews are gassed. She does not believe the worst of these. The Führer who dreamed up *Landjahr* lagers and one-pot Sunday dinners would never order such unconscionable things. It is one thing to deport the Jews, another to murder them. The stories smack of Allied propaganda – the kind written on the leaflets that the RAF drops.

But, all the same, they are unsettling.

In the future, when Ania tries to explain this to her daughter, words will fail her. She knew of the horrors and she didn't. She *half knew* – but there is no word for that. She knew it the way you know something is happening far away in a distant land, something you have no control over: earthquake refugees living in squalid conditions or victims in a foreign war.

But it wasn't a foreign war, it was your war! her daughter will insist.

True, Ania admits. *But it didn't feel that way.*

Until the Warthegau.

For life in this new lager, Ania packs warm clothing, a small book of photos, blankets for the boys, nails, a hammer, a wooden spoon, a potato peeler, and her precious paring knife. This winnowing down to the essentials is good practice for the future, though she doesn't know that yet. The lager will be furnished, but these are items you can't count on finding anymore.

The trip east is as spartan as the landscape. The Brandts ride in an army transport train, in a car reserved for 'civilian settlers.' Their fellow passengers are a group of young women, members of the BDM, out spreading the 'domestic culture and hygiene of Germandom' to the ignorant peasant peoples of the east, and many ex-soldiers like Rainer – injured men or those too old for active duty but still capable of farm and police work. She is the only mother with children. Wolfgang is sick for most of the trip. Anselm, at seven, stares out of the window, fascinated by the military transports at the stations they pass. He has never seen so many SS men in their long, swishing coats and black boots.

Anselm is the one to point out the train in Schwerin: a long line of cattle cars stuffed with human beings, their frightened faces visible through the small windows at the top.

'Why are those people riding in the animal cars?' he asks.

'There aren't enough civilian cars,' Ania suggests. The sight is jarring, though. In Dortmund, the Jewish transports from France and the Netherlands were overcrowded passenger trains; apparently it is not so in the east.

'Are there bathrooms in the cars?' Anselm persists. 'Where are they going?'

'Maybe chamber pots,' Ania answers. 'To camps in the east.'

'Enough questions,' Rainer barks. It is one of the few times he speaks.

'Look.' Anselm nudges her. He points his chin towards the first car, behind the engine, an open goods wagon with no roof. In this one, Ania can see the people clearly. They are standing because it is too crowded to sit. Along the side, a row of faces stare out at hip height – children. With wide eyes, they watch as their train pulls ahead. When the two cars are side by side, Ania finds herself staring into one particular woman's face. She is not old, not young, a mother holding a baby in her arms. For an instant, their eyes connect. And the woman's gaze is so full of despair it takes Ania's breath.

Beside her, Wolfgang throws up.

In that moment, Ania understands that they are headed to a terrible place.

CHAPTER TWENTY-NINE

THE WARTHEGAU, 1943

The lager in the Warthegau is in a converted slaughterhouse. No matter how many times Ania scrubs the floors, the walls, the wide kitchen table, it stinks of blood.

And the boys here are tougher than those at the previous lagers. Some are orphaned. Most are from big industrial cities. They have been sent here to escape the bombing, but also because they exhibit a certain kind of physical and mental promise. They are here to provide labour for the local farms and to seed the east with good German citizens, and also to be hardened into future SS men. This is a new development. 'If this is the task, what is my role? And what about Anselm and Wolfgang?' Ania demands during one of her early arguments with Rainer.

'You begged me to come along,' he says coldly. 'It was your choice.'

'But I didn't know what I was choosing!'

'I told you it would be different' is Rainer's response. And Ania is blindsided by the truth of this. Her desperation to leave Gudrun's apartment and bomb-besieged Dortmund made her stupid. She should have asked more questions. She will rue her lack of curiosity, her ability to see things only as she wanted to, for the rest of her life.

Rainer has been given a handful of new materials, and he shares them with Ania for the first time once they are installed. They are full of fiery quotes from Hitler and the handsome Reich's youth leader, Baldur von Schirach.

'Those who want to live, let them fight, and those who do not want to fight in this world of eternal struggle do not deserve to live.'

'He alone who owns the youth owns the future.'

'I want brutal, domineering, fearless, and cruel youth. . . . The free, magnificent beast of prey must again flash from their eyes.'

All the friendly rhetoric of togetherness is gone, along with any celebration of a wholesome, simple way of life.

'"Cruel"?' Ania asks Rainer. 'Are these boys really supposed to be cruel?'

Rainer gives a non-committal shrug. This new Rainer is stern and silent all the time – less like a partner and more like an unreliable room-mate. At night he drinks vodka and grows moody and speaks to the boys in a sarcastic snarl. Ania is a little bit afraid of him.

As far as she can tell, the lager boys are cruel and domineering already. This is not their first lager – many have been living in youth homes where they have been sent to escape the bomb-threatened cities for years. In their free time, which is plentiful, they improvise hard games: a ball toss in which the loser is beaten on the back with sticks, a race in which the winner walks on the other boys in his hobnailed work boots. Everything is a contest of strength and power – they beat one another black and blue over who sleeps on the top bunk, who takes the first freezing bath, who has to muck out the latrine. The same boys always win. When Ania attempts to stop them, Rainer intervenes: 'Why?' he asks. 'They will need to be hard.'

'But they can still be human, can't they?' she asks.

This is the first time Rainer slaps her. It comes out of nowhere. He is standing beside her as she washes the dishes and, at first, when his hand arcs towards her face, Ania thinks it is a plate flying out of the sink. She steps back in shock.

'Don't talk that way,' he says as she raises a hand to her blood-ied lip. 'For your own good.'

There is no more strolling through green wheat fields at dusk singing German folk songs. There are no more Sunday-morning hikes and campfire games. There is no more decent heating, clothing, or food.

Rainer broods and sulks and spends hours polishing his boots. His face has become set in a bitter expression. He has no passion left – not for the ideals that they set out with, not for Hitler, and certainly not for Ania. Here in the Warthegau, he doesn't even attempt intercourse. He sleeps in a spartan room off the boys' dor-mitory, while Ania shares a room off the kitchen with their sons. One night before he slapped her she knocked on his door, in a combination of loneliness and determination. *Can I come in?* she asked, blushing, holding her nightgown at the throat. But when Rainer opened the door, he only looked at her with a kind of weary pity. *It's late for conversation, Ania. Go to bed.*

Ania's days involve long shuffles through the mud to the post office where their rations and supplies are delivered. Like a goat, she tows cartons of potatoes, flour, and salt pork in a cart with a shoulder yoke. She keeps Anselm and Wolfgang beside her in the kitchen. Rainer does not approve, but she insists. Her boys are too young to run around with the others. And it isn't only their age that makes them vulnerable – they are softer than the rest. Hitler has not yet weaned them of their mother. She can see that Rainer is embarrassed by this.

One day, Ania comes upon a group of boys behind the barn forcing the smallest, youngest ones to swallow live toads. 'Stop it!' she yells, despite Rainer's instructions. 'Stop this nonsense! You are not animals!' They turn their astonished faces towards her. Some are transparently relieved, others challenging. Heiner Mohrer, one of the largest and meanest of the group, curls his lip and tips an imaginary cap. 'Of course, *gnädige Frau*,' he says. But she can hear them restart the game as soon as she is out of sight.

Rainer makes Heiner something like an assistant. He is as tall as Rainer and broader, from a family of Hamburg dockworkers, all of whom died in the bombing. He routinely picks on the small boys, knocking the wash they are carrying to the ground, tripping them as they rise from the table. And he speaks rudely to Ania. 'You are looking fine today, Frau Brandt,' he says in the insolent manner of a boy who knows a certain kind of women. In another life, before the Warthegau, Rainer would have boxed the ears of anyone who spoke like that to his wife. But the new Rainer pretends he doesn't hear.

The land around the lager is as bad as the place itself. The fields stretch on and on and, at this time of year, are nothing but kilometres of frozen mud. The village, a cluster of modest, thatch-roofed houses, is mostly empty. The simple country folk who built these homes have been 'resettled' farther east or sent to work as labourers in the Reich. Of the original occupants, only a handful are left.

'How did they choose who would stay?' she asks Herr Beinecke, a local man turned member of the Nazi Order Police. He scowls at her. 'It was easy,' he says. 'We eliminated the partisans.'

The word has become a sort of catchall: Communists and Jews and Polish nationalists and anyone who is not ready to work for the Nazis. 'Were there so many?' Ania asks.

'Almost everyone,' Herr Beinecke replies.

Now she hears that the townspeople were not 'resettled' but driven into the woods and murdered by local *Hilfswillige*, or 'volunteers,' and a traveling SS *Einsatzgruppe*. The *Hilfswillige* are the only locals still alive. To 'volunteer' apparently meant not to die. She learns all this from the youngest boy in the lager, Gerald Eisenblatt, a sweet, out-of-place fifteen-year-old from Essen whose mother, a widowed seamstress, sent Ania a letter early on: *Thank you for caring for my son. He is a good boy. I promise he will cause you no trouble. And I appreciate in advance all you will do for him.* Ania could imagine her, poor woman, small like Gerald, wan with worry, her fingers covered with needle pricks. And in her own loneliness, she felt kinship. In an attempt to protect Gerald from the others, Ania invites him to help her in the kitchen as often as she can. He tells her things the boys see around the countryside and hear from the farmers on whose land they work.

'And what about the women and children of the partisans?' she asks Gerald, though in her heart she already knows. He glances at her as if to assess what she can handle. 'Eliminated,' he answers. Ania does not doubt that he is telling the truth. She can feel the steady crackle of cruelty in the air.

It makes her frightened of the locals who still live in the town, and of all the members of the Wehrmacht and SS who pass through. At night she dreams about the dead townspeople whose simple houses and belongings are left: the bucket hanging on the edge of a gate, the single sunflower growing in a small garden, the laundry line stretched between a tree and a windowsill.

The Brandts have lived at the lager for a year when the orphans come. Little ones. Two- and three-year-olds, and one infant. They arrive in the back of an SS transport truck, supervised by a young officer who finds it funny to give them swigs of whisky from his flask. The babies look surprised and spit it out. One of them cannot walk – he is a big, handsome boy who pulls himself around on his bottom, taking everything in with his wide, imperturbable eyes. They are staying only one night. The lager, it turns out, serves as a rendezvous point. Members of the Brown Sisters, a female division of the SS, will come for the babies.

Ania is aghast.

'Where will they take them?' she asks. 'Orphanages? Foster families?'

The SS man shrugs. 'The Brown Sisters will decide.'

'Decide what?'

'Where they will take them.'

'Enough questions, Ania,' Rainer barks.

While she waits, cold spreads up from her gut. Ania hopes that the Brown Sisters, as women, will be sympathetic. But she is not optimistic. The BDM girls she has met in the east have been a hard lot, tough or lonely enough to want to come here and instruct the recalcitrant locals in 'proper cooking' and hand-washing and God knows what else. These BDM women are suspicious of her as the wife of a lager leader, which is unheard of here in the east. And the Brown Sisters are a level up from the BDM women she has met.

Ania throws herself into caring for the babies, who are hungry, cold, and wet. The boys of the lager are out assisting a local *Wehrbauer* as he slaughters his pigs. Anselm and Wolfgang act as her assistants, tearing an old sheet into nappies, mixing a thin gruel to feed the orphans, playing peekaboo. Ania rocks the grouchy ones to sleep, swaying gently, humming as she once did with her own sons. The SS men drink vodka and watch. At one point, the youngest soldier stands over a baby lying on a blanket and nudges it with his boot.

'For God's sake!' Ania says, snatching it up, and the man laughs.

Her favourite is a roly-poly one who looks to be almost two but still can't walk. When she lifts him, he reaches his little hand up from time to time to fondle her ear. When Ania turns to smile at him, he looks surprised, as if he thought her ear belonged to someone else.

When the Brown Sisters arrive, there are only two of them: a meek, moon-faced girl who can't be much older than eighteen and says almost nothing, and her superior, who introduces herself as Sister Margarete. She is a short woman with a clipped manner, unmarried and childless, but full of exact information about how to deal with babies. Which is: harshly. She makes no remarks about the sweet dimple on this one's chin, or the way another puts his hand to his head. To her, they are clearly cargo to be transported. The cold in Ania's gut turns into panic.

Margarete observes the babies and takes notes. She measures their height and weight, the length of their foreheads, the circumferences of their skulls. And she does not allow Ania to help her handle them, preferring the assistance of the SS men, who seem as dismayed by this as Ania is.

'Where will you take them?' Ania asks.

'Different places,' Margarete answers.

'To foster parents?'

'If they are suitable.'

'And if they aren't?' Ania tries to ask it casually. She can feel Rainer's eyes telling her to shut up.

'That is confidential,' Sister Margarete snaps.

'We can keep them,' Ania says. The words come out in a rush. 'We can care for them here with the boys until the war ends.'

Sister Margarete fixes her with an intent look. 'That is impossible,' she says. 'And the idea is inappropriate for a person in your place.'

Ania looks down and bites her lip. *Let them all be suitable*, Ania prays. *Please God, let them all be delivered to kind homes.* She is afraid for the little dark-haired girl – so pretty with her big brown eyes, but not very German looking. Sister Margarete spends extra time on her measurements.

Ania picks up the chubby one and holds him close. He reaches immediately for her ear.

When Margarete has finished her measuring, she announces that she and her assistant will not spend the night. They would like to reach Posen before dark.

'So will you take them all?' Ania manages, despite the hard ball in her throat.

'These four,' Margarete says and gestures as if she is speaking about a few cuts of meat. Already she and her assistant have taken the first of the babies out to their car, the back of which is filled with metal washtubs lined with blankets, improvised bassinets.

In her arms, one of the babies starts to shriek. 'Scharführer Meister and Unterscharführer Haberman will take the others.'

'The others' are the roly-poly boy in Ania's arms and the little dark-haired girl.

'Where?' Ania asks, above the babies' crying. 'Where will you take them?' Her voice is loud and growing hysterical.

'Ania.' Rainer puts a hand on her arm. The boy in her arms begins to cry.

The younger of the two SS men shrugs. 'Chelmno. Unless we take them to the forest and shoot them first.'

'No!' Ania nearly chokes. 'You can't.'

'Don't frighten the woman,' the older soldier says to his compatriot. 'We'll take them to a camp.'

When the man reaches for the baby, he clings to Ania, wailing louder. But this makes no difference to the man, who peels him from her arms.

On Ania's other side, Rainer holds her fast.

In the years to come, Ania will remember this as the end of Ania Fortzmann. Not at the moment when she took her sons and stole out into the predawn to disappear into the west. Not in the ruined bomb cellar under the Dresden *Hauptbahnhof* when she took the papers from her dead friend's dress.

For years, she will sift through this memory of the babies, through the racket of her own tears and the screaming and Rainer's voice telling her to shush – looking for some lost grain of action. She will try to remember running after the SS man, prying the baby from his arms, or at least attempting this. It doesn't matter that the outcome would have been the same. It would have made a difference to *her*.

But it isn't there.

She simply stood and watched and wept. And she let them go.

*　　*　　*

Shortly after the Brown Sisters' visit, Rainer receives orders requesting two of his best boys to report for duty at a nearby labour camp. They are shutting it down and moving its prisoners farther west into the Reich. The boys are to assist with the prisoner transport. Rainer selects Heiner, the bully, and Gerald Eisenblatt.

But on the morning of their departure, Rainer doesn't come out of his room.

'You'll have to do it,' he says when Ania knocks on his door. He is lying in bed, one arm thrown across his face, still in his nightclothes.

Ania stares at him, appalled. 'I won't,' she says.

Rainer turns and faces the wall.

So Ania, creature of duty and slave to her own fear of punishment, takes them herself. Arthur Greiser, the leader of the Warthegau, is known for his harsh response to insubordination, and she has her own sons to think about.

She kisses her sons and tells them to stay in their room, pretend they are sick.

And as dawn is breaking, Ania and the two boys set off. A weak grey light illuminates the road through the winter haze. There is always haze here, a dulling white cloud of steam that rises from the manure in the fields and hovers in the air.

Heiner sees the journey as an opportunity for unfettered bullying, which he begins by tossing pebbles at Gerald's narrow back. 'Stop it!' Ania commands. 'Stop it this instant.'

But Heiner just laughs. 'What will you do – send me back?'

'I will tell whoever is to oversee you.'

'What, that your "best and brightest" don't follow your orders?' He hoots with delight at his own cleverness and begins flinging even larger stones at the smaller boy. Gerald yelps and turns to hit Heiner with his own stealthily palmed rock. In an instant they have fallen into a flailing heap.

'Stop! Stop it!' Ania shouts, slapping at Heiner's back. They are on a long stretch of uninhabited road and her voice sounds like the chirping of an irrelevant bird. She can only stand and stare at them. Gerald is beyond her help. By what sleight of hand did her enthusiasm for national service, for shaping young men and building community, turn into this?

'You should be ashamed,' she says, speaking equally to herself.

When they stand, Gerald is bleeding. His lip is split, and he has a black eye. She takes the handkerchief from her pocket, spits on it, and wipes his cuts.

They continue the rest of their walk in merciful silence, occasionally interrupted by Heiner's tuneless whistling. From Gerald she hears a quiet, choked breathing sound. His face has swollen to a livid purple; she tries not to think of his mother. It will be up to Ania to explain his condition to the authorities.

The station at Kutno is packed with people. Since Stalingrad, the Russians have been advancing. The chickens are coming home to roost. Everyone in the east knows it, never mind what Hitler and Goebbels and *Der Stürmer* tell them to believe. Here are the first waves of evidence: wizened grandmothers, bedraggled young women and babies, old men with long faces and an air of desperation, all fleeing before the advancing Russian troops.

Ania and the boys are the only ones waiting on this side of the tracks. The camp where they are headed is farther east. Hitler has ordered Germans in the territories to stay put, but meanwhile Himmler quietly moves their prisoners deeper into the Reich.

'Will we take the prisoners west by train?' Gerald asks.

Ania has no idea. Truthfully, she has not given the details of their task much thought. Ania has become skilled at not thinking beyond her own sons.

It is late afternoon when they arrive. The sky is vast and grey. The station has no name, and there is no town or village anywhere in sight – only a fence surrounding long, low barracks beside a giant quarry. Ania is confused. She has understood the camp to supply labour for an SS farm. But this does not look like a farm.

Even Heiner seems cowed. They make their way along the fence towards what appears to be the front gate, flanked on both sides by rudimentary guard booths, from which two SS men emerge. 'Halt!' one shouts.

Ania and the boys freeze.

An eerie silence follows, punctuated by the whirring and hammering of heavy machinery. The men continue their approach.

It occurs to Ania that she is expected to speak.

'We've come from Lager 428, in the Warthegau,' she says. 'I am delivering trainees.'

The older of the two men holds out his hand for the papers. The younger one grins and nicks his chin towards Gerald's swollen face.

The man glances up from the papers and eyes Heiner and Gerald, his gaze lingering on the black eye. Then he nods. Apparently they are in the right place.

He gestures for the boys to walk.

As they continue towards the gate, they can see the activity on the other side. Prisoners are sorting piles of stones and loading them into wagons bound for a cement works. A group of them pull an impossibly heavy-looking cart. And, as Ania watches, something becomes clear: they are all women.

Ania stops and stares.

'Move along,' the SS man barks, and Ania complies automatically. But she keeps her eyes on the women. As she watches, one of them sinks to her knees, causing confusion down the line – the others continue to pull, even though she is still attached to the rope of her harness. Her body sags forward but cannot completely drop. No one stops, and for a grisly moment, she is pulled along, in danger of being run over. Then the accompanying guard lunges forward and slices the rope that holds her and she tumbles to the ground. The woman behind her manages to kick her body to the side, out of the way of the wheel.

Without thinking, Ania stops and covers her mouth.

'*Nha?*' The younger guard grins. '*Arbeit macht frie.*' Ania can make out the words despite his Polish accent. A grim parody of what she once understood them to mean: *Work will free you.* Reeducation through labour, Hitler's promise of redemption through hard work.

On the other side of the fence, the fallen woman gets to her knees. Ania's whole body is swept with relief. She is all right! But then, in one motion, the guard smacks her with the butt of his rifle. She falls sideways, this time facing the gate.

'Frau Brandt!' the senior SS man says sharply. 'Unterscharführer Pretski will take your boys to their quarters. You will follow me to sign the papers. There is a train due in half an hour that you can take back.'

As if underwater, Ania returns her eyes to the boys, these fifteen-year-olds she has delivered to this hell. 'Heil Hitler!' Heiner says loudly and salutes. Gerald, more shakily, follows suit.

Ania knows what is required of her. But she cannot move her arm, or open her mouth.

Their eyes are all on her.

'*Mach's gut,*' she says in something like a whisper as, on the other side, the woman is dragged away.

All the way back to the lager, Ania thinks of the boys. Of horrible Heiner and kind Gerald and the fact that she is the one who delivered them to that place. She thinks of Gerald's unwitting mother, in some drab apartment, missing her son. And she thinks of Otto Smeltz, the first boy she betrayed. She is no better than those SS men with the babies. All these years she has been putting one foot before the other, imagining herself a good person, a good mother, someone labouring for a just cause.

And she thinks of the woman hanging from the cart, the way she fell, slumped at the waist like a rag doll. When she crawled to her knees and looked out towards Ania, her face was empty, filled only with pain and the most basic remnant of life. But once, it had been the face of a mother or wife. Possibly of a sister or an aunt or a best friend. And underneath the layers of time, the face of someone's child, a girl some mother clothed and fed and held.

Above Ania, the moon is nearly full and the stars are as bright as always. *Cassiopeia, Orion, Arachne* . . . The names of the constellations return to her in her father's voice. They are all in their places, a buffer against the chaos and indifference of the universe.

It is what is down here below them in the mud that is all wrong.

When Ania arrives at the lager, it is nearly three in the morning. But she does not crawl into her bed. Propelled by a barely tamped-down horror, she packs her paring knife, a blood sausage, and a loaf of bread. Nothing sentimental. Only what they will need to survive. When she is done, she wakes her boys and leads them out into the dawn. Her urgency is so compelling they demand no explanation.

And so the night she delivers Heiner and Gerald to their fate becomes the morning Ania and her sons join the flow of displaced persons, severed from themselves.

CHAPTER THIRTY

FRÜHLINGHAUSEN, DECEMBER 1950

The Frühlinghausen Benita returned to was shockingly un-changed. On the surface there were amendments, of course. The mental hospital was gone, for example – the building had burned to the ground, and the patients, Benita thought with her new post-war black humour, had probably all been euthanised. There was no more foul-smelling fertiliser pit beside the cannery and no more dingy Krensig Strasse. The ancient, mouldering thatched roofs had proved incendiary when a nearby stretch of train track was bombed. This was no surprise to Benita. For the last half century those cottages had been waiting for an opportunity to self-destruct.

But Frühlinghausen was still home to the same stupid people Benita had always wanted to escape. The once promising young Nazi mayor had turned into a beefy, middle-aged pig farmer with green-tinged glasses that made him look sinister. Fearless Fräulein Brebel, one-time leader of Benita's BDM group, was now a middle-school teacher – so much for denazification! And the boys who had courted Benita were all either dead or married; running their family's farms or working at the cannery. The stolid red-brick Catholic church Frau Gruber had dragged her children to every Sunday morning was once again well attended, its shattered stained-glass window replaced with an ugly pane of wavy yellow glass.

Of the Gruber family, only Gertrud and Lotte remained. Frau Gruber had died before the war began in earnest, and Benita's brothers lay beside her in the town graveyard: Georg, the youngest, shot God knows where in Russia, and Hans, dead of an infection caught in a military hospital. Sophie, the second-oldest Gruber daughter, had married an American soldier and moved to a place called Kansas. This was both marvellous and galling to Benita. How could plain, quiet Sophie, who had always been so content in Frühlinghausen, have been the one to escape?

Lotte and Gertrud lived side by side in a row of new stucco cottages with matching lace curtains over the windows and tiny gardens full of practical plantings: potatoes, cabbage, carrots, and parsley. It made Benita want to cry.

'Tired of life in the castle?' Lotte said with a smirk when Benita first stepped off the train.

Gertrud was kinder. 'Mother would be happy that you came back.'

But unfortunately Benita was staying with Lotte, whose children had already left home. Her daughter had married the local butcher, and her son was studying in Braunschweig to become a government clerk. The Grubers (now Freiholzes, thanks to Lotte's unpleasant husband, Gephardt) were moving up in the world. Benita found this a good joke. But there was no one to share it with.

The beginning of December marked three months since Benita had been back. Lotte, who was always prickly, was now downright peevish. Whether this was because of Benita's continued presence or Gephardt's prolonged absence was impossible to know. Gephardt had gone south to see his ailing mother shortly after Benita's arrival, and for the last two weeks Lotte had eagerly awaited his return. Maybe the delay brought to mind the long years she had spent raising children while he did God knows what in a Siberian labour camp. Or maybe the constant effort of preparing a hot dinner in expectation set her on edge. Benita slunk around the house like a person trying not to wake a sleeping baby. But even so, she managed to get on Lotte's nerves.

'Benita,' Lotte said when Benita let herself into the cottage one afternoon, 'have you thought about applying for a job at Weseman's?'

Benita had not even unwrapped her scarf.

Weseman's had opened recently – a narrow grocery with no windows and a heavy smell of cigarette smoke, long shelves of canned and packaged goods. These were not in high demand in Frühlinghausen, where almost everyone still grew their own produce, canned their own fruit, and bought their meat from the butcher. Benita had set foot inside the place exactly once.

'Lotte, let poor Benita catch her breath,' Gertrud chided from the table where she sat cracking nuts for Christmas cookies.

'Isn't that what she was just doing? Strolling around in the fresh air?'

'It's all right,' Benita said, shedding her coat. She knew better than to bristle at Lotte's barbs. 'Are they looking for someone?'

'I should think so – I heard Trude complaining about the long hours – dawn till dusk and no one to fill in besides her and Horst. Apparently she never sees him anymore – though I don't know if that's really much to complain about.' Lotte slipped into an imitation of a man with a stiff back and pained face. Lotte had once been the class clown, a brash, big-boned, and funny girl everyone was slightly afraid of, and she maintained a little of this demeanour as an adult.

'Lot-te,' Gertrud chided. 'Horst is a nice man.'

'Who said he wasn't?' Lotte cracked a walnut with particular violence.

She and Gertrud had their own way of communicating – a kind

of closeness achieved through years of living side by side, sharing the profound and the mundane. Benita existed entirely outside its confines, a *subject* of their conversation rather than a participant. 'Well, he is nice,' Gertrud said to Benita. 'It's true.'

Obviously they had discussed the job already; Benita was their mutual problem to solve.

'I'll go tomorrow,' Benita said.

She had tried to find work already. First at the local kindergarten, but she had no experience. Then with Frau Kurtzdorf, the town seamstress, but she did not know how to work a sewing machine. She had even applied at a department store a long bus ride away in Bremel but was told she was too old. Too old! The portly Dutchman conducting the interview had given her a lascivious once-over even as he pronounced this. It made her furious and despairing in turn.

But what could she do but keep trying? Lotte needed money for coal and provisions. Gephardt either could or would not work; it was unclear which. In any case he contributed nothing by way of household income, and beneath her scornful demeanour Lotte was worn out. She worked long hours in the canning factory office. Benita could not blame her for wanting support, and she did not want to be a burden.

Standing in the small, chilly parlour with its familiar lamp on the table – the same one Frau Gruber had kept in a place of honour in her own dingy parlour – Benita knew she should sit down beside Gertrud and help shell the walnuts, that she should make conversation and inquire whether there was any news of Gephardt, or ask what the church had planned for the first Sunday of Advent or whether Gertrud's children were over their colds. But she could not. 'I have a headache – I'm going to lie down a moment,' she said instead.

'Of course you are,' Lotte retorted, raising her eyebrows in Gertrud's direction. 'That's our Benita.'

*   *   *

Upstairs, Benita sank onto her narrow bed and looked at the photograph of Martin that hung beside it. In it, he was about nine; his arms were outstretched, his hair ruffled by wind. It was taken in the field below Burg Lingenfels. The grass rose to his knees, and Benita could almost hear the skylarks and swallows, the papery rustle of grasshoppers. It had been a beautiful, warm afternoon – a picnic with Marianne and Ania and all the children, at the end of their time living in the castle. There had been resistance to the plan in the beginning – Elisabeth had wanted to stay inside and read her book, Fritz had complained of a toothache, and Benita herself had wanted to go into Tollingen to shop for a new hat. But Marianne had prevailed – it was the perfect day for a picnic, she insisted. And she wanted to take photographs with her new camera. Photographs of a picnic! Both Ania and Benita had been appalled. In their experience, cameras were precious, delicate tools, reserved exclusively for formal portraits – not toys to be toted along to take pictures of sweaty, disorderly children running wild. But how right Marianne had been to insist! The day had been wonderful – one of the happiest of Benita's life. And in the photograph of Martin running, Marianne had captured a rare and unguarded moment of joy. Here was the thing Benita was most proud of: She had raised a boy capable of such feeling. Somehow, despite everything, he could experience this.

Why did you decide to go back to Frühlinghausen? he had asked in his first letter, and she had answered as best she could: There was no reason for her to rely on Marianne's hospitality any longer. And it was important to be near her sisters; Lotte needed her help with the house . . . She knew her answers were thin. But Martin seemed to have accepted them because he had not asked again.

In his last letter he had written of an invitation.

A wealthy classmate from an old family had asked him to spend the winter holiday skiing with them in Switzerland. He was reluctant to accept. *I don't want to leave you alone at Christmas, Mother,* he wrote. *I could stay with you in Frühlinghausen. Does Lotte have room?* The thought depressed Benita. She hated the idea of him here among Lotte, Gertrud, and their families. He would have to sit beside Gephardt in the dingy church pew she had loathed as a child. He would have to eat with people who gobbled their food in silence and wiped their mouths with the backs of their hands. This was not what she had raised him to be.

No, she had insisted. *Accept the invitation. You can and come visit in the new year. It will be good for you to learn how to ski.* So he would spend Christmas on the slopes of St Moritz with some happy family of dukes and duchesses. It was better this way, but at the same time her heart ached. She would content herself with his image and letters and the knowledge that he was happy.

The next day she steeled herself for an interview at Weseman's.

Lotte, being Lotte, had gone over first thing in the morning and laid the groundwork. God knows what embarrassing things she had told them. In any case, she reported, the owners were happy to meet with Benita. In fact, Trude Weseman remembered her from their days together in the BDM.

This startled Benita. She did not remember a Trude Weseman.

Lotte stared at her impatiently. Trude *Schultz*. She had married a Weseman.

A face presented itself to Benita: pale and large eyed, with pimply skin and dark hair pulled back into tight braids. Of course! Benita felt the stirring of hope. They had shared experience to go on – not friendship, but a connection: all those long hours with Fräulein Brebel, singing Nazi *Volkslieder* and slogging through arduous Sunday hikes. All that ridiculous homemaker training, stamping butter and aerating batter and generally learning skills the war would render useless. There would, maybe, be something to laugh about.

But when she arrived, she did not recognise the woman who opened the door. Over the years Trude had grown stout. And her pimples had given way to pockmarks. Her hair had gone prematurely grey. Benita realised with dismay that she had seen this woman around town once or twice already and not acknowledged their connection.

'Trude!' she said warmly, offering her best smile.

Trude nodded her head curtly, rejecting Benita's familiar tone.

Had she felt snubbed by their recent encounters? Benita resolved to be particularly self-deprecating and complimentary. 'How long it's been since the days of Fräulein Brebel,' she said. 'And you look wonderful. Not a day older.'

'I certainly look days older.' Trude sniffed, shaking her head. 'Come this way – Horst is in the parlour.'

Benita followed.

Had Trude not liked her as a girl? She could not remember. But often someone had been sweet on someone who was sweet on Benita and this had made for hard feelings . . . Maybe Trude had hankered after Paul Henike? Or Axel Pittman? Those years were a great meaningless fuzz in Benita's mind. Following the woman's stiff back down the hall, Benita reproached her teenage self. What had she done back then? And why had she cared so little?

In the parlour, Horst rose from behind a messy desk. He was a thin, balding man with stooped shoulders and a tired air, quite like Lotte's imitation.

Benita extended her hand. 'So nice to meet you,' she began. 'Frühlinghausen is lucky to have your store.'

Trude made an impatient gesture. 'Ach, sit down, sit down.' She waved away Benita's words.

Stung, Benita complied. So did Horst. It was clear who was in charge. Horst offered an apologetic smile.

'So Frau Gruber – pardon – Frau *Fledermann* is looking for a position as a shop assistant,' Trude stated flatly. 'What are the days we need help on our schedule?'

'Well.' Horst rustled the papers on his desk. 'We could work around the times Frau Fledermann has available as—'

'Come, Horst,' Trude broke in. 'What are the hours on the schedule in front of you?'

'I'm very flexible,' Benita offered. 'I'm sure I could—'

'Do you have experience with a cash register?' Trude interrupted.

'Not with a cash register, no,' Benita began. 'But I could learn—'

'So you don't know it already?' Trude asked, as if this were preposterous.

'No.' Benita shook her head.

At his desk, Horst cleared his throat.

Trude let out a sharp bark of laughter. 'So then – surely you did not think we would take you on out of charity?'

Benita looked at her. Her face was the embodiment of Frühlinghausen, all the meanness and small-mindedness Benita had always despised – only transformed from an indifferent force to a specific, ugly power, a highly evolved venom to which she was uniquely susceptible. 'No,' Benita said with as much dignity as she could summon, and gathered her bag and hat. 'I know you have none of that.'

She walked through the town like a blind woman. And in her humiliation, she did not notice the telltale signs that Gephardt had returned – the hat and boots in the doorway vestibule, the dirty plate and napkin on the table. She made her way upstairs without even removing her coat.

In her small room under the eaves she was greeted by a surprise: an unfamiliar steamer trunk, an old suitcase, and a carpetbag she recognised.

The sight jolted Benita, momentarily, from her misery. Her belongings. She had asked Marianne to pack them for Gephardt to retrieve; his mother lived not far from Tollingen. Marianne had objected. Wouldn't Benita come herself so they could have a chance to visit? But Benita had remained steadfast. And Gephardt, for all his usual crankiness, was oddly amenable to playing porter. Maybe he was curious to see where Benita had been living, or to meet this 'Countess Marianne' (a meeting that was at once comical and horrifying for Benita to imagine).

In any case, he had obviously returned. And with him, her old life.

Benita stood in the middle of the room and listened, but the house was silent. Her possessions, piled on the small rug, seemed utterly unassimilable. The fine porcelain jewellery box Marianne had given her, the pretty scarves, the high-heeled shoes she had bought in Munich last year, her favourite dresses. The idea of these treasures *here*, in this house, in Frühlinghausen, depressed her. Who was there to look pretty for? Even if there were someone, she wouldn't want him. She missed Franz with a physical ache. He had known her – really *known* her, the best and the worst parts. He was the narrow bridge that connected the two.

A step sounded in the hall outside her room.

'I nearly broke my back carrying all that upstairs,' Gephardt grumbled from the doorway. He was a glowering, unpleasant man, once a catch by Frühlinghausen standards, but he had thickened and calcified over time. Now he had a gut like a pregnant woman's belly and restive eyes that made Benita shudder – God knows what he had done during his time in the SS.

'I'm sorry.' Benita sighed. 'Thank you.' She looked down, feeling the sting of her own dependence. Trude Weseman was right – she *was* a charity case.

Gephardt did not move from the doorway.

When Benita lifted her eyes, he was staring at her with a scornful, evaluative expression, one arm braced across the door, blocking the exit. It gave her a start.

'Where is Lotte?' she asked.

He made a choked snort. 'Where's Lotte?' he repeated, still staring. With a chill, she recognised this look, with its particular mix of anger and lust.

Benita drew herself up. 'Come now,' she said. 'There's no need to be childish.'

'Childish?' he repeated, taking a step towards her, breathing fast.

Mercifully, from downstairs came the sound of the front door opening.

'Lotte?' Benita called in a falsely light tone. 'Is that you?'

'Who else?' Lotte snapped.

Gephardt glared at Benita.

'Gephardt?' Lotte exclaimed, apparently noting the signs of his return that Benita had missed. 'Are you back?!'

For a moment he didn't speak. Benita returned his glare. 'I'm here,' he answered finally, turning on his heel.

After he left, Benita shut the door behind him and leaned against it for what seemed like an eternity.

That evening, she feigned a headache and did not go downstairs to dinner. Instead she stayed in her room and opened the chest. She did so with a sense of duty rather than pleasure. First there were the creams and perfumes she had collected over the past year, as the stores again began to stock such items. Then the combs for her hair, the scarves, the brooch Franz had given her.

And beneath these, papers – the forms Marianne had helped her fill out as an *Opfer*, Martin's notes from school, her marriage licence, written in stark indecipherable Nazi script she shuddered to look at. She had half a mind to burn it. And then the shoebox of Franz's letters, tied prettily with a red-and-white ribbon. She had knotted the packet herself and imagined rereading the letters together with Franz, one day when they were old. She could barely look at them now. But as she moved to replace the lid, she caught sight of something else. A longer, thinner envelope much handled and slightly yellowed.

To my wife, Benita Fledermann was written across the front in a familiar, elegant script. The blood rushed to her head and away, leaving her faint. Here was Connie's letter. The one Marianne had given her so many years ago. The one she had never opened. She had entirely forgotten that it existed.

From downstairs Benita could hear Lotte and Gephardt's conversation, the shrill warble of her sister's voice and her husband's low, insolent grunts. Raindrops pattered on the sloped roof. She lifted the letter gingerly, half expecting it to disappear at her touch.

How could she have forgotten?

The fact was preposterous. What kind of woman would forget a letter from her dead husband? Why had she never read it? In the beginning, she had been too angry. This was true. But afterwards . . . afterwards she had simply let it slip. It filled her with shame.

Benita opened the envelope. The letter was not long. But at first, her eyes refused to make sense of the words, which swam and jostled on the page. Gradually, though, they fell into place.

My dearest Benita, it read. She could hear Connie's voice. It had been so many years since she had heard it. *If you are reading this, it means the plot I have given my life for has failed. That Hitler is still in power and I am dead.*

She felt that time rise up around her – the flat in Berlin, Martin playing marbles on the floor. The restless loneliness and anger. The shriek of the air-raid siren.

I am sorry then that I put this spike between us for nothing. That is what I most regret.

I never meant to keep secrets from you, my love. I only wanted to protect you. The less you knew, the safer you would be. I could not let you bear responsibility for my actions. And I don't even know if you agree with them. Our love is not a part of world events and politics. Our love has always been its own country.

Benita, I am so sorry for the ways I have hurt you. I know

I have not been the husband you dreamed of. I have been foolish. I have been selfish. I have acted sometimes with my own interests, and our country's interests, at heart. But I have always believed our future as individuals is fused with Germany's. If I, as a human being, don't act against Hitler, I cannot live with myself. If we Germans don't put out our own demon, he will never be exorcised.

My dearest, I write this by way of explanation, if you should want one.

But what I most want to say is that I loved you from the moment I saw you on the day of the Anschluss, by the mill-pond, in your solemn little uniform. And I never stopped. Even now, as you read this. Be happy. Care for our son. Raise him to know happiness as you do. And I will be with you.

Yours always,

Connie

Benita set the letter down. Connie – her dear Connie, whom she had never even said goodbye to. Whom she had hated – really *hated* – for so long. But he had always been strong. He had lived his life on a plane of grand ideals and all-encompassing rights and wrongs. His view had been much longer than the trappings of his own life. And she had been the little mouse who could see no farther than her own nose, stumbling over roots and stones, oblivious to the oncoming storm.

She sat for a long time. Night deepened outside. The rain passed and stars shone. A sliver of a moon rose, shedding no light.

Her collection of objects lay in heaps, no more substantial than the scraps of leaves and paper a bird might use to shore up her nest. Somewhere, out in the world, Franz Muller moved through life, serving dinner to Clotilde and his father on the yellow table-cloth, or working late in his coffin shop. And somewhere Marianne was doing . . . God knows what: writing, organising, dining with friends – Marianne never just sat. And Martin, her own son

– Benita imagined him in his room at Salem, head bent over his books, improving his life.

There was a purpose to each of their lives. Even Franz was responsible for old Herr Muller and Clotilde. Only Benita had no purpose. She had already raised her son. All she could do now was hold him back. She was a woman built for love. But love was dead – at least to her and to her generation. There was no place left for it in this world. And yet, she had never wanted anything else.

In the dark, she removed her dress and jewellery and lay down on the bed. She took one of the pills Lotte's doctor had prescribed to help her sleep. And as the warm, floating feeling of a dream came on, she shook another pill into her hand. She saw Connie's face as it was when he had come to her that last night, and it felt almost possible to go back, to turn to him and say *Goodbye* and *Good luck*. To give him her blessing. And she saw Martin in her arms, as a baby, his sweet, innocent face lighting up when she bent towards him. To this too she could return.

She took a few more pills, and then the rest, swallowed them with one gulp. And then she lay back down.

CHAPTER THIRTY-ONE

FRÜHLINGHAUSEN, DECEMBER 1950

The train ride from Tollingen to Frühlinghausen was long and full of transfers. Three minutes to change trains in Frankfurt, seven in Kassel, twenty in Göttingen . . . everything was once again on time. In the cities, bombed-out remains of buildings had been oddly integrated into the general forward motion of life – like assimilated amputations, noticeable only to strangers, such as those passing through on trains.

Marianne and Martin managed, for the last leg of their journey, to find an empty compartment. It was not a busy travel time: midday, midweek, children at school, adults at work. Everyone was caught up in the reassuring web of industry. Only the travellers had come unstuck.

'When the war ended, why did my mother go to you instead of her family?' Martin asked, startling Marianne. She had almost forgotten he was sitting across from her, wrapped in his own cloak of grief. He had grown tall in the last months at school, and his legs sprawled across the aisle, his shoulders hunched forward like folded wings.

'It made sense at the time,' Marianne said. 'Everything was mixed up. No one was where they started. And I don't think—' She stopped herself. She was unsure what Benita had relayed to Martin about her family.

'What?' Martin pressed.

Marianne sighed. 'I don't think she was close to her family.'

Martin turned to stare back out of the window. One after another poor, dilapidated farm flew past – prosperity had returned to Germany but not to this corner of the country. Martin did not ask the obvious question: Why, then, had Benita gone back to Frühlinghausen in September? His mother must have offered him some sort of explanation. And whatever it was, it had not turned him against Marianne. For that she was grateful. Benita had 'died in her sleep,' according to the telegram. But Marianne had understood. It was her fault Benita was dead. Her meddling had killed her. She would never outlive this.

What Martin understood of his mother's death remained unclear.

He was an inscrutable boy. Not just now, in his grief, but always. Unlike Fritz, no matter where Martin went, he was well liked. He was popular with his peers and with his teachers, the kind of boy parents were happy to invite to their homes. He was agreeable and excelled in school, but what he cared about, what he felt passion for, remained mysterious. He had inherited his father's likability without his streak of rebellion and strong-mindedness.

'Will you recognise your aunts?' she asked him.

'Lotte and Gertrud?' Martin looked worried. He had met them only a few times.

'Never mind,' Marianne said. 'We'll find them together.'

Martin did recognise them, though, thank God, because Marianne never would have identified the two drab, middle-aged ladies waiting on the platform as Benita's sisters. One was tall and square jawed and wore incongruously peaky cat-eye glasses. Her greying hair was tucked into several neat but unartful rolls. The other was medium height and softer in appearance, with a wide, doughy face and bright blue eyes. Neither looked anything like Benita. Where had she come from?

'Tante Lotte? Tante Gertrud?' Martin asked, approaching the women with childish uncertainty. The taller of the two nodded. But she offered no smile, no warm greeting, no expression of condolence – only a grim nod and a handshake – one for Martin and one for Marianne. At least the dough-faced sister, who introduced herself as Gertrud, gave Martin an awkward pat on the shoulder. Marianne felt sorrow for her dead friend – how could a woman who had so loved beauty and fine things have lived here with these stark sisters, in this ugly place?

A memory rose to the surface: a day in the early summer, shortly before they had moved from Burg Lingenfels. She and Benita and Ania and all the children had taken a picnic out to the hillside – an old tablecloth from Weisslau, embroidered by Albrecht's grandmother, a basket of cold meatballs and potato salad, pickles, fresh plums, a thermos of coffee, and Ania's butter cake with raisins. The hayfield buzzed with insects and meadowlarks and smelled of hot grass and flowering nettles. Below them a field of rapeseed bloomed a brilliant, other-worldly yellow. The air above shimmered with heat. Marianne had brought a camera, the first one she had ever owned, and snapped pictures of the children running helter-skelter. *This is what we live for, isn't it?* Benita had said, her face flushed with happiness.

On this cold December day, Frühlinghausen was the opposite of this. From the train station, Lotte and Gertrud took them directly to the cemetery. They wanted to show Martin his mother's plot before the service and the burial, scheduled for the following day. *Probably because he was expected to pay for it* was Marianne's uncharitable thought.

Should she be buried here in Frühlinghausen? Lotte had asked Marianne during their one telephone conversation. Where else? Not beside Connie, whose remains had been disposed of as a traitor's – buried in some pit or burned in a Nazi crematorium. No one had ever been told exactly where. Marianne felt revulsion towards the whole endeavour of burial. Bodies, so precious in life, then suddenly in death so awkward and full of horror. She would be cremated and have her ashes scattered at the castle. None of this delicate balance between earthly preservation and rot.

The sisters had hired a local farmer with a wagon to take them to the graveyard, and they rode in silence. Marianne squeezed Martin's hand as the horse jerked over the cobblestones.

The cemetery was a humble place at the very edge of town, enclosed by an ugly new cement wall. At one end, it was bordered by fields, ploughed and turned, nothing but clods of earth at this time of year, stretching towards the horizon. At the other sat the last of a row of grubby brick cottages. Two boys kicked a soccer ball in the backyard, bouncing it off the cemetery wall. Otherwise there was only the sound of wind blowing across the fields and the caw of a raven from above. The wagon driver grinned and nodded as they climbed down as if they were off to a party.

The graves were elevated in the traditional way – small, coffin-sized plots bordered by stone, planted with flowers, all scraggly and dead. Lotte led them to the spot already dug out for Benita, beside her mother: ILSE GRUBER, 1880–1940. Marianne blinked tears back fiercely. This was not the time and place to cry. She was aware of Martin, standing still as a statue beside her.

'It's a nice place,' Lotte asserted crisply. 'People take care of the graves. Gertrud and I come once a week to visit Mother and our brothers, so we will be here often. This is a yellow rose-bush.' She pointed at a trimmed stalk, tied up for winter. 'And here we plant pansies and lavender; the ivy is good too because it covers so much . . .' The subject of the flowers made her talkative, but Marianne only half listened. This was where Benita would lie, returned to the roots she had tried so hard to leave behind, and a part of her life that Marianne had never known. But what *had* she known? Very little, maybe. Not of Benita and her love affair, or of Ania, who was not Ania, and with whom she had not spoken since that day in the castle. Standing at the grave, Marianne was suddenly aware of her own blindness; her dearest friends were like dreams she had woken from. How had she missed so much?

'What's that?' Martin asked, bringing her back to the present moment. He pointed at a small cart beside a pile of soil.

'Turnover,' Lotte said, following his hand. 'Every thirty years they dig up the graves to make room for new ones.'

'Oh.' Martin nodded, but his eyes looked shocked.

'If there is a marker, they will preserve it, of course,' Lotte continued in her matter-of-fact way. 'But often with the old graves there is none.' She sniffed. 'It keeps the cemetery' – she searched for the word – 'fresh; no grave is forgotten, because no one here has been dead for more than thirty years.'

Marianne stared. She thought of her own family plot in Pomerania with its ancient graves – her grandparents and great-grandparents and their parents before them, in the shade of a giant chestnut tree, and of the von Lingenfels cemetery in Weisslau, with its plots dating back to the eighteenth century. Certainly there was no one left to tend these. Did the Poles, who had taken their land, roll the graveyard right into the wheat field beside it? Apparently, this was the new way – a rapid turnover of bodies.

'And after thirty years?' Marianne asked. 'No one is remembered?'

Lotte stared at her with a blank expression. 'Remembered, maybe, but not tended. Not *maintained*.'

Later, after the funeral and after Marianne had brought Martin back to school, she returned to Tollingen. No one was there to greet her. She walked from the train station to the town square and stared up at her flat. Its windows looked dark and sad in the shadow of evening, and she could not bring herself to go inside.

Behind her, in the square, the Wild Boar began setting its outdoor tables. Mothers pulled their children home to supper, shop workers closed shutters, lovers strolled hand in hand. And there were men on the streets again, smoking cigarettes and hurrying home to their families, happily returned to everyday life. She felt a pang of sadness for Albrecht, for Connie, for all those who had not lived to see this new life.

She could not go upstairs to the kitchen she had once shared with Benita and make herself a lonely egg and toast. She could not sit in the twilit parlour and sort through Albrecht's papers. She could not pass by all those empty rooms – Benita's, Martin's, her own children's. And she could not go to visit Ania, sit in her warm kitchen, remember Benita together, and be comforted.

Marianne left her bag behind the stairs in the foyer and walked towards the river at the edge of town. At least she could sit here and mourn, among the bones of all the poor souls who had died on its banks. She could lie on the grass and look at the stars and be lulled by the rush of the river's poisons. But as she neared the riverbank, she realised she was not alone. A figure, half obscured by shadow, stood with his back to the water, swaying a little on his toes. His lips moved slightly, and she could hear his low, murmuring voice, speaking a language she did not understand. Eventually his words came to an end.

'Excuse me,' she said as he turned and took in her presence.

He was a young man, maybe twenty-five, even if his face was much older. He wore a black hat and his hair in long curls: a Jewish DP from one of the few remaining camps.

'It's allowed,' he said. Marianne stared at him, confused. 'It's allowed to pray here,' he clarified.

'Of course.' She stepped back, startled that he thought she would question this. 'Did you know someone? Among the dead?'

The man scowled and then squinted at her as if trying to read her intent.

'I knew them *all*,' he said. The words hung between them.

'I also came here to pray,' Marianne said, realising as she spoke that this was true.

Above them, the first stars of evening were suddenly visible, like holes in a thin cloth, revealing a great light behind the darkness. The river shone a pale and other-worldly violet.

The man regarded her intently, and Marianne found herself awaiting some sort of verdict.

Finally, he ducked his head.

'Well, go on then,' he said. 'You can be here forever with that task.' He turned to go.

'And you?' Marianne said.

He looked back at her. 'I leave tomorrow for America.'

And looking at him, this young stranger with an old face, Marianne felt the truth of his words and his weariness. But through this, she heard the word *America,* as if for the first time. Not as the name of an enemy nation or as an Ally. Not as the originator of bombs and oranges and chocolate or as the creator of all the paperwork she had so tirelessly filled out for so many refugees. She heard it as the name of a place where a person could begin again.

Long after the man had departed, the word blew around in her mind, like a scrap of paper, alluring and brightly coloured, hinting at another life.

PART IV

CHAPTER THIRTY-TWO

DEER ISLE, MAINE, JULY 1991

The road to Marianne's home on the coast of Maine was as winding and lovely as the name von Lingenfels, which Martin had always thought beautiful, though it lost some of its lightness on the American tongue. But Martin was not an American, even after so many years living in New England. He was a German, as this visit reminded him. A German who was more than an hour late, which was not a promising start.

His tardiness was fitting, though. As a boy he had always been late. He could feel the old pattern of behaviour rising, his tendency to fulfill other people's narratives, usually at a cost to himself. So he was to be the hapless teenager, Marianne the overbearing parent, picking up his mother's slack. Never mind that he was now in his fifties and she was eighty-three, and he had not seen her for God knows how long. She had written to say she had a proposal. And while he wasn't generally up for proposals since his most recent divorce, he could not refuse Marianne. It had always been that way.

The turn off Route 114 onto Marianne's little clamshell strewn 'Way' was marked by a profusion of beach plum blossoms, which she had not mentioned in her directions. Possibly because at her age she did not venture far enough to have seen them, but more likely because a thicket of flowers and shiny purple berries was not the sort of thing Marianne made note of, while the sturdy aluminium mailbox, now all but obscured by the bushes, was.

Her house was the last of the seven or eight that lined the road, and when Martin pulled around the corner, he was struck not only by its loveliness – a little grey shingled cottage, with a peaked roof and wrap-around porch – but by its utter Americanness. It was rough-hewn and impermanent looking. Its wide sliding glass doors lent it a quality of carefree openness. Such a great contrast to Burg Lingenfels. *Americans can face the world with open arms,* Marianne had once said, *because the world hasn't yet come to knock it down.*

Before he could climb out of the car, the front door opened and there she was: Marianne von Lingenfels – at once totally recognisable and completely changed. She walked with a cane and wore a pair of thick, squarish glasses, but her grey hair was pulled back from her face in the same practical manner it had always been, with a clip on each side, just above her ears. And her voice, barking his name, rang straight from his past.

'Marianne,' Martin said, slamming the car door behind him. A broad, pure smile spread across her wrinkled face. Here she was, unmoored from the circumstances that for him had always defined her – in America, in *Maine,* for Christ's sake. Yet unlike Martin, who was a chameleon, an adapter to even the strangest situations, Marianne remained completely herself.

From the shore came the sound of the surf, and overhead the seagulls screeched. The front door of the house swung open again and a mournful-faced black woman with her hair braided close against her skull emerged. 'You all right, Marianne?' she asked softly.

'Oh, yes,' Marianne said, keeping her eyes on Martin. Her smile remained fixed – an outpouring of happiness. 'Alice, this is my dear friend Martin.'

Martin climbed the steps and extended his hand, which Alice

accepted shyly. Then he turned to Marianne, grasped her gnarled fingers between his, and kissed her delicate shrivelled cheeks.

'*Ach, Martin,*' she said, clinging to his hands. '*Du bist das Ebenbild deines Vaters.*' *You are the picture of your father.*

Martin continued to smile, but the words resurrected the old, familiar dismay. His father the resister, the great man, the almost-liberator of Germany and almost-saver of so many millions of lives. Marianne had always shone a bright light on the chasm between Martin and this man.

'Come, have a cup of coffee. Or maybe you would like something stronger – a glass of schnapps after your journey,' Marianne said, speaking in English now.

'Coffee would be fine,' Martin replied.

'Sit,' Marianne commanded when they had reached the covered part of the porch where a set of mildewy wicker furniture was grouped like so many pigeons, facing the sea. 'Alice will bring it.'

Martin complied. From here, one could see down to a short, T-shaped jetty, sticking like a cross into the water. The sun on the rocks was strong and bright.

Marianne lowered herself into the armchair opposite Martin, which looked as uncomfortable as his. Comfort, it seemed, was no more relevant to Marianne now than it had been when she was young.

'So how *are* you, Marianne?' Martin said, trying to strike a jovial tone.

'Oh, Martin,' she said, sighing. 'As well as possible for a person of my age. I am a lucky woman.'

'Not old at all,' Martin responded, aware as soon as he said it that she would find the statement ridiculous. 'You look marvellous.'

'Thank you.' Marianne bobbed her head patiently. 'And what of you, Martin Fledermann?' She smiled. 'It was New York, I think, where I saw you last, no?'

'Yes, it was,' Martin said, the day coming clear in his own head with her prompting. He had gone to see her in some big, featureless building on the Upper East Side where she had been living at the time. They drank tea and ate buttered *Pfefferkuchen* and looked out over the city through a draughty picture window, surrounded by all the old things – dark Biedermeier armoires and claw-footed tables, thick white embroidered curtains, and the dusty needle-point portrait of Grossmutter von Lingenfels. Martin had just divorced his second wife, a subject he had been preoccupied with not discussing and that now loomed over the memory as if in fact she had been there – a lovely, sorrowful presence, full of reproach. The rest of the visit, what he and Marianne had discussed, how she had looked, was obliterated from his mind.

'You were working on something – a book – I can't remember the subject now.'

'Ah yes, right.' Martin nodded. 'I'm still working on it.'

'Still?' Marianne raised her eyebrows. 'The same book?'

'The same book,' Martin tried to say with self-deprecating humour, but it came out sounding bitter. The truth was that the book had become the bane of his existence. He had begun his career as a professor with a burst of glory – a lauded first book about post-war anti-Fascist architecture, various academic prizes, and tenure at a well-regarded American university. But then he was gripped by a crippling stiflement. He was meant to write a book that came to terms with something larger than the architecture of renewal. He was meant to write a book that would, in some way, relate to his father, the hero and resister. But that book refused to come.

He leaned back and was rewarded with a stab of broken wicker into his spine.

'That is a long time.' Marianne frowned, studying him.

A probing silence threatened.

'How did you come to this place?' Martin asked. 'It's so . . .' He searched for the word – *primal* presented itself, but Marianne was too German – *he* was too German – to use the word without discomfort. 'Obscure,' he filled in.

Marianne laughed. 'It was difficult for you to find, I think.'

'No, no.' Martin tamped down his instinct to bristle. 'I mean, just this corner of the country – it's not anywhere Elisabeth and Katarina come, is it?'

Elisabeth and Katarina, those dark-haired girls he had spent so much time with as a boy, now lived unfathomable lives in the brash, historyless American west. They too had been drawn here, to this continent of new beginnings, fellow children of Burg Lingenfels. Of the von Lingenfels family, only Fritz, a copyright lawyer at an international law firm, remained in Germany.

'No, no, Katarina vacations in Mexico – or the Caribbean.' Marianne waved his question away. 'And Elisabeth doesn't vacation.'

'Well, it's a long way from Burg Lingenfels.'

'Ha! I should say so.' Marianne laughed. 'And you are in New Hampshire still, I understand from Irena – she is in better touch with me than you are! She sends a Christmas card at least.'

'Does she? Irena?' Martin was startled. He tried to imagine his daughter, the inscrutable suburban schoolteacher she had become, writing to Marianne.

'Every year, last year with a picture of her babies – those sweet little things. To think you are a grandfather, Martin!'

Martin shook his head. It was incredible, actually. He was only fifty-two. Irena was a child of his youth. He had been too young, only twenty-four when he had her, and now she was a mother herself – also too young, in his estimation. Fatherhood had slipped between his fingers, and time hiccupped forward. Now here he was a grandparent. Too late! Too late! Grandparenthood taunted him. *You can't go back and be a father now.*

'I'm not a very good one, I'm afraid,' Martin said.

'*Ach.*' Marianne waved this away too. 'I'm sure you are.'

Martin said nothing. Sitting here, on this weather-beaten porch, with its brittle railings and the dull pounding of the sea below, he felt a grey bloom of failure. This was why it had been so long since he had last seen Marianne. She was the gardener of this ugly flower. She knew just how to turn its face to the sun.

He was relieved to hear Alice opening the screen door, bearing a tray with Marianne's good coffee pot (pale blue with tiny white flowers, how familiar it still was), a carton of milk, and two practical white mugs that had replaced the Meissen china of the old days.

'Have we no jug for the cream?' Marianne frowned. 'This looks not fine.'

'No, ma'am,' Alice murmured. 'No jug.'

'*Ach*, well. So it is.' Marianne sighed. 'But surely there is a sugar bowl.'

Alice nodded and returned to search for one.

'She is Rwandan,' Marianne asserted when she had left. 'Her husband was killed in the civil war there. And her son.'

'My God. How terrible.'

'She is very good. Very honest.'

Martin nodded. Marianne had always been comfortable with such sweeping moral pronouncements.

'You see,' Marianne said, smiling, 'I like always to surround myself with widows.'

'I suppose so.' Martin tried to smile back.

'I miss your mother, you know,' Marianne said. 'She was not one for a houseful of widows.'

The comment jarred him. He was so rarely around anyone who spoke of his mother.

'But she lived in one,' Martin said.

'I think of that man she saw,' Marianne continued, fixing her gaze on the jetty. 'After the war. The ex-Nazi.'

'Herr Muller,' Martin offered, though his own memory of the man was hazy at best. He had been astonished when Marianne told him of his mother's affair, so many years ago. But he had not been alarmed. His own memories of the man were positive. He had shared his Christmas chocolate with him on that long-ago day.

'I was very hard on her about him,' Marianne continued. 'I

think, if she loved him and he loved her . . .' She shook her head. 'This is the main thing, isn't it?'

At that moment, Alice reappeared, carrying a cereal bowl half filled with sugar.

'Aha, well,' Marianne said, breaking the sombre mood, 'we live in elegance here, don't we, Alice?'

'Maybe so.' Alice smiled shyly. She had a scar on her neck, Martin noticed, a thin white line that snaked down from her ear.

'Love is the thing, we agree, is it not?' Marianne asked.

Alice looked from Marianne to Martin. 'Yes, ma'am,' she said when it became clear that Marianne was addressing her. 'Love is great.'

'You see?' Marianne said to Martin. 'This is what I mean to say: love is great.'

Martin felt suddenly consumingly tired. The heaviness of the exchange, the awkwardness of the moment – what had he expected?

'Would you like anything else?' Alice asked in her soft, pleasantly accented voice.

'No, no – except a schnapps for Martin. He needs one, I think.'

It was maybe an hour or two later, with the sun softening to forgiving afternoon ripeness, that Marianne posed the question. It wasn't a question, actually.

She placed a card in front of him – thick white stationery like a wedding invitation. The return address caught his eye: Burg Lingenfels.

Inside was a postcard with a black-and-white photograph of a woman squinting at the camera, shielding her eyes against the sun, one rubber booted foot propped on a low wall. Marianne, at the cistern.

MARIANNE VON LINGENFELS: MORAL COMPASS OF THE RESISTANCE was printed underneath.

Martin looked up at her, surprised.

'Yes, it's me. A biography.' Marianne made a gesture of dismissal.

'That's wonderful,' Martin said, turning the card over. '*A remarkable story of a woman at the heart of one of the most courageous stands against evil in our time . . .*' he began to read.

'Oh, it's a little much,' Marianne said, though she could not fully conceal her pride. 'But that's not the point. There is a party. This autumn. At Burg Lingenfels.'

Martin sat back. '*A weekend of talks, discussions, and meditations on the subject of resistance,*' he read aloud.

'Martin,' Marianne said, leaning forward, 'I want you to take me there. And I want to find Ania and bring her, too. I want to invite you both – as my guests.'

Martin sighed. 'I would love to, Marianne, but I don't know—'

'Stop.' She lifted a hand. 'Don't say no. I won't let you say no. Think about it first. It is the wish of an old woman. Think of it, if you want, as my last wish.'

Martin looked at her: the thin grey hair, the fragile, papery skin of her face. 'Why do you want me to come with you?'

Marianne cocked her head to the side. 'Why do you think, Martin Fledermann?'

'Because I am my father's son.' He sighed.

'No,' Marianne said, knitting her brows. 'Because you are your *mother's* son.'

It was not decided in that moment.

The sun sank lower in the sky, and at Marianne's formidable insistence, Martin took her for a swim.

'Swim where?' he asked when she proposed the idea.

'Where?' Marianne laughed. 'Look around you, Martin Fledermann. The sea.'

The swimming trunks she provided were folded dustily on the

top shelf of the towel closet: a voluminous pair of brightly flowered shorts – a style Martin dimly recalled from his early days in America as 'jams.' Her son-in-law's, apparently. Martin was a good swimmer, albeit out of practice. As a boy, he had been the star of the Salem swimming team. But it was years since he had swum in the ocean, and never with an eighty-three-year-old.

Marianne wore a blue-skirted suit with violent splotches of purple. Against this, her skin was a pale greenish-grey, finely webbed with wrinkles. Her arm was looped through a bright pink inner tube.

'Ah,' she said, beaming. 'My swim escort.'

'You really want to do this?' he asked, as lightly as possible, though in fact he felt vaguely panicked. He might be responsible for Marianne von Lingenfels's drowning. People would shake their heads and wonder what sort of idiot had allowed an old woman to climb into the cold northern Atlantic Ocean.

'Come,' Marianne said. 'We will have an adventure.' She wrapped his hand under her arm and clutched it against her bony rib cage.

From the porch, there was a dusty path and a set of wooden steps over the rocks, which led to the jetty. His bare feet smarted against the rough ground, and a rivulet of sweat trickled down through the thin patch of hair on his chest. It was still blazing hot in the direct sun, but he did not falter.

And walking, he was struck suddenly by the memory of swimming in the small, gravel-shored German lake where they would picnic on Sundays after the war. '*Schwimmen!*' Marianne would bark at his mother and Ania and their children. '*Nicht sitzen!*' To Marianne, sitting and eating and skimming stones without first plunging in and swimming at least as far as the float was tantamount to sloth. She herself would swim all the way to the other side with her oddly effective head-above-the-water version of the crawl. She was so utterly German in those moments, so determined and so filled with the folksy belief in physical activity and the trappings of innocence, it was hard to separate her from the Teutonic forces she and Albrecht and Martin's father had spent their lives conspiring against. And it was with simmering resentment that Martin would set out behind her, overtake her, and swim until his lungs almost burst.

'So what now?' he asked when they reached the jetty. Waves crashed against the rocks of the shore and sucked back out, leaving eddies scurrying in the crevices.

'There is a ladder at the end,' Marianne said. 'You should go in first' – she handed him the inner tube – 'and hold this for me.'

'All right.' Martin accepted the plastic ring. The metal planks whistled in the wind.

Martin yelped when his bare feet came down on the jetty's gleaming surface. He ran forward and, with one ungraceful jump, dived into the water.

A shock ran through his body at the cold. He swam out a few lengths and watched Marianne as she navigated her own cleverly aqua-sock-shod way along the jetty, holding the rails on either side. At the end, she removed her glasses and looped them over the railing by their strap. Then she stood, squinting down at him.

'It's bracing!' Martin called, shielding his eyes with one hand. 'Are you sure—?'

By way of answer, Marianne began the serious business of lowering herself down the ladder. Her foot paddled the air once, twice, before finding purchase on the top rung, and in the bright sun, her pale, naked limbs shone like some dangerous evolutionary beacon, beckoning the darkest forces of the sea. The ropy veins on her legs seemed treacherous and parasitic – strangling her fragile limbs. But when her feet entered the cold water, she did not flinch.

'Bring the doughnut here,' she directed. 'You hold it steady while I sit.'

Martin did as instructed.

And then, with a surprisingly tremendous splash and a great bobbing jerk, she was in. Through the spray and the swelling waves, Martin held on. The water peeled away from his eyes, and there she was, in her doughnut, like some delicate hatchling in a postapocalyptic nest.

'Are you all right?' he asked, tossing his hair from his eyes.

'Yes,' Marianne said, adjusting herself. 'Yes.' And as she repeated it, her look of discomfort disappeared. 'This is lovely.'

'It is,' Martin echoed, realising it was true. His body tingled pleasantly in the cold. The water rising and falling around his neck was featherlight.

'See?' Marianne said, smiling through the spray. 'Now promise that you'll come back to Burg Lingenfels with me.'

And looking at her small, frail form, Martin felt all the resentment and resistance of the afternoon fall away. How could he refuse? She was Marianne von Lingenfels.

'All right,' he said, taking hold of the string to her inner tube like some marine beast of burden and swimming out to sea.

CHAPTER THIRTY-THREE

CAMBRIDGE, MASSACHUSETTS, JULY 1991

Ania Kellerman had flown 5,000 kilometres, taken the train another 120, collected extra heart and blood pressure prescriptions, suspended bread and milk delivery for three weeks, found, washed, and packed her old but still good trench coat, and filled half her suitcase with good German chocolate, in part so her daughter could show her the house that now stood before them. It was large and grey and beautiful, built in that graceful American style with wooden clapboards and columned porches Americans referred to as 'Victorian' in a confusing homage to an empire they had overthrown. It was certainly unlike most of the houses in England. Or in Germany, for that matter, where homes were built of stone or stucco or brick – never something as precious and impermanent as wood.

'Well?' Marianne – or 'Mary,' as she was called here in America – asked.

'Can we get out of the car?' Ania said, gazing up at the peaked roof.

Mary frowned. It was a demonstrative look, meant to note this example of motherly hardness or wrongness or, at best, ineptitude. The people of today wanted delicate handling, Mary among them. Ania knew this, but she was too stubborn to comply – and anyway, she did not know how.

Ania waited as Mary went around the car to open her door, an unnecessary rule her daughter had established following an incident in the airport car park in which, in Mary's estimation, Ania had nearly been killed. This was not founded in reality: Ania had looked before opening her door and the minivan pulling into the next space had been at least half a metre away, but Mary had an overactive imagination, especially when it came to catastrophe. And Ania appreciated being cared for this way. When her daughter opened her door, she swung her feet out onto the kerb and stood with relative ease. She was lucky to be so fit for an eighty-year-old woman.

Ania used Carsten's walking stick for support as she stood before the house. This was the place Mary intended to raise her children post-divorce. She had bought it herself. There were three floors, the uppermost under a steeply gabled roof. Tall, elegant black shutters framed the windows, and on the second floor, a cream-coloured panel was carved with an overflowing bowl of fruit and above this, less successfully rendered, a flag inscribed with the date 1864.

Ania regarded the clapboards, which were caked with layers of poorly scraped paint. The sill on the third-floor window was brown and rotten where it met the glass.

'So?' Mary prodded. 'You haven't said a word!'

'It is a beautiful house,' Ania said sadly.

'So why the tragedy?'

Ania shook her head. 'It is too old.'

Mary laughed. 'That's the best part! They don't make houses like this anymore. I love its oldness.'

Ania regarded her daughter, the young American she had become in the twenty years she had lived here. Mary honestly believed that you could update the electrical system, rebrick the chimney, brace the foundations, and cover over the past with a fine, clean coat of paint, and instead of a fragile, seam-filled heap of expired goods, you would have a fresh new house. She had become American enough to assign a moral value to the house's age.

At forty-one, Mary was a beautiful woman, with thick, honey-coloured hair and a long, intelligent face. She was ageing like an American, though: deep lines between her brows and along the sides of her mouth. Too much smiling. Too much emotion on parade. It was a young country. It mistook the theatre of expression for honesty. If Mary had lived like a German, she would look ten years younger.

'You really don't like it?' Mary asked, growing more wrinkles by the minute, her face contorted into a tableau of surprise.

'I like it,' Ania said.

'Then what is it?'

Ania shrugged. It was a useful gesture with her grown children – a sort of what-do-I-know disclaimer about her general lack of knowledge or understanding of the modern world.

'It's dead,' Ania said finally. 'The things it is made of – they are past their time.'

'Aha,' Mary said, bristling in earnest now. 'So now things that aren't alive can die, too. I see. How wonderful.'

Ania could see her daughter's vexation, all the layers of it: the history of disappointments her mother had doled out to her, all the ways Ania had rebuked and judged and misunderstood her, all the times her blunt and unromantic nature had quashed the joys of Mary's young life. And then there were the surface layers of anxiety about the purchase, which was, in Mary's own words, the biggest financial decision of her life. The sum she had paid struck Ania as exotically expensive, a sign of how discordant her own sense of value was – a language founded on different root words.

Ania took a breath and thought about Jesus, whom she did not believe in but whose teachings, as she understood them from the Bible, seemed in her old age to provide a sound road map for life.

She reached out and placed her hand on Mary's cheek, which was soft and slightly creamy with moisturiser. 'Child, it is a beautiful place. I am an old woman – don't listen to me.'

'Sure, sure, sure,' Mary said crossly, sounding more German now. 'You're only an old woman who happens to be my mother, why would I want your approval?'

Ania looked back at her daughter. *Lightness, lightness,* she told herself. This was what such moments required. She bucked the urge to sigh, to shake her head, to honestly reflect the vast gulf between them, and laughed instead.

'You have this,' she said. 'You will always have my approval.'

Later, when they were back in the car and Mary had found it in herself to speak to her mother again (a product of her talkative nature as well as her obsessive deliberating on the purchase), she began to lay out her plans.

'I don't have to fix everything at once. I'll chip away at it, piece by piece. You know that from living on the farm. You and Father did it your whole life.'

In Ania's mind, she saw Carsten's farm as it had been when she first arrived. The dark washroom with its always-chilly flagstone floor, the toilet at the end of the hall that dropped refuse down a long pipe into a pit.

'If I could have lived somewhere else, I would have,' Ania said with a sigh. 'If we had had the money to tear it down and build a new house, we would have. To me, old things are work. Not romance.'

'Well, they're not *romance* to me, either,' Mary said.

Outside the window, American life flew by – the giant cars, the eclectic, colourful signs for gyms and clothing stores and fast-food restaurants, supermarkets and gas stations with inflatable balloon figures bobbing goofily in the wind. As well as the boarded-up concrete bunkers of obsolete supermarket chains, failed Chinese food shops and electronics outlets, left standing like rotten teeth in an otherwise healthy smile. It didn't matter. There was room for everything. It was a free country. The past was nothing to be ashamed of here.

In Germany, Ania lived in a retirement home, near Lake Constance. It was not far from Carsten's farm or Burg Lingenfels – an hour by car, maybe – but she never went back. For ten years, after Carsten died, Wolfgang had worked the farm with minimal success. Their plot of land was too small to compete with the vast farming conglomerates Germany had established in the former east. Hitler's *Lebensraum* aims achieved, this time in peace. So Wolfgang had sold the farm and moved north, near Lübeck, where he ran a farm equipment dealership.

At the front door of the bland, modern condominium in Newton where Mary had lived since her divorce, there was a large manila envelope.

Mary glanced at the sender and tucked it under her arm as she turned her key. She looked discouraged. Ania felt a pang of guilt. She had hurt her daughter's feelings. And over what? There was no purpose to this disagreement. She was an old woman. And her point of view was more dead, more irrelevant than the house.

The door swung open and sounds of children's exuberant playing came from upstairs. 'Helloo-oo,' Mary called out, tossing the package on the front hall table.

Martin Fledermann. Ania caught the name on the corner of the envelope and felt a rush of adrenalin.

'You are in touch with Martin?' she asked.

'It's for you,' Mary said over her shoulder as she walked up the steps to the family room. 'But don't open it now – I want to show you.'

Ania stared at the package, absorbing this development. A package for her from Martin Fledermann, the tall, handsome, successful man whose nose she had once wiped, whose brow she had mopped when he was sick, whose little pants and shirts and sweaters she had mended and hemmed and layered on his body to make sure he was warm enough for the long walk to school. He was now a university professor here in America.

'Mama!' Mary's six-year-old son, Gabriel, cried, flying across the floor and into his mother's arms, wrapping his skinny, pyjama-clad legs around hers, and burying his face in her belly. It was wonderful how free today's children were, that a boy would offer such an affectionate, unregulated greeting.

'Can I order a pizza?' Sarah, Gabriel's more even-tempered nine-year-old sister, asked from around the corner.

'Yes! Pizza, pizza, pizza!' Gabriel echoed, releasing his mother and bouncing in excitement. 'I love pizza!'

'Did you get the chance to defrost that soup?' Mary called to Perla, the young woman who picked the children up from school and spent the afternoon with them. Mary was a lawyer for some sort of American non-profit organisation devoted to protecting the rights of immigrants. The relevance of her work as the daughter of a Nazi was not lost on Ania. What an amazing country this was.

'I make it in the freedgerator but eets not soft yet—' Perla replied, and her light, soft-vowelled voice trilled on, accompanied by fervent, excited interruptions from Gabriel and dotted with questions from Mary's lower, flatter tone.

Ania's eyes drifted back to the package. She had hoped Martin would drive down from New Hampshire to see her, but the 'timing had not worked' for such a reunion, and she had tried to conceal her disappointment. He was the one person she had remained in touch with from the castle. But now here was this package – whatever it might be. It pleased her to think that he had made the effort to send her something, and that he and Mary had spoken about it. They were children from two different chapters of her life, in touch only because she had introduced them. By the time Mary was born, Martin was nearly a teenager, away at boarding school.

'Hi, Omi,' Gabriel said from the top step, and Ania realised she had missed his greeting the first time. At his mother's prodding, surely, from the way she stood beside him, one hand on his small shoulder.

'Ah! Hello, my child!' Ania said in her brightest language-school English, clapping her hands together.

'Hello.' Gabriel became suddenly shy, rolling his head against his mother's hip, bending one leg so he could grab his ankle. He was an unfamiliar specimen to Ania – an exotic hothouse flower from this time of plenty. She found him both vexing and lovely.

'Did you finish the puzzle?' she asked, selecting her words carefully. For many years now, she had squeezed into a tiny desk at the local elementary school for night classes in English so she might learn the language that would be her grandchildren's. But now when she needed them, the words seemed buried in quicksand.

Gabriel shook his head a little sadly. 'It's too hard for me.'

'No,' Ania said. 'That cannot be. Come show your omi.'

The boy did not move from his mother's side. He was a perceptive child and seemed to understand that he owed his grandmother some particular respect or delicacy. But he was not a natural pleaser. He lived in his own world with its own prescriptions and edicts, which he was not in the habit of amending. Ania could see this sort of thing now, in the luxury of her old age. How her own children had been, what they had loved and hated . . . there had been no time for such reflections when they were young. It gave her a pang of sadness, looking at Gabriel here, and knowing him this well.

'Go on,' his mother said, giving him a little push. 'I bet Omi can help you.'

And so Ania extended her hand and tried, with her smile, to show him she understood his reluctance and did not hold it against him, that she was not actually scary even though she was so old. But he did not look up at her. He took her cool fingers in his own warm hand and pulled her across the floor like a burden.

*   *   *

Mary had been stubborn as a girl. Ania remembered this much. More nuance, more understanding she had not granted the child. She had been born in the beginning of the *Wirtschaftswunder* – that somnambulant time of sudden plenty that had swept Germany like a dream. They had been poor in comparison to Mary's classmates in town, but compared to Anselm and Wolfgang, Mary was raised in the lap of luxury and good fortune, with milk and eggs and chocolate to eat, new shoes to wear, and even, when she turned five years old, a car to share with the Glebers. Unlike her half brothers, Mary had grown up without typhoid and diphtheria and rape. She had not been pressed into overcrowded trains and transport vehicles and fetid, swarming, waterless DP camps full of war-hardened souls. She had always had school, and clothing, and medicine, and a roof over her head.

And most of all she never had to lie.

Had Ania held this against her? Was this why, so many years later, when Mary was an ordinary eleven-year-old who wanted a pair of fine shoes for dancing class or complained about the slow bus ride home from school, Ania would rage about her spoiledness? Once, she had locked her daughter into the pitch-dark smokehouse for a whole afternoon among the gory, half-cured hams and sides of bacon hanging from the ceiling. Many times, she had shouted and threatened absurd punishments for minor infractions. It made Ania sick with regret to think back on those days. Her meanness haunted her in the soft, innocent faces of Mary's children.

But somehow she and Mary had come through. Somehow, they had even become close. It was as if the five thousand kilometres Mary had put between them had given her the space she needed to forgive her mother. They spoke on the phone every Sunday evening. And each autumn, for three weeks, Ania flew across the ocean to stay with her daughter. Who loved her, improbably enough.

Mary sent her large-print books and special reading lights, photos of her children, homeopathic remedies for her bad back and arthritis. When she visited Germany, she took Ania to the movies and introduced her to chamber music and drove her to the cemetery where Carsten was buried. She was Ania's most thoughtful and attentive child. Anselm and Wolfgang were dutiful sons, but neither ever thought about what might make Ania laugh or feel less lonely or more comfortable or better informed. Mary, on the other hand, tried to understand her. She tried to do for her mother what her mother had never done for her.

Mary did not mention the package again until after dinner, when the children had been elaborately and painfully put to bed (there was homework to help with, night lights to leave on, snacks to bring upstairs, as if they were being prepared for a frightening and arduous journey rather than the luxury of sleep). It was nearly nine thirty when Mary emerged, looking haggard. Ania sat at the dining room table sewing a skirt at the sewing machine she had given Marianne so many years ago and that she used, every time she came to visit, to make some new dress or article of clothing for her granddaughter.

'Another schnapps?' Mary asked her mother hopefully as she poured herself one more half glass of wine from the open bottle on the counter. Ania agreed, even though the schnapps did nothing for her anymore – too many old-age medications had dulled her receptors, even her taste buds. But her poor tired daughter should not have to drink alone.

Mary refilled Ania's glass and started to sit before jumping up again, her hands thrown into the air. 'The package! I almost forgot!'

She disappeared into the front hall and reemerged with it. The sight sent a small, prescient shiver through Ania.

'So.' Mary slid the package towards her mother and collapsed into her chair. 'Put away your sewing. Enough work for one day.' She waved her hand as if the project were frivolous nonsense.

This condescension was the price Ania had to pay for their years of fighting. It was a small one.

Obediently, she folded the piece of skirt she was sewing and turned off the machine.

'Okay, so let's open it!' Mary said.

'You want me to?' Ania asked.

'Go on. I know what it is already!' Mary took a sip of her wine.

Ania fumbled with the puffy envelope closure until Mary finally snatched it away and tore what turned out to be a neat pull-tab made expressly for this purpose. She pushed it back across the table to her mother.

Inside was a note folded over a large, formal-looking white envelope addressed to *Ania Kellerman* in an alarmingly familiar hand.

Dear Ania, it read.

It would be a great honour if you would join us at this event. It has been too many years. I would like to invite you to come to Burg Lingenfels as my guest so we could spend time together and know each other again.

Yours,

Marianne von Lingenfels

Ania felt the room swim and her hands begin to shake. It had been nearly fifty years since she had seen her once dearest friend.

'Look inside, Mother – go on,' Mary ordered.

Inside she found a photograph of Marianne, just as she remembered her, in rubber boots with tweed trousers ballooning over them. Ania recognised the bucket she was holding, too – what a precious object it had been then, metal, and dented on one side; they had used it for everything. Even in shadow, you could see the bright intensity of Marianne's expression, daring whoever saw the picture to laugh at her – the young countess in washerwoman's garb.

A party to celebrate the launch of Marianne von Lingenfels: Moral Compass of the Resistance. A book by someone named Claire Weiss. *Five o'clock in the evening, the 21st of October 1991, the Falkenberg Institute, Burg Lingenfels, Ehrenheim, Germany.*

'Frau von Lingenfels is inviting you – and me too, if you want my company – as her guests. And Martin will be there as well. I've spoken to him.' Mary's excitement was palpable.

Ania stared at the photograph. The smell of limestone, stagnant water, and chestnut blossoms rose up around her, the particular bounty of a head of cabbage.

Involuntarily, she pushed the envelope away.

'Oh, Mutti!' Mary's face fell. 'I think we should go, don't you?'

She grabbed the card and studied the photo. 'I never understood why you and Frau von Lingenfels fell out. It was such an important time of your life!

'Oh, Mutch!' she exclaimed, looking at Ania's face. 'Never mind.' She pushed the card back into its envelope. 'I thought you would be excited! Your long-lost friend . . . it was supposed to be a nice surprise.'

But Ania was suddenly immersed in another time and place – the kitchen of Burg Lingenfels, dimly lit and boarded up. Rainer at the table, the smell of sickness. And the look of innocent surprise turning to shock on Marianne's face.

From a distance came the thundering, bumping rush of a city bus. Mary picked up her empty wineglass and Ania's untouched schnapps. Ania heard the sound of the tap running, the dishwasher opening and shutting. Mary walked around the living space, turning off the lights. Around Ania, the apartment became a twinkling landscape of artificial brightness – the flickering green panels of the entertainment centre, the glowing red light switches, a stuffed bear with a purple digital screen in place of a heart. Densely packed, mysteriously animated: this was life on the other side of the apocalypse.

Mary sat beside Ania and took her mother's hand in her own. 'I think it would be wonderful to make this trip together – to go back and see these people and that place. I can leave the kids with their dad. You could tell me more about that time of your life.'

Ania leaned back in her chair. The idea was preposterous, really. There would be too much to explain, too many questions to address.

But her sweet daughter was looking at her, asking for answers. Not simply half the story this time, but the whole truth.

'Maybe,' she said. 'Let me think about it first.'

CHAPTER THIRTY-FOUR

BURG LINGENFELS, OCTOBER 1991

Burg Lingenfels is now home to the Falkenberg Institute of Moral and Ethical Inquiry. From the start, Marianne has been a great supporter of the institute. The founder is a distant cousin, and the son of a fellow member of the resistance. The gift of Burg Lingenfels was a boon for the institute. Now academics and intellectuals from all over the world apply for its cushy fellowships: a six-month stay in a German castle, access to the significant library, a gourmet chef. What better conditions for contemplating the moral and ethical challenges of civilised life?

Claire Weiss, the author of the biography, was a fellow at the institute some years ago, and the castle was, in fact, where she 'discovered' Marianne, as she says, as if Marianne were a starlet, or some sort of rare mineral. Claire is a force of nature – a modern lipstick-and-high-heel-wearing feminist. She was drawn especially to the story of Marianne as a woman in a man's world, though Marianne herself never felt particularly constrained by this. After all, as she has pointed out to Claire, if she were a man, she would be dead.

In the last five years, the castle has been 'redesigned' by a notable architect. Marianne has seen the brochures and pictures, but it is still shocking to stand before it. When she climbs out of the airport shuttle, her knees feel weak. The old bridge remains, thank God, and the moat is filled with remarkably clean-looking water, but the battered, metal-reinforced door has been replaced by a glossy, heavily grained slab of wood. To Marianne, it looks like a marbled cut of meat. Plate glass windows have been cut into the crumbling limestone where the small, deep-set openings used to be, and the grand stone hall features an enormous chandelier of modern Chihuly glass.

'Different, I am sure,' the director says with a nervous laugh. 'Shall we allow you some time to rest before I give you the full tour?'

Behind her, Alice clutches her bag to her chest. She did not want to come – Marianne had to wheedle and plead and even promise a church tour: Alice is suspicious of Germans and also very devout.

'Let's go now,' Marianne says, despite her light-headedness.

'Are you sure?' Martin asks. He has flown with them from Boston, and for the umpteenth time Marianne is grateful for his company. He was meant to come along. Her own children would be too sceptical and full of judgement. And, anyway, Katarina hates to travel and Elisabeth is busy with important prior engagements. Fritz will arrive on Sunday in time to hear Marianne's speech.

'I'm not tired,' Marianne assures him, although it isn't quite true.

The grand rooms at the front of the castle are mostly the same, but in the back, where they all lived after the war, everything is changed. The kitchen is gone – no more giant oven, and no more cistern. It has been subdivided into a hive of glass-walled cubicles. The pantry and washroom are the new kitchen, outfitted in a modern institutional style. The bedrooms where they once slept have become offices with plush carpeting and sleek white desks.

Ghosts look on over Marianne's shoulder, their voices loud in her ears: the countess, Albrecht, Connie . . . and Benita – what would they make of this transformation? After a while, Marianne stops nodding and smiling. Martin can carry on the chit-chat. It is more exhausting than she imagined, absorbing all this.

The front rooms upstairs, where the countess once housed her most dignified visitors, is now 'guest accommodation.' The tour ends here, and Alice commands Marianne to rest.

Marianne lies on the bed she has been given, hands folded over her chest. She is *tired,* but not sleepy – and the air in this sealed and modernised room feels too close, the mattress too soft. Ania Kellerman is due to arrive tonight. The uneasy thrill of anticipation is agitating.

With some effort, Marianne rises from the bed. Outside the window, staff members cover small tables with white cloths. In the light wind, these flare out, reminding her of sheets – unfurled from windows, hung from church steeples, *we surrender, we surrender, don't shoot.* That time is so near in her mind these days. Not the war, not the failed assassination, not the time leading up to it, about which she has written and been extensively interviewed – but the end, and afterwards. This is not yet fossilised into a clear narrative.

At quarter to five, Alice returns.

'Time to dress.' She sighs. 'But you didn't sleep.'

First, Alice helps her into the supportive hose Marianne has to wear underneath her skirt to stop her blood from pooling, or seizing, or whatever it is. She holds on to Alice's strong back while the younger woman rolls the stockings up over her puffy, mottled knees. It strikes Marianne as funny that Alice is now more familiar with Marianne's body than she is herself.

After the hose, Alice helps Marianne pull on her tweed skirt and grey silk blouse. Before she left, Elisabeth sent her a navy-blue tunic and a buttonless jacket composed of a lovely half-cashmere fabric for the occasion. *Something to wear on your big day,* the card read, as if Marianne was a child going off to perform in a spelling bee. There is not enough air in a room for Marianne and Elisabeth to share. They have learned this the hard way, but acceptance of the fact has made life easier. Now they see each other twice a year, for a weekend in the early summer and for the American holiday of Thanksgiving. For both occasions, Katarina, Fritz, and their children are present to diffuse the tension. Elisabeth never married. She is now the president of a well-regarded university, a celebrity in her own right. This navy-blue lounge suit is the sort of thing she wears to family holidays or weekend brunch. For speeches or awards or television appearances, she always wears crisp Angela Merkel suits. Marianne can overlook the insult inherent in this, but she will not wear the outfit.

'How do I look?' she asks.

'Beautiful,' Alice says. 'Like yourself.'

In the mirror, an old woman with a stern expression stares back.

Downstairs, the first party of the weekend has begun.

Various fellows – mostly Europeans and a few Africans, a small cadre of Chinese dissidents – mill around a table of wine and hors d'oeuvres: fancy cheeses and pickles and ham toasts, platters of shrimp cocktail and chicken satay, a funny mixture of European and American cuisine. The countess would approve of such eclecticism. But the Falkenberg Institute itself would be far too serious for the countess's taste.

Marianne is overwhelmed by the internationalness of the world represented here. So many cultures and backgrounds in a castle built to protect some probably illiterate, surely small-minded feudal overlord. There was a point in her life, not so long ago, in which the castle's transformation, the diversity of this audience, would have seemed like insurance against the rise of another Nazi-like regime. But now the connection feels obscure. Her hip aches, and her face is stiff. There are so many people in the world. This, above all, is what Marianne sees demonstrated here.

Claire arrives and makes a beeline for Marianne, full of questions and ideas, accompanied by people she would like to introduce. She is lovely with her thick, dark hair piled messily on top of her head, wearing a bright red low-cut blouse. Marianne thinks of Benita, who lived at a time when it was impossible to be both intellectual and voluptuous. It gives her a pang of sadness. Unlike Claire, Benita was a prisoner of her own beauty.

'How was the trip? Did you request the vegetarian meal? What do you think of the renovation?' Claire takes Marianne's arm and leads her through the party, whispering information and making introductions. There is a German woman studying Sophie Scholl and a Swiss 'fan' of Marianne's, and the man organising Albrecht's letters into a new book. Marianne shakes hands and tries to listen and absorb. But her eyes keep flickering to the door. How silly that she did not arrange for a more private place to first meet Ania.

And then there she is. An old woman stands in the doorway with someone who must be her daughter: little Mary, Marianne's namesake. Ania is smaller than she remembers and uses a stick, but her back is surprisingly straight. Her hair hangs around her face in a neat and sensible bowl cut. But her face! It is old, wizened with wrinkles of every direction and stripe. She looks into the room with an expression that is at once tremendously sorrowful and alert. When her eyes land on Marianne, they ignite. And she is Ania again – full of the same unique and unflappable strength. How familiar she is still, from the forward jut of her head to the intense seriousness of her gaze.

'Ah, this is the guest you have been waiting for,' Claire says, following Marianne's gaze. 'You must introduce me!' It has become clear to Marianne that she has spoken remarkably little of Ania or Benita to Claire, despite all their long hours of interviews. The fact makes her uncomfortable, as if the women are secrets she has kept.

Somehow, with the help of Martin, who swoops in from the side, Marianne makes her way over to her friend.

'Frau von Lingenfels!' Ania's daughter exclaims with a smile – she has a kind, attractive, if slightly beleaguered face.

Ania is silent, but her eyes are bright as she reaches for Marianne's hand. And grasping it in her own – brittle, aged, claw on claw – she gives it a squeeze.

'I always knew we would see each other again,' Ania says.

'Of course,' Marianne answers, though to her, this did not always seem evident.

The last time Marianne saw Ania was the day before Rainer died. It was late November 1950 and winter had set in. Before that, she had not seen her friend in weeks, not since that horrible day she had walked up the hill to the castle and discovered Rainer.

Wolfgang had appeared at Marianne's door, blue with cold, stamping his feet, blowing on his hands. He was thin and raw-boned in the manner of a growing calf and shifted uncomfortably on his feet. For the first time, possibly ever, Marianne had felt something soft and genuine for him. 'Don't just stand there letting in the cold air,' she ordered, as if he were her own son.

Uneasy silence descended as she opened and closed the bare cupboards to find coffee and milk to serve.

'How can I help you?' she asked when he was seated at the kitchen table with a cup of coffee between his palms.

Wolfgang cleared his throat. At thirteen he still had a boy's manner, although his voice was low and his chin awkwardly whiskered. 'Herr Brandt – my father' – his eyes darted to meet hers and then away again – 'is very ill. He can't sleep. My mother wondered if you had any laudanum.'

Marianne regarded the boy. His face betrayed great discomfort: Embarrassment? Pain? Sadness? Probably all three.

'I don't,' she said. 'But I imagine I can get you some.'

'Thank you,' he stammered. 'My mother will appreciate—'

'You have been dealt a bad hand,' she said, cutting him off. 'But it isn't your fault.'

He shifted uncomfortably in his seat.

'You are not responsible for your parents' mistakes.'

The words emerged from her mouth without forethought, inspired by the young man's miserable face. But were they true? Hadn't she taught her own children to accept their father's heroism as part of their inheritance? So wouldn't this also be true in reverse?

She stood for a moment, staring at him, until he lifted his eyes.

'When do you need this?' she asked.

She delivered the medicine herself.

Inside the castle, it smelled of coal smoke and sickness. The man lay on a mattress beside the stove. He was paler and more skeletal than he had been when Marianne first saw him. Sweat shone on his face.

When Marianne entered, he did not appear to notice.

She held out the bag of laudanum for Ania to take. Doktor Schaeffer had been generous. *A toothache,* she had told him.

Marianne did not venture far into the room. What had once been a sanctuary had been perverted.

'Thank you, Marianne,' Ania said in an unfamiliar, penitent way, her eyes downcast. 'He has been screaming . . .' Her voice trailed off. With her words, the threat of discovery hung over them both.

'Doktor Schaeffer said four drops mixed with water in the morning,' Marianne said. 'Again in the middle of the day and then in the evening. And, if necessary, in the middle of the night. Not to be exceeded,' Marianne continued. 'He was very strong on this.'

Ania lifted her eyes.

Not to be exceeded. In that instant, Marianne understood. She felt a rush of cold and then hot. How had she not grasped Ania's intention from the start?

From the mattress the man hacked a horrible, airless cough.

She could feel Ania's eyes, begging her for something – permission? Forgiveness? Marianne's whole body recoiled at the thought.

'Marianne,' Ania finally said, 'you are a good woman.'

Marianne did not respond.

But all the way down the hill her friend's words repeated themselves in her head, not as a statement, but as a question.

And the following day, Rainer was dead.

It is not difficult for Marianne and Ania to extract themselves from the party. Claire is preoccupied with making connections. And when you are old, you can get away with anything.

Martin and Mary, their twin tugboats, guide them out of the throng and settle them in the library like children, with plates of snacks and glasses of water. Through the glass doors, Marianne sees them talking. Is Mary married? Divorced? She can't remember. Mary throws her head back and laughs, dangly earrings swinging at her neck. Martin lounges against the exposed stone with his hands thrust into his pockets and his face downturned, smiling the bemused smile that has always made women want to please him. Grey hair aside, he looks like the teenage boy Marianne remembers. His father flashes before her eyes: the same stance, same smile, same way of looking – as Martin does now, with eyebrows raised – disarmingly incredulous. A bright flash of sun.

Soon the party will move to the music room for a concert. But Marianne and Ania will remain. This is the heart of what Marianne came here for, after all – this chance to talk with Ania, to set straight the past.

'Tell me about Anselm,' Marianne says.

'He is a pharmacist. But not happy.' Ania shakes her head.

'Why?'

Ania shrugs. It is an old Ania gesture – self-deprecating rather than indifferent. 'I don't think he can be. I never taught him how.'

'You gave him a good life,' Marianne says.

The real subject lurks between them – all the questions Marianne never asked.

'I don't know,' Ania says. 'I did what I thought was right. But I don't think I'm a good judge of that.'

'Ha!' Marianne says. 'Our whole generation, no?'

Ania shakes her head with this new air of tragedy that she has adopted in old age. She is too serious to laugh.

Slowly, they make their way backwards through time.

Wolfgang lives in the north of Germany and has no children, only a stern and unfriendly wife. Anselm is married with two daughters and works in a pharmacy, rather than as the chemist he once dreamed of becoming. Fritz lives in Berlin and is as good-humoured as always, with three children, a dog, and a pretty, artistic wife fifteen years younger than he is. Katarina, in Denver, teaching, Elisabeth, with her speeches . . . Marianne rattles through the information.

'Did you ever tell your children about Rainer?' Ania asks, finally diving in.

Marianne looks at her friend. 'I never told anyone.'

For a moment they are silent. The sound of the party in the next room floats through the French doors.

Ania shakes her head, looks across the room at the fireplace – the one, it strikes Marianne for the first time, that she sat in front of with Connie after the countess's last party. A memory rises of that long-ago kiss. She can still feel its surprise and thrill.

'I'm sorry,' Ania says. 'I'm sorry I was not honest with you from the beginning.'

'*Ach.*' Marianne waves this away. She did not come here for apologies. 'We are beyond that.' She leans forward. 'But now I want to know everything I did not want to know then.'

'About Rainer?' Ania asks doubtfully.

'About *you*,' Marianne says. 'Ania Brandt. Not Ania Kellerman or Ania Grabarek.'

Ania sighs. From the other room, Marianne can hear Claire's loud, bubbling laugh. The fire sparks and pops.

'All right,' Ania says, taking a deep breath.

CHAPTER THIRTY-FIVE

BURG LINGENFELS, OCTOBER 1991

Ania does not believe in heaven. She does not even believe in God.

It is a funny thing, though. When she looks back over the snaking trail of her life, the rises and falls and hairpin turns, the muddy sloughs where the path becomes almost invisible, she feels an urgent need to judge. To weigh the good against the evil in a manner that is, at heart, religious – to examine the small and large choices she has made that amount to her complete mark on the world.

There are actions that tilt her towards heaven: her work at the DP camp, her patience as Carsten's wife, her various small acts of kindness on the journey west. Then there are those that tilt her towards hell: the lies she has told and perpetuated, the sacrifices she asked of her boys, the fact that she was a Nazi, not only in name but in lived reality. And in these times of moral calculation – usually at two or three in the morning, lying in bed – it is those babies that tilt her into the abyss. The fact that she stood there and let them go.

There is nothing she can do about this now. Your actions are your actions. At the end of your life you have done what you have done. This is what she tried to impress upon her own children. Although probably she did not impress this on them at all. After all, actions speak louder than words.

Her boys, Anselm and Wolfgang, always knew she was pragmatic rather than good. And now that Mary has been to Burg Lingenfels, she knows this as well.

*You let Frau von Lingenfels believe you were someone else? Would
you ever have confessed if your husband had not shown up?* Mary had
been worse than angry. She had been horrified. On her last visit
to the US, Ania had confessed all to her daughter, who had only
known pieces: That Ania was married before Carsten, yes. That
this first husband was still alive when she remarried, no. That she
had run a year-on-the-land programme, yes. That she had let her
best friends believe she was someone else, no. Her mother, about
whom she had, as a schoolgirl, once written an essay entitled 'My
Hero', was not only a Nazi but a liar! And worse than a liar, a fake!
She railed at her and Ania bore it. Mary was right. She did not try
to defend herself. There was no defence. *Should I leave tomorrow?*
she had asked.

That's not the point! Mary had said. As if there actually were *a
point*.

They had not spoken for days.

Then slowly, somehow, Mary forgave her. *You did what you had
to do to survive.* Somehow, Ania still has her daughter's love if not
her respect. There is a new distance between them, which makes
her sad. But it is, after all, less punishment than she deserves.

Burg Lingenfels is smaller than Ania remembers it. In her mind,
it has become giant, a castle fit for Sleeping Beauty with great for-
bidding halls and acres of freezing, closed-off rooms.

Ania wakes early, before breakfast is served, according to the
small leather-bound handbook beside her bed. *A guide to help visitors navigate* was how the guest-and-fellow coordinator phrased
it, as if she and Mary were ships charting their way across an
unfamiliar sea. It irritated her, this way of speaking. She is a true
farmer's wife in the end. So many years of living with Carsten

made her wary of fancy talk. Or maybe it is her experience as a Nazi that made her suspicious of metaphor, euphemism, and figures of speech.

On the bed beside hers Mary is asleep, snoring gently, her dark hair a mess on the pillow. Ania feels a swell of tenderness for her tired daughter. This is meant to be a vacation for her, not all tending to her mother's needs. The poor girl (she will always be a girl to Ania) deserves rest – all that endless childcare after long days at the office. All that keeping up with schedules, lessons, and appointments, the self-imposed stresses of modern life.

Ania swings her legs off the bed and reaches for her cane. With effort, she rises and makes her way to the bathroom, where her face in the mirror is, even now, after so many years, a surprise. When she thinks of herself, she doesn't think of all these wrinkles, all this grey. Never mind. She splashes water on her face and neck and combs her hair. Then, careful to be quiet, she reenters the bedroom and fumbles over the clothing draped on the chair.

'Mother?' Mary's sleepy voice comes from the other bed.

'Shhhh,' Ania says. 'It's early. Go back to sleep.'

'Do you need help?' Mary asks, sitting.

'No, no,' Ania says, more crossly than she intends. 'What do you think I do at home?'

'All right,' Mary mumbles, and lies back down.

Outside, the sky is turning pink. Long, wavy arms of sunlight reach across the hillside, which is more naked than it used to be. All farmland now, where before it was forest. Germany has become the agricultural wonder Hitler always imagined, every metre planted with crops or windmills or endless flats of solar panels that stretch out alongside the highways. No scrap of wasted space. Even the patches of woods serve as sound barriers to shield towns against the roar of the autobahn, or screens to mask gravel mines or irrigation.

Ania lets herself out through the new, elegant front door and starts down the smoothly paved drive.

The closest section of forest behind the castle remains. Spiky peaks of the pines rise like a mountain range at the edge of the meadow. From here it looks just as it always did. Ania would like to cross the uneven grass and enter, but she doesn't trust her footing on the rutted earth, so she sits on the stone wall beside the road and remembers.

These woods are where she and her boys buried Rainer. They wrapped his wasted body in a sheet and carried it from the castle, light as a child's. Ania felt nothing but relief. He was no longer her husband but her secret, a man who had made the wrong choice at every turn. And she had made her own bad choice in him. He was the second great mistake of her life. Her first was believing in Hitler. And in the awkward, distinctly human weight of Rainer's body – the cold, lifeless shoulder bumping against her leg with every step – she felt the extremity of her bad judgement.

The grave was shallow, the earth was nearly frozen, and when Rainer's body lay at the bottom, Ania and her boys paused by unspoken agreement. She did not pray: What would she have prayed for? And from whom? A God she was certain did not exist? If there was a hell, Rainer was bound for it.

But as she stood, she willed herself to remember the boy she had befriended so many years ago in her father's waiting room. The boy who had walked his own sickly father to Doktor Fortzmann's once a week for treatment, who had allowed the old man to lean heavily on his narrow shoulders, offering him sips of water from a canteen he had thought to pack. He was a good son. And in the beginning, he had been a good husband: considerate, enthusiastic, dutiful. He had been steady in his love – so utterly convinced from an early age that she was meant to be his wife.

And as they stood above his lifeless body, it occurred to Ania that the darkness in him was her fault. She had never returned his passion. She had never loved him enough. Maybe his sins as well as her own rested on her back.

Beside her, Wolfgang toed the earth sullenly. Anselm was more inscrutable, face bowed, hands deep in his pockets. She could not ask him what he was thinking; there was too much water under the bridge. But still there was a solace in their togetherness. If she had taught her boys one thing, it was silence – they could navigate its shoals and currents like born sailors. And in its open waters, they met one another – three ships blinking their lights across the darkness, communicating without language, enough to say, *I know you, we come from the same country.*

It was two weeks later that Ania learned of Benita's death.

And with this death, she was alone in her mourning. Her sons had always kept their distance from the beautiful young mother in their midst. And Marianne, who surely shared her grief, would never speak to her again.

Ania learned of her friend's death from Martin. He sent a brief note stating the time and place of the funeral, which, by the time she received the information, had already passed.

Sitting in the parlour of the drafty old farmhouse with Carsten, Ania dropped the letter to her lap.

'Eh?' Carsten asked from his chair, startled by the abruptness of her movement.

The fire glowed in the coal stove, the baby purred, asleep in Ania's arms. 'Benita is dead,' she managed to say.

Her husband's eyes widened. 'How?'

Ania shook her head. Her body felt light with shock.

'She was a fine one,' Carsten said, shaking his own head. And the pronouncement seemed not so much an observation as an analysis. *A fine one.* Too fine for this time of rough, animal realities and ugliness.

Dear Benita, whose dreaminess and impracticality had been a reminder of all that was beautiful and light. She had always made Ania laugh. Was it the end of her affair with Herr Muller that had killed her? She had seemed so distraught on that day in the hospital . . . It would be like Benita to die for love. But Ania had no one to ask.

In her solitary sadness, she hung pine branches and oranges pierced with cloves across their foyer the way Benita had taught her. They lent the house an air of spicy sweetness. And when Ania walked beneath them with the baby, little Mary craned her neck to see these ordinary objects that bobbed and glimmered in the dark, made beautiful by their suspension.

This morning, as Ania sits on the stone wall, the castle begins to stir with life. A man opens red sun umbrellas on a new, attractive rooftop terrace. Someone tugs back curtains across the plate glass windows on the first floor. It is good to see the castle in its new life; it has become such a useful, democratic place, housing all these well-meaning people from every corner of the world. They are trying to understand all sorts of complicated things: what makes humans cruel or kind, and how we might all live together in peace. Ania appreciates their efforts, although she is sceptical that they will ever find an answer. Hitler always said there were too many people on earth. Too many people in Germany – such a small country, so many people . . . But then of course it turned out his answer to this was not a solution, but a symptom of the disease. He was the rat in the maze that begins to eat the others.

Ania is about to rise and head back towards the castle when she sees a form approaching. A woman, her hair blowing upward in the wind. Mary.

Ania lifts her arms in a wave. Mary's hands are shoved deep inside the pockets of her jacket – stiff looking with a collar and a waxy, rubberised sheen. An odd garment, designed for some specific circumstance but worn generally – like those pants with all the pockets and loops and strings attached, or the slick clothes Ania always associated with gymnastics that are now worn for anything that involves movement – grown men ride bicycles in slippery, skintight garments. Ania is too old to understand such things.

'Couldn't go back to sleep,' Mary says when she is closer. 'I miss the kids.'

The children – the idea of them belongs to another world, another life. It takes Ania a moment to register her daughter's meaning.

'They will survive,' she says. 'But of course you do.'

Mary sighs and sits on the wall beside her mother.

'It's a beautiful view,' she says. 'I forgot how beautiful it is here, in this part of the world.'

Ania too has forgotten. Impulsively, she links her arm through Mary's. It is the sort of gesture she has not made since their fight.

To her relief, Mary gives it a squeeze. It brings tears to her eyes.

'I don't deserve you,' Ania says. 'I did so many things wrong. I lived my life wrong.'

'But you know *now*—' Mary says, turning to her. 'You take responsibility for your mistakes. You ask for forgiveness—'

Ania starts in such a way that she nearly falls. 'Forgiveness! God forbid!' She crosses herself, the gesture coming to her across the years. 'I would *never* ask for that.'

Mary is quiet. 'You *admit*,' she says finally. 'That counts for something.'

'Does it?' Ania asks.

'I think so,' Mary says.

Ania would like to ask: In what sort of calculation? She can see it is important to Mary to believe this. She is an American after all; she has been swept up in the culture of talk – of belief in psychotherapy and confession, of television shows in which people reclaim their innocence through voicing their regrets.

In Ania's view, no talk in the world can change the past.

If Mary knew about those babies, she would know that taking

responsibility doesn't matter. It can't bring them back. It can't return them to their lives, to their parents. And there is no atonement for all the lies Ania told herself instead of acting – that the babies were going to an orphanage, or foster families, or God knows what other acceptable end, even as she hung her head over the latrine and threw up. This is what Ania will pay for: not only her inaction, but her self-deception, for narrating away evil while staring it in the face. How can she tell her daughter this?

Instead she squeezes Mary's arm and appreciates her kindness. Her *understanding*. This is why people have children, even when they believe the world is going to hell, even when life is nothing but uncertainty. In hopes of being understood.

CHAPTER THIRTY-SIX

BURG LINGENFELS, OCTOBER 1991

Marianne sits at the desk in the strange visiting-dignitary bedroom she has been assigned and tries to prepare her speech. *Not a 'speech,' just 'remarks'*, Claire corrected her. *Nothing too complicated.* She wonders whether Claire is nervous about what she will say. After all, the book is Claire's narrative, but the life is still hers.

Before she left home, Marianne prepared some funny anecdotes from her time in the resistance, a few cautionary parables, a recognition of contemporary resisters around the world. But now what she wrote seems grandiose, full of overblown rhetoric.

She and Ania spent hours talking in the library last night. Ania's life is three-dimensional now – no, not merely three-dimensional, but three faced. Ania Fortzmann, Ania Brandt, Ania Grabarek – why did Marianne never know of these? In her mind, these faces are no longer broken into *good* or *bad*, *true* or *false*. They have been laid bare, a collection of choices and circumstances.

Why didn't you try to tell me all this after Rainer died? Marianne asked her friend. *Why didn't you explain yourself?*

Because you wouldn't have cared, Ania said. *And you were right.*

Marianne did not protest. She saw herself that day in the castle, standing in the kitchen doorway, staring at Ania and the dying man. She had not been interested in knowledge. It was too close to the war, to Albrecht's death, to all the deaths. Knowledge would have been too much to stomach.

Benita's life also has become more whole to Marianne on this trip. Spending time with Martin brings his mother back. He is compelling in the same way Benita was: not just his handsomeness, but something more intangible. His *aura*, the New Age word comes to Marianne's mind. Marianne has always scoffed at the idea of such vagaries, but here, against the backdrop of this ancient castle, in this last chapter of her life, the idea of an 'aura' or an 'energy' feels true and important, as real as action, the gold standard around which she has built her life. This is why people were drawn to Benita, why Connie fell in love with her.

There is a light knock on the door, and before she turns, a child rushes in, followed by her son, Fritz. 'Omi!' the little girl calls, her curly hair flying behind her in a wild mop. Nicola, Fritz's youngest – a little girl as exuberant and incautious as her father was as a child. Of all her grandchildren, Marianne loves her best.

'Nicola,' Marianne exclaims, 'what a nice surprise!'

'I brought her with me. Angela is sick,' Fritz explains, crossing the room and bending to kiss his mother. 'She promised to be quiet – isn't that right?' He turns to his daughter. 'Quiet as a mouse during Omi's speech.'

'Like a mouse,' Nicola proclaims, scrunching her face into an approximation of mouseness and tiptoeing delightedly around the room.

'Oh, be however you want,' Marianne says, wishing there was no speech, and no party to attend.

'Aha! Here it is!' Fritz exclaims, catching sight of the hardcover lying on the desk beside her. 'Do I finally get a copy of the book about my famous mother?' He lifts it and begins reading the back, which is full of airy quotes from academics and journalists.

For a moment, in his concentration, he reminds her of Albrecht. Tall, slightly stoop shouldered, holding the book at arm's length.

'Oh, Fritzl,' Marianne says, reverting to his childhood nick-name. 'I am your *mother.* You don't need that book.'

Marianne goes downstairs to the reception in a combination of panic and mental haze. The visit from Fritz and Nicola has kept her from any further preparing of what she would like to say. Though she suspects it was not going to come clear anyway.

Despite Alice's entreaties, Marianne has not changed her clothes. She wears her beige cardigan and pleated khaki skirt, a pair of horrible, comfortable walking shoes. It doesn't matter. Of this much she is certain, at least.

When she enters the room, she is startled to see so many people. There must be two hundred in attendance, fellows, academ-ics from Humboldt and the Free University, contacts of Claire's and the director's, and then – dear God, she has almost forgot-ten – those she invited herself: old Eberhardt von Strallen and his middle-aged daughter, Irmgard Teitelman, Mamie Kaltenbrun-ner, Peter Weber – they have come all the way from Hamburg! – old, long-lost friends. And is that one of the von Oberst children, now a middle-aged man? She recognises the distinctive forward-jutting chin.

'There you are!' Martin says, appearing beside her to take her elbow and steer her towards her seat. He does not seem fazed by her appearance. His aura may resemble his mother's, but his man-ners and charm are all Connie Fledermann. Marianne reaches up and pats his hand.

When she is settled, the director rises and moves to the podium. 'I am so proud to be here, to be part of this celebration of an im-portant book by a past fellow of the Falkenberg Institute. A book that examines the very essence of resistance and moral clarity. What does it take for a person to be able to recognise evil as it un-folds? To see with foresight and acuity . . .'

Marianne listens uncomfortably.

When he finishes, Claire rises and takes the stage. She looks more serious today, in a black dress and funny, dark-rimmed glasses, a string of bright red Chinese beads around her neck.

'It has been my great good fortune to be a transcriber to this marvellous and heroic woman – a woman whose courage and moral backbone stayed stick straight in a time when most others bent, a woman in a world whose intellectual and political circles were dominated by men . . .'

The words make Marianne squirm. She thinks of all those in the audience, whom she has known in so many different places and at so many different crossroads of her life. Certainly she has not always been so infallible.

'I would like to invite Marianne forward to offer a few words,' Claire says. For a long moment, and with a sense of growing panic, Marianne remains frozen in her seat.

But then Martin is standing before her, offering his arm. He has come all the way from America to Burg Lingenfels at her request. She allows him to lead her up to the podium.

The audience looks at her expectantly.

And as Marianne stares back, more faces become clear: a von Kreisberg cousin whose name she can't remember, but whose mother hosted her and the children on their flight from Weisslau, and there, beside him, the kind librarian from the Document Centre, and standing against the wall, two childhood girlfriends of Elisabeth's.

'When will she talk?' Nicola's four-year-old voice says from the back of the room, where Fritz holds her in his arms. A few audience members laugh.

Marianne takes a deep breath. She must say something. But an apology is all that comes to mind. She is not sure for what.

'You would think . . .' she says finally, and her voice sounds foreign to her own ears. 'You would think from this introduction that I must be a very wonderful person.' There is more laughter. The audience is relieved that she has opened her mouth. 'And that

I must have answers and secrets of how to be good and . . . how to see evil and resist it, and everything else Claire said.'

Outside, a crow squawks from the parapet.

'Instead,' Marianne continues, 'I look out at you and I see so many familiar faces – so many people I have known and not known, so many people I have lost . . . And I see, most of all, my own blind spots.'

The audience is very quiet. In the front row, Claire looks anxious.

And as Marianne stands, gripping the podium, her eyes find Ania, sitting in the front row, between her daughter and Martin. She is so small – such a tiny person. How is it that in all those years Marianne never noticed this? And her face, her dear face, so deeply lined and etched with grooves and wrinkles, the bed of a violent river.

Ania returns her gaze. And as the silence grows, she nods, ever so slightly, as if to say, *Go on, continue. I am here, no matter what you say.*

A memory rises in Marianne's mind: That night, so many years ago, when she and Ania waited together while the Russians feasted. The dark, uneasy quiet of the castle, the flickering shadows of the fire, and, outside, the suspended carcass of Gilda's body. She can hear the crackle of sparks and the strange sounds of the men's voices gathering into a low and other-worldly song. How grateful she had been to have Ania beside her – a fellow adult and human being, connected not through allegiance to any group or party or particular way of thinking but through the reality of the moment, through their shared will to get through the next hours, the next day, and the one after, and through their shared determination to keep their children safe.

It is the great regret of her life that she lost this – no, that she forsook it. And that she lost Benita, too – her sweet, flawed friend, fellow widow and human being, whom Marianne can see now that she, in her own way, betrayed.

'I want to say,' she begins again, 'I want to say that I have not always tried hard enough to *know*. That this "moral compass" Claire talks about may not have been as helpful in my own personal life as it was in the wider political context. Sometimes it is easier to see clearly from a distance. And what is up close – what is up close' – she falters – 'is harder to make out.'

In the audience someone coughs.

'There is so much grey between the black and the white . . . and this is where most of us live, trying—'

Marianne loses her place. Trying what? Confusion presses in on her. Not just of the moment, the words, but the greater confusion of life itself – the whole murky, impulsive side of human interaction, the tangled knots of influence and emotion. A vast, primordial soup she has spent her life trying to negate.

'—trying, but so often failing, to bend towards the light.'

Marianne can feel her tongue dry in her mouth. The world grows dim, and there is an odd buzzing sound. She meets the eyes of the Chinese scholar she was introduced to last night. What does she know of him? Of his experience? The world is too vast to *know* in all its corners.

Then, all at once, her knees give out.

Her vision goes before her consciousness.

But she can feel, suddenly, a strong pair of arms, catching her, holding her up. 'I'm sorry,' she says, or tries to say.

'Shhhh . . .' She recognises Martin's voice. 'We need our heroes. No more apologies.'

Then all is quiet.

CHAPTER THIRTY-SEVEN

BURG LINGENFELS, OCTOBER 1991

Martin wakes in bed next to Mary. He can't think of her as Mari-anne, which is what she would like to be called. Mary, it turns out, is a nickname she has always disliked.

Last night, when Marianne revived, the castle was filled with jubilant relief. Thank God! Imagine if she had died, right there on the castle floor, killed by the effort of straying beyond the clarity that has defined her life. When her eyes opened, even stoic Ania wept with relief. And the party that followed was a real bash. The Sophie Scholl scholar played the fiddle, and a Russian philosopher taught a group of guests to dance the *barynya*. And the food was excellent: delicate white trout, new potatoes, and 'homegrown' carrots from the castle kitchen garden, now a vast organic nursery. For dessert, Martin's favourite: fluffy, shredded pancakes known as *Kaiserschmarnn*, a local speciality. And of course lots of champagne. Mary and Martin were among the last guests to depart.

Mary is not the sort of woman Martin usually pursues. She is a little scattered and too modern, really. He is generally drawn to cool, steady women with unrufflable feathers. But there is, un-derneath her disorganised charm, a kind of emotional steadiness. And she has a good sense of humour, which is a surprise coming from the daughter of Ania and Carsten Kellerman, whom Martin remembers as a German version of *American Gothic*.

Though apparently, what did he know?

Mary shared her mother's revelations with him last night. A secret past, a Nazi husband still alive when she married Carsten. It is to Marianne's credit, Martin supposes, that she never told him any of this. It is possible that in his usual sidestepping way, he never really asked her why she and Ania fell so completely out of touch. Like many members of his generation, he has made a career of avoiding difficult questions.

'Can you imagine?' Mary asked as they lay side by side. 'My mother was nursing one husband by day and sleeping with another at night.'

No, Martin agreed, he couldn't. But this is at the bottom of the list of things he can't imagine: Auschwitz, Treblinka, believing in Hitler, the mother of a fatherless boy committing suicide. And there are actually whole swathes of his own experience that he can't imagine: living in an orphanage for children of traitors, spending nights in bomb shelters, reclaiming his mother from some rats' nest of Russian soldiers . . .

Anyway, he likes Mary, and he feels connected to her through this place. They are both products of the same mess.

He runs a finger down her brow and nose, coming to rest on her lips.

Her eyes fly open, and her look of surprise makes him laugh.

'Oh my God,' she says, sitting bolt upright. 'I hope my mother isn't awake yet.'

'You make me feel so young.' Martin laughs. 'I haven't worried about anyone's mother since I was seventeen.'

'Ha!' Mary fumbles with the sheet, tucking it awkwardly around her body, stripping it from him as she stands. 'Sorry!' She blushes.

But Martin is too old to be ashamed of his nakedness. 'Here.' He hands her a pair of gold hoop earrings from beside the bed.

'You look as though you do this every day,' she says. 'Sleep with a weirdly connected stranger in a castle where you spent a traumatic childhood,' she clarifies.

'Not *every* day.'

'Every other,' Mary says, smiling.

And looking at her – this middle-aged American daughter of Carsten and Ania's, standing naked on the ancient stone floor of Burg Lingenfels – Martin is filled with an unfamiliar, buoyant happiness.

There is a farewell breakfast this morning in the great hall, after which the guests will disperse: Mary to drive Ania the two hours back to her retirement home on Lake Constance ('Can *you* persuade her to move to America to live near me?' she had begged Martin last night); Marianne to the hospital in Munich for tests. The woman has the constitution of an ox, but her fainting spell should be fully evaluated, Fritz and Martin together insisted.

Martin himself will go north. First to Frühlinghausen to visit his mother's grave and his aunt Gertrud, the one member of Benita's family with whom he is still in touch. After Frühlinghausen, he has one more stop: to visit Liesel 'Falkman,' his long-lost friend. For years as a boy, he dreamed of her, though he never spoke of this. And then, before coming here, he tracked her down and wrote to her, and she wrote back. Of course she remembers him, although she tries not to think about that time much. She spent the rest of her childhood, such as it was, living with her aunt in the flat where he and Marianne had left her – in a part of Berlin that ended up behind the wall, in the east. Now that Germany is one again, she has moved to Hamburg. She is an accountant with two grown children, long ago divorced.

At first he was dismayed by these details. What did this ordinary life have to do with the fierce, intelligent Liesel of his youth? But he has bucked his tendency to avoid possible disappointment and booked his return flight out of Hamburg. He has made a reservation at the Hotel Atlantic for them to have lunch.

On his way down to the breakfast, Martin pauses on the landing. The Sophie Scholl scholar and Russian philosopher are listening to Claire, who is waving her arms, holding forth. And Mary, who has beaten him downstairs, sits with her mother, talking to Fritz. There is warmth between them, and Ania looks happy, or as happy as she can with her tragic face.

Marianne presides from the wheelchair she has been relegated to while her granddaughter scrambles around on her lap. She looks smaller than usual, and tired: some spark of righteousness has been extinguished. But all the same, from her seat at the centre she emanates Marianne-ness.

The great hall itself is just as Martin remembers it from childhood – cavernous, dim, and chilly. And standing here, he feels the chafing layers of time, the inscrutable ghost of himself as a little boy colliding with the shifty construct of himself as a middle-aged man. And all around, he feels the press of other, lesser-known ghosts: Marianne as a young woman; his mother as a bride-to-be; the Nazi occupiers with their shiny leather boots; the harvest party's ill-fated Jewish guests; the frightened townspeople hiding from the Americans; centuries of gouty princes and counts and long-suffering servants. They all seem to be climbing these steps. And their movements have an urgent restlessness.

Through this, Martin hears Marianne's voice. 'Here he is,' she is saying. 'My favourite guest.'

Martin looks around.

'Martin Fledermann,' she says as if they are the only two people in the hall.

He feels the force of her love for him and it makes him proud. Smiling back, he approaches, holding out his hand.

CHAPTER THIRTY-EIGHT

BURG LINGENFELS, 1991

Clotilde Muller likes to walk her dogs on the grounds of the Falkenberg Institute. Not only because it is beautiful but because it makes her feel close to her father now that he is dead. She can imagine him hacking away at the thicket of trees in the once unruly woods, now a carefully maintained park criss-crossed by well-signed gravel paths. She had been coming here for years before she learned of the time her father had spent at the castle chopping wood.

To be fair, Clotilde did not ask him many questions. She is a woman of few words, and Franz Muller was a man of even fewer. All a question gets is an answer, and in her experience you don't always want those. As a gardener, she knows that if you turn over a rock, you will find worms and potato bugs. Sometimes even a snake. And as a German, she knows that if you start poking through a shoebox of photographs, you'll find Nazi uniforms and swastikas and children with their arms raised in *Heil Hitler* salutes.

And then what? Does that help you love the cranky old father whose laundry and dentures and toilet bowl you have to clean? To treasure the grandparent whose dementia already tests your patience? Clotilde knows she was lucky in this regard. Her father was kind and mild-mannered and easy to get along with until the end. And his silence was a gift.

Even when he broke this, it was not to unburden himself. It was to provide her with the facts. Which, after all their years living together, she never knew. Because she never asked.

So.

He had been drafted into the reserve police and sent to the east late in the war, assigned to load Jews and Slavs and other 'undesirables' onto Treblinka-bound trucks. *Did you know where they were going?* Clotilde asked. He hesitated. *Not in the beginning, but then, yes.*

And once he knew, he asked to be transferred to another 'less intensive' detail, and they granted his request. He became, instead, a courier of documents, shuttling sealed envelopes between army groups.

It was that easy? Clotilde asked. *You just had to ask to be transferred and they did it?*

He was silent for some time, his meaty hands spread on top of the hospital sheet. *Yes,* he said finally, *at least in my case.*

But he felt, at the time, that he had been selfish asking for this special treatment. That it meant someone else in his unit had to do the job of sending women and children to their deaths. So his resistance was not out of moral clarity, but out of a selfish cowardice.

What nonsense, Clotilde said. *You did the right thing! The question is why didn't everyone else? Don't belittle it.*

But her father did not concede.

He looked out of the hospital window and, after that day, they never spoke of it.

There was a time when Clotilde imagined a different life for herself, one with a husband and children and her own home, maybe somewhere else. But her father was an easy man to live with, and a surprisingly good cook. She has a job she loves as a gardener in the

town park. And she has her dogs. And based on what she understands of history and sees of the present, dogs are a superior species.

Clotilde remembers Burg Lingenfels as it was when she was a
teenager: abandoned, graffitied, its windows broken and weeds
pushing through its ancient stones. Frau von Lingenfels, the
woman who owned it, had moved to the United States. And in her
absence, it became a haven for vagrants and local teenagers up
to no good. Clotilde was lured there one night by a migrant farm
worker for an experience she doesn't care to remember, certainly
nothing the castle hadn't seen before. After that she stayed away.

But now the castle is grand once again, inhabited by intellectuals from all over the world. The Falkenberg Institute proclaims
itself to be 'a site of moral inquiry'. Fellows come here to ask questions. Well, leave them to it.

Clotilde comes here not to inquire, but to follow her father's
wishes.

There is a grave in the forest behind the castle that he asked
her to visit. A body he buried with his own hands. Franz Muller
didn't know much about the man – he was a Russian prisoner,
released from the local stalag after the war. He had arrived at Burg
Lingenfels with a band of fellow former prisoners: all hungry,
weak, and diseased. And in these woods, he had come across her
father. There was an altercation. And there was a woman present, a woman with whom her father had been in love. This is the
difficult part, because Clotilde remembers this woman. She was
beautiful, with light eyes and pale hair. She was introduced to Clotilde as her father's future bride, and Clotilde, as an eleven-year-
old, had concocted a wealth of lovely fantasies around her: this
woman would become her mother and teach her to sew and buy
underwear and other embarrassing girl items, maybe even give
her a little brother or sister so she would no longer be alone. But
then *poof*, the woman disappeared. No marriage, no courtship, no
further mention of her. It was one of the great disappointments of
Clotilde's young life.

Anyway, this woman, Benita Fledermann was her name, somehow came across Clotilde's father and this Russian. And something happened: the man attacked her or she attacked him, and the man was killed. *You killed him?* Clotilde had asked her father, who nodded solemnly. But he had never been a good liar. *Or she killed him?* Clotilde had pressed. *It doesn't matter,* he answered. *We killed him.*

This was a crime punishable by death – the murder of a former enemy combatant, a violation of the ceasefire. So Franz buried the man. And the time being what it was, no one came looking. No one even noticed he was gone.

But the man lay on Franz Muller's conscience, as much as any of the victims he felt responsible for in the east. He had carved a small cross on the tree above the grave, and he visited once a month. He cleared the nastiest weeds and brought flowers and, most of all, stood there and listened to the forest and tried to show respect.

At some point, her father had researched the man at the local archive and discovered an article in the town paper from around that time, more of a newsletter really, released by the occupying Americans, naming a Fyodor Ivanov, former inmate of Stalag VIIA, missing, last seen outside Ehrenheim with his former stalag comrades. It was one of many such listings – missing persons took up a whole page. And Franz had not known how to pursue it further. He had only an elementary-school education. He was not a researcher. And Ivanov was a common Russian name.

Some years ago, another body was discovered in these same woods. This was right before Franz Muller died, and he had followed the story with interest. The bones were entered into an official process run by the German Office, the state agency responsible for such findings. They were analysed and bundled into black plastic, stored temporarily in the town's morgue. DNA testing revealed they belonged to a German male, approximately thirty-eight years old, with evidence of combat injuries and death from a wasting sickness. No definitive identity was established. The bones were reinterred in a cardboard box in the Ehrenheim cemetery.

Were the bones of that man, whoever he was, any better off now than they were before they were found? This was the question Franz Muller asked. He honestly didn't know. Clotilde could decide, once he was gone, what she should do. Her father's secret is now her responsibility.

She is still undecided. Maybe someday she will go to the authorities and set the official exhuming process in motion. Maybe they will dig up the bones and discover enough information to separate *this* specific Fyodor Ivanov from all the others declared dead or missing at the time. Maybe his family will be tracked to some corner of what is now Belarus and contacted by a tireless employee of the German Office whose job it is to conduct this sort of postmortem search. And maybe this will bring someone closure, or stir their anger, or reopen wounds. But it won't bring back the man.

For now, Clotilde maintains her father's tradition. She visits the grave and ensures it is not entirely overgrown. She brings flowers from her garden or sometimes a special stone she has found on a trip. The original cross Franz Muller carved into the trunk has grown up out of sight, and there is a new one, a stripe he gouged into the bark maybe fifteen years ago, which itself has moved up. Any passers-by who might stumble upon the site would probably imagine it an animal's grave or a child's fairy house. Maybe they would stop and wonder for a moment. But most probably not.

When she visits, Clotilde follows her father's instructions. In the dappled light beneath the tall pine, she tries to think of the varied beauties of life: the watchful way her dogs look on as she stands in silence; the sight of crocus heads pushing through the melting snow; the fact that human beings are compelled to construct cathedrals and sing lullabies and create art; that they devote themselves to obscure causes and esoteric fields of knowledge; that the world population grows by eighty million people each year.

She conjures these things in her mind and hopes they have meaning.

And she doesn't say a word.

ACKNOWLEDGMENTS

This book took me seven years to write, so first of all I would like to thank my family – my children, Tilde, Helen, and William, for hanging in there through the ups and downs of writing and long hours in the library; and my husband, Preble, for his patience and kindness, his first readings, and his belief in me.

I couldn't have written this book without the many hours of interviews I conducted with my grandmother, and without the stories my mother told me when I was a girl and that my aunt, Annegret Falter, continued telling me after my mother died.

This book also would not exist without the recollections and insights many others shared with me. First and foremost, I'd like to thank Dorothea von Haeften for sharing her own mother's story and memoir, and for generally introducing me to the story of the courageous men and women of the German Resistance. And Annegret Falter, for not only telling me stories but answering a million questions, tracking down facts, and helping connect the pieces. Friedrich-Christoph von Saldern and Ellen von Winterfeld, Mechtilt Reike, Heidewig Ellerman, and Constanze von Salmuth (through her film) all offered their memories to me. My father, John, believed in this book from the beginning and provided acute insights as a reader and sounding board. Petra and Jürgen Schrewe have always generously opened their home to me.

I am indebted to a great many histories, films, and memoirs as well. *Frauen* by Alison Owings, *Ordinary Men* by Christopher

Browning, *Black Earth* by Timothy Snyder, *DP: Europe's Displaced Persons, 1945–1951* by Mark Wyman, everything by Gitta Sereny, Victor Klemperer's diaries, *The Past Is Myself* by Christabel Bielenberg, *Memories of Kreisau and the German Resistance* by Freya von Moltke, *Battleground Berlin* by Ruth Andreas-Friedrich, *On Hitler's Mountain* by Irmgard Hunt, *Hitler's Children: The Hitler Youth and the SS* by Gerhard Rempel, *Courageous Hearts* by Dorothee von Meding, *Backing Hitler* by Robert Gellately, *The German War* by Nicholas Stargardt, *Not I: Memoirs of a German Childhood* by Joachim Fest, *A Woman in Berlin,* and Hava Kohav Beller's moving film *The Restless Conscience,* among many others.

Also to my readers Karen Schwartz, Risa Miller, Dehn Gilmore, and Anjali Singh for their invaluable help at various stages of the process. My amazing agent Eric Simonoff and his colleague Raffaella de Angelis. My fierce and energetic editor, Jessica Williams, who has put blood, sweat, and tears into this book, and been a real partner in bringing it out into the world. Laura Cherkas, who went through it with a fine-tooth comb. The whole team at William Morrow – Kelly Rudolph, Liate Stehlik, Lynn Grady, Katherine Turro, and Doug Jones – for all their enthusiasm and hard work.

I'm also forever grateful to Alexandra Fernholz, Leonie Goetzens, Judith Hintner, Sofia Folkesson, and Hanna Ahlin for their kindness and support. And to the MacDowell Colony and the Public Library of Brookline for offering me a quiet place to write.

ABOUT THE AUTHOR

JESSICA SHATTUCK is the award-winning author of *The Hazards of Good Breeding*, which was a *New York Times* Notable Book and finalist for the PEN/Winship Award, and *Perfect Life*. Her writing has appeared in the *New York Times, New Yorker, Glamour, Mother Jones, Wired,* and *The Believer,* among other publications. A graduate of Harvard University, she received her MFA from Columbia University. She lives with her husband and three children in Brookline, Massachusetts.